THE PENGUIN BOOK OF

•

EROTIC STORIES
BY WOMEN

•

EDITED BY RICHARD GLYN JONES
AND A. SUSAN WILLIAMS

VIKING

VIKING

Published by the Penguin Group
Penguin Books Ltd, 27 Wrights Lane, London W8 5TZ, England
Penguin Books USA Inc., 375 Hudson Street, New York, New York 10014, USA
Penguin Books Australia Ltd, Ringwood, Victoria, Australia
Penguin Books Canada Ltd, 10 Alcorn Avenue, Toronto, Ontario, Canada M4V 3B2
Penguin Books (NZ) Ltd, 182–190 Wairau Road, Auckland 10, New Zealand

Penguin Books Ltd, Registered Offices: Harmondsworth, Middlesex, England

First published 1995
1 3 5 7 9 10 8 6 4 2
First edition

Typeset by Datix International Limited, Bungay, Suffolk
Printed in England by Clays Ltd, St Ives plc

Set in 10.5/12.5pt Monophoto Garamond

A CIP catalogue record for this book is available from the British Library

ISBN 0–670–86620–2

CONTENTS

•

The introductions to the individual stories are by Richard Glyn Jones.

INTRODUCTION

This anthology contains stories with an erotic theme that have been written by women from all over the world – from countries as far apart as Japan, France, Botswana, Peru and Russia. Since the time span covers more than a hundred years, from the 1880s to the present day, it is a rich and diverse collection, reflecting very different historical moments and cultural frameworks. Iva Pekárková, a Czech woman who is making her name as an author following the collapse of socialism in Eastern Europe, has drawn on a different set of experiences from Anna-Elisabeth Weirauch, who lived and wrote in Weimar Germany. Equally, Alifa Rifaat, living in late twentieth-century Egypt,[1] is engaging with moral and sexual values that are quite unlike those facing Kathy Acker, living in the very secular USA of the same period.

Within this broad range, we have imposed our own constraints. All the stories are self-contained and complete in themselves, even when they have been extracted from longer works. Many are by authors who are well known in their own countries and abroad, like Gertrude Stein of the USA and Simone de Beauvoir of France; other stories are the work of exciting new writers, like Evelyn Lau of Canada. The material has been arranged in chronological order, so as to illustrate the unfolding story of women's erotic fiction over the last hundred years.

An introduction to a collection of erotic fiction is bound to consider the meaning of 'erotic'. The word derives from ἐρωτικος, which was used in ancient Greece to mean 'of or caused by love; given to love, fond'; it was closely connected to 'Eros', the name of the Greek god of love and desire.[2] All these meanings are contained today within the English word 'erotic': *The Oxford English Dictionary* defines it as an adjective 'pertaining to the sexual passion; treating of love; amatory'. So far, so good.

A closer look at 'erotic', however, reveals that its meaning is not so straightforward. We do not know to what extent the Greek word was used to describe sexual passion felt by *women*. Athens in the fifth century BC has been praised as the cradle of demo-cracy (ruled by the people), but it would be more accurate to describe it as an andro-cracy (ruled by men, at least those in the more powerful strata of society). The majority of the population – women and slaves – were excluded from civic life. They produced virtually none of the ancient Greek literature that we read today,[3] so it is impossible to know what they thought about anything, let alone erotic desire. In any case, love and sex involving women was regarded by Athenian society as much inferior to male homosexual relations. 'For the Greek man,' explains the historian Eva Canterella, 'the homosexual relationship was a privileged outlet for exchange of experience, and he found in it an answer to his greatest needs. To relegate women to a purely biological role was perfectly natural.'[4]

Some feminist scholars have objected to the term 'erotic': Sarah Hoagland argues that it belongs too much to 'homopatriarchal greco-Christian tradition'.[5] However, there are few words in the English language that do not reflect in some way the centuries of violence and exploitation that have marked the history of the English-speaking world. It would be an impossible task to abandon all these words; it seems more reasonable to use them in a way that is understood by most people and conveys the intended meaning. Accordingly, all the stories in this anthology are underpinned by the sexual passion and love identified in *The Oxford English Diction-ary*'s definition of 'erotic' – *but from a woman's point of view*.

Until very recently, writing by women and for women has been markedly absent from collections and books of erotic fiction. In the whole of Terence J. Deakin's *Catalogi Librorum Eroticorum* (1964),[6] which purports to list all the major bibliographies of erotica and a large number of secondary materials, only one woman's name appears.[7] This does not mean that most erotic art has been produced by men; it simply means that the erotica that is available and written about has been produced by men. Some women authors have concealed the erotic elements of their fiction by embedding them deeply within the text. Gertrude Stein's story, 'Didn't Nelly and Lilly Love You', is representative of her 'explicit treatment of lesbian subject-matter disguised by stylistic devices'.[8] Other writers have managed to disclaim responsibility for their erotic art through a narrative device. Radclyffe Hall, for example, in 'Miss Ogilvy Finds Herself', cloaks her sexual fantasy in the fabric of a dream; this device enables her to avoid ownership both of her erotic fantasy and of same-sex desire.

In the Western world today, the genre of erotic writing is no longer an exclusive club for men, according to Linda Grant in *Sexing the Millennium* (1993).[9] Women now have many more opportunities to write freely, as the publication of this Penguin anthology demonstrates. In some other parts of the world, however, there has been less change. Svetlana Boym, the author of 'Romances of the Era of Stagnation', has commented that 'Russian and East European women's erotica is extremely scarce ... One could arguably say that [my story] is as erotic as it gets in our puritanical Russian climate, at least as far as women's prose goes.'[10]

The nature and experience of women's sexuality have been the subject of much discussion and debate by feminist writers, historians and activists.[11] Simone de Beauvoir, the French author of *The Second Sex* (1949), believed that a woman's sexuality is intrinsically different from a man's. 'Her eroticism, and therefore her sexual world,' she wrote, 'have a special form of their own and therefore cannot fail to engender a sensuality, a sensitivity, of a special nature.'[12] This argument, which is borne out in 'Marcelle', a story by de Beauvoir in this anthology, has been echoed by the American poet and essayist, Adrienne Rich. In female terms, claims Rich, the erotic is 'that which is unconfined to any single part of the body or solely to the body itself, as an energy not only diffuse but ... omnipresent'. For this and other reasons, adds Rich, lesbianism is quite different from male homosexuality (even though lesbians are widely regarded as female versions of male homosexuals).[13]

For the most part, it is men rather than women who pay for anonymous or impersonal sex – whether straight or gay – with those who can be hired on city streets. Evelyn Lau, the author of 'Fetish Night' in this volume, has described how it felt to have her body bought for sex. She became a prostitute at the age of fourteen and recalls that '... some of [the punters] would bring out photographs of their wives and children from their wallets. I have no sympathy for that now. It was awful, what they asked you to do and the way they treated you. You were disposable to them.'[14]

This difference still raises interesting questions about female and male sexuality. These questions have no simple answers, according to Ann Oakley, a British feminist and novelist who has written a story for this book. 'In a culture that defines women's attitudes to sex in a particular way,' she observes, 'it is very difficult to unearth the evidence that they may define it differently.'[15]

This Penguin anthology of erotic stories by women seeks to contribute in some way towards the unearthing of this evidence, by revealing aspects of sexuality – and ways of writing about it – that are uniquely female. To discuss the ways in which women's writing is different from men's is, of course, to risk regarding men's work as the normative benchmark. Here we see 'the massive and constant pull of men's centrality', to use the words of Joanna Russ, an American feminist who has contributed a story to this anthology.[16] But because of the domination of the erotic genre by male-centred narrative conventions and language, anyone wishing to write from a different point of view needs to analyse the form and function of men's fiction.

In many stories written by men, women are presented simply as the object of desire, while men are the active subject; there is little reciprocity of sexual pleasure and emotion. According to the British feminist critic Joan Smith, author of the controversial *Misogynies* (1989), 'there's very little erotic writing which reflects women's real sexual experiences of their fantasies'. She argues that Pauline Réage's *Story of O* (1954), one of the few bestselling erotic novels to have been written by a woman, simply replicates the language and assumptions of male sexual discourse, in which men dominate women.[17] This is the story of a woman who becomes the sex slave of a group of men who torture, rape, abuse, beat and humiliate her, until she surrenders all freedom and will.

While much of the recent wave of erotic fiction aimed at a female market is free of this kind of degradation, it still employs the conventions underpinning male-centred erotica. The Black Lace novels,[18] for example, which lurch from one shudder of ecstasy to another, qualify as innovative only through their sustained focus on women's sexual experience. *The Blue Hotel* is one example:

> In a trice she had him hard. To her frustration, she had become too slippery, too excited at the feeling of sliding her lips over the springing shaft of flesh. Then she had him tight

in her hand, forcing that glorious nine inches of heated manhood upwards, pressing into the tightness of the membranes of her maidenhead. All she had needed to do was to sink herself on to it, and the deed would have been done. *But he had rolled her and been on top of her in a second, in control . . .*

Then he had thrust . . . [italics added][19]

. . . and so on. Typically, the man takes control and the woman is put in 'her place', both physically and metaphorically.

Many of the authors represented in this anthology have rejected these conventions and attitudes and found new ways of writing about desire. Luce Irigaray, an influential French feminist, has argued that the subversion of male conventions of writing about women is a priority for women authors: 'the female body is not to remain the object of men's discourse or their various arts but [to] become the object of a female subjectivity experiencing and identifying itself'.[20] Some women achieve this by working within the genres of fantasy and science fiction, which enable them to create worlds that are free of the gendered assumptions attached to the society in which they live. Examples of such writing in this volume are Joanna Russ's 'An Old-fashioned Girl' and L. A. Hall's 'Harmonizing Polarities'.

Ann Oakley sought to foreground a woman's pleasure in her depiction of a heterosexual relationship in *The Men's Room* (1988). When the novel was serialized for television, this was carried through to the screenplay; it showed male as well as female nudity, unlike most television programmes with scenes of love-making. However, complaints to the BBC about the showing of male genitals led to their disappearance from the programme (nobody complained about the close-ups of the woman's body).[21] Paradoxically, this removal of the phallus can be seen as a sign of phallocentric control.

Oakley prevents any possibility of such distortion in 'The Bee Sucks', which she wrote especially for this anthology. For most of this story, the chief male character believes that he is firmly in control – of his wife, of his lover in the brief sexual encounter described in the story, and of the bees that he is paid to destroy. Then, just moments after he 'grasped her left buttock *in a controlling action*', his control is shown to be a vain illusion. Bessie Head, too, in 'The Collector of Treasures', shatters the illusion of male control when the heroine of her story, whose husband has come home 'for some sex' (which she cannot refuse because 'Black women didn't have that kind of power'), takes drastic action.

Reflections on the nature of erotic fiction lead invariably to discussions about pornography, which became an important issue for feminists in the 1970s. In 1985, Andrea Dworkin and Catherine MacKinnon drafted a model anti-pornography law, on the grounds that pornography relates to the subordination of women and is a violation of women's civil rights; erotica was differentiated from pornography as being 'sexually explicit materials premised on equality'.[22] The right to produce and consume pornography has been defended by other women, however, as a cornerstone of free expression in democratic society. Joanna Russ has mockingly called this debate 'the Great PP Controversy or the "Puritans" v. the "Perverts".'[23] L. A. Hall, a contributor to this anthology who is also a historian of sexuality, has remarked that some critics of pornography 'write about it in a way that is quite pornographic in itself, full of gruesome *frisson*, sex as danger – rather like the attraction of horror novels'.[24]

Questions about sexuality, power and pornography can only be answered when women and men write freely about these subjects, relating them to the real world in which they live. This anthology is a unique attempt, we believe, to bring together into one volume erotic fiction by women from all over the world. The collection acknowledges and confirms women's right to shape and define their own sexuality, rather than having it shaped and defined by men. It does not simply celebrate desire and sex, but shows that many sexual relationships are riddled with complex and difficult issues of power. It also reveals that for many women, the meaning of 'erotic' extends beyond what is narrowly sexual to the emotional world of desire;[25] in the words of the poet and essayist Audre Lorde, it becomes 'those physical, emotional, and psychic expressions of what is deepest and strongest and richest within each of us, being shared: the passion of love, its deepest meanings'.[26]

NOTES TO INTRODUCTION

1. Her translator, Denys Johnson-Davies, writes that her point of view is quite different from that of Western feminists: 'For her there is nothing romantic about adultery: it is, quite simply, a sin . . . It is part of a woman's role in life to see that a marriage, whether successful or not from her standpoint, continues' – in Translator's Foreword to Alifa Rifaat, *Distant View of a Minaret and Other Stories*, London, Quartet Books, 1983, pp. vii-ix.

2. Liddell and Scott's *Greek–English Lexicon*.

3. An exception was Sappho, the lyric poet of the late seventh century BC; however, Sappho lived on the isle of Lesbos, not in Athens.

4. Eva Canterella, *Pandora's Daughters: The Role and Status of Women in Greek and Roman Antiquity*, Baltimore, Johns Hopkins, 1987, p. 46.

5. Sarah Hoagland, *Lesbian Ethics: Towards New Values*, Palo Alto, California, Institute of Lesbian Studies, 1988, p. 165.

6. London, Cecil & Amelia Woolf, 1964.

7. In the reference for Marion Zimmer Bradley and Gene Damon's *Checklist: A Complete Cumulative Checklist of Lesbian, Variant, and Homosexual Fiction in English*, 1960.

8. Lillian Faderman, *Surpassing the Love of Men* (1981), London, The Women's Press, 1985, p. 402.

9. Linda Grant, *Sexing the Millennium*, London, HarperCollins, 1993, especially chapter 12, pp. 235–59.

10. Personal communication by Svetlana Boym to ASW, 12 December 1994.

11. Their differing views are brought together in the journalism, history, sociology, fiction and poetry that are collected in *Desire: The Politics of Sexuality*, eds Ann Snitow, Christine Stansell and Sharon Thompson, London, Virago, 1984.

12. Simone de Beauvoir, *The Second Sex* (1949), translated by H. M. Parshley, New York, Bantam Books, 1970, p. 688.

13. Adrienne Rich, 'Compulsory Heterosexuality and Lesbian Existence', in *Desire: The Politics of Sexuality*, op. cit., p. 228.

14. 'Andrew Billen meets Evelyn Lau, Ex-prostitute turned Author', 'Life Magazine', *Observer*, 4 December 1994, p. 8.

15. Personal communication by Ann Oakley to ASW, 12 December 1994.

16. Joanna Russ, *Magic Mommas, Trembling Sisters, Puritans and Perverts*, Trumansburg, New York, The Crossing Press, 1985, p. 14.

17. Joan Smith, 'Pornography? There Just isn't Enough', *Guardian*, 17 September 1994, p. 5.

18. Sold by a major British women's publishing house as 'Erotic fiction for women'.

19. Cherri Pickford, *The Blue Hotel*, London, Black Lace, 1993, pp. 205–6.

20. Luce Irigaray, 'Writing as a Woman' (September 1987), in Irigaray, *Je, Tu, Nous: Toward a Culture of Difference*, translated from the French by Alison Martin, London, Routledge, 1993, p. 59.

21. Personal communication by Ann Oakley to ASW, 30 December 1994.

22. *Pornography and Sexual Violence: Evidence of the Links*, London, Everywoman Ltd, 1988, p. 2.

23. Joanna Russ, 'News from the Front' in *Magic Mommas, Trembling Sisters, Puritans and Perverts*, op. cit., p. 65.

24. Personal communication by L. A. Hall to ASW, 30 November 1994. Hall's publications on the history of sexuality include *Hidden Anxieties: Male Sexuality 1900–1950*, Cambridge, Polity Press, 1991, and (with Roy Porter) *The Facts of Life: The Creation of Sexual Knowledge in Britain 1650–1950*, New Haven and London, Yale University Press, 1995.

25. This connection between sex and desire has been explored by a number of women scholars, including Audre Lorde, Teresa de Lauretis and Marilyn Frye. Carolyn Allen usefully examines their views in 'The Erotics of Nora's Narrative in Djuna Barnes's *Nightwood*', *Signs*, Vol. 19, Number 1 (Autumn 1993), pp. 177–200.

26. Audre Lorde, 'Uses of the Erotic: The Erotic as Power', in her *Sister Outsider*, Trumansburg, New York, The Crossing Press, 1985, p. 56.

LA MARQUISE DE MANNOURY D'ECTOT
Violette
(1882)

One of the very few pre-twentieth-century erotic novels that can confidently be ascribed to a woman is Le Roman de Violette, *which was published privately and anonymously in Brussels in 1882. Most authorities agree that its author was a Frenchwoman, the Marquise de Mannoury d'Ectot, née Le Blanc. An intellectual who during the Second Empire entertained the important poets and artists of the day at her country mansion near Argentan, she wrote three novels exposing the depravity of the reign of Napoleon II before falling on hard times.*

Violette is the story of a frightened young housemaid who flees her employers to seek refuge with the narrator and, as the following episode shows, it has a quality most unusual in nineteenth-century erotica: tenderness.

I was thirty years of age when I made the acquaintance of Violette.

I lived at the time on the fourth floor of a rather fine house in the rue de Rivoli, just beneath rooms occupied by domestics and young girls employed in a linen-drapery establishment on the ground floor under the arcades.

I was then on intimate terms with a very handsome and aristocratic lady. Her complexion was of that description which Théophile Gautier celebrates in his *Emaux et camées*; her hair was such as that with which Aeschylus adorns Electra's head and which he compares to the fair corn of Argolide. But the lady had become rather too plump and stout at an early period of her career, and, highly incensed at her premature embonpoint, displeased with herself and all the world, she worried all those who approached her, as if they should be made responsible for her misfortune.

As a consequence, our intimacy went on the decline, and though I duly provided for all her wants and whims, I made no effort to bring into closer vicinity our respective bedchambers, situated at opposite ends of the suite of rooms. I had made choice of my own for the sake of the fine view on the Tuileries. I aspired already to be an author, and truly nothing can be finer, sweeter, more refreshing for a writer than the sight of this sombre mass of foliage formed by the ancient trees of the garden.

In summer, the wood pigeons sport and frolic about the tall boughs till twilight, when calm and silence begin to reign in their aerial abodes.

At ten o'clock, the tattoo is heard and the gates are closed, and when the night is fine the moon slowly sails along the heavens, leaving its silvery track on the lofty treetops.

Sometimes a light breeze makes the pale light tremble in the rustling leaves, which then seem to awaken, to live, and breathe of love and pleasure.

And by degrees, the noises of the big city grow more and more faint and distant to the ear which rests in the enjoyment of this delightful silence, while the eye gazes admiringly on the château and the dark, deep and majestic masses of the huge trees. Often I would thus remain for hours at my window, dreaming and wrapped in thought.

What were the subjects of my dreams? I could hardly tell. I probably dreamt of what one dreams when one is thirty years of age: of love, of the women one has seen, and more often still, of those unseen as yet.

And, in truth, are not the charms of the unknown fair ones the most potent of all?

There are men, unfavoured by nature, whose hearts never thrill under a ray of sunlight. They live on as if in a kind of semi-darkness and accomplish as a duty, not as a joy, the act which is the supreme happiness of life, and which brings such rapture to the senses that if it lasted a minute instead of lasting five seconds it would kill even a Hercules. These men in their passage through life, eat, drink, and sleep; they indeed beget children, but they will never be able to say: I have loved! And surely is there anything worth living for, unless it be love?

I was wrapped in one of those dreams which have neither horizon nor limits, in which heaven and earth are mingled; I had just heard the bell in the neighbouring clock tower chime two o'clock, when I thought I heard a knock at my door. But perhaps I was mistaken, so I listened. The knock was repeated. Wondering who could come to visit me at this unwonted hour, I ran to the door and opened it. A young girl, almost a child, slipped in and said:

'Oh! let me take refuge here, monsieur, I beseech you!'

I motioned to her to be silent, and softly shut the door. I then encircled her waist with my arm and took her to my bedroom. There I was enabled to have a view of the bird just escaped from its cage and which had flown to me for protection.

My supposition was correct. It was indeed a lovely girl, barely fifteen, straight and pliant as a reed, though her form already showed signs of womanhood.

I placed my hand on her bosom by chance, and I felt a living globe as firm as marble.

The mere contact sent a thrill through my veins. There are indeed women who have received from nature the fascinating gift of exciting sensual desires at the slightest touch.

'How frightened I was!' she murmured.

'Really?'

'Oh yes! How fortunate that you were not yet in bed!'

'And what was the cause of that great fright?'

'Monsieur Béruchet.'

'Who is this Monsieur Béruchet?'

'The husband of the seamstress with whom I work below.'

'And pray tell me, what did this Monsieur Béruchet do to you?'

'But you will keep me all night, will you not?'

'I shall keep you as long as you like. It is not my custom to turn pretty girls out of doors.'

'Oh! I am only a little girl. I am not a pretty girl.'

'Well, well!'

I gave a look at her bosom and what I saw through the half-opened chemise gave me reason to think that she was not such a little girl as all that.

'Tomorrow, at break of day, I must go,' she murmured softly.

'And where will you go?'

'To my sister's.'

'Your sister? And where does your sister live?'

'Number 4, rue Chaptal.'

'Your sister lives in the rue Chaptal?'

'Yes, on the first floor. She has two rooms, and will lend me one.'

'And tell me, what is your sister doing in the rue Chaptal?'

'She works for milliners' shops. Monsieur Ernest helps her.'

'Is she older than you?'

'Yes; two years older.'

'What is her name?'

'Marguerite.'

'And what is yours?'

'Violette.'

'It seems that in your family they like names of flowers?'

'Oh yes! Mamma did like them so!'

'Is your mother no more?'

'No, monsieur.'

'What was her name?'

'Rose, monsieur.

'Well, they did like the names of flowers! And your father?'

'Oh! he is quite well.'

'And what is his trade?'

'He is a keeper at the gates of Lille.'

'What is his name?'

'Rouchat.'

'But I perceive that I have been asking you questions for an hour, and I have not yet inquired of you why Monsieur Béruchet frightened you so?'

'Because he always tried to kiss me.'

'You don't say so!'

'He followed me everywhere, and I never dared go without a light in the back shop, because I always made sure of finding him there.'

'Then you did not like him to kiss you?'

'Oh! Not at all!'

'And why were you displeased so?'

'Because he is so ugly, and then I thought that he did not only want to kiss me.'

'But what did he want else?'

'I do not know.'

I looked at her to see whether she was not making fun of me. But I perceived, from her innocent look, that she was perfectly in earnest.

'Well then, what did he do, besides kissing you?'

'He came up to my room yesterday when I was in bed; at least I think it was he, and he tried to open my door.'

'Did he say anything?'

'No. But during the day, he said, "Do not shut your door as you did yesterday, little one. I have something of importance to tell you."'

'And you locked your door all the same?'

'Oh yes, I did! More securely than ever.'

'Did he come?'

'Yes, he did come. He tried all he could to open the door. He tapped and tapped; then he knocked louder. Then he said, "Do open the door. It is I, little Violette."'

'You may well imagine that I gave no reply. I was shaking with fright in my bed. The more he said, "It is I," the more he called me darling Violette, the more I put my blanket over my head. At last, after waiting at least half an hour, he went away grumbling.

'All day he looked sulky, so that I was in hopes he would leave me alone tonight. I was half undressed, as you see me, when I thought of bolting the door. But the bolt had been taken off during the day and there was no lock there; so, without losing a moment, I ran off and knocked at your door. Oh! how lucky I did so!'

And the child threw her arms around my neck.

'So you're not frightened of me?'

'Oh! no.'

'And if I wished to kiss you, would you run away?'

'See now,' said she, and she applied her humid and fresh mouth to my parched lips.

I could not help keeping my lips on hers for some seconds while I caressed her teeth with the tip of my tongue. She closed her eyes and leant her head backwards, saying, 'Oh! how nice, that kind of kiss!'

'You've never been kissed that way?' I inquired.

'No,' said she, passing her tongue over her burning lips. 'Is it the usual way?'

'Yes; when you love the person.'

'Then, do you love me?'

'If I am not yet in love with you, I am afraid I shall soon be.'

'Just like me!'

'So much the better!'

'And what do people do who love one another?'

'They exchange kisses as we have just done.'

'Is that all?'

'Yes.'

'Well, that is funny. It seemed to me I wished for something else; as if this kiss, however sweet it may be, were only the beginning of love.'

'What did you feel?'

'I cannot say; a kind of languid sensation in all my body. A pleasure such as I have experienced sometimes in dreams.'

'And when you awoke after these dreams, how did you feel?'

'I was quite exhausted.'

'Did you never have that sensation except in a dream?'

'Yes; indeed, just now, when you kissed me.'

'Am I then the first man who ever kissed you?'

'In that way, you are. My father often kissed me, but it was not at all the same thing.'

'Then you are still a virgin?'

'Virgin, what does that mean?'

Evidently, from her tone, she was sincere!

I took pity, or rather I felt respect for that innocence which then put itself so entirely at my mercy. It seemed as if it were a crime to rob her of that sweet treasure which she unconsciously possessed and which, when once given away, is lost for ever.

'And now let us talk seriously, my dear girl,' I said releasing her from my embrace.

'Oh! you are not going to send me away, surely?'

'No, I am too happy to have you here.' Then, after a pause: 'Listen,' I said, 'this is what we are going to do. We will go and fetch your clothes.'

'Very well. And where shall I go?'

'That's my business. First of all let us go to your room?.'

'And Monsieur Béruchet?'

'It is probable that he has left, for it is nearly three o'clock in the morning.'

'What shall we do in my room?'

'We will take away all your things.'

'And then?'

'And then I shall take you with your little luggage to a room in town, whence you will write to Monsieur Béruchet a letter which I shall dictate. Are you willing?'

'Oh! I shall do all you bid me.'

How charming this confidence of innocence and youth! The darling girl, she would certainly have done all I bade her, there and then.

We went up to the lockless room, and put her scanty belongings in a carpet bag.

Violette finished dressing herself, we came downstairs, and as there were no cabs about, we set out arm in arm, as happy and light-hearted as two school chums, and repaired to the rue Saint-Augustin, where I kept a room for a night's debauch when I felt so inclined.

An hour later, I was home again, without having tried to make further progress in my amours with Violette.

. . .

The room which I kept in the rue Saint-Augustin was not in a lodging house. It was a room which I had furnished myself, in view of its destination, with such *recherché* as would have satisfied the most dainty lady.

It was hung all round in nacarat velvet; the window curtains and bed curtains were of the same material. The bed was covered with velvet also, and the whole set off by torsades and bands of gold satin.

A looking-glass occupied the whole of the wall beside the bed and corresponded with the mirror placed between the two windows so that images were reproduced 'ad infinitum'.

The rest of the furniture was in keeping with this elegant decoration. A bath was hidden in a sofa and a large bearskin made the pretty feet which rested on it look still whiter.

A pretty little lady's maid, whose only functions were to keep the room in order and to attend to the different lady visitors, had her room on the same landing.

I bade her prepare a bath in the dressing-room without awaking the occupier of the bedroom.

We entered without a light, and I only lit a night lamp in a vase of rose-coloured Bohemian glass. Then I turned away to allow the young girl to undress freely, an operation which in her innocence she would have done in my presence. After which I kissed her on both eyes, bade her good-night and returned home as I said before.

In spite of the emotions of the day, Violette went to bed, where she nestled like a little pussy. She said goodbye with a yawn, and I am sure she must have been fast asleep before I was well in the street.

As for me, the case was different, and I could not close my eyes. I confess, that bosom from which my hand had rebounded, that mouth which had been glued to my lips, that half-opened chemise which had disclosed such lovely treasures – the recollection kept me awake and in a state of great excitement.

I am certain male readers will not ask for any explanation of my conduct, for they fully understand why I stopped halfway.

But lady readers, more inquisitive or more ignorant of certain articles of our code, will surely wish to know why I went no further.

I must say that it was not for lack of desire, but Violette, as I stated before, was barely fifteen years old, and then she was so innocent that it would have seemed like a crime to take possession of charms given away, so to speak, without any consciousness of the seriousness of the act. And again, I must add, that I am one of those who delight in the relish of all the preliminary delicacies of love, all the voluptuousness of its most complicated pleasures.

Innocence is a flower which should be left unculled as long as possible on its stalk, and should be plucked only leaf by leaf.

A rosebud will sometimes be a week in bursting into a full-blown flower. Besides, I like pleasure without attendant remorse; and within the walls of the city which so well defended itself against the invader in 1792 there existed a veteran whose old age I respected.

The worthy man did not seem as if he would have committed suicide on account of the mishap of his eldest daughter, but perhaps he loved more tenderly his youngest – perhaps he had formed for her future plans which I did not like to upset. Besides, I have always noticed that with patience everything goes well for everybody.

I thus pondered till daybreak. Pent up with fatigue, I at last closed my eyes and slept on till eight o'clock.

I got up hastily, as Violette must have been an earlier riser. I told my man that I should probably not be home for breakfast, I hailed a cab, and in five minutes was at the house in the rue Saint-Augustin.

I went upstairs four steps at a time, and my heart beat as if this were my first love.

I entered the room noiselessly. Not only was Violette fast asleep, but she had not even moved.

However, the blankets were partly drawn back, and, as her chemise was half opened, one of her breasts was exposed to my view.

She was charming thus, with her head thrown back and nearly hidden by her luxuriant locks: she then looked like a picture by Giorgione.

Her bosom was marvellously plump and as white as snow. Though a brunette the nipples of her breasts were rosy and like strawberries. I leant over her and applied my lips lightly to one of them; it stiffened instantly, whilst a slight shudder ran through her frame. Had I only chosen to pull off the sheets, I am sure she would not have opened her eyes.

But I preferred awaiting the close of her slumbers.

I took a seat near the bed and held one of her hands in mine.

By the light of the night lamp, I examined that hand; it was small, of a comely shape, rather short like the hands of Spaniards, and the nails were rosy, pointed, but the forefinger bore evidences of needlework. While I was thus occupied, she suddenly opened her eyes and uttered a joyful exclamation.

'Oh!' said she, 'you are here, how happy I am! If I had not seen you on waking up I should have thought it was all a dream. Did you never leave me, then?'

'I did,' I replied. 'I left you for four or five hours, which seemed like ages, but I returned, hoping to be the first object on which you should set eyes on waking up.'

'And how long have you been here?'

'For half an hour.'

'You should have woken me.'

'I should never have thought of doing so.'

'You did not even kiss me!'

'Yes, I did, I kissed one of your pretty little rosebuds.'

'Which!'

'That one on the left.'

She uncovered it with a genuine air of innocence and tried to touch it with her lips.

'Oh! how tiresome!' said she. 'I cannot kiss it in my turn.'

'And why should you like to kiss it in your turn?'

'To place my lips where yours have lain.'

She renewed the attempt.

'I can't do it. Well!' said she, 'you gave it a kiss just now for your own sake, let your lips touch it now for "my" sake.'

Thereupon I leant over her, and taking the rosebud between my lips I caressed it with the tip of my tongue.

She gave a little cry of pleasure: 'Oh! how nice!'

'As nice as yesterday's kiss?'

'Oh! yesterday's kiss. It is so long since, I cannot remember.'

'Shall I begin again?'

'You know I should like you to, since you told me that was the proper way to kiss people you loved.'

'But I don't know yet whether I love you.'

'As for me, I am quite sure I do love you dearly. So do not kiss me if you don't like to do it, but I shall kiss you all the same.'

And, as on the previous day, she glued her lips to mine, with this difference, that, this time, her tongue touched my teeth.

I could not have got away had I wished to do so, she hugged me so tightly.

Her head fell back, and, with half-closed eyes she murmured, 'Oh! how I love you!'

The kiss made me mad. I snatched her, so to speak, from the bed, and pressing her closely to my heart I covered her bosoms with kisses.

'Oh! what are you doing, I feel quite faint?'

These words brought me to my senses, for it was not thus, by surprise, that I wished to possess her.

'Dear girl,' said I, 'I have had a bath got ready for you in the dressing-room.' With these words I carried her there in my arms.

'Ah!' said she, sighing, 'how comfortable I feel in your arms.'

The bath was just warm enough. I put her in it after having poured in half a bottle of eau de Cologne. I then lit the fire and placed the bearskin rug in front of it.

Then I brought out a dressing-gown of white cashmere and put before an armchair a pair of small red Turkish slippers with gold embroidery.

After a quarter of an hour, my little bather came out quite shivering and ran to the fire.

'Oh, how nice and warm', she said, and she sat on the bearskin at my feet.

She was charming in her cambric peignoir of such a transparent texture that the skin could be seen through it. She looked round and said: 'Dear me, how pretty everything is here. Am I to live in this place?'

'Yes, if you like, but we must have somebody's permission.'

'Whose?'

'Your father's.'

'My father's! But will he not be glad when he knows I have a beautiful room and plenty of leisure time for study?'

'To study what?'

'Ah! I had forgotten. I must explain.'

'Do, my dear girl, by all means. You know you must tell me all,' said I, kissing her.

'You remember one day you gave me a ticket for a play?'

'Yes; I do remember.'

'It was for the Porte-Saint-Martin theatre, where they played *Antony* by M. Dumas.'

'It is an immoral play, not at all fit for little girls to see.'

'I did not think so at all. I was quite taken up with it, and ever since that day, I told my sister and Monsieur Ernest that I wished to appear on the stage.'

'You don't say so?'

'Then Monsieur Ernest and my sister exchanged glances. "Well," said my sister, "if she has any taste at all for it, it would be preferable to milliner's business."

'"And then," said Monsieur Ernest, "with my journal, the *Gazette des Théâtres* I can give her a lift."

'"Well! that will be just the thing for her."

'Madame Béruchet was told that I should sleep at my sister's and that I should not return till next day. After the play we returned to the rue Chaptal and I began to repeat the principal scenes which I remembered, and I set to acting, all the while moving my arms about like this –'

But meanwhile Violette unconsciously opened her peignoir and disclosed some lovely treasures to my view.

I took her in my arms, sat her on my knee, and she nestled lovingly against me.

'What next?' I asked.

'Monsieur Ernest then said, that if my mind was made up, as two or three years must elapse before I made my début, I must let my father know of the plan.'

' "And during these two or three years, how will she live?" asked Marguerite.

' "What a question to ask!" replied Monsier Ernest. "She is pretty, and a pretty girl need not want anything. From fifteen to eighteen she will find a protector. Besides she eats no more than a little bird. What does she require? A nest and a little seed." '

I shrugged my shoulders while casting a glance at the poor little creature nestling in my arms as in a cradle.

'Then,' resumed Violette, 'the next day they wrote to papa.'

'And what did papa reply?'

'He replied: "You are two poor orphans thrown upon the world without any other protector than an old man of sixty-seven, who may at any moment be taken away from you. Therefore, do the best you can, but never do anything which would make the poor old soldier ashamed of you." '

'Did you keep that letter?'

'Yes, I did.'

'Where is it?'

'In the pocket of one of my gowns. Then I thought of you. I said: Since he gave me tickets for the play, he must be acquainted with the managers of theatres. I always put it off till next day. But the affair with Monsieur Béruchet decided all. Will you do all you can to help me in studying for the stage?'

'I will indeed. I promise you.'

'How good you are.' And Violette threw her arms round my neck, and so doing lay bare the treasures of her bosom. This time, I confess, I lost my head; my hand glided down her body and rested on a spot covered with hair as soft and fine as silk.

When Violette felt my hand, her whole body seemed to vibrate; her head fell back, her mouth was half-opened, while her eyes were nearly closed. And yet, I had hardly touched her.

I was mad with passion, and carrying her to the bed, I knelt before her and placed my mouth where my hand had been. I experienced then the supreme pleasure of one's lips in contact with virginity.

From this moment, Violette uttered inarticulate words, till a spasm of pleasure thrilled through her whole body.

I got up and gazed on her while she was recovering. She opened her eyes, tried to sit up, and murmured, 'Oh! how delicious it was! Can we begin again?'

Suddenly she got up and looking intently at me, she asked,

'Is it not very wicked?'

I sat near her on the bed.

'Has anybody ever spoken to you seriously?'

'Yes, sometimes father did, when I was a child, to scold me.'

'I don't mean that. I mean to ask you whether you could understand anyone who should talk to you seriously?'

'Not perhaps if it were a stranger. But I believe I can understand anything you say to me.'

'Well then, listen.'

She clasped her arms round my neck, fixed her eyes on mine and with an attentive air said: 'Now speak; I listen.'

'Woman, when created, certainly received the same rights as man, that is the right of obeying one's natural instincts.

'Well, Society being ruled by men, who are stronger than women, certain laws have been forced on women. Chastity is imposed on girls, and fidelity on married women.

'Men, in framing these laws, have reserved for themselves the right of satisfying their passions, without thinking that in order to indulge them they must cause women to break the laws which they laid down for them.

'These women give them happiness, but shame is their own lot.'

'That is very injust,' remarked Violette.

'Yes, my dear, truly so. Therefore have certain women risen up and said: "What does Society offer me in exchange for the bondage in which she keeps me? Marriage with a man I shall not probably love, who will take me at eighteen years of age, who will enjoy me and make me unhappy all my life. I had rather remain outside Society, follow my own inclination and love whom I please. I shall be a woman of Nature not of Society."

'From Society's conventional point of view, what we have done was wrong. From Nature's point of view we have only given satisfaction to our legitimate desires.

'Did you understand?'

'Quite well.'

'Well, think of this all day. This evening you can let me know whether you want to be Nature's woman or that of Society.'

I rang the bell and the maid came. Violette was in her bed, showing only her head. 'Madame Léonie,' I said, 'you will please attend to all this young lady's wants; you will have her food sent by Chevet, her pastry from Julien's. There is Bordeaux wine in the cupboard and 300 francs in this drawer.

'Ah! I forgot. Send for a dressmaker to measure the young lady for two simple but tasteful dresses, with bonnets to match.'

When I returned in the evening, Violette ran up to me, and, throwing herself into my arms, she said:

'I thought of what you told me.'

'All day?'

'No; for five minutes, and I prefer to be Nature's woman.'

'You do not wish to return to Monsieur Béruchet?'

'Oh no!'

'You wish to return to your sister's?' Violette made no reply.

'Do you think it inconvenient to return to your sister's?'

'I am afraid it may not please Monsieur Ernest.'

'Who is that Monsieur Ernest?'

'A young man who visits my sister and who is a journalist.'

'What makes you think that he would not like to see you with your sister?'

'Because when, by chance, Madame Béruchet sent me for an errand, and I quickly ran to kiss my sister when M. Ernest was there, he looked quite sulky. He went into the other room with Marguerite and locked the door. One day I remained because the lady had told me to wait for an answer, and that seemed to put them both out of temper.'

'Well, then, there is an end of it. You shall be the woman of Nature.'

. . .

Dear girl! It was indeed nature, but a delightful nature, which inspired her.

I had some excellent books in my library. She had been reading all day.

'Did you feel dull?' I asked.

'Yes, on account of your absence; but not otherwise.'

'What did you read?'

'I read *Valentine*.'

'Then I am not surprised,' I replied. 'That book is a masterpiece.'

'I do not know; but what I do know is that it made me cry all the time.'

I rang the bell for Madame Léonie.

'Get tea ready,' I said.

Then I asked Violette: 'Do you like tea?'

'I don't know. I never tasted it.'

When tea was ready, I asked Violette whether she required the services of Léonie any longer. She said no; so I shut the door and locked it.

'Are you going to remain here?'

'If you will allow me.'

'All night?'

'All night!'

'Oh, how nice! Then we can go to bed together like two good little friends.'

'Just so. Have you ever slept with any of your girl friends?'

'At school, when I was quite little; but not since then, except when I slept with my sister.'

'What did you do then?'

'I used to say good night; I kissed her, and we both went to sleep.'

'Is that all?'

'That is all.'

'And if we slept together, do you think that would be all?'

'I hardly know; but it seems to me there should be something else.'

'But then, what could we do together?'

She shrugged her shoulders.

'Perhaps what you did to me this morning!' she said, embracing me.

I took her in my arms and put her on my knees. She was silent for some time; then she smiled, and said, 'Can you guess what I should like?'

'No.'

'I should like to be learned.'

'Learned! Why would you like to be learned, of all things in the world?'

'To understand what I do not understand.'

'What is it you do not understand?'

'A good many things. For instance, you asked me whether I was a virgin?'

'Yes.'

'Well, I replied I did not know, and you burst out laughing.'

'That is correct.'

'Well, what is it to be a virgin?'

'A virgin is a young lady who has never been caressed by any man.'

'Then I am no longer a virgin now?'

'How's that?'

'Why, it seems to me that you caressed me this morning.'

'But there are different ways of caressing, my dear girl. The kisses I gave you this morning, though very sweet . . .'

'Oh yes, they were sweet! They were indeed!'

'However sweet, they do not destroy virginity.'

'And what are those that do take away one's virginity?'

'I should first explain to you what is virginity.'

'Do explain it to me, then.'

'It is no easy matter.'

'Oh no. You are *so* clever!'

'Well, virginity is the physical and moral state of a girl who, like you, has not had a lover.'

'But what is having a lover?'

'It is doing with a man certain things by which children are begotten and brought into the world.'

'Did we not do these things?'

'No.'

'Then you are not my lover?'

'I am only as yet your sweetheart.'

'When will you be my lover?'

'In as long a time as possible.'

'I suppose it is because you would dislike it?'

'Not at all; just the reverse. It is the thing that I should like above all things in the world.'

'Oh dear! How tiresome! I no longer understand you.'

'To be the lover of a woman, pretty little Violette, is to be, in the alphabet of love's pleasures, at the letter Z of the ordinary alphabet. There are twenty-four letters to learn before you come to the end of that series whose first letter, the letter A, is a kiss on the hand.'

I took her little hand and kissed it.

'And what you did to me this morning – what letter was it?'

I was fain to confess that it stood very close to letter Z, and that I had omitted many vowels and consonants to get to that stage.

'You are chaffing me!'

'No, indeed I am not, sweet darling. I should like to make this alphabet last as long as possible – this charming alphabet of love, of which each letter is a caress and each caress is bliss. I should wish to take off little by little that robe of innocence, just as I shall pluck one by one all the different articles of your apparel from your person.

'If you were dressed, each portion that I should take off would disclose something new to me – something unknown, something charming: the neck, the shoulder, the bosom, and, by degrees, all the rest. Like a brute, I divested you of all in a moment. You did not know the value of all that you gave away.'

'Then I have done wrong?'

'No, no! I loved you too much, too passionately, to proceed otherwise.'

I slipped off her gown, and then she sat on my knee clad only in her chemise.

'You wish to know what is virginity,' I said, losing all control of myself. 'Well, I will tell you; but draw near – nearer still – your lips on mine.'

I pressed her to my breast; she clasped her arms round my neck, sighing and panting with amorous excitement.

'Do you feel my hand?' I asked.

'Oh, yes!' said she, with a shiver through her whole frame.

'And my finger, do you feel it too?'

'Yes . . . Yes . . .'

'I am now touching what they call the maidenhead. When once this is broken through you cease to be a virgin, and you become a woman. Well, what I wish is to caress you only in such a way that you shall keep that maidenhead as long as possible. Do you understand?'

Directly my finger was fixed there, Violette gave no other answer than by caressing me fondly and muttering passionate words. Then she entwined her body round mine, uttered inarticulate exclamations, sighed, and suddenly she loosed her hold of me; her head fell back, and she lay as if in a swoon. I undressed rapidly, tore off her chemise, and stretched her against me in the bed.

She soon recovered, and said, 'Oh! I am dead!'

'Dead!' I cried. 'You dead! Just as if you said I was dead. Oh, no! on the contrary, we are beginning to live.' And I covered her with kisses which made her writhe as if they had been so many bites. Then she began in her turn to bite me with little passionate cries. Each time our lips met there was a pause, full of voluptuous pleasure.

Suddenly she gave a cry of astonishment, and seized with both hands the unknown object which had caused her surprise, as if the veil were torn asunder.

'I understand,' said she, 'it is with that . . . But it is quite impossible.'

'Violette, my sweet darling, I can no longer restrain myself; I shall become mad!'

I tried to tear myself away from her embraces.

'No,' she said. 'Remain, if you love me. Do not be afraid of hurting me. I wish it.'

She then slipped under me, clasped her arms round my neck, twined her thighs round mine, pushing her body against my own.

'I wish it,' she repeated . . . 'I wish it.'

Suddenly she gave a little shriek.

All my fine resolutions had vanished. At the same time that Violette began to understand what was a maidenhead, she had lost her own.

On hearing her cry out, I stopped.

'Oh no,' said she, 'go on! . . . go on! . . . You hurt me; but if you did not hurt me, I should be too happy! I wish to have pain! Go on; do not stop! Do, dear Christian! my beloved! my friend! Oh! I shall go mad!

'Oh! it is like fire! Oh! I die! . . . Take me, take all!'

Ah! Muhammad fully knew by what dream he should enthral man when he gave his disciples the sensual Paradise – a bottomless abyss of voluptuous rapture always renewed.

We spent a night full of bliss – of passionate caresses, and never closed our eyes till daybreak.

'Ah!' she said, on waking up and embracing me, 'I hope now I am no longer a virgin.'

•

KATE CHOPIN
The Storm
(1900)

The 1890s brought fin de siècle *decadence along with major advances for the women's movement. Kate Chopin began writing her Louisiana stories after the deaths of virtually all the members of her family within a short space of time, and in them she tackled the problems facing women with a frankness hitherto rare. Her first novel,* At Fault *(1891), and the stories in* Bayou Folk *(1894), concern the possibilities and perils of female emancipation. A* Night in Accidie *(1897) was castigated for its unabashed sensuality, and her greatest novel,* The Awakening *(1899), provoked such outrage that it effectively ended her literary career.*

Amid such controversy 'The Storm', a more explicit sequel to her celebrated story 'The 'Cadian Ball', was never even offered for publication in Kate Chopin's lifetime, and was discovered only after her death in 1904.

I

The leaves were so still that even Bibi thought it was going to rain. Bobinôt, who was accustomed to converse on terms of perfect equality with his little son, called the child's attention to certain sombre clouds that were rolling with sinister intention from the west, accompanied by a sullen, threatening roar. They were at Friedheimer's store and decided to remain there till the storm had passed. They sat within the door on two empty kegs. Bibi was four years old and looked very wise.

'Mama'll be 'fraid, yes,' he suggested with blinking eyes.

'She'll shut the house. Maybe she got Sylvie helpin' her this evenin',' Bobinôt responded reassuringly.

'No; she ent got Sylvie. Sylvie was helpin' her yistiday,' piped Bibi.

Bobinôt arose and going across to the counter purchased a can of shrimps, of which Calixta was very fond. Then he returned to his perch on the keg and sat stolidly holding the can of shrimps while the storm burst. It shook the wooden store and seemed to be ripping great furrows in the distant field. Bibi laid his little hand on his father's knee and was not afraid.

II

Calixta, at home, felt no uneasiness for their safety. She sat at a side window sewing furiously on a sewing-machine. She was greatly occupied and did not notice the approaching storm. But she felt very warm and often stopped to mop her face on which the perspiration gathered in beads. She unfastened her white sacque at the throat. It began to grow dark, and suddenly realizing the situation she got up hurriedly and went about closing windows and doors.

Out on the small front gallery she had hung Bobinôt's Sunday clothes to air and she hastened out to gather them before the rain fell. As she stepped outside, Alcée Laballière rode in at the gate. She had not seen him very often since her marriage, and never alone. She stood there with Bobinôt's coat in her hands, and the big rain drops began to fall. Alcée rode his horse under the shelter of a side projection where the chickens had huddled and there were ploughs and a harrow piled up in the corner.

'May I come and wait on your gallery till the storm is over, Calixta?' he asked.

'Come 'long in, M'sieur Alcée.'

His voice and her own startled her as if from a trance, and she seized Bobinôt's vest. Alcée, mounting to the porch, grabbed the trousers and snatched Bibi's braided jacket that was about to be carried away by a sudden gust of wind. He expressed an intention to remain outside, but it was soon apparent that he might as well have been out in the open: the water beat in upon the boards in driving sheets, and he went inside, closing the door after him. It was even necessary to put something beneath the door to keep the water out.

'My! what a rain! It's good two years since it rain' like that,' exclaimed Calixta as she rolled up a piece of bagging and Alcée helped her to thrust it beneath the crack.

She was a little fuller of figure than five years before when she married; but she had lost nothing of her vivacity. Her blue eyes still retained their melting quality; and her yellow hair, dishevelled by the wind and rain, kinked more stubbornly than ever about her ears and temples.

The rain beat upon the low, shingled roof with a force and clatter that threatened to break an entrance and deluge them there. They were in the dining-room – the sitting-room – the general utility room. Adjoining was her bedroom, with Bibi's couch alongside her own. The door stood open, and the room with its white, monumental bed, its closed shutters, looked dim and mysterious.

Alcée flung himself into a rocker and Calixta nervously began to gather up from the floor the lengths of a cotton sheet which she had been sewing.

'If this keeps up, *Dieu sait* if the levees goin' to stan' it!' she exclaimed.

'What have you got to do with the levees?'

'I got enough to do! An' there's Bobinôt with Bibi out in that storm – if he only didn' left Friedheimer's!'

'Let us hope, Calixta, that Bobinôt's got sense enough to come in out of a cyclone.'

She went and stood at the window with a greatly disturbed look on her face. She wiped the frame that was clouded with moisture. It was stiflingly hot. Alcée got up and joined her at the window, looking over her shoulder. The rain was coming down in sheets obscuring the view of far-off cabins and enveloping the distant wood in a grey mist. The playing of the lightning was incessant. A bolt struck a tall chinaberry tree at the edge of the field. It filled all visible space with a blinding glare and the crash seemed to invade the very boards they stood upon.

Calixta put her hands to her eyes, and with a cry, staggered backward. Alcée's arm encircled her, and for an instant he drew her close and spasmodically to him.

'*Bonté!*' she cried, releasing herself from his encircling arm and retreating from the window, 'the house'll go next! If I only knew w'ere Bibi was!' She would not compose herself; she would not be seated. Alcée clasped her shoulders and looked into her face. The contact of her warm, palpitating body when he had unthinkingly drawn her into his arms, had aroused all the old-time infatuation and desire for her flesh.

'Calixta,' he said, 'don't be frightened. Nothing can happen. The house is too low to be struck, with so many tall trees standing about. There! aren't you going to be quiet? say, aren't you?' He pushed her hair back from her face that was warm and steaming. Her lips were as red and moist as pomegranate seed. Her white neck and a glimpse of her full, firm bosom disturbed him powerfully. As she glanced up at him the fear in her liquid blue eyes had given place to a drowsy gleam that unconsciously betrayed a sensuous desire. He looked down into her eyes and there was nothing for him to do but to gather her lips in a kiss. It reminded him of Assumption.

'Do you remember – in Assumption, Calixta?' he asked in a low voice broken by passion. Oh! she remembered; for in Assumption he had kissed her and kissed and kissed her; until his senses would wellnigh fail, and to save her he would resort to a desperate flight. If she was not an immaculate dove in those days, she was still inviolate; a passionate creature whose very defencelessness had made her defence, against which his honour forbade him to prevail. Now – well, now – her lips seemed in a manner free to be tasted, as well as her round, white throat and her whiter breasts.

They did not heed the crashing torrents, and the roar of the elements made her laugh as she lay in his arms. She was a revelation in that dim, mysterious chamber; as white as the couch she lay upon. Her firm, elastic flesh that was knowing for the first time its birthright, was like a creamy lily that the sun invites to contribute its breath and perfume to the undying life of the world.

The generous abundance of her passion, without guile or trickery, was like a white flame which penetrated and found response in depths of his own sensuous nature that had never yet been reached.

When he touched her breasts they gave themselves up in quivering ecstasy, inviting his lips. Her mouth was a fountain of delight. And when he possessed her, they seemed to swoon together at the very borderland of life's mystery.

He stayed cushioned upon her, breathless, dazed, enervated, with his heart beating like a hammer upon her. With one hand she clasped his head, her lips lightly touching his forehead. The other hand stroked with a soothing rhythm his muscular shoulders.

The growl of the thunder was distant and passing away. The rain beat softly upon the shingles, inviting them to drowsiness and sleep. But they dared not yield.

The rain was over; and the sun was turning the glistening green world into a palace of gems. Calixta, on the gallery, watched Alcée ride away. He turned and smiled at her with a beaming face; and she lifted her pretty chin in the air and laughed aloud.

III

Bobinôt and Bibi, trudging home, stopped without at the cistern to make themselves presentable.

'My! Bibi, w'at will yo' mama say! You ought to be ashame'. You oughtn' put on those good pants. Look at 'em! An' that mud on yo' collar! How you got that mud on yo' collar, Bibi? I never saw such a boy!' Bibi was the picture of pathetic resignation. Bobinôt was the embodiment of serious solicitude as he strove to remove from his own person and his son's the signs of their tramp over heavy roads and through wet fields. He scraped the mud off Bibi's bare legs and feet with a stick and carefully removed all traces from his heavy brogans. Then, prepared for the worst – the meeting with an over-scrupulous housewife, they entered cautiously at the back door.

Calixta was preparing supper. She had set the table and was dripping coffee at the hearth. She sprang up as they came in.

'Oh, Bobinôt! You back! My! but I was uneasy. W'ere you been during the rain? An' Bibi? he ain't wet? he ain't hurt?' She had clasped Bibi and was kissing him effusively. Bobinôt's explanations and apologies which he had been composing all along the way, died on his lips as Calixta felt him to see if he were dry, and seemed to express nothing but satisfaction at their safe return.

'I brought you some shrimps, Calixta,' offered Bobinôt, hauling the can from his ample side pocket and laying it on the table.

'Shrimps! Oh, Bobinôt! you too good fo' anything!' and she gave him a smacking kiss on the cheek that resounded. '*J'vous réponds*, we'll have a feas' tonight! umph-umph!'

Bobinôt and Bibi began to relax and enjoy themselves, and when the three seated themselves at table they laughed much and so loud that anyone might have heard them as far away as Laballière's.

IV

Alcée Laballière wrote to his wife, Clarisse, that night. It was a loving letter, full of tender solicitude. He told her not to hurry back, but if she and the babies liked it at Biloxi, to stay a month

longer. He was getting on nicely; and though he missed them, he
was willing to bear the separation a while longer – realizing that
their health and pleasure were the first things to be considered.

v

As for Clarisse, she was charmed upon receiving her husband's
letter. She and the babies were doing well. The society was agree-
able; many of her old friends and acquaintances were at the bay.
And the first free breath since her marriage seemed to restore the
pleasant liberty of her maiden days. Devoted as she was to her
husband, their intimate conjugal life was something which she was
more than willing to forego for a while.

So the storm passed and every one was happy.

•

KATHERINE MANSFIELD
Leves Amores
(1907)

*Katherine Mansfield's economical short stories (she wrote no novels) were
usually small slices of life, describing a few significant hours in the lives of
her characters and concentrating on some small event that encapsulates both
the protagonist and the larger meaning of the story. Often they evoked her
New Zealand childhood, as in 'Prelude' (1918), or sensitively portrayed
women ('A Dill Pickle', 1920). Mansfield's own life was troubled by
unhappy relationships with both men and women, and she was already ill
with tuberculosis when she married John Middleton Murray in 1918.*

*Because the sexual and political elements in her stories were so subtly
expressed they were often missed altogether, though to dismiss this as 'double-
talk', as some contemporary critics have, is harsh given the restrictions on
plain speaking that prevailed at the time. 'Leves Amores', which like Kate
Chopin's 'The Storm' remained unpublished in the author's lifetime and was
discovered only recently, seems to indicate that Katherine Mansfield would
have spoken more plainly if she could.*

I can never forget the Thistle Hotel. I can never forget that strange
winter night.

I had asked her to dine with me, and then go to the Opera. My room was opposite hers. She said she would come but – could I lace up her evening bodice, it was hooks at the back. Very well.

It was still daylight when I knocked at the door and entered. In her petticoat bodice and a full silk petticoat she was washing, sponging her face and neck. She said she was finished, and I might sit on the bed and wait for her. So I looked round at the dreary room. The one filthy window faced the street. She could see the choked, dust-grimed window of a wash-house opposite. For furniture, the room contained a low bed, draped with revolting, yellow, vine-patterned curtains, a chair, a wardrobe with a piece of cracked mirror attached, a washstand. But the wallpaper hurt me physically. It hung in tattered strips from the wall. In its less discoloured and faded patches I could trace the pattern of roses – buds and flowers – and the frieze was a conventional design of birds, of what genus the good God alone knows.

And this was where she lived. I watched her curiously. She was pulling on long, thin stockings, and saying 'damn' when she could not find her suspenders. And I felt within me a certainty that nothing beautiful could ever happen in that room, and for her I felt contempt, a little tolerance, a very little pity.

A dull, grey light hovered over everything; it seemed to accentuate the thin tawdriness of her clothes, the squalor of her life, she, too, looked dull and grey and tired. And I sat on the bed, and thought: 'Come, this Old Age. I have forgotten passion, I have been left behind in the beautiful golden procession of Youth. Now I am seeing life in the dressing-room of the theatre.'

So we dined somewhere and went to the Opera. It was late, when we came out into the crowded night street, late and cold. She gathered up her long skirts. Silently we walked back to the Thistle Hotel, down the white pathway fringed with beautiful golden lilies, up the amethyst-shadowed staircase.

Was Youth dead? . . . *Was* Youth dead?

She told me as we walked along the corridor to her room that she was glad the night had come. I did not ask why. I was glad, too. It seemed a secret between us. So I went with her into her room to undo those troublesome hooks. She lit a little candle on an enamel bracket. The light filled the room with darkness. Like a sleepy child she slipped out of her frock and then, suddenly, turned to me and flung her arms round my neck. Every bird upon the bulging frieze broke into song. Every rose upon the tattered paper budded and formed into blossom. Yes, even the green vine upon the bed curtains wreathed itself into strange chaplets and garlands, twined round us in a leafy embrace, held us with a thousand clinging tendrils.

And Youth was not dead.

•

ANNA-ELISABETH WEIRAUCH
Forbidden Love
(1919)

If writers like Kate Chopin and Katherine Mansfield had been experiencing difficulties in publishing their more intimate thoughts in Britain and the USA, in Germany in the early years of the century things could be made a little more plain. Anna-Elisabeth Weirauch's Der Skorpion *(the significance of the title becomes apparent in the concluding episode below) was first published in 1919, when its sensitive portrayal of a romance between two young women, in sharp contrast to the bourgeois household from which Myra flees, caused some outrage; this did not prevent the author from continuing to develop the story into a fully-fledged trilogy, however.* Der Skorpion *was not translated into English until 1932, since when it has acquired something of a cult following under the title* Of Love Forbidden.

Myra sat on the window-sill in the bright, friendly mansard room, smoking a cigarette and polishing her nails. On the white cover of the sewing-table which Myra had degraded or advanced to a dressing-table, a thick, little, black book lay open – the New Testament.

The door was pushed ajar and her cousin Hermann insinuated himself through the crack. But he stopped midway and stood toying with the latch.

'Coming down for supper, or have you still got a headache?' he asked laconically.

'Shut the door, child,' Myra commanded in a low voice. She did not want the cigarette smoke to float downstairs and assail Aunt Antonia's sensitive nostrils.

The boy closed the door but continued to toy with the latch.

'Why do you hang on to the door?' asked Myra, amused. 'Come in, come in! Take a seat!'

The boy hesitated. 'Of course, we're not supposed to come up here,' he ventured. 'But if your headache is better, I guess you can't be sick any more!'

'Sick?' said Myra in some surprise. 'Are you supposed not to come up here because I'm sick?'

'Yes,' said the twelve-year-old, too shrewdly for his age, 'because it's contagious!'

'Ah, Mannie!' Myra uttered a short laugh. 'My sickness certainly isn't contagious.'

'What kind of a sickness have you?' The boy drew nearer curiously.

Myra hesitated. The boy cast a covetous glance at the cigarettes.

'Give me one!' he begged suddenly.

'Certainly,' said Myra. 'As many as you like. But you've got to mail a letter for me, secretly, so that not a soul sees you. Can you be depended on?' Myra glanced at him sharply and searchingly. The boy's honour was touched.

'Do you think I'd let myself get caught?' he said with conviction. 'What do you think I am, a dummy?'

He received the cigarettes and the letter and stowed them so artfully in his blouse that Myra smiled. 'This is not the first thing he's hidden from his mother's sharp eyes,' she thought.

But he was still reluctant to go. He hesitated for a while and then came out with it. 'Say, what kind of sickness *have* you?'

Myra wondered what she should tell him. Then her glance fell on the cigarette case. 'Well, Mannie,' she said after a pause, 'I was bitten by a scorpion, and now the poison is all through my blood. And you know, the only thing that will cure a scorpion's bite is scorpion's poison. It's all superstition that it's contagious. It's only phalanges that are so poisonous you die from washing in a basin that's been used by somebody bitten by one. Your mother has mixed them up.'

'Then it's not contagious?' asked the boy, venturing a step nearer.

'No!' Myra shook her head with a doleful smile, 'I believe that people can die of it – but it's not contagious.'

*

Young Hermann, who undertook to convey the letter to the post office with much secrecy and a most important air, was firmly convinced that it must be a love letter which had been confided to him. He would have been greatly astonished could he have learned that the letter spoke more of him, of little Hermann himself, than of love.

'Formerly I used to hate my uncle's children,' Myra wrote after a matter-of-fact recital of the events of the past few days. 'I had no reason to hate them except that they had such protruding ears. Tell me, dear, what has changed me so completely? Now I see character in every childish action, I see destinies inextricably bound up with those characters.

'I have made a discovery, Olga. You'll laugh at me. My Aunt Antonia has closed the bookcase to me and laid the New Testament on my table. I have a suspicion that she meant to punish me with it. A year ago, at the height of my rebellion, I flung it against the wall and would never have believed that I could actually read it again. And yet we've made friends once more! What a glorious book it is! But you'll laugh at my discovery of the fact. Is there anything beautiful on earth that you do not know and love?'

Uncle Jurgen and Aunt Antonia were most agreeably surprised by Myra's behaviour. They had expected an unmanageable child whom it would be necessary to tame, if the occasion required, by force. They found a quite perfect and lovable young lady. Hence they disliked to be always restricting and supervising her, and allowed her one liberty after another.

Myra took full advantage of these liberties and began preparations for her flight. Day or night, she had never had any other intention and her constant preoccupation with such plans kept her in a state of almost wantonly happy excitement.

But the first problem was where to find money. Myra sold everything with which she could possibly dispense. Still it was not enough. She began to dispose of articles from the household. But that was difficult and impractical. In the first place, it might be discovered before she was gone, and then all would be lost. In the second place, the results did not repay the trouble it required, and it hurt her to see valuable things given away for a song.

One day Uncle Jurgen received a large sum of money by mail, and locked it away in the desk, in Myra's presence.

Myra stared as if hypnotized at the locked desk. Here was all she needed, but how could she get at it?

She lay all night without sleeping, or even trying to. Her mind was working feverishly. Should she break open the desk that night? There was no train at that hour which would be certain to bring her to the city before daybreak.

The next day Myra procured a half-dozen keys from the locksmith. She told him some story about a key to the bookcase which she had lost, and was delighted at the assured and unembarrassed manner with which she told it.

That night she stole down and tried the keys. Nearly all were easy to insert, but they did not unlock the desk.

Next day she asked for her uncle's keys in order to get a book from the library. While she was kneeling in front of the bookcase, she removed the key to the desk from the ring. In its place, she attached one resembling it.

She took a book from the case without seeing what it was.

As she handed the keys back to Uncle Jurgen, she felt sure he must hear the furious throbbing of her pulses. She thought her face must be as white as chalk and made an effort to set her frozen lips in a smile.

Her uncle took the keys without glancing up from his newspaper, and with a brief 'Thanks', thrust them into his trousers pocket.

Myra packed her suitcase and sent a telegram. Late in the afternoon, she carried the suitcase to the station.

At half-past seven they sat down to supper. The train left at half-past eight. During supper Myra complained of a headache. At her request her uncle gave her a headache tablet and advised her to lie down immediately.

Myra said 'good night' while the others were still at table.

In order to reach the stairs from the dining-room, she had to pass through the darkened living-room. While she listened to their voices in the adjoining room, expecting at every moment to hear a chair scrape as someone rose, she unlocked the desk and crammed a handful of bills into her pocket.

In the hall her coat was hanging, a piece of forethought. She slipped into it and opened the little rear door that gave on the garden. She did not dare pass the dining-room windows in front.

There was nothing difficult about swinging herself over the low garden fence. She looked back once. That side of the house was completely dark. She listened. Not a door opened or window rattled. Then she turned and ran as if the Devil were after her, across the fields, to the station.

During the journey on the train, she fought against an agony of fear. She saw herself pursued, handcuffed. The train seemed to crawl along at an intolerable pace, and to stop much longer than required at each station.

With sudden terror she thought of the possibility that her telegram might not arrive in time or that Olga might not be at home to receive it.

And what in God's name was she to do if Olga were not at the station!

To go home was impossible. She could already feel the strait-jacket and handcuffs. Should she rush through the night to Olga? Ring a strange doorbell and wake up the people in the pension? What right had she to do that?

There was nothing left but to take a room for a night at a hotel. But where would she be safe? Early next morning they would be searching everywhere for her. She shuddered to think of what lay ahead.

There were moments, too, when she regarded her own actions with astonishment, terrified by her daring. Suddenly feeling the bills crinkling in her waist, she asked herself with amazement, 'Good God, how did I ever manage to do it?'

At eleven twenty the train arrived at the depot. The light and the tumult in the buzzing hall, whose vast vault was lost in darkness, was still more alarming than the silent night of the fields.

But Olga Radó was there.

Amidst that sea of hurrying, scurrying, searching people she stood perfectly still, but drawn up a little taller than usual. Sur-rounded by stupid, stolid, deformed faces, her own pale face shone brightly. From under her dark brows, which were knitted as if threateningly, her dark eyes sparkled and peered along the line of coaches.

Myra flung open the door before the train stopped. Regardless of all, she forced her way through the crowd, jabbing her suitcase into people's knee joints. She stretched out her hand, no, she clutched like a falling man at a support, crying between tears and laughter, 'Olga!'

Olga's face, which had turned abruptly to her, remained grave. Not the ghost of a smile relaxed those tense features.

'Myra!' she said in her deep voice. 'My child! What folly are you up to now!'

Myra was a little taken aback. Not much. She would have preferred another reception – but what difference did these words make to her or the tone of these words? Olga was there. She gazed into her face, listened to her voice.

Now everything was all right.

'Are you angry?' asked Myra, her eyes laughing, while she clung to Olga's hand. 'If you really are angry, you old Philistine, I won't even dare confess all the wicked things I've done!'

'I'm not angry,' said Olga earnestly, 'I simply refuse to be in any way responsible. If you've run away, that's your affair. I have not influenced you to it by a single word, a single glance. I knew nothing about it. I want to get that straight now and forever!'

'Yes,' said Myra, 'but as soon as you've got it straight, perhaps you'll tell me whether or not you're glad to see me.'

'If I must be candid,' said Olga with a vague smile and without looking at Myra, 'I'm not unglad you're here, but I'm a little disturbed. Have you reflected at all as to what is to become of you now?'

Myra had thought about it. But reflected? No, that was certainly not the right word. She had thought of herself as coming to Olga in order to be with Olga, to remain with Olga. She had pictured herself in Olga's comfortable room, the one room in which she had known happy hours, had meant to hide herself there, never to go into the street, never to go home – now she was aware of the folly of the idea and did not dare to declare it to the shrewd eyes watching her.

'I don't know,' she said pitifully. 'I only know that I can never go home, never, never, never, never! I'll look for a job as a nursemaid or a chambermaid – anything!'

'Do what you like as far as I'm concerned!' Olga stood and closed her eyes for a moment as if in mortal terror. 'You are positively brutal, Myra! Don't you see how you're going to incriminate me! I can't accept responsibility for this, I can't!'

They were still standing on the platform, which was by then almost emptied of its swarming crowds. Only a few night travellers were still hurrying toward the exit.

Myra felt tired and shattered; the light suitcase was like a ton in her hand. The draught in the vast hall made her shiver.

'Can't we sit down in the waiting-room for ten minutes?' she asked dejectedly. 'Perhaps if I think about it quietly, something will occur to me that I can do. But if you feel so tired, why don't you go home?'

'Yes,' said Olga, 'and leave you sitting here alone all night in the depot! Have you gone clean crazy, my dear child?'

They sat in the empty waiting-room and Myra related the story of her flight. She took the crinkled bills out of her waist and thrust them into her pocket.

Myra had almost expected Olga to laugh. While she was telling the story, the whole business struck her like an incredibly comical adventure. But Olga's face remained intensely serious.

'And now?' she asked.

'I'm going to a hotel!'

'And I?'

'You are going back to your pension!'

'I won't leave you alone.'

'Come with me, then,' said Myra with a flame of hope.

'Yes,' said Olga bitterly, 'and the first thing tomorrow morning the police will come and arrest us. No, thank you. I'll probably be accused of making you commit grand larceny.'

'Then,' said Myra after further reflection, 'in that case we'll have to behave like real embezzlers. That is, take the next train and keep going. We'll simply get off at some station or other and go to a hotel. From there I'll write my father, and beg him first of all to straighten out the money business. Perhaps he'll be reasonable and I'll be able to come to some agreement with him. In six months, I'll receive my grandmother's legacy. If my father won't give me anything, I'll borrow against my legacy: it can be done somehow.' Myra looked at the huge schedule. 'The next train leaves at midnight!'

Olga's face had lost its stern expression. Her eyes were laughing with a deep joy. But she still hesitated.

'You're absolutely crazy!' she said. 'No nightdress, no toothbrush!'

'I have linen enough,' said Myra eagerly, 'and we can buy a toothbrush!'

'What ideas you do have!' said Olga slowly.

Myra saw she was already half convinced.

'Grand ideas!' she said radiantly. 'Fascinating, entrancing ideas. Don't you think so?'

'Yes, but *I* never would have thought of it,' said Olga emphatically. '*You* talked me into it. It's your idea and no one else's!'

'Absolutely! I'm much too proud of it to let anybody else claim the authorship.'

The midnight train was a passenger train. They sat alone in a compartment for non-smokers, that was dimly illuminated by the blue-shaded light in the ceiling.

They played at flight. They stooped whenever anybody passed outside. They breathed freely again as soon as the train had started. Myra did her hair differently so as not to be recognized.

'You know,' said Myra mysteriously, 'we certainly ought not to get off at the place our tickets call for. If we do, they'll be after us immediately. We'll simply get off at some other stop.'

'Yes,' Olga agreed, 'seven stops from here. Seven is a mystic number.'

Myra was enthusiastic. 'It's beautiful, it's wonderful! We go on, and we don't know where. We get off, and we don't know where. We'll wake up early tomorrow morning in a strange city, and won't know the name of it.'

'How strange that sounds!' said Olga, paraphrasing the words. 'Like something really profound! We live – and we don't know how! We love – and we don't know why! We die – and we don't know when!'

'No,' said Myra, 'I don't know when! Thank God. But I do know why! Also, thank God!'

The ghost of a shadow seemed to pass over Olga's face as if she wished not to hear what Myra said. 'I used to long so dreadfully to know when I would die,' she said reflectively. 'I think it is so unjust for us to know absolutely nothing about how much time we have before us. We ought to have a right to regulate that! I used to envy a friend of mine who died of tuberculosis. She knew exactly – so much of my lung is left, I can live so much longer provided I economize, provided I spare myself. Or I have the choice of squandering the rest, of throwing away what's left. That must be beautiful! As it is, you know, I never can leave my room until it is cleaned up, because I suffer so from the fixed idea – who knows if I shall ever return. The thought is so appalling to me that some time I may have just to step out of life and leave everything in disorder behind me!'

Myra was on the verge of tears. She wanted to conceal, to dispel the sadness that was tormenting her, so she said with affected rudeness, 'Don't you think you're really insane? Perhaps you'll be good enough to choose some other topic of conversation for this dismal night-journey! If you don't, I'm going to sit in the next compartment until you've finished your meditations.'

'Child!' said Olga, smiling and clasping her hand. 'You are quite right! Scold me! It's because of my stupid oracle!'

'Oracle?' said Myra, astounded.

'Haven't you found that out about me yet? I'm like these old peasant women who, whenever they are in trouble, stick a knitting-needle in the Bible and fish out a quotation.'

'But you haven't got a knitting-needle,' said Myra, laughing.

'Nor a Bible either! The Bible must be an heirloom. A new one is no good. But you really don't have to have a Bible for that purpose: you can take any book and open it. It's remarkable, what answers you sometimes find. I asked yesterday, for example – when your telegram came – whether I should go to the depot . . .'

'And?' asked Myra in suspense.

'Oh, it's all silliness,' said Olga with a wry smile. She turned away and stared intently out of the window into the black night that was flitting by them.

'Of course, it's silliness,' said Myra sincerely. 'But it worries you all the same. And you won't see how really silly it is until you've told me. So tell me – then we can laugh at it altogether.'

Olga turned to her again. She was trying to maintain an uncertain smile.

'When Radomonte Gozaga entered Genoa – in some campaign of vengeance or other, I don't remember just what – he wore a doublet on which was embroidered a scorpion. Under it was the legend, *Qui vivens laedit, morte medetur*. "What life wounds is healed in death." Is that an answer or not?'

Myra seized Olga's hand. She must rend some veil that the words, which had been uttered with such effort, had thrown over her.

'You are certainly insane!' she said. But her voice did not ring true. She had to clear her throat of a sudden huskiness.

The brake ground under the coaches. 'The sixth stop!' said Myra mysteriously, her eyes big. 'The next is our fate. I hope to heaven it isn't a large city.'

When the train was once more in motion, they began to make ready to get off. The next stop might be ten minutes or an hour distant – they did not know.

They had placed their suitcase on the seat, and were standing side by side at the window, their faces pressed against the pane in an effort to penetrate the darkness rushing past.

'There are lots of woods in this country,' said Olga, 'pine woods!'

'Yes,' Myra exulted, 'we'll go walking in them tomorrow.'

The woods ended. Again, broad fields. Then at a distance they could not estimate, as though set between the gently rolling furrows, a tiny light twinkled. Another, and another.

'Look! Look!' cried Myra, in raptures. 'Maybe that's our stop.'

The train was slowing, creaking, puffing. Wooden columns flashed out suddenly, supporting the roof of a narrow shelter. The train stopped.

Olga seized the suitcase, lifted the latch and sprang down the high steps. Myra followed her, in a strange dreamy trance. She was worn out by the two sleepless nights; her senses, sharpened a thousandfold, seemed to notice everything. The thin film of hoar-frost that covered the earth, the coarse faces of two women in peasant's attire who hurried past, the conductor's long-drawn shout, the red hands in knitted mittens of the man at the guard gates, the little dark room, its walls pasted up with bills, and the worn benches, the whistle of the departing train behind her – all was impressed on her mind with ineradicable distinctness.

Olga pushed open a door, descended a flight of stone steps, and they were standing on the uneven flagstones of a broad square, feebly illuminated by the lights of the station.

Left and right – pitch darkness. As far as they could see –

nothing but bare, twisted trees, unpaved, sodden paths, slightly frozen over.

At a little distance there was something that resembled the beginning of a street.

Olga stood still and looked at Myra with a smile. 'Well,' she said, 'are you shivering already? What would you give now to be safe at home under an eiderdown, with the electric light to turn on whenever you want it?'

'Nothing at all!' said Myra defiantly. 'On the contrary, I think it's extremely pleasant right here. And if we don't find any accommodation, I shall mind it for your sake only. It was I who led you into this excursion!'

'Oh, for all I care,' said Olga deprecatingly, 'for all I care, we can spend the night on those benches in the station. But if you're afraid, we can go back and ask the man at the guard gates if there's a hotel.'

'No,' Myra insisted, 'don't ask. Let's go on.'

The street broadened to a kind of market-place. On one side, was a long, squat, grey box with a broad roof, sloping low, and several dormer windows. Over the broad arch of the dark entrance a tin star was swaying, not unlike a shaving-basin, while a big blue lantern, swinging from a beautifully curved arm, illuminated the words: 'At the Sign of the Blue Star. Hotel and stable accommodation.'

'Look,' said Olga, 'even a hotel!'

They looked for a night bell. They felt a metal knob, tugged at it and succeeded in evoking a shrill ring that made them start, so hair-raisingly did it shatter the silence.

Steps, voices, a light.

A sleepy-looking individual appeared in the doorway, slippers on his bare feet, a jacket held closed under his chin with his left hand.

Olga took over the management of negotiations.

She told the sleep-drunk man a long tale of the train by which they had just arrived, and how the Blue Star had been recommended to her even in Berlin, and how she regretted having had to disturb his slumbers, but the trains arrived at such uncomfortable hours, and they couldn't remain on the streets, and, of course, the people at the station had directed them here.

He conducted them into a big, dark, cold room. It was evidently the Blue Star's 'imperial suite'.

The high, broad bed, the ponderous plush sofa almost vanished in the vast room. Between the windows stood a huge, gold-framed mirror before which, on the console, were wax flowers under glass, while the walls were elegant with numerous gay prints, most of them in heavy gold frames.

'Mine host' stooped and lit a gas heater. A long row of little pointed blue flames puffed up, were mirrored in a reflector of grooved copper that cast a warm and ruddy glow on the shabby carpet.

'Splendid!' said Olga, tossing her gloves on the big, round, plush-covered table. 'Now it will be warm here, too. That's simply ideal! No, sir, we don't need another thing. We should like to have breakfast here in the morning. Is this the bell – splendid! Thank you! Good night!'

The door closed behind him.

'Wonderful!' said Olga, including it all in a wide embrace.

'Are you serious?' asked Myra timidly. 'I was afraid your sense of beauty would be in constant agony! Those pictures! And those artificial flowers, and the plush upholstery!'

'Simply splendid!' said Olga. 'It just couldn't be any different. I'd have been terribly disappointed if those fighting stags were not here, or that wonderful Empire maiden with the apple tree in bloom. Do you think I want to see Chippendale furniture in the Blue Star? God forbid! As it is, I think it's simply heavenly!'

Myra unpacked her suitcase, spread night-gowns on the bed, set bottles and boxes on the wash-table. Olga walked about noiselessly, whistling with soft, sweet flute tones. She stopped before each picture, studying it with childish enthusiasm, while she made up long stories about it.

'Here,' said Myra, laying her silk kimono on the chair, 'you can put that on.'

'And you?'

'I have my wrapper, that's all right for me.'

'Wonderful,' she said, 'simply wonderful! Now all I need is warm feet. Then I'll be absolutely happy.'

She rolled a chair up to the gas heater and began to take off her shoes.

'Shall I help you?' asked Myra, eager to serve.

'I never heard of such a thing!' said Olga provoked. 'Why, I wouldn't let my maid do such a thing for me!'

'That's another matter,' said Myra, smiling. 'It's a distinction that one does not confer on maids.'

'You're certainly insane!' Again that sudden deep crimson pulsed into Olga's cheeks.

She had drawn off her stockings and was holding her bare feet toward the flame. She raised her arms and slowly ran Myra's brush over the hair that fell in heavy black curls about her neck.

Myra jumped up and turned out the light.

'Now,' she said with a laugh, 'you can have a painting made of yourself, or a chromo, and frame it in gold and hang it on the walls here. Title: *Au coin du feu*, or The Witch, or Firelight, or something just as good. How can anybody be so shamelessly lovely? Child, what a marvellous foot you have! But so cold, they're always like ice!'

She clasped both hands about Olga's foot. It was as beautiful in line and colour as if a master hand had chiselled it out of marble. But it was as cold as stone.

Myra endeavoured to warm it in her hands, but then she could not resist temptation – she set her lips upon its cool, smooth, white skin.

Olga broke away, sprang up and ran through the dark room to the window.

'Olga!' cried Myra, terrified, and rose, hesitantly. 'What is the matter? What's wrong with you?'

No answer. Myra went over to her. But when she reached the window and stretched out her hand toward her, Olga dodged as if hunted, along the wall.

She stood, cowering, in a corner, Myra barring her way.

Her lovely pale face gleamed weirdly in the dark. Her tense features were at once frightened and threatening, like a wounded animal's, that sees itself surrounded and prepares to defend itself desperately.

Myra shrank from the expression of those compressed lips, those darkly glowing eyes. Timidly she laid her hand on Olga's arms, which were folded across her breast.

Olga started and cowered deeper in her corner.

'Go away!' she said through clenched teeth. 'Let me be!'

'You must not stand in your bare feet on the bare floor,' said Myra on the verge of tears. 'You'll catch your death of cold. I don't

want you to do anything but sit by the heater. I can sleep in the
hall, in front of the door, or I can take another room, or I can jump
out the window. But come out of that corner, I can't bear to look
at you a minute longer!'

She seized her by both shoulders, but Olga shook her off.

'Let me be!' she said angrily. 'Can't you see that you're torturing
me to death? How can anybody be so stupidly cruel?'

Her voice broke and suddenly her face was covered with tears.

Myra could control herself no longer. Her eyes, too, brimmed
over.

'I don't understand!' she said with quivering lips. 'If I'm so
hateful to you that you can't stand me, what are you here for? Why
do you have anything to do with me? No one can like a person
whose presence is a torture to him. But I know why you can't stand
me!'

'Why?' asked Olga astonished.

Myra shook her head in silence, still struggling with her tears.

'Why can't I stand you?' Olga demanded more urgently. 'Answer
me! I want to know!'

Myra still avoided looking at her. 'Because I love you too much!'
she said bitterly and sadly. 'It must be dreadful to be loved by
someone whom you do not love! Almost disgusting!'

'Idiot,' said Olga and stroked Myra's hair very tenderly.

'Oh, don't,' said Myra and disengaged herself from the hand.
'There's no use forcing one's self.'

Olga let her arms drop heavily.

'One must force one's self,' she said, breathing softly but with an
effort. 'If I did not force myself, I would so smother you with
caresses that you'd be frightened to death and run away.'

Myra felt the pulse throbbing in her neck so that she could
scarcely breathe.

'Don't do it,' she said. 'Though I would certainly never run
away, I might go mad with happiness!'

Then Olga slowly raised both her slender white arms and laid
them on Myra's shoulders. Myra felt their powerful, delicious
pressure grow tenser and tenser.

Since Olga was barefoot, their faces were almost on a level.
Their eyes bored into one another, gravely, unflinchingly, while
they felt in every vein the terrible throbbing of their hearts.

Then they bent toward one another, like two thirsting souls.

They did not release one another again. They walked through the room, nestling close together, they sat on the edge of the bed in one another's arms.

The coarse, damp sheets exhaled a chill miasma.

They did not speak. But like a murmuring music, they heard the droning pulse of one another's hearts, and the breath that came quicker and quicker.

Then they lay nestling one against the other like children tired with play, while their lips brushed eyelids and cheeks as gently, as softly, as a butterfly a swaying flower.

'Little one!' said Olga, and all the bells pealed in her voice. 'My beautiful, my good one!'

'My dear,' said Myra. 'Oh you miracle of heaven! What are you really? Are you a wild creature? Or a god? Or the spirit of a white orchid?'

'I don't know,' said Olga. 'I believe I am a god. But an hour ago I was a poor tortured creature. Are you not proud, little girl, to be able to work such miracles?'

'I wish I could work miracles,' said Myra longingly.

Olga laughed a hard laugh. 'Then you'd change me into a man!' she said.

'God forbid!' cried Myra, clasping her in both arms. 'Never! Never! Never! But if I could work miracles, I'd never let this night end. I would make it last for ever!'

The red glow of the copper behind the gas flame filled the room with a warm light. The little pointed flames trembled gently, and the bright spot on the worn gay carpet trembled, too.

Olga leaned on her elbows, supporting her head in her hands. Between her white fingers her black curls peeped. In her pale face, her clear dark eyes glowed in infinite majesty and clarity, like twin stars.

'For ever!' she said softly. 'Everything that is God, is eternal! Do you not feel that this night belongs to God? Time is an invention of the Devil. Satan invented the passage of time in order to make man apostate to God. But God remains eternal. Satan invented much else, besides, sickness, pain, vermin and money. Above all – money! But time came and the passage of time, and could never be dispelled again. Now they are a part of every invention of the

Devil. But what is God's is eternal. New happiness always effaces old pain as if it had never been. And happiness endures. No pain can efface it. Don't you feel that something has happened to your soul that must remain with it beyond all death? Don't you feel that this hour has changed you beyond any power of death to change?'

'Yes,' said Myra. 'And more than any birth. I was born today – not twenty years ago. Now I can say to myself for the first time consciously: "I live!" '

'*We* live!' said Olga, clasping her to her, with an exultation in her voice that was like the jubilant cry of a wild bird rising in flight.

'We live, sweetheart! For ever, and ever, and ever, we live!'

Translated by Whittaker Chambers

•

COLETTE
Mitsou
(1919)

Her popular Claudine *books were published under her husband's pseudonym, Willy. When they separated in 1904 she used the name Colette Willy, which she later shortened to just Colette. She worked as a music-hall dancer and actress, and became a prolific writer, finding even greater success with the* Chérie *series in the 1920s, and with* Gigi *(1945), which inspired the famous musical.*

Many of her works, both fact and fiction, were based upon her own experiences and show her preoccupation with issues of sexual politics. As The Feminist Companion to Literature in English *notes, Colette's enormous* oeuvre *'is remarkable for its lyricism and its extraordinary crossing and mixing of genders and genres, social classes and cultures . . . [she] alters the rules of literary play'.*

On another level, Colette came to epitomize France's reputation for sauciness. Certainly, 'Mitsou' could not have been openly published in Britain or America in 1919.

Mitsou's apartment. She enters, ahead of Robert. He blinks in the electric light and advances rather awkwardly, cautiously avoiding the furniture. Mitsou turns to look at him. She had flung herself so wildly into his waiting taxi, and the journey passed so quickly (sloppy kisses, some casual chat – 'Was it a good audience? Not too tired?' 'What did you *do* for those two hours?' etc.) that she hasn't had a chance to find out whether he is still 'sulking', as she childishly calls it. No, he's not sulking, but he is wary. He is looking at these unfamiliar doors, the Gothic chandelier – the whole room, whose opulence is so bourgeois that it makes him think of the suburbs, with their net curtains and deep-pile carpets. And there waiting for them is the wonderful bed: a double bed with rather coarse sheets, pillows with little blue bows on them and a silk eiderdown – a huge bed, for sleep and for love. 'If she gets me anywhere near that bed,' thinks Robert, 'I'm done for.' Apart from anything else, he's falling asleep on his feet.

MITSOU: Now we can be comfortable, darling; there's no one here but us. Come, let me show you. Here's the bathroom. I'll run you a bath right now. (*He hears water running, and smirks. He has already had one bath, that morning; now he can have as many as he likes.*) This is the boudoir. That door leads out on to the landing, and that's the lav. Come here, I'll show you how to switch on the light.
ROBERT (*with male bashfulness*):   Never mind, Mitsou. I'll figure it out.
MITSOU: That's what everyone says, then in the night you want to have a pee and you bump into everything, and you end up in the kitchen. Just *come and see*: the switch is on the left-hand side. You're not embarrassed that I'm showing you the lav? God, you're so difficult! You're not shy about asking for a drink, but you won't see what everyone needs after they've had a drink. Now, here's the sitting-room.

Robert follows her and his eyes take in the Sea Island silk cushions and the imitation Dresden. He can only think about that bed. Those big fat pillows that are so cool when you slip your arm underneath. The musical bounce of the mattress. The smooth white plane of the sheet. To collapse on to it, one leg that way, one leg this, and fall aslee ... 'Asleep?' He starts. 'I didn't come here to *sleep*.'

ROBERT: What are you thinking about, Mitsou?
MITSOU (*lifting her eyes modestly*):   I was thinking that I would

undress in the boudoir. The bath is ready; I'll only be ten minutes, then I'll run one for you, and then . . .

ROBERT (*looking longingly at the bed*): Then we'll go to bed!

MITSOU (*flattered*): Darling! (*She flings her arms around his neck, kisses him, and scurries off.*)

Robert, abandoned for a moment, goes over to the bed. 'Dare I?' he murmurs to himself; 'Dare I just rest my cheek on that pillow while I'm waiting? No, don't be a damned fool! If my face so much as touches that white linen, when Mitsou comes back she'll find a wallowing beast in boots, snoring his head off.' He sinks into an armchair and tries to think of Mitsou. He is asleep instantly: the rigid sleep of the soldier, sitting up with head erect and face set. This brief petrification conceals a series of brief dreams in which war and youth (for him not far apart) are intermingled memories. Great pools of darkening blood, flashes of fire, a holiday home in the country, a flat-bottomed boat on a sunny river. Barefoot, he's a little boy again, scooping for tadpoles in the water with a straw hat, when Mitsou returns and shakes him.

MITSOU (*in a peach-coloured wrap, her hair loose – flushed and very brave*): Here I am. I'm ready.

ROBERT (*pleased to note that she is not wearing pyjamas*): My darling! Ready for the sacrifice.

He takes her in his arms, then turns serious again because she is naked and because she is trembling.

ROBERT (*very solemn*): Mitsou, I'm so sorry. These clothes – may I go to the bathroom?

MITSOU (*very solemn too*): Yes. I've run your bath. I think everything is there.

He goes. He relishes the hot water, splashing with his feet in the bath, soaping himself with the loofah, appreciating Mitsou's thoughtfulness in providing a new tablet of soap, clean towels, bath-salts and scented toilet water.

Meanwhile, she is shyly climbing into the bed. She is still trembling slightly and notices that the pink ribbon on her silk wrap is quivering. She listens attentively to the muffled sounds coming from the bathroom. Suddenly she thinks of an evening the previous week when Fluff bounded down the staircase at the Empyrée to

meet her date, shamelessly calling, 'Whoopee, girls! There's going
to be some loving tonight! There's going to be some loving
tonight!' (only 'loving' wasn't the word she used). Mitsou doesn't
feel like bounding or yelling. She ponders for a minute, then shakes
her head: 'Yes, but Fluff's wasn't a *love* affair.'

Then she remembers with shame an earlier occasion, when she
gave herself, with frigid politeness, to a Respectable Man, whose
caresses were not what she required. 'How remote it all seems! I
don't know where I am, I'll never know . . . I'm turning into an
old maid.' She sighs – and Robert is back, without knocking. He's
wearing a bathrobe.

MITSOU (*sitting up straight in the bed*):   But I put out pyjamas for
you! On the chair over there.

ROBERT (*whose bath has completely revived him*):   You don't want me
to wear someone else's pyjamas?

He lets the bathrobe fall to the floor and stands before her naked,
very sure of himself: pearls before swine, as Mitsou considers any
fellow who hasn't actually got a paunch to be 'a fine figure of a
man'. She averts her eyes, which is a pity, shrinks to one side of the
bed and says: 'You're sure to catch cold.'

With one leap he is on the bed, opens the bedclothes, dives in
and slips his left arm around Mitsou's waist. He hugs her to him,
and squeezes her whole body against his. She gives a little squeak
like a squashed animal, then remains silently pressed against him,
breathing fast.

ROBERT (*triumphantly*):   Ah! Ah!

But he would be hard-pressed to say whether his cry of victory is to
do with attaining Mitsou or the bedlinen, which caresses the whole
length of his body with the distinctive sweetness of strong linen
that he has recalled so often. Close to his face is another, younger
face with wide eyes that are very dark in the subdued light: a fresh
round face framed by disordered hair. His nose is almost touching
hers: a tiny nose which makes kissing her so easy. His breath still
bears the faint smell of toothpaste and of the toilet water she had
rubbed on her cheeks. With his bare knees he pries apart her two
knees, still encased in their silk wrap, and settles one leg comfortably
between her smooth thighs. They feel wonderfully round, and her

flesh is firm and resilient. This is a nice position. If he was brave enough he would say to this unfamiliar young woman with whom he is so intimately entangled: 'Darling, why don't we just stay like this? Let's go to sleep if we want to, or talk a little. Or we could cuddle for a while – but just cuddle, without any of *that*. We can go further if we feel like it. We may wake up excited in the night . . .

'But alas, I can't call a truce now, can I? We're both afraid of letting the other one down, so I must lift or open your silky veil – which feels rather nice, as a matter of fact. I've got to end our friendly hug. I must get busy, and you've got to do your bit too. Afterwards we'll be thrilled, like kids who smash a window to get some fresh air. Later, they may realize that the window had its uses. Maybe it was better than this draught. Oh well, let's go!'

He doesn't just think this last bit – he says it:

ROBERT: Let's go!
MITSOU (*puzzled*):   Go where?
ROBERT (*tenderly, for she really is delightful*):   My dear, what a nuisance I am. Let's get on with it – stop pretending to be Paul and Virginie, and to hell with all fig leaves!
MITSOU (*quite happy, for the moment, to have no idea what he's talking about*):   Yes, of course.

But her eyelids close, and her fingers remain as chaste as her eyes.

ROBERT (*whispering*):   Mitsou, are you asleep?
MITSOU (*whispering too*):   Sound asleep.

She peeps from under her eyelashes at this handsome, naked faun crouching over her. He laughs, because he can see the black and white of her mischievous eyes. She responds with a little nervous laugh of her own. They are both close to the simple, lovely joy of animals at play – the friendly biting, rolling and tussling. But neither of them can forget their obligation to make love, that seemingly unavoidable engagement. 'Let's go!'

Good-naturedly, he gives it his best effort, which his youth soon transforms into something warmer. His love-making follows the standard procedure. First, the mouth; yes, definitely the mouth. Next comes the throat – never forget the throat. It hardly fills his cupped hands, but is straight enough to warrant the lingering, respectful attention he gives it.

MITSOU (*excited, almost crying*):   Oh!

Her cry, together with the drooping curve of her mouth and the hope that she might really cry, excite the intruder more than he expected. He skimps all the stages which the most elementary manuals of love-making prescribe. In one bound, Robert has everything that his pale subject has to offer. She is prone beneath him, her hair streaming; she has offered no resistance. For a moment he pauses to savour fully, deep within, the pleasure of what he has got. The slow rhythm commences, to the tune of an unheard dirge: the dance of two bodies joined together as if they were closing and healing a wound.

In Mitsou's bedroom, for the first time, a wonderful image is thrown on to the lace-covered wall at the head of her bed: it is the shadow of a rider's naked body, broad-shouldered and narrow-waisted, arched over his invisible mount.

Newly translated for this book by Marie Smith

•

GERTRUDE STEIN
Didn't Nelly and Lilly Love You
(1922)

Abandoning her studies in psychology and medicine, Gertrude Stein left the USA and eventually settled in Paris in 1903, where she quickly became a central figure amongst the artistic avant-garde *and embarked on a lifelong affair with Alice B. Toklas. While sitting for Picasso's portrait of her she wrote her first major work,* Three Lives *(1909) and began to develop the style that she later described as 'insistence', which involved repetition-with-variations in rhythms that were meant to invoke a 'continuous present'. By the 1920s she had become famous as a writer, critic and personality, and, although her style was mocked, recent scholarship credits her as an important precursor of post-structuralist and feminist theory.*

In some of her earlier writing, Stein's lesbian experiences were fictionalized as heterosexual ones. Later, as in 'Didn't Nelly and Lilly Love You', the erotic content is deeply embedded within the prose, as perhaps it had to be; in the same decade, Radclyffe Hall's The Well of Loneliness *was the subject of public outrage and a prosecution for obscene libel.*

How sweetly we are fed.
Credit me that ingratitude is instinctive.
Credit me understanding the repetition of religion.
How sweetly we are winsome.
Credit me with origin of crediting and editing and obliging building so that we can see the same tree.
The same as the tree.

Part one

He prepared in that way.
What did he say.
He said didn't Nelly and Lilly love you.
May we describe the dream.
We are sending the wine and bringing the poem.
Now guess stress.
Distress guess.
Florence in Italy.
Florence in the United States and Italy.
California in France.
California in France and America.
Now you know why occasionally very occasionally they never parted.
Hear them speak.
They speak.
Fierce and tender I send her.
Didn't Nelly and Lilly love you.
She was beset.
Climb it.
Climate.
When he arose.
Was it a rose it was a rose, was it a rose he arose and he said I know where it has led, it has led to changing a heel. We were on a hill and he was very still, he settled to come and tell whether, would he could he did he or should he, and would he, she wound around the town. She wound around the town and he was nervous. Can we ever. Can we ever, can we ever recognize the spot.

As I have said it is an instinct, ingratitude, recognizing the spot, loving her dearly, asking her to do it again and breaking her coral chain is an instinct. Didn't Nelly and Lilly love you.

Once upon a time when Poland had a capital and Washington was the capital of the United States there was born in Allegheny in the state of Pennsylvania the seventh child of a father and a mother. The father had many a brother, the mother was as a mother what would be reasonably certain to necessitate kindling not only religion but travelling. And so they travelled to what was then a capital kingdom which had in it no relation to eliminate any education unaccompanied by intoxication.

Two years old.

Three years old certainly and not weather beaten nor anxious nor reliant nor attending. He attended to the breathing. She came swinging her breathing as she came registering that as a separate suggestion.

In San Francisco in the state of California representative antagonism had not any meaning.

She came not to corrupt impeding but just to tower. How can we have a tower there. We haven't. We have extending.

I extend to you.

And do you too.

Thank you. I was there.

This was received and then there was not a separation but a resultant registration. I register that it was I caused it to be registered that there was a birth and a reception. I received and she I received can you see how a word could have the third part first. Two syllables. She and as for me, I said she can see, and she can see. I can see. I can see.

A division.

I was told it was cold, it was cold I was told.

Tolled for me, the whistle on the steamer, and we went by train the whistle on the steamer whistled and we went by train. She went north to Seattle and she went by train and in Seattle there is a great deal of rain. And I I went back to the petted section of France Austria and arithmetic and I always forgot the languages which are related to their view.

Can you colour trees green and violets blue and I love you and salt water too. Can you colour trees green and violets too and all for you.

It is the custom when there is imitation to speak the language that resembles green. It is the custom when there is tangling to colour the silks the colour of roses and green. It is the custom when the country is willing to leave the colouring in green and vermilion. I often wonder about pink and about rose and about green. We knew what we felt. We felt felt. Austria made felt and I felt that the ruler, do not despise a coloured ruler, I felt that no one was any cruder.

How can you control weddings. When all is said one is wedded to bed. She came and saw and seeing cried I am your bride. And I said. I understand the language. Don't Nelly and Lilly love you. Didn't Nelly and Lilly love you.

It is a coincidence, he has studied the connection between a coincidence and extermination. It was a coincidence that he moved there and that she stayed there and that they were and that he came to be there and she came not to be fair, she was darker than another, how can a sky be pale and how can a lily be so common that it makes a hedge. I do know that she never met him there and that he never knew and that she never knew, and that his father and his mother, and that her mother and her father and her brother, that neither the one nor the other one, ever regret contradiction. We never met. No we never have met. No we did not meet and was it so sweet, and was it so sweet, indeed was it sweet at all. When you don't love wind or colder weather was it sweet at all. Was it at all sweet. I feel nearly as well as ever. Better. Yes very much better. Now actually what happened was this. She was born in California and he was born in Allegheny, Pennsylvania. She was born and raised there but was well aware and why should she not be well aware that to declare that in the distance to declare where in the distance, she went there, when she was littler than a twin, because after all ingratitude is a twin, didn't Nelly and Lilly love you, she went there when she was younger than allowing for that reason. She was seven years old. There we are. She was not at home. How are you all at home.

He was at home. Where was he at home. He was at home in his home. Thank you again and again for everything and also for the earring. They have not met that is to say, receive her. He received her. He had received. And now how radiantly do witnesses see sunshine. How radiantly do they like remarks and fencing. When you think of visiting do you really think of meeting with pleasure. I do not meet you because you are present.

I love her with an a because I say that she is not afraid. How can I tell you of the meeting. How can I tell you that she wrote, that I did not write, that we quote, I quote every body. What do I quote. She quotes this. Don't Nelly and Lilly love you. And I remember that I did say it and I deny it and I say I said. Not so quickly and I really said, What did you really say. I really said what was in my head. I am afraid that I said. Didn't Nelly and Lilly love you. What kind of circumstance was it when I said what she said that I said. It was very well said. Didn't Nelly and Lilly love you.

The circumstances were that we were talking of the relative heat of the countries which we inhabit. I inhabit a warm country. And so do I. And I inhabit a country in which the heat is so great that probably you would not care to walk about in the heat of the day. That is quite true. And you. As for me I do prefer and now I say I did prefer such heat. And now I say we will come this way. Follow me suddenly. And where do we permit ourselves to declare our fond affection. Here. And we say. I passionately may. May I say, I passionately may say, can you obey. Remember the position. Remember the attention that you pay to what I say. I cannot thrust you away. He was perfectly sure that he could endure what he would say. What did he say that day. She said, anyway I can sway with the circles in that way. We have never mentioned circles yet.

Care for me. I care for you in every possible way. Didn't Nelly and Lilly love you.

By columns, I figure by columns.

Did you hear that in the right way.

We mentioned that we had intended to meet brother by brother and brother by brother. This meant no defeat for us or for another. This meant that our future would be for ourselves alone. And so we proceeded. And on the next day I gave the list away, the list of the second day. Do please give the list of the second day. Winding and discrimination and as sister and I do not know when frivolity is acceptable as success and gold, no one knows that gold was to be sold and gold was to have been held. I hold what I have to have held.

And now the real reason why when she wrote she never mentioned me.

Godiva revisited or an excellent retaliation.

She called him a pope and she never inquired just in which way I was inspired. Didn't Nelly and Lilly love you. I addressed this question when I wondered about arms and tears. And was I ever ridiculous. I am afraid I could merit chastity. Can cedars deceive, can cedars deceive as they deceive.

I never deceive cyclamen. And why not when they are radiant. I said, this way in this way or for this anyway or because of this in their way I said can you say, I said had you said what we had said we could resume. The way to resume is to resume. Did the question ever cause confusion. No indeed her mind is clear. Cover in that place they cover in that place they cover the cyclamen in that place. Cyclamen categorically expresses reddening and re-reddening. In this way brown and coral in this way a deep voice and a credit to me. Are you a credit to me. Cause me to stir. I stir the decision. I decide to win my bride. She is my bride and more beside.

I have ceased to apply ages to ages.

And now reason about lettering.

The letter which announced her birth also announced that the forest that in the spring they had not made the excursion because he had reason to mean arranging everything. Can you be what, can you be very hot in April, the end of April the thirtieth of April for instance. Can you become heated motion by tradition by voluntary rushing. And then carry me there and reason for me. I reason for her. I have a reason for her. From then on cauliflowers cauliflowers can have mauve colouring. In warm climates where they are long and not green. Come to me for baths.

Indians are not stout nor do they shout red indians where there are windows. She remembered the obstruction. I didn't sadly. And now where can carelessness be intentional. In that month.

Loving birthday wishes to my husband.

All that is fairest brightest and best. On this your birthday dear Husband be your guest.

Birthday greetings to my dear wife.

My darling wife may all that's good in life be yours today and lasting happiness be yours that shall not pass away. And as the years roll around all gladness may you find and every hour be brighter than the one you leave behind.

When they kindly met and were not meeting as it were where they had representatives when they kindly met they met to be asked will you come and see me.

She came late I state that she came late and I said what was it that I said I said I am not accustomed to wait.

We were so wifely.

She has any quantity of energy and a great deal to do.

When she came late she did not wait and I did not wait and indeed why wait. I love you. Didn't Nelly and Lilly love you.

How can I handle feathers, accompaniments, stations, astrakhan furs, arms and doves, and bitter winter. The winter is not bitter when it blows. And we know we were raised in a temperate climate. Climate and the affections, you know climate and the affections. Why can she in April have a Spanish shawl. Why can she have a Spanish shawl at all. Because I gave it to her.

We went away day before yesterday and she followed later. Who were we. She and I say we. When we went away she followed later and I met her. Did you get here. No I met her and she had lost her key. She found it again immediately. Then we were not together, we were not together whether we were there or whether we went there we went there together.

Do you remember whether we were evidently anxious to be together. Were we evidently anxious to know that a description had been left to identify why we cry.

How can I ever thank you, do you think I can ever thank, really thank and then thank.

Do you think that you are going to be true. Truly you somehow managed to impress us all. Where can we credit an Italian. Italian Italian who says Florence is Italian. Who says California is France. Who says they can hesitate to glance away. You did stay. And then didn't Nelly and Lilly love you.

Do you wish to be there at all. Didn't Nelly and Lilly love you.

Do you wish to be there at all. Mutter to me.

We came to pass there in time and she said moonlight is warmer in the summer. And I said I can explain nearly all lizards and their constipation. Lizards do not go away they stay. Real lizards do not go away they stay. Real lizards I mean coloured green and living on the wall and when they make a mistake they fall. How do you very, how do you very nearly do what you do mean to do. How do you very nearly do, how do you do. We never were blaming Amelia or Eugenia nor Maddalena nor even Harriet, Carrie, Estelle Jane nor Sarah. Didn't they have hours in which to pray. What do you say, didn't they have hours in which to pray. Where did they stay. Did we stay any way. How can I mix summer with winter, this summer with this winter and this winter with that winter and that summer and that summer and this winter. And then we had a terrace there. How do you care how do you come to care here and there. Here and there I said here and there I said here and there.

Can you decline history. I have this word here, the history of a tear. He David often asked and did she make you cry. Try. This was at home this was at home she was at home, she was to be at home.

Can I remember the house where I was born. Can I remember the day that she mentioned to me. I said to her you always please me and she said to me I do not reply I expect to reply by and by and I said do you know that he said by and by is easily said and I said I certainly said I can share that and that and that. And she said, what. And I said I can share that and that and that. And she said you can share that and that and that. I said let me [be] beginning again with the neglected addresses. The first address was the one in which I addressed you as having come to this city. I said to you, how do you do. I also said do you like French bread. After that we knew that no one was present when we were able to say that we had intended to stay away. This is one way of demoralizing their comfort. How comfortable is Isadora. Isadora, how comfortable is Isadora. We knew how to quote. We knew that songs are religious, we knew that quarters are one fourth of the whole and we knew that Nelly and Lilly, didn't Nelly and Lilly love you, we knew that warm and cold that warm and cold and temperate climate and the affections we knew the history of places. I place you.

Continue.

We continue as above.

We cannot consider it as at all likely that Creoles are difficult to placate. How many kinds of Creoles are there, there are Scotch Creoles, Portuguese and French and she was neither Scotch, Portuguese nor French. She was not a Creole. The wonder of it was not that she was not a Creole. The wonder of it was not that I permitted that I did permit, I did not permit, the wonder of it was

not national neither was it religious neither was it personal neither
was it an excrescence. The wonder of it was that I have never been
willing to remember that there could be any other, any other door
or doors any other chair or chairs any other and they had asked and
this door does it lead to the street or does it lead to another door.
Is there another door there. We felt that we dwelt in marble halls
and that we had no other plans. And in Italy and in Italy they do
paint marble. And in Italy they do paint in the manner of marble.
Florence is in Italy and California in France. Now do not startle
suddenly do not startle them suddenly.

We can meet, we can meet, we can meet them on the street. We
can meet also we can also meet merrily very merrily when we are
not certain of distances. The distance from there to there, all the
distance from there to there. Rounder and rounder where is he
around her.

I fancy, I fancy that the history of his recollection is clear. I fancy
that he has been that he has often been told that it clearly that it
very clearly is as the history of his recollection is, clear. He said I
can spare you an occasion in which together we will meet as they
meet them.

The history or histories of a birth place and travelling.

Do you remember just why you said is it to this I have been led.
I have not been led away, let us say I have been led in this way.
Why say what you do say. Let me tell you the history of fireworks.
Saint John is the patron saint of a city not named after him. They
celebrate the day of his martyrdom by celebrations. We never
repent, we turn our backs away we say can we say, Caesars can we
say do as I say. Caesars do not turn away but stay. I put the Caesars
to bed and this is what I said, I want you to do instead, instead of
what, said the Caesars, instead of not doing it and this is what I
said. But as I was saying the celebrating did not cease, it was
necessary that I should walk and what did she say, let us wait for
the day to come and I said marines and navies and she said, does no
one wait there. And I said yes, and she said yes and I said oh yes.
How can you collect all the advantages there are when there are a
great many advantages.

We will not mention what was said when she said that she
questioned me as to what I had said. I said I knew and she said you
know and we said, no we are not to go. And now how about the

vow. I know now that restitution and you can not declare reparation a restitution nor restitution a reparation, you can declare that you are there. There you are.

Pardon me did you say that she was born when she was born. Certainly I said something. Collect me, collect for me. Collect for me, in the same way as you recollect clearly.

The history of this is that there are that there are weddings which are placed by royalty as they are placed and weddings which are in their place by the autumn summer winter spring and February. February and April say February and April. How do you do.

Coloured ribbons of notes.

No one can say of them that they decided to be wide. No one can say of them that they decided beside. No one can say of them that they decided that the bride, can they exercise their pride. A bride beside, can you say that a wedded existence can have precedence. I precede you. And now for the story.

Once upon a time there was a little boy. It was requested that he be a beauty and all that. Thank you so much.

If a railroad train is moving and another train is moving and both of them are in the station waiting why do we not have the same phenomena in a motor car. This shows us to be a receiver of flattering. She does not flatter me.

She came readily. She was weaned but before that, how very expectedly signs did not fail. Quail. Do you quail before me. I didn't.

Erect and right, and Mexico is no toy. No one knows how a toy is made.

Once more I refer to the meaning of birth and blessing. Dilatory do date what you ate and drank. The third. The first the third the first. Now do you refer to dates or ages.

Leave me to be, what, I do not leave you.

Readily made readily made, why is it readily made.

To aid, to aid to aid and an aid. She is an aid to all whom she aids. She aids me and I am sure that she has aided Lilly and Nelly.

Aid and added, to aid to be added. I am sure that she has been added to me. She has not said, mountains. Mountains exist as wholes.

Now please tell me about fishes.

Fishes, stones, shot and pebbles and not shells are dangerous to the teeth.

If fishes were wishes the ocean would be all of our desire. But they are not. We wish for land and sea and for a birthday and for cows and flowers. Our wishes have been expressed. We may say that the history of Didn't Nelly and Lilly love you is the history of wishes guessed expressed and gratified. Didn't Nelly and Lilly love you.

It happened once upon a time that there was easily marriage and a marriage relation. Can you witness a marriage. In the marriage when all the exchange is resolved upon is a marriage where cleaning can be done and ought to be done and where a bountiful providence enriches the music boxes. In relieving music there is no jealousy and yet how could twenty years after more than twenty years after be resolute. They resolved to shove. I can guess what is the price of water and more than water. Why do you mention just what was resolved. I resolve to recognize you and I do. And I resolve to read the rest of it to you. Do you please me. Oh so much.

I have resolved not to say that I agreed to their saying what I had said. And was it denied. Not at my side.

Now we will mention the wedding. If you please. Will the bride acquiesce. She could say yes and I could write many to find such a pleasant opportunity.

And now I will tell of charm. What is charm. The Americans and the Spaniards have it, and the elegance of radiography, all smile when they think that they have the world beneath them. What is the difference between under and beneath. Teeth. Teeth remain firm. Teeth remain firm. Pet me tenderly and save me from alarm. I have no sense of a pastime. Our pastime is to measure beds rather to measure beds.

Can you be fairly necessary to me. Didn't Nelly and Lilly love you. Tell me what you said.

Now I had best fasten it to the door.

Let me remember that I can not pretend to have bettered the answer. You had better give an answer. And I said can you remember that I said, I was not resolutely led. And be wise here, remember how can you have played. I remember asking you this thing, can you have played.

I remember your mentioning hours of practising. I remember your embellishing my illustrations and I also remember coercion. Coercion and cohesion.

Have I refused to beguile. A reason for all this comes to this as an opening. I did not say didn't Nelly and Lilly love you all day. I said I have been very happy today. We mean to read clauses and clauses and phrases and phrases and books and books and writing and reading. We mean to smear the water over the rabbits and inundate the dry earth. The earth is not so dry. In that case we mean to say we began and we began. Come to me to the satisfaction of the garden. The public garden. We stay at home and decide that publicity is our pride. Come and stay. Hear me. Do you hear me. Come and stay. Do you hear me.

Now I wish to tell what she resembles I wish to tell this very well.

She resembles at the same time everything I have mentioned. In the historical sense there is nearly every satisfaction and in this particular we are not deceived. I know my history.

A historical novel is one which enriches all who bore colours and stones and fires. To be fierce and tender to be warm and established, to have celebrations and to lean closely all these establish a past a present and a future. The history of establishment is a history of bliss.

Now in fighting history we find acknowledgements. I acknowledge that you are often precious.

When they began to assist when he began to assist when she began to assist, when he and she began to assist they began to assist them. He began to assist when there was mention of cleanliness and a fountain. And she, she was measured and measured. How sweetly the vowel the already eased country and city, the flooded merchants and almost all the trains established communication. I do not mention others than those that were concerned in mingling in elaborately mingling their addresses. Count on me. Oh yes and what do I see, I see public bathing places and a division. She and a servant came between, she and I never hesitated before that door, she and I cry. We did not know then that we were crying loudly. And please do not hurry to me. It took all that time and when we arranged for the time well in a manner of speaking we arranged very well for the time. We arranged that at that time that doors and then again summer we arranged at that time that suspicions were not poignant nor were objects placed. We plan what we plan. And what we planned. We smile at the bay.

There was no water there was no water there there was no water there there was no water there.

Didn't Nelly and Lilly love you and they were mentioned together. They were not in that respect remarkable and yet how did you know their name. Their name was not the same.

Didn't Nelly and Lilly love you. The occasion was radish, a radish, a red dish, in the sun, tears in the sun do not cool the cheek. Tears in the sun do not run do not run away, do not run away to be the same anyway. And now close it to close the heat out. Close it to close the heat out.

I have promised that I will not mention my iniquities. I take great pleasure in promising.

The splendid example the splendid example here the splendid example, to be here, the splendid example in order to be here, in order that there is to be here that the example is to be here, in order that there is to be here the example in order that the splendid example is to be here, in order that the splendid example is to be here in order that it is to be here it is necessary to admit coercion. Did he kick and scream in the stream and did she dare, did she dare to respond. I respond you respond, he responds and he says yes there is a splendid example.

I find some words very annoying. Annoying is easily met. I annoy him yet. She annoys him yet. I feel that that moment is past. Now indeed there is no speed. Now indeed currents and wild horses. We have forgotten horses. Didn't Nelly and Lilly love you.

She meddled with this she meddled with this then. He did not ascertain what the wedding meant to him. He said I miss I do not miss, I do not miss, he said I do not mistake you, he said I am not mistaken, and he said I am not patiently waiting and he said hearing and everything and he said how can you mean to be beside, and he said, besides and he said I am beside myself and he said I can do as I said and he said I do do what there is to do and he said do you say that you wish to please me and he said by that time I have said that he believes that he himself has read something of a composition and he said how willing I am to wish no invention and he said I do not say dwell and spreading and he said I will find you an hourglass and she said thank you for that intention. He said that the advantage was that he had a great many ways of marking what he saw and he said I lean to you and she said I am satisfied with repetition.

How can you make weddings a wedding. How can you make of weddings a wedding.

How can you make of operas a single piece of phonetic writing. They made many reasons for individual reorganization.

Then came the exact day. Didn't Nelly and Lilly love you.

I can tell you all about tenderness.

Now listen to me carefully.

History can rush along. And what do we do.

We agree you agree I agree and I agree. You agree we agree and I agree. I agree. You agree we agree I agree.

Now then compare glass and a violin. Compare glass and a violin.

This makes us suddenly know that I told you so.

We find that there was really no need of men and women. Sisters. What are sisters, and sisters and brothers. What are sisters and brothers. We found piles of linen and silver and a credit to men and women. And when we happily settled. And when we happily settled the south. We do not go north to go south, nor do we go to the centre repeatedly. We go and we stay and we purchase we may purchase the things that are meant to be suddenly seen.

How can every day suit a queen. And how can decisions meddle easily with all the wall being divided into three parts. I can tell how you mean to say this. I can tell how you mean to say this.

First we gather together. Then we correct couples and after that we arrange medals. More often we tower.

In the meantime we make famous that which is meant to be called readable. About this we have a difference of opinion. Some select a cord and others wood and both together make a fire. We have changed our stove to a chimney and our metal to silver our pink to grey and monkeys and our yellow to assistance. Then when we were all ready we said which. And I said I wish to stay and she said I stay and they said how can you delay and we said it is better to be settled than not and we said go away and he said I can easily go on that day. We we were there we we were there we we were there and we are to be called, we are to be called the resident reader. Then come to see me. We have never changed the wording of that word. Come to see us here.

When we were able to contract we contracted for a door to a door. Thank you that was a success. And then there is every reason to be pleased with actualities. When I arouse myself I say, I did not say it in that way. And in the same ready way they say and in the same ready way they do say.

I do not repeat a title. I feel that I have thought that. Thoughts are revealed by evidence of nationality. And when this access is in process and when this process is praiseworthy, how many praises do you hear. I hear you praise me and I say thanks for yesterday and today. And tomorrow we do not doubt. Then clearly you see what I have never objected to and you. Can you believe my word. Arrangement, we arrange in the best way for the beginning.

It is very peculiar it is very strange that authors are visited. It it very peculiar that collections are visited. It is very strange that everybody is visited. It is very peculiar that in front of them and more often than that that in front of them they do not believe in repetition. I repeat that nearly everything is eaten cooked. Except salad. And she is very fond of that. Nearly everything has been mentioned excepting irresistible onslaught. And why do they hesitate to say that he was unnecessary yesterday and today. He knew when he was occasionally repeating. He knew when he was occasionally repeating this he knew when he was occasionally repeating that. Didn't Nelly and Lilly love you. We haven't seen Nelly since then. Didn't Nelly and Lilly love you. We haven't seen Lilly since then.

And now to withstand history. History has this meaning, it covers them and it uncovers them and it uncovers them and it covers them. Let me tell the history of letter paper.

We were easily deceived by our intention of illustrating a rose by a rose. We were not easily deceived. We did not deceive them nor did they deceive us nor did we deceive them. We were not betrayed nor were we unreasonable. We did indeed know that history had this meaning. We did know that happiness and remarkable happiness we did know that remarkably happiness we did know that they outdistanced double impressions. We also did know that we had not undertaken sheets and initials and also illustrations unnecessarily. We surmised that we were equally to be measured by the rose and by the table. Upon the table and upon the table we replaced no one. We added increased coloration and we added white and vermilion. Not really she said and we said, he said and we said that a rose had just this signification. How nearly we were not certain that this did happen then. By this I mean that I can not recollect the historical present yet. I cannot regret this lack of concentration nor indeed can we be represented as uncertain yet. She knows and I know where these things grow and we know what we mean to bestow. I mean to bestow and I do bestow, how do you bestow, I bestow almost all the dates. I date it today. Today is the day.

I reflect that you reflect about me. I reflect what you reflect about me. I reflect about the conditions of matrimony.

If you were used to this, if you were at all used to this then what would you miss. He said I think of the standard of bliss. Standard has two meanings it can be a banner or an estimate. Standard has in this sense two meanings, I mean to express a wish.

I wish that I were seen to be in the meantime what was annexed. Reflect for me. Tell me that around about that around and about, tell me that around and about that I around and about. Satisfy me sentimentally, and now for a fetish. When I thrill along, when I drill along, soldiers drill to their song I sing of the prohibition of what of reflection. I reflect together.

I see you and you see me I reflect you and you reflect me when this you see repeat for me what I repeat when I repeat pleasantly. I repeat what I have said. What have I said.

I have mentioned that a part of reflections is the history of reflections. Let me tell you further. For instance if it had not been that there was a continuing would loving be indulged in and would there be calculation. I calculate in threes and fours and I in twenties and I in ones and twos and I in the third dimension. I calculate that a horn a motor horn I calculate that a horn is necessary to this end and now I speak above all noise.

Remember me to you.

I reflect upon the causes that there are for recognition, I recognize older ages and I recognize pillows and I recognize finishers. I also recognize curtains and weddings and I also recognize complicated wishes. What do you wish me to do.

This is the history of reflections.

It was very singular that there has never been ready the recoil from capital. A capital is a principal city and capital is possession and capital is to be very well pleased.

In this sense rapidity is certain to be measured. I rapidly measure the older addresses and he wonders do they rebuild operas. Operas are encouraged and so are beds of roses.

In the history of reflection we have ultimately and beginning we begin intimately in considering the history of reflections I have this as my authority. Almost all the changes are stereoscopic and all the emblems are multiplied. I multiply for you.

Now then press this for me.

And teach me a whim.

Let us colour letters.

The history of reflections is measured by radical symbolism. And why do I astonish abruptly. Send me sentences. I send them the sentences they read in their start. We start apart.

Colour me heartily and hear me specifically. And how did he know that I was enamoured. Please do not finish this temporarily and why do you not say, history is this, history with us is this, the history of reflections is this. This is the history.

I mix I mix I mix what do I mix. I do not mix a bird and a bettle nor a second enough. I mix in the necessities of papers. I hear her turning leaves. And then I look up and I say how sweetly camellias may how sweetly camellias may. And now for the organization.

The history of reflections.

I attend to them. When you see all of them being used and when you invite them when you do invite them to feel them let me relate. Do you see that you state that you translate. I translate. Naturally, I naturally relate.

The milk of religion is this, cream and orange and citron. The milk of religion is this, come to their close union. Believe my engagement.

I feel that I refer to that reflection.

I cannot organize oil.

In wondering in very nearly wondering. In very nearly wondering whether there is deliberation. She says. Yes. There is deliberation.

In wondering about rendering that there and in there. How can you practically follow me.

When this you see remember me.

By closing mountains to mounting and winning water wealthily how you utter more than they said. They said yes, I wish, come to me, say what you have said, do not be remarkable, have the suggestion made, freely be sensitive, see the occasion narrowed. Now let me tell this to her.

You know exactly what I have said what I have prayed and what I am. You know exactly for what I wish. I wish that the fish are fishes. And that a cow is a cow. I wish this and I say when in this way I pray, I pray you to do as I do. I do do as you do. In this way you reflect me. I reflect you.

When you hear me speaking creditably. When you hear me speaking creditably you find it to have the value of their stage. Now I have said I mean to be favourable.

How rarely incubation neglects thoughts.

In this way I think the same. They do not reflect birthdays. Call me too easily.

I can manage I can manage that.

I can manage to have the rest said. I say you can conceive. I say can you conceive why I stay. I say can you conceive of an invitation today. In this way reflections take their place.

I reflect about Abraham and about how that name came to be famous. Also how it happened sentences came to make a blessing. I bless you for all of this.

I merely do not see why he wished to remain unintelligible. Do you see why he wished to remain unintelligible. Do you understand why syllables separated in such a way that around them there was audacity. Believe me.

I cannot tie a knot in wool.

For this reason and for this reason alone I have no opposition, I have no one in opposition. For this reason and for this reason, for this reason and for this reason I do not call subjects subjects. Have they no choice, do they not choose citizens. And what can you please, how can you please where can you please. You know very well that I do remain to please. And now let me not feel that I have not said that this has led to their frustration. I do not indelibly deter them. He said that there was that trace. Who traces them for them. I can be hourly faithful. And I do see what I have said what I have said.

I wish to remember this presently. I mention it here because I feel that it will impress. I wish to mention the practicability of housing a cow. In this way cities prosper and Caesars render that which Caesars owe. I do not say this to intimidate Caesars nor do I implore I sweetly caress and impress. Caesars do not reflect they do so well show by the daily activity how useful how tender and how strong and how a Caesar will do no wrong.

Mark me I am expressed.

Thank you very much for your kind attention.

He understands this, I understand that, I understand this, he understands this and he understands that. And then excellent dwindling.

Come to me Francis and friends.

I have developed their relative retention. Do not apply selection to respect. Respect the carpet and the floor and the door and the rest of the pleasure. I please myself too.

Come to me too.

Come to me too today.

Come to me and tell me what did you do yesterday.

I cannot very well elaborate the earnestness of categories. And colour too.

Pardon me when I say he is not selfish.

I blend the glass and the goose. They usually do this for pleasure.

Pleasure is not partaken of because of annoyance nor houses nor is it really a saddler. We have almost forgotten a saddler.

We really admire more savings than ever. And do arouse me. Follow me fairly often. Follow me fairly separately. This is not their reflection nor indeed their relation. They relate themselves to bestowal. Please seize with ease.

An orthodox wedding is an orthodox wedding.

When you have the principal witness decorated, I cannot end there where double where they double together. Where they doubly caress. Caress tenderness. And now accustom me to counselling. I counsel you to listen and to remember that more than one that more than one that more than one. How can you furnish accentuation. Do believe me when you hear me. And now roses for camellias. Did he believe me. Prepare to emerge. I urge you. And you ought to know that willingly that you say as willingly as I am willing I need this splendid suggestion. Explain ribbons to those who wear ribbons. I do not ordinarily infer that there is more favour more in their favour that there is more in their favour. I do not ordinarily mean all this as their spectacle. To be spectacular. How do you mean. To be started in a wire. Why wire.

Eighty nine and ninety. And no less. How curious the handsome is as handsome does. How curiously it sounds.

I have always had a great many responsibilities. I am responsible for this.

Are you responsible for the shilling.

I have always had a great many responsibilities and I am responsible for everything.

And I am very willing to understand strength and resolution. I am very resolute and I admit that the selection of it has been a great pleasure to me. I have selected willing. Are you willing to remember that a cousin is in relation has relation to resemblance and restoration. I restore this to you. When you are through are you a Jew.

Don't explain restlessness.

And now save me for this.

I am earnest and prepared and there is no one to say how are you able to keep it a subject.

She has been told to be gay.

And now I reflect hurriedly and necessarily.

I reflect hurriedly and necessarily and I accustom I occasionally accustom I am accustomed to rest and rising. And in the meantime she says, she has explained that credible witnesses do say that they have decided as to relative climates.

We have often wondered why they relate this of climate. Climate and the affections. How often have I said they quote that. Climate and the affections and interruptions and can you recollect marriage. Of course you can't certainly you can't. Certainly you can not.

I have wondered about engrossing civil ceremony. Have you.

And what does nobility do.

And what does royalty do.

And what do they do.

In this way I cleverly arouse and really rally them. I can not complain in ecstasy. I said what word would best suit the expression of my appreciation. And she suggested, exquisite. I said I considered daisy more decorative and she and I said we will say that. I'll say it.

Consider the rapidly growing waterfall. I can remember the word cascade and the word carousel. For merry-go-round.

I have come to increasing isolated reflections by very simply asserting that at all that they come at all, that they easily come and that it is necessary that they come at all. I furnish them this in that case. I have reference to the extent of the use of that single instance.

Climate and the affections. I have often been quoted as quoting that.

Plan a repetition a general repetition a general of rivers.

We have said that we thoroughly understand that a city in order to have distinction must replace seas by rivers. Seas by rivers. We have thoroughly understood that we need houses when and where we wanted them and that we have repeatedly the pleasure of refusing. How can you be playful and precious. And how can you be so actually reached that even foreigners are famous.

We have come to come there.

And now reach this for me and hand it to me.

Thank you.

And now eagerly satisfy me.

And now pray say yes.

And now consider how unnecessary it has been.

And now tell me again what you have told me.

There there, I say, there there.

There there, an excellent pair.

I stand firmly and I say, rapidly I say he rapidly makes deference necessary.

I defer to you.

And you.

And you.

She and he, he and she, they decide it this way. They have a thousand chances in this.

Now then repeat quietly what you have said. I have said that I do not believe that I do not believe that we reflect more than they say that we reflect. I say that indeed we reflect popularity as well as authority as well as masterpieces and joy. We reflect about this, we decide alternately. We alternate between hiding and precision. Which is the more precise.

This is nice.

Which is the more precise.

How soon will you be fair.

If you are not fair to me what care I how fair you be.

This is very nice.

You understand that I undertake to perpetuate what I state.

I state this and I stare.

At a waist-line.

Can you believe that colours and colours that there are colours called to be presently called established.

And now smile at me determinedly.

I determine myself that this is not a fancy that very really and presently I will establish rows and rows of roses.

A rose is a rose is a rose is a rose.

Satisfy all the dates.

We find that dates are more delicious.

Now then call me again.

In a minute.

And now we find that a bath after breakfast.

That a bath after our breakfast. That you must breakfast. That there must be relation in religion and in civil ceremony, that all ceremony is civil. As for us we often reflect as to whether suddenness is religious or civil or perhaps both.

I think it is not at all present in absence. Because really if they were present and they were they anticipated what. Each other. I anticipate you.

Thank you for that.

Thank you more and more and merrily.

I thank you pleasantly courageously and courteously.

And now no insistence. I do not insist.

Let us converse respectfully.

I respect this in you. And you mean to allow the Atlantic to allow an Atlantic very nearly the Atlantic we have determined to press this to press them.

Come and call.

I call for you freshly.

Respond with ease.

I want to tell you about the trees. I have been very well satisfied and I do not mind displeasing them.

He says that he knows all of the directions that he takes. He says that he knows that accidents are found all around. He also says that he cannot diminish water and all of that is not ready. Are you ready.

We reflect about hurry. I hurry to you. And you hurry. You are in a hurry. I am in a hurry too. I have an extra reason for saying come again.

Now then fresh and refresh. You refresh them for me. I refresh them and you say fish is fresh. It always is. It always is. I say can you supply me today and I say and I say yes.

I say yes and he says yes and they say yes and we say I guess yes. I say I guess yes.

I say I guess yes and we say yes and you say do you see any connection between yes and yesterday. I will repeat this. Do you see any connection between yes and yesterday.

I congratulate you. Upon what. Upon what she is and upon what he is. I congratulate you upon what he is and upon what she is.

I congratulate you upon meaning to be crowned. I am to be carefully crowned. I am to be carefully kept there. He kept him right there. I am going to be carefully kept right there.

Now say to me. I have always had a great many responsibilities. Now say to me I am prepared to be prepared. Now say to me do you wish me to do this. Now say to me and what do you say. Now say to me, certain reasons are your reasons. And now say to me what did you say. You say this to me and we decide together not one before the other. Again and again. Again and again and again. I was not dreadfully embarrassed. I wasn't either. Nor was I at all troubled. Neither was I. Nor did I bother you. No you did not do that. And how often have I said, that you said you did not organize charity. You did not you do organize charity. I am charitable. I am charitable, I am genuinely charitable. And the instance. Consider the instance, consider transport in this instance.

Do not find it selfish. I think of her. I prefer to think of her.

I am being led I am being led I am being gently led to bed.

I am being led I am being led I am being gently led.

This is not nervousness.

I find that they return that they do return. I find that they do return, I find that they do return. He says that it is the fault of the sand. Is it.

And now respected wife let me speak. I wish to say that every day that Katherine barometer today. I wish to say every day, that daisy does stay. I have always had a great many responsibilities, in pointing out reparations does she in pointing out reparations I have earned what I have earned.

Let me know what comes first. Let me know about her restraint. Have I as much real real occasion to enliven me.

Now then again. Now then and again. Now then and again and then now then again.

I have every realization.

There was a way of assisting him, there was a way of insisting for him there was a way of persisting with him there was a way of recording an arbitrary collision. And he said how is the driving there and she said. Stop him. Alright.

I love my love and she loves me, I can reflect and so can she. She can be responsible for me and I can see this responsibility.

I often decline praise.

He murmured about excess.

They murmured about excess not about excess of tenderness. They murmured about excess I exceed the limit.

I have been carefully careful.

Mister and Mrs Picasso, and their boy. I made a joke. Mr and Mrs ourselves and we make it they, they make it say that we make it pay.

Yes indeed we do, yes indeed we do.

I return the line and they incline to reproduce the twine. In this way we say that the hand leads the way. This is a description of Mr Man Ray.

Have you been at all interfered with.

Have you been at all interfered with. The meaning of this is have you been at all interfered with.

When you have seen the result of reflection, and reflection does result in this, when you have seen the result of reflection, reflection does result in this.

Have you seen the result of secondary merriment. Second to none he said, she said, they have said second to none.

Under the circumstances under these circumstances under the circumstances marry me again.

I am a husband who is very very good I have a character that covers me like a hood and must be understood which it is by my wife whom I love with all my life and who makes it understood that she isn't made of wood and that my character which covers me like a hood is very well understood by my wife.

There was a chance that Mr and Mrs Peale did know that they were telegraphing after telephoning and telephoning in order to know why they were so reasonably sure that they stood to win. I like that phrase we can assume that we have won. I like that phrase.

How talented every one who kisses is. They kissed the current and they kissed there.

How shall we win an ordinary apostrophe.

How can you remain extraordinarily permanent.

I have always been fond of permanent.

Chauvinism à part c'est trop tard.

Do not regulate window ribbons.

Now I will tell all about her success at the salon.

She exhibited a picture which was painted. It was a small picture graceful and undistinguished delicate and pretentious and with it there went a condition. The condition was this, authors must not be readers. All their astonishment was be fair, be very fair. And why did they resolve to accept and to accept. Why did they resolve to accept and to accept. Why did they resolve to accept and to accept. Why did they resolve to accept and to accept.

Come again and waver.

I do resolve that merchants who sell water, and water is so dear to me, I am resolved that merchants who sell more water than candles merchants who sell more water than candles have this interest for me.

I interest myself generally in them. And for them not at all for them not at all for them.

How suddenly we scented the weather. How suddenly. Now reflect. I do reflect. I fasten it firmly.

What was it signed. It was signed for you.

Now then.

Again and again.

What did you say.

She knew what to do.

How do you do.

It was very easily arranged that they should encourage exactly where and when they had represented them. Where and why do you say you mean this.

I do very fairly, he is very fairly, they very fairly understand me.

They very fairly understand me and I do authorize them to address it.

Address it address it.

Address it.

He is very merry.

She is very merry.

Do not neglect a tooth, do not neglect a tooth, do not neglect a tooth, do not neglect positive poison, do not neglect ingredients and do not neglect do not nearly neglect to say that.

Not this evening.

What did she say.

And now once more get into the rhapsody, others rhapsodize, we are accustomed to think of it as Christian, others rhapsodize.

Now and the moon.

I was so astonished at the alteration he made in the glove, she wanted it to catch, what, you know, she wanted it to match.

I can breathe easily today and I say, and I say to you I did not mean, I did not mean to deprive you of responsibility. I have always had a great deal of responsibility. I did not mean I did not mean I did not mean to detain you by questioning this and by careful market. Now then say it, careful market. I did not mean to detain you by a careful summary. Careful, carefully, he carried that to the Indian. One little Indian two little Indian three little Indian boys, four little five little six little seven little eight little Indian boys. To an American an Indian means a red-skin not an inhabitant of the Indies, east or west.

A wife hangs on her husband that is what Shakespeare says a loving wife hangs on her husband that is what she does.

I have heard almost all the announcements they have made.

I have indeed wondered if a chinese skirt and a chinese dog and a chinese letter and a chinese cross, he is rarely cross, I have often wondered if it is representative.

And now happily we are said to be in the eye and in the mind an artist. My husband says of me that I have the eye but not the hand of an artist. My husband says of me that he thinks remarkably.

I have been so often interpolated.

My brother says that I should not interest myself in what, you would be astonished, you would be astonished.

I answer we know the interest we take.

And now may we say that we have been interested.

May we say that a pleasure has been a pleasure.

May we say come pleasantly.

May we say that we have always had a great many responsibilities and now we do not consider it this.

I plan and I have a plan.

I plan that the weather will be such that it will be a pleasure to use a fan.

I have been agreeably able to colour it adequately.

And now there was no hurry.

There was no hurry now.

There is no hurry.

I have planned for their care.

I care for them.

I do care.

Do you see them often.

Do you remember how we decided that indeed if he came we would have it said that there would be no admittance. Do you remember that we decided that we had entertained him as frequently as we would and that now when he came we would have him told that we would not receive him. Do you remember that.

She always calls after you and says grumblingly one might say she always adds violently but you do not fear I do not fear, I do not fear and she may hear, I do not fear that he may hear.

Hear hear.

This in a way is the custom.

The custom is that they see to that as a custom. Their custom is to remain advantageous. I do not freely recollect speaking. So have continents.

Did you hear what she said, they are going to have summer time in April in New York city and Chicago. Listen to her and you will hear her. They are going to have summer time in April in New York city and Chicago.

I have been moved to tears.

And were there eggs which were supplanted by flour and flour by milk and milk by wrestling.

I know about wrestling. And how about Sofia, Sofia differs from the girl because she has the letter the extra letter and I know what I see when I hear. I do not hear them at all.

You were pleased not to hear them. I was very pleased not to hear them.

I know that there is no flattery in this. I know that there isn't.

Now then let us tell this to one another.

Do you remember how often we bought cake. Do you remember how often we bought venison. Do you remember how often we bought what we needed.

I feel that none of it is in it in the same way. What did you say. I said that I was certain that I had not put it in in the same way.

What did you say.

I said yes and the name of an acquaintance.

I said yes and the name of the acquaintance.

And now able to state what I know.

I mean that I was sitting there in the chair and that when there what do I mean, what do I really mean. What do you mean.

What do you mean.

I come to realize that responsibilities are used in this way. I am useful. Yes I am useful. And decorative. Yes and decorative. Yes and decorative. And acceptable. Yes and acceptable. And announced. Yes I am announced. Whom shall I announce. You might just as well announce what you feel which is faith in Caesars. All of them say yes. And I say yes.

Now then as to appetite. We have a very good appetite.

He remembers that to quote. What did he quote. He quoted the quota. Lindo. Why is Lindo a quantity. Why is Lindo a quantity of that of which it is composed. Lindo a quantity. Lindo Webb. A quantity of which it is composed. I gently feel of it. This makes it the other way. What did you say. I said I did there first, first in the sense of before, in the sense of before this. That before this.

The canon of Italy the canon of Italy makes the noise and we say, they say she says we say that he says unfortunately he unfortunately says all that he says this is our criticism of that. Meet it but do not greet it. Meet it as the best way to meet him. He is around the sound. He is the declaration of the canon. The canon the Italian canon, the canon of Italy is not debasing. Do believe in honey, they do not they believe in oil. I say and we say and she, she is right. She has been right and she is right and she will be right and fitfully when I say to him, I say to him I beg your pardon. This distresses me and makes me ashamed and I say never today. Never at all today.

I mean to be human nature's daily food. I mean to be.

And now explain exactly what you mean by prunes and figs and apples and why you have plenty of confidence. Why have you plenty of confidence. Because wishes are horses and beggars do ride. This is equally true of asparagus. We see.

Responsibilities

Sonatinas are all there and they are not to be followed by prayer there they are to be followed by the songs as sung, she ought not to be living there. I know that result. I know that result. A sonatina followed by another is plenty good enough, I feel no musical estrangement.

It is the same story and now I will say it like this, a window in the roof is the what is it, and it often makes the rising around, the rising of the conclusion.

Oh shut up.

Have you been educated by the brother of a sailor. I'd hate to be put to music.

I think that all of this is very unpleasant and not very affable. Do you not feel that way about it. I do.

Now come to think of it all for there are the three men and there is the one man and when she sings there you are and when she sings, she is the one who has the remarkable opportunity. She has that as inauguration just as has the president.

They think of babies of work of resignation and of black-smithing. They do occasionally repeat that they remember salt.

He has had so much to eat. He has so much to eat. And this makes him reasonable and repetitional. She is not imprisoned by gestures. She is not at all imprisoned by gestures. She is not at all imprisoned by gestures.

That is just the same that is just the same as that.

He leans gleefully.

Don't forget it and don't forget that it is not a mother but a father. She says it is not a mother but a father. She says it is not a mother but a father. She says it is not a mother but a father. She says that it is not a mother but it is a father.

She knows everything but the third, third what, but the third congratulation.

Do remember me for this I do not want to be persistent. I do not want to have them sing. A sonatina will be followed by another.

Thank you.

Do you do you indeed.

He said I will tell you this to move you.

Recall, do you recall this at all. I recall that I said that when I was not equal to myself I would attend to the others and I am doing it. I said that when I was very nearly explained I would not measure by soldiers. Soldiers how do you mean soldiers how do you mean by soldiers. I said I would not measure them for that.

Where are they.

Why are they filling the room up with wood-work. Did you say wood-work. Are you sure that you meant what you said.

The first one wasn't good but the second one was very nice.

She says she said, early to bed. And she did not say that it was easily done, nor was there any rain. In Spain there is no rain. When this you see remember me.

There is no rain in Spain.

When this you see remember me.

And now I adhere to what I have said. I have said that I can offer no opinion.

Do not blame him fully.

And now to distinguish this one from that one.

Do not repeat it as formerly. I am more than ever attached to myself.

Early yes early with it and have you spoken of the barometer.

We have four knees.

Cut into their little tall shelters is what the municipality has decided to do.

We know how to blame them.

Mike would say force them to engage builders, and do not force anybody to exchange cotton for a collar. Do not face hats. How did you think of that.

Now then carry a gun. A gun carriage. That made you laugh.

Let me repeat the text the context. A gun carriage we do not think of a carriage because today. What is today.

Do not forget what it will cost, do not forget that she is not to be crossed, do not forget that words are clear to her, very clear indeed. Do you indeed love me.

He considers he considers you to be perfect.

And what do you consider me. I consider you to be aware of that.

We want to see the Robinson tree and there were more trees there than there had been.

What is sweating, that's what I like, says Mike.

The Lieutenant-Colonel was found dead with a bullet in the back of his head and his handkerchief in his hand.

I gather from what I saw at the door that you wanted me to come in before.

I can erase, I can place I can face I can face and erase I can erase and place I can face and place. I can place and face I can face and place and erase. I can erase that and place this and face that. I can place and I can erase I can erase and I can place this. I can place that and erase this. I can erase this and face this and I can place this.

•

MAY SINCLAIR
The Villa Désirée
(1926)

In Britain in the 1920s, May Sinclair was generally regarded as one of the most important writers of the day, alongside Dorothy Richardson and Virginia Woolf. Despite the reprinting of most of her work in recent years, she is still underrated.

Her interest in women's suffrage and psychoanalysis influenced the form and content of her novels, such as The Divine Fire *(1904),* The Three Sisters *(1914) and* The Life and Death of Harriet Frean *(1922), while her short stories often dealt with sexuality in supernatural terms; 'Where Their Fire is Not Quenched', which is often reprinted, is a chilling depiction of adulterous lovers doomed eternally to relive their joyless affair, while the story below terrifyingly imagines a man's lust as a tangible entity.*

I

He had arranged it all for her. She was to stay a week in Cannes with her aunt and then to go on to Roquebrune by herself, and he was to follow her there. She, Mildred Eve, supposed he could follow her anywhere, since they were engaged now.

There had been difficulties, but Louis Carson had got over all of them by lending her the Villa Désirée. She would be all right there, he said. The caretakers, Narcisse and Armandine, would look after her; Armandine was an excellent cook; and she wouldn't be five hundred yards from her friends, the Derings. It was so like him to think of it, to plan it all out for her. And when he came down? Oh, when he came down he would go to the Cap Martin Hotel, of course.

He understood everything without any tiresome explaining. She couldn't afford the hotels at Cap Martin and Monte Carlo; and though the Derings had asked her to stay with them, she really couldn't dump herself down on them like that, almost in the middle of their honeymoon.

Their honeymoon – she could have bitten her tongue out for saying it, for not remembering. It was awful of her to go talking to Louis Carson about honeymoons, after the appalling tragedy of *his*.

There were things she hadn't been told, that she hadn't liked to ask: Where it had happened? And how? And how long ago? She only knew it was on his wedding-night, that he had gone in to the poor little girl of a bride and found her dead there, in the bed.

They said she had died in a sort of fit.

You had only to look at him to see that something terrible had happened to him some time. You saw it when his face was doing nothing: a queer, agonized look that made him strange to her while it lasted. It was more than suffering; it was almost as if he could be cruel, only he never was, he never could be. *People* were cruel, if you liked; they said his face put them off. Mildred could see what they meant. It might have put *her* off, perhaps, if she hadn't known what he had gone through. But the first time she had met him he had been pointed out to her as the man to whom just that appalling thing had happened. So far from putting her off, that was what had drawn her to him from the beginning, made her pity him first, then love him. Their engagement had come quick, in the third week of their acquaintance.

When she asked herself, 'After all, what do I know about him,' she had her answer, 'I know *that*.' She felt that already she had entered into a mystical union with him through compassion. She *liked* the strangeness that kept other people away and left him to her altogether. He was more her own that way.

There was (Mildred Eve didn't deny it) his personal magic, the fascination of his almost abnormal beauty. His black, white, and blue. The intensely blue eyes under the straight black bars of the eyebrows, the perfect, pure, white face suddenly masked by the black moustache and small, black, pointed beard. And the rich vivid smile he had for her, the lighting up of the blue, the flash of white teeth in the black mask.

He had smiled then at her embarrassment as the awful word leaped out at him. He had taken it from her and turned the sharp edge of it.

'It would never do,' he had said, 'to spoil the *honeymoon*. You'd much better have my villa. Some day, quite soon, it'll be yours, too. You know I like anticipating things.'

That was always the excuse he made for his generosities. He had said it again when he engaged her seat in the *train de luxe* from Paris and wouldn't let her pay for it. (She had wanted to travel third class.) He was only anticipating, he said.

He was seeing her off now at the Gare de Lyons, standing on the platform with a great sheaf of blush roses in his arms. She, on the high step of the railway carriage, stood above him, swinging in the open doorway. His face was on a level with her feet; they gleamed white through the fine black stockings. Suddenly he thrust his face forwards and kissed her feet. As the train moved he ran beside it and tossed the roses into her lap.

And then she sat in the hurrying train, holding the great sheaf of blush roses in her lap, and smiling at them as she dreamed. She was in the Riviera Express; the Riviera Express. Next week she would be in Roquebrune, at the Villa Désirée. She read the three letters woven into the edges of the grey cloth cushions: P.L.M.: Paris – Lyons – Méditerranée, Paris – Lyons – Méditerranée, over and over again. They sang themselves to the rhythm of the wheels; they wove their pattern into her dream. Every now and then, when the other passengers weren't looking, she lifted the roses to her face and kissed them.

She hardly knew how she dragged herself through the long dull week with her aunt at Cannes.

And now it was over and she was by herself at Roquebrune.

The steep narrow lane went past the Derings' house and up the face of the hill. It led up into a little olive wood, and above the wood she saw the garden terraces. The sunlight beat in and out of their golden yellow walls. Tier above tier, the blazing terraces rose, holding up their ranks of spindle-stemmed lemon and orange trees. On the topmost terrace the Villa Désirée stood white and hushed between two palms, two tall poles each topped by a head of dark-green, curving, sharp-pointed blades. A grey scrub of olive trees straggled up the hill behind it and on each side.

Rolf and Martha Dering waited for her with Narcisse and Armandine on the steps of the veranda.

'Why on earth didn't you come to us?' they said.

'I didn't want to spoil your honeymoon.'

'Honeymoon, what rot! We've got over *that* silliness. Anyhow, it's our third week of it.'

They were detached and cool in their happiness.

She went in with them, led by Narcisse and Armandine. The caretakers, subservient to Mildred Eve and visibly inimical to the Derings, left them together in the *salon*. It was very bright and French and fragile and worn; all faded grey and old greenish gilt; the gilt chairs and settees carved like picture frames round the gilded cane. The hot light beat in through the long windows open to the terrace, drawing up a faint powdery smell from the old floor.

Rolf Dering stared at the room, sniffing, with fine nostrils in a sort of bleak disgust.

'You'd much better have come to us,' he said.

'Oh, but – it's charming.'

'Do you *think* so?' Martha said. She was looking at her intently.

Mildred saw that they expected her to feel something, she wasn't sure what, something that they felt. They were subtle and fastidious.

'It does look a little queer and – unlived in,' she said, straining for the precise impression.

'I should say,' said Martha, 'it had been too much lived in, if you ask me.'

'Oh no. That's only dust you smell. I think, perhaps, the windows haven't been open very long.'

She resented this criticism of Louis's villa.

Armandine appeared at the doorway. Her little, slant, Chinesy eyes were screwed up and smiling. She wanted to know if Madame wouldn't like to go up and look at her room.

'We'll all go up and look at it,' said Rolf.

They followed Armandine up the steep, slender, curling staircase. A closed door faced them on the landing. Armandine opened it, and the hot golden light streamed out to them again.

The room was all golden white; it was like a great white tank

filled with blond water where things shimmered, submerged in the
stream; the white-painted chairs and dressing-table, the high white-
painted bed, the pink-and-white striped ottoman at its foot; all
vivid and still, yet quivering in the stillness, with the hot throb,
throb of the light.

'*Voilà*, Madame,' said Armandine.

They didn't answer. They stood, fixed in the room, held by the
stillness, staring, all three of them, at the high white bed that rose
up, enormous, with its piled mattresses and pillows, the long white
counterpane hanging straight and steep, like a curtain, to the floor.

Rolf turned to Armandine.

'Why have you given Madame this room?'

Armandine shrugged her fat shoulders. Her small, Chinesy eyes
blinked at him, slanting, inimical.

'Monsieur's orders, Monsieur. It is the best room in the house. It
was Madame's room.'

'I know. That's *why* –'

'But no, Monsieur. Nobody would dislike to sleep in Madame's
room. The poor little thing, she was so pretty, so sweet, so young,
Monsieur. Surely Madame will not dislike the room.'

'Who *was* – Madame?'

'But, Monsieur's wife, Madame. Madame Carson. Poor Monsieur,
it was so sad –'

'Rolf,' said Mildred, 'did he bring her here – on their
honeymoon?'

'Yes.'

'Yes, Madame. She died here. It was so sad. Is there anything I
can do for Madame?'

'No, thank you, Armandine.'

'Then I will get ready the tea.'

She turned again in the doorway, crooning in her thick, Provençal
voice. '*Madame* does not dislike her room?'

'No, Armandine. No. It's a beautiful room.'

The door closed on Armandine. Martha opened it again to see
whether she were listening on the landing. Then she broke out:

'Mildred – you know you loathe it. It's beastly. The whole place
is beastly.'

'You can't stay in it,' said Rolf.

'Why not? Do you mean, because of Madame?'

Martha and Rolf were looking at each other, as if they were both asking what they should say. They said nothing.

'Oh, her poor little ghost won't hurt me, if that's what you mean.'

'Nonsense,' Martha said. 'Of course it isn't.'

'What is it, then?'

'It's so beastly lonely, Mildred,' said Rolf.

'Not with Narcisse and Armandine.'

'Well, I wouldn't sleep a night in the place,' Martha said, 'if there wasn't any other on the Riviera. I don't like the look of it.'

Mildred went to the open lattice, turning her back on the high, rather frightening bed. Down there below the terraces she saw the grey flicker of the olive woods and, beyond them, the sea. Martha was wrong. The place was beautiful; it was adorable. She wasn't going to be afraid of poor little Madame. Louis had loved her. He loved the place. That was why he had lent it her.

She turned. Rolf had gone down again. She was alone with Martha. Martha was saying something.

'Mildred – where's Mr Carson?'

'In Paris. Why?'

'I thought he was coming here.'

'So he is, later on.'

'To the villa?'

'No. Of course not. To Cap Martin.' She laughed. 'So *that's* what you're thinking of, is it?'

She could understand her friend's fears of haunted houses, but not these previsions of impropriety.

Martha looked shy and ashamed.

'Yes,' she said. 'I suppose so.'

'How horrid of you! You might have trusted me.'

'I do trust you.' Martha held her a minute with her clear loving eyes. 'Are you sure you can trust *him*?'

'Trust him? Do *you* trust Rolf?'

'Ah – if it was like that, Mildred –'

'It *is* like that.'

'You're really not afraid?'

'What is there to be afraid of? Poor little Madame?'

'I didn't mean Madame. I meant Monsieur.'

'Oh – wait till you've seen him.'

'Is he *very* beautiful?'

'Yes. But it isn't *that*, Martha. I can't tell you what it is.'

They went downstairs, hand in hand, in the streaming light. Rolf waited for them on the veranda. They were taking Mildred back to dine with them.

'Won't you let me tell Armandine you're stopping the night?' he said.

'No, I won't. I don't want Armandine to think I'm frightened.'

She meant she didn't want Louis to think she was frightened. Besides, she was not frightened.

'Well, if you find you don't like it, you must come to us,' he said.

And they showed her the little spare room next to theirs, with its camp-bed made up, the bedclothes turned back, all ready for her, any time of the night, in case she changed her mind. The front door was on the latch.

'You've only to open it, and creep in here and be safe,' Rolf said.

II

Armandine – subservient and no longer inimical, now that the Derings were not there – Armandine had put the candle and matches on the night table and the bell which, she said, would summon her if Madame wanted anything in the night. And she had left her.

As the door closed softly behind Armandine, Mildred drew in her breath with a slight gasp. Her face in the looking-glass, between the tall lighted candles, showed its mouth half-open, and she was aware that her heart shook slightly in its beating. She was angry with the face in the glass with its foolish mouth gaping. She said to herself: Is it possible I'm frightened? It was not possible. Rolf and Martha had made her walk too fast up the hill, that was all. Her heart always did that when she walked too fast uphill, and she supposed that her mouth always gaped when it did it.

She clenched her teeth and let her heart choke her till it stopped shaking.

She was quiet now. But the test would come when she had blown out the candles and had to cross the room in the dark to the bed.

The flame bent backwards before the light puff she gave, and righted itself. She blew harder, twice, with a sense of spinning out the time. The flame writhed and went out. She extinguished the other candle at one breath. The red point of the wick pricked the darkness for a second and died, too, with a small crackling sound. At the far end of the room the high bed glimmered. She thought: Martha was right. The bed *is* awful.

She could feel her mouth set in a hard grin of defiance as she went to it, slowly, too proud to be frightened. And then suddenly, halfway, she thought about Madame.

The awful thing was, climbing into that high funeral bed that Madame had died in. Your back felt so undefended. But once she was safe between the bedclothes it would be all right. It would be all right so long as she didn't think about Madame. Very well, then, she wouldn't think about her. You could frighten yourself into anything by thinking.

Deliberately, by an intense effort of her will, she turned the sad image of Madame out of her mind and found herself thinking about Louis Carson.

This was Louis's house, the place he used to come to when he wanted to be happy. She made out that he had sent her there because he wanted to be happy in it again. She was there to drive away the unhappiness, the memory of poor little Madame. Or, perhaps, because the place was sacred to him; because they were both so sacred, she and the young dead bride who hadn't been his wife. Perhaps he didn't think about her as dead at all; he didn't want her to be driven away. The room she had died in was not awful to him. He had the faithfulness for which death doesn't exist. She wouldn't have loved him if he hadn't been faithful. You could be faithful and yet marry again.

She was convinced that whatever she was there for, it was for some beautiful reason. Anything Louis did, anything he thought or felt or wanted, would be beautiful. She thought of Louis standing on the platform in the Paris station, his beautiful face looking up at her; its sudden darting forward to kiss her feet. She drifted again into her happy hypnotizing dream, and was fast asleep before midnight.

She woke with a sense of intolerable compulsion, as if she were being dragged violently up out of her sleep. The room was grey in the twilight of the unrisen moon.

And she was not alone.

She knew that there was something there. Something that gave up the secret of the room and made it frightful and obscene. The greyness was frightful and obscene. It gathered itself together; it became the containing shell of the horror.

The thing that had waked her was there with her in the room.

For she knew she was awake. Apart from her supernatural certainty, one physical sense, detached from the horror, was alert. It heard the ticking of the clock on the chimney-piece, the hard sharp shirring of the palm leaves outside, as the wind rubbed their knife blades together. These sounds were witnesses to the fact that she was awake, and that therefore the thing that was going to happen would be real. At the first sight of the greyness she had shut her eyes again, afraid to look into the room, because she knew that what she would see there was real. But she had no more power over her eyelids than she had had over her sleep. They opened under the same intolerable compulsion. And the supernatural thing forced itself now on her sight.

It stood a little in front of her by the bedside. From the breasts downwards its body was unfinished, rudimentary, not quite born. The grey shell was still pregnant with its loathsome shapelessness. But the face – the face was perfect in absolute horror. And it was Louis Carson's face.

Between the black bars of the eyebrows and the black pointed beard she saw it, drawn back, distorted in an obscene agony, corrupt and malignant. The face and the body, flesh and yet not flesh, they were the essence made manifest of untold, unearthly abominations.

It came on to her, bending over her, peering at her, so close that the piled mattresses now hid the lower half of its body. And the frightful thing about it was that it was blind, parted from all controlling and absolving clarity, flesh and yet not flesh. It looked for her without seeing her; and she knew that, unless she could save herself that instant, it would find what it looked for. Even now, behind the barrier of the piled-up mattresses, the unfinished form defined and completed itself; she could feel it shake with the agitation of its birth.

Her heart staggered and stopped in her breast, as if her breast had been clamped down on to her backbone. She struggled against

wave after wave of faintness; for the moment that she lost consciousness the appalling presence there would have its way with her. All
her will rose up against it. She dragged herself upright in the bed,
suddenly, and spoke to it:

'Louis! What are you doing there?'

At her cry it went, without moving; sucked back into the
greyness that had borne it.

She thought: 'It'll come back. It'll come back. Even if I don't see
it I shall know it's in the room.'

She knew what she would do. She would get up and go to the
Derings. She longed for the open air, for Rolf and Martha, for the
strong earth under her feet.

She lit the candle on the night table and got up. She still felt
that It was there, and that standing upon the floor she was more
vulnerable, more exposed to it. Her terror was too extreme for her
to stay and dress herself. She thrust her bare feet into her shoes,
slipped her travelling coat over her nightgown and went downstairs and out through the house door, sliding back the bolts
without a sound. She remembered that Rolf had left a lantern for
her in the veranda, in case she should want it – as if they had
known.

She lit the lantern and made her way down the villa garden,
stumbling from terrace to terrace, through the olive wood and the
steep lane to the Derings' house. Far down the hill she could see a
light in the window of the spare room. The house door was on the
latch. She went through and on into the lamp-lit room that waited
for her.

She knew again what she would do. She would go away before
Louis Carson could come to her. She would go away tomorrow,
and never come back again. Rolf and Martha would bring her
things down from the villa; he would take her into Italy in his car.
She would get away from Louis Carson for ever. She would get
away up through Italy.

III

Rolf had come back from the villa with her things and he had
brought her a letter. It had been sent up that morning from Cap
Martin.

It was from Louis Carson.

My darling Mildred,

You see I couldn't wait a fortnight without seeing you. I *had* to come. I'm here at the Cap Martin Hotel.

I'll be with you some time between half-past ten and eleven –

Below, at the bottom of the lane, Rolf's car waited. It was half-past ten. If they went now they would meet Carson coming up the lane. They must wait till he had passed the house and gone up through the olive wood.

Martha had brought hot coffee and rolls. They sat down at the other side of the table and looked at her with kind anxious eyes as she turned sideways, watching the lane.

'Rolf,' she said suddenly, 'do you know anything about Louis Carson?'

She could see them looking now at each other.

'Nothing. Only the things the people here say.'

'What sort of things?'

'Don't tell her, Rolf.'

'Yes. He *must* tell me. I've got to know.'

She had no feeling left but horror, horror that nothing could intensify.

'There's not much. Except that he was always having women with him up there. Not particularly nice women. He seems,' Rolf said, 'to have been rather an appalling beast.'

'Must have been,' said Martha, 'to have brought his poor little wife there, after –'

'Rolf, what did Mrs Carson die of?'

'Don't ask *me*,' he said.

But Martha answered: 'She died of fright. She saw something. I told you the place was beastly.'

Rolf shrugged his shoulders.

'Why, you said you felt it yourself. We both felt it.'

'Because we knew about the beastly things he did there.'

'*She* didn't know. I tell you, she saw something.'

Mildred turned her white face to them.

'I saw it too.'

'You?'

'What? What did you see?'

'Him. Louis Carson.'

'He must be dead, then, if you saw his ghost.'

'The ghosts of poor dead people don't kill you. It was what he *is*. All that beastliness in a face. A face.'

She could hear them draw in their breath short and sharp. 'Where?'

'There. In that room. Close by the bed. It was looking for me. I saw what *she* saw.'

She could see them frown now, incredulous, forcing themselves to disbelieve. She could hear them talking, their voices beating off the horror.

'Oh, but she couldn't. He wasn't there.'

'He heard her scream first.'

'Yes. He was in the other room, you know.'

'*It* wasn't. He can't keep it back.'

'Keep it back?'

'No. He was waiting to go to her.'

Her voice was dull and heavy with realization. She felt herself struggling, helpless, against their stolidity, their unbelief.

'Look at that,' she said. She pushed Carson's letter across to them.

'He was waiting to go to her,' she repeated. 'And – last night – he was waiting to come to me.'

They stared at her, stupefied.

'Oh, can't you *see*?' she cried. 'It didn't wait. It got there before him.'

●

RADCLYFFE HALL
Miss Ogilvy Finds Herself
(1926)

Her early resemblance to her father brought abuse from her mother, who deserted the family shortly afterwards. When her father died in 1898, Marguerite Radclyffe-Hall was eighteen, rich and calling herself 'Peter', later 'John'. She wrote several volumes of poetry which expressed sentimental love for girls, then short stories and novels exploring social and sexual issues, such as The Unlit Lamp *(1924) and* Adam's Breed *(1926), the latter winning several awards.*

The storm of controversy stirred up by The Well of Loneliness *(1928) has been noted earlier. It is an explicit (for its day) study of a lesbian writer much like the author, whose suffering she compares to that of Christ, and its nucleus is to be found in 'Miss Ogilvy Finds Herself'. Here, however, the protagonist's sexual fantasy is still disguised in heterosexual terms.*

Miss Ogilvy stood on the quay at Calais and surveyed the disbanding of her unit, the unit that together with the coming of war had completely altered the complexion of her life, at all events for three years.

Miss Ogilvy's thin, pale lips were set sternly and her forehead was puckered in an effort of attention, in an effort to memorize every small detail of every old war-weary battered motor on whose side still appeared the merciful emblem that had set Miss Ogilvy free.

Miss Ogilvy's mind was jerking a little, trying to regain its accustomed balance, trying to readjust itself quickly to this sudden and paralysing change. Her tall, awkward body with its queer look of strength, its broad, flat bosom and thick legs and ankles, as though in response to her jerking mind, moved uneasily, rocking backwards and forwards. She had this trick of rocking on her feet in moments of controlled agitation. As usual, her hands were thrust deep into her pockets, they seldom seemed to come out of her pockets unless it were to light a cigarette, and as though she were still standing firm under fire while the wounded were placed in her ambulances, she suddenly straddled her legs very slightly and lifted her head and listened. She was standing firm under fire at that moment, the fire of a desperate regret.

Some girls came towards her, young, tired-looking creatures whose eyes were too bright from long strain and excitement. They had all been members of that glorious unit, and they still wore the queer little forage-caps and the short, clumsy tunics of the French Militaire. They still slouched in walking and smoked Caporals in emulation of the Poilus. Like their founder and leader these girls were all English, but like her they had chosen to serve England's ally, fearlessly thrusting right up to the trenches in search of the wounded and dying. They had seen some fine things in the course of three years, not the least fine of which was the cold, hard-faced woman who, commanding, domineering, even hectoring at times, had yet been possessed of so dauntless a courage and of so insistent a vitality that it vitalized the whole unit.

'It's rotten!' Miss Ogilvy heard someone saying. 'It's rotten, this breaking up of our unit!' And the high, rather childish voice of the speaker sounded perilously near to tears.

Miss Ogilvy looked at the girl almost gently, and it seemed, for a moment, as though some deep feeling were about to find expression in words. But Miss Ogilvy's feelings had been held in abeyance so long that they seldom dared become vocal, so she merely said 'Oh?' on a rising inflection – her method of checking emotion.

They were swinging the ambulance cars in mid-air, those of them that were destined to go back to England, swinging them up like sacks of potatoes, then lowering them with much clanging of chains to the deck of the waiting steamer. The porters were shoving and shouting and quarrelling, pausing now and again to make meaningless gestures; while a pompous official was becoming quite angry as he pointed at Miss Ogilvy's own special car – it annoyed him, it was bulky and difficult to move.

'*Bon Dieu! Mais dépêchez-vous donc!*' he bawled, as though he were bullying the motor.

Then Miss Ogilvy's heart gave a sudden, thick thud to see this undignified, pitiful ending; and she turned and patted the gallant old car as though she were patting a well-beloved horse, as though she would say: 'Yes, I know how it feels – never mind, we'll go down together.'

II

Miss Ogilvy sat in the railway carriage on her way from Dover to London. The soft English landscape sped smoothly past: small homesteads, small churches, small pastures, small lanes with small hedges; all small like England itself, all small like Miss Ogilvy's future. And sitting there still arrayed in her tunic, with her forage cap resting on her knees, she was conscious of a sense of complete frustration; thinking less of those glorious years at the front and of all that had gone to the making of her, than of all that had gone to the marring of her from the days of her earliest childhood.

She saw herself as a queer little girl, aggressive and awkward

because of her shyness; a queer little girl who loathed sisters and
dolls, preferring the stable-boys as companions, preferring to play
with footballs and tops, and occasional catapults. She saw herself
climbing the tallest beech trees, arrayed in old breeches illicitly
come by. She remembered insisting with tears and some temper
that her real name was William and not Wilhelmina. All these
childish pretences and illusions she remembered, and the bitterness
that came after. For Miss Ogilvy had found as her life went on that
in this world it is better to be one with the herd, that the world has
no wish to understand those who cannot conform to its stereotyped
pattern. True enough, in her youth she had gloried in her strength,
lifting weights, swinging clubs and developing muscles, but presently this had grown irksome to her; it had seemed to lead
nowhere, she being a woman, and then as her mother had often
protested: muscles looked so appalling in evening dress – a young
girl ought not to have muscles.

Miss Ogilvy's relation to the opposite sex was unusual and at that
time added much to her worries, for no less than three men had wished
to propose, to the genuine amazement of the world and her mother.
Miss Ogilvy's instinct made her like and trust men, for whom she had a
pronounced fellow-feeling; she would always have chosen them as her
friends and companions in preference to girls or women; she would
dearly have loved to share in their sports, their business, their ideas and
their wide-flung interests. But men had not wanted her, except the
three who had found in her strangeness a definite attraction, and those
would-be suitors she had actually feared, regarding them with
aversion. Towards young girls and women she was shy and respectful,
apologetic and sometimes admiring. But their fads and their foibles,
none of which she could share, while amusing her very often in secret,
set her outside the sphere of their intimate lives, so that in the end she
must blaze a lone trail through the difficulties of her nature.

'I can't understand you,' her mother had said, 'you're a very odd
creature – now when I was your age . . .'

And her daughter had nodded, feeling sympathetic. There were
two younger girls who also gave trouble, though in their case the
trouble was fighting for husbands who were scarce enough even in
those days. It was finally decided, at Miss Ogilvy's request, to allow
her to leave the field clear for her sisters. She would remain in the
country with her father when the others went up for the Season.

Followed long, uneventful years spent in sport, while Sarah and Fanny toiled, sweated and gambled in the matrimonial market. Neither ever succeeded in netting a husband, and when the Squire died leaving very little money, Miss Ogilvy found to her great surprise that they looked upon her as a brother. They had so often jibed at her in the past, that at first she could scarcely believe her senses, but before very long it became all too real: she it was who must straighten out endless muddles, who must make the dreary arrangements for the move, who must find a cheap but genteel house in London and, once there, who must cope with the family accounts which she only, it seemed, could balance.

It would be: 'You might see to that, Wilhelmina; you write, you've got such a good head for business.' Or: 'I wish you'd go down and explain to that man that we really can't pay his account till next quarter.' Or: 'This money for the grocer is five shillings short. Do run over my sum, Wilhelmina.'

Her mother, grown feeble, discovered in this daughter a staff upon which she could lean with safety. Miss Ogilvy genuinely loved her mother, and was therefore quite prepared to be leaned on; but when Sarah and Fanny began to lean too with the full weight of endless neurotic symptoms incubated in resentful virginity, Miss Ogilvy found herself staggering a little. For Sarah and Fanny were grown hard to bear, with their mania for telling their symptoms to doctors, with their unstable nerves and their acrid tongues and the secret dislike they now felt for their mother. Indeed, when old Mrs Ogilvy died, she was unmourned except by her eldest daughter who actually felt a void in her life – the unforeseen void that the ailing and weak will not infrequently leave behind them.

At about this time an aunt also died, bequeathing her fortune to her niece Wilhelmina, who, however, was too weary to gird up her loins and set forth in search of exciting adventure – all she did was to move her protesting sisters to a little estate she had purchased in Surrey. This experiment was only a partial success, for Miss Ogilvy failed to make friends of her neighbours; thus at fifty-five she had grown rather dour, as is often the way with shy, lonely people.

When the war came she had just begun settling down – people do settle down in their fifty-sixth year – she was feeling quite glad that her hair was grey, that the garden took up so much of her

time, that, in fact, the beat of her blood was slowing. But all this
was changed when war was declared; on that day Miss Ogilvy's
pulses throbbed wildly.

'My God! If only I were a man!' she burst out, as she glared at
Sarah and Fanny, 'if only I had been born a man!' Something in her
was feeling deeply defrauded.

Sarah and Fanny were soon knitting socks and mittens and
mufflers and Jaeger trench-helmets. Other ladies were busily working at depots, making swabs at the Squire's, or splints at the
Parson's; but Miss Ogilvy scowled and did none of these things –
she was not at all like other ladies.

For nearly twelve months she worried officials with a view to
getting a job out in France – not in their way but in hers, and that
was the trouble. She wished to go up to the front-line trenches, she
wished to be actually under fire, she informed the harassed officials.

To all her inquiries she received the same answer: 'We regret that
we cannot accept your offer.' But once thoroughly roused she was
hard to subdue, for her shyness had left her as though by magic.

Sarah and Fanny shrugged angular shoulders: 'There's plenty of
work here at home,' they remarked, 'though of course it's not quite
so melodramatic!'

'Oh . . .?' queried their sister on a rising note of impatience – and
she promptly cut off her hair: 'That'll jar them!' she thought with
satisfaction.

Then she went up to London, formed her admirable unit and
finally got it accepted by the French, despite renewed opposition.

In London she had found herself quite at her ease, for many
another of her kind was in London doing excellent work for the
nation. It was really surprising how many cropped heads had
suddenly appeared as it were out of space; how many Miss Ogilvies,
losing their shyness, had come forward asserting their right to
serve, asserting their claim to attention.

There followed those turbulent years at the front, full of courage
and hardship and high endeavour; and during those years Miss
Ogilvy forgot the bad joke that Nature seemed to have played her.
She was given the rank of a French lieutenant and she lived in a
kind of blissful illusion; appalling reality lay on all sides and yet she
managed to live in illusion. She was competent, fearless, devoted
and untiring. What then? Could any man hope to do better? She

was nearly fifty-eight, yet she walked with a stride, and at times she even swaggered a little.

Poor Miss Ogilvy sitting so glumly in the train with her manly trench boots and her forage cap! Poor all the Miss Ogilvies back from the war with their tunics, their trench boots, and their childish illusions! Wars come and wars go but the world does not change; it will always forget an indebtedness which it thinks it expedient not to remember.

III

When Miss Ogilvy returned to her home in Surrey it was only to find that her sisters were ailing from the usual imaginary causes, and this to a woman who had seen the real thing was intolerable, so that she looked with distaste at Sarah and then at Fanny. Fanny was certainly not prepossessing, she was suffering from a spurious attack of hay fever.

'Stop sneezing!' commanded Miss Ogilvy, in the voice that had so much impressed the unit. But as Fanny was not in the least impressed, she naturally went on sneezing.

Miss Ogilvy's desk was piled mountain-high with endless tiresome letters and papers: circulars, bills, months-old correspondence, the gardener's accounts, an agent's report on some fields that required land draining. She seated herself before this collection; then she sighed, it all seemed so absurdly trivial.

'Will you let your hair grow again?' Fanny inquired . . . she and Sarah had followed her into the study. 'I'm certain the Vicar would be glad if you did.'

'Oh?' murmured Miss Ogilvy, rather too blandly.

'Wilhelmina!'

'Yes?'

'You will do it, won't you?'

'Do what?'

'Let your hair grow; we all wish you would.'

'Why should I?'

'Oh, well, it will look less odd, especially now that the war is over – in a small place like this people notice such things.'

'I entirely agree with Fanny,' announced Sarah.

Sarah had become very self-assertive, no doubt through having mismanaged the estate during the years of her sister's absence.

They had quite a heated dispute one morning over the south herbaceous border.

'Whose garden is this?' Miss Ogilvy asked sharply. 'I insist on auricula-eyed sweet Williams! I even took the trouble to write from France, but it seems that my letter has been ignored.'

'Don't shout,' rebuked Sarah, 'you're not in France now!'

Miss Ogilvy could gladly have boxed her ears: 'I only wish to God I were,' she muttered.

Another dispute followed close on its heels, and this time it happened to be over the dinner. Sarah and Fanny were living on weeds – at least that was the way Miss Ogilvy put it.

'We've become vegetarians,' Sarah said grandly.

'You've become two damn tiresome cranks!' snapped their sister.

Now it never had been Miss Ogilvy's way to indulge in acid recriminations, but somehow, these days, she forgot to say: 'Oh?' quite so often as expediency demanded. It may have been Fanny's perpetual sneezing that had got on her nerves; or it may have been Sarah, or the gardener, or the Vicar, or even the canary; though it really did not matter very much what it was just so long as she found a convenient peg upon which to hang her growing irritation.

'This won't do at all,' Miss Ogilvy thought sternly, 'life's not worth so much fuss, I must pull myself together.' But it seemed this was easier said than done; not a day passed without her losing her temper and that over some trifle: 'No, this won't do at all – it just mustn't be,' she thought sternly.

Everyone pitied Sarah and Fanny: 'Such a dreadful, violent old thing,' said the neighbours.

But Sarah and Fanny had their revenge: 'Poor darling, it's shell-shock, you know,' they murmured.

Thus Miss Ogilvy's prowess was whittled away until she herself was beginning to doubt it. Had she ever been that courageous person who had faced death in France with such perfect composure? Had she ever stood tranquilly under fire, without turning a hair, while she issued her orders? Had she ever been treated with marked respect? She herself was beginning to doubt it.

Sometimes she would see an old member of the unit, a girl who, more faithful to her than the others, would take the trouble to run down to Surrey. These visits, however, were seldom enlivening.

'Oh, well . . . here we are . . .' Miss Ogilvy would mutter.

But one day the girl smiled and shook her blond head: 'I'm not –
I'm going to be married.'

Strange thoughts had come to Miss Ogilvy, unbidden, thoughts
that had stayed for many an hour after the girl's departure. Alone
in her study she had suddenly shivered, feeling a sense of complete
desolation. With cold hands she had lighted a cigarette.

'I must be ill or something,' she had mused, as she stared at her
trembling fingers.

After this she would sometimes cry out in her sleep, living over
in dreams God knows what emotions; returning, maybe to the
battlefield of France. Her hair turned snow-white; it was not
unbecoming yet she fretted about it.

'I'm growing very old,' she would sigh as she brushed her thick
mop before the glass; and then she would peer at her wrinkles.

For now that it had happened she hated being old; it no longer
appeared such an easy solution of those difficulties that had always
beset her. And this she resented most bitterly, so that she became
the prey of self-pity, and of other undesirable states in which the
body will torment the mind, and the mind, in its turn, the body.
Then Miss Ogilvy straightened her ageing back, in spite of the fact
that of late it had ached with muscular rheumatism, and she faced
herself squarely and came to a resolve.

'I'm off!' she announced abruptly one day; and that evening she
packed her kit-bag.

IV

Near the south coast of Devon there exists a small island that is still
very little known to the world, but which nevertheless can boast an
hotel, the only building upon it. Miss Ogilvy had chosen this place
quite at random, it was marked on her map by scarcely more than a
dot, but somehow she had liked the look of that dot and had set
forth alone to explore it.

She found herself standing on the mainland one morning looking
at a vague blur of green through the mist, a vague blur of green
that rose out of the Channel like a tidal wave suddenly suspended.
Miss Ogilvy was filled with a sense of adventure; she had not felt
like this since the ending of war.

'I was right to come here, very right indeed. I'm going to shake
off all my troubles,' she decided.

A fisherman's boat was parting the mist, and before it was properly beached, in she bundled.

'I hope they're expecting me?' she said gaily.

'They du be expecting you,' the man answered.

The sea, which is generally rough off that coast, was indulging itself in an oily ground-swell; the broad, glossy swells struck the side of the boat, then broke and sprayed over Miss Ogilvy's ankles.

The fisherman grinned: 'Feeling all right?' he queried. 'It du be tiresome most times about these parts.' But the mist had suddenly drifted away and Miss Ogilvy was staring wide-eyed at the island.

She saw a long shoal of jagged black rocks, and between them the curve of a small sloping beach, and above that the lift of the island itself, and above that again, blue heaven. Near the beach stood the little two-storeyed hotel which was thatched, and built entirely of timber; for the rest she could make out no signs of life apart from a host of white seagulls.

Then Miss Ogilvy said a curious thing. She said: 'On the south-west side of that place there was once a cave – a very large cave. I remember that it was some way from the sea.'

'There du be a cave still,' the fisherman told her, 'but it's just above highwater level.'

'A-ah,' murmured Miss Ogilvy thoughtfully, as though to herself; then she looked embarrassed.

The little hotel proved both comfortable and clean, the hostess both pleasant and comely. Miss Ogilvy started unpacking her bag, changed her mind and went for a stroll round the island. The island was covered with turf and thistles and traversed by narrow green paths thick with daisies. It had four rock-bound coves of which the south-western was by far the most difficult of access. For just here the island descended abruptly as though it were hurtling down to the water; and just here the shale was most treacherous and the tide-swept rocks most aggressively pointed. Here it was that the seagulls, grown fearless of man by reason of his absurd limitations, built their nests on the ledges and reared countless young, who multiplied, in their turn, every season. Yes, and here it was that Miss Ogilvy, greatly marvelling, stood and stared across at a cave; much too near the crumbling edge for her safety, but by now completely indifferent to caution.

'I remember ... I remember ...' she kept repeating. Then: 'That's all very well, but what do I remember?'

She was conscious of somehow remembering all wrong, of her memory being distorted and coloured – perhaps by the endless things she had seen since her eyes had last rested upon that cave. This worried her sorely, far more than the fact that she should be remembering the cave at all, she who had never set foot on the island before that actual morning. Indeed, except for the sense of wrongness when she struggled to piece her memories together, she was steeped in a very profound contentment which surged over her spirit, wave upon wave.

'It's extremely odd,' pondered Miss Ogilvy. Then she laughed, so pleased did she feel with its oddness.

v

That night after supper she talked to her hostess, who was only too glad, it seemed, to be questioned. She owned the whole island and was proud of the fact, as she very well might be, decided her boarder. Some curious things had been found on the island, according to comely Mrs Nanceskivel: bronze arrowheads, pieces of ancient stone celts; and once they had dug up a man's skull and thigh bone – this had happened while they were sinking a well. Would Miss Ogilvy care to have a look at the bones? They were kept in a cupboard in the scullery.

Miss Ogilvy nodded.

'Then I'll fetch him this moment,' said Mrs Nanceskivel, briskly.

In less than two minutes she was back with the box that contained those poor remnants of a man, and Miss Ogilvy, who had risen from her chair, was gazing down at those remnants. As she did so her mouth was sternly compressed, but her face and her neck flushed darkly.

Mrs Nanceskivel was pointing to the skull: 'Look, miss, he was killed,' she remarked rather proudly, 'and they tell me that the axe that killed him was bronze. He's thousands and thousands of years old, they tell me. Our local doctor knows a lot about such things and he wants me to send these bones to an expert; they ought to belong to the nation, he says. But I know what would happen, they'd come digging up my island, and I won't have people digging up my island, I've got enough worry with the rabbits as it is.' But Miss Ogilvy could no longer hear the words for the pounding of the blood in her temples.

She was filled with a sudden, inexplicable fury against the

innocent Mrs Nanceskivel: 'You ... you ...' she began, then checked herself, fearful of what she might say to the woman.

For her sense of outrage was overwhelming as she stared at those bones that were kept in the scullery; moreover, she knew how such men had been buried, which made the outrage seem all the more shameful. They had buried such men in deep, well-dug pits surmounted by four stout stones at their corners – four stout stones there had been and a covering stone. And all this Miss Ogilvy knew as by instinct, having no concrete knowledge on which to draw. But she knew it right down in the depths of her soul, and she hated Mrs Nanceskivel.

And now she was swept by another emotion that was even more strange and more devastating: such a grief as she had not conceived could exist; a terrible unassuageable grief, without hope, without respite, without palliation, so that with something akin to despair she touched the long gash in the skull. Then her eyes, that had never wept since her childhood, filled slowly with large, hot, difficult tears. She must blink very hard, then close her eyelids, turn away from the lamp and say rather loudly; 'Thanks, Mrs Nanceskivel. It's past eleven – I think I'll be going upstairs.'

VI

Miss Ogilvy closed the door of her bedroom, after which she stood quite still to consider: 'Is it shell-shock?' she muttered incredulously, 'I wonder, can it be shell-shock?'

She began to pace slowly about the room, smoking a Caporal. As usual her hands were deep in her pockets; she could feel small, familiar things in those pockets and she gripped them, glad of their presence. Then all of a sudden she was terribly tired, so tired that she flung herself down on the bed, unable to stand any longer.

She thought that she lay there struggling to reason, that her eyes were closed in the painful effort, and that as she closed them she continued to puff the inevitable cigarette. At least that was what she thought at one moment – the next, she was out in a sunset evening, and a large red sun was sinking slowly to the rim of a distant sea.

Miss Ogilvy knew that she was herself, that is to say she was conscious of her being, and yet she was not Miss Ogilvy at all, nor had she a memory of her. All that she now saw was very familiar, all that she now did was what she should do, and all that she now was seemed perfectly natural. Indeed, she did not think of these things; there seemed no reason for thinking about them.

She was walking with bare feet on turf that felt springy and was greatly enjoying the sensation; she had always enjoyed it, ever since as an infant she had learned to crawl on this turf. On either hand stretched rolling green uplands, while at her back she knew that there were forests; but in front, far away, lay the gleam of the sea towards which the big sun was sinking. The air was cool and intensely still, with never so much as a ripple or bird song. It was wonderfully pure – one might almost say young – but Miss Ogilvy thought of it merely as air. Having always breathed it she took it for granted, as she took the soft turf and the uplands.

She pictured herself as immensely tall; she was feeling immensely tall at the moment. As a matter of fact she was five feet eight which, however, was quite a considerable height when compared to that of her fellow tribesmen. She was wearing a single garment of pelts which came to her knees and left her arms sleeveless. Her arms and her legs, which were closely tattooed with blue zigzag lines, were extremely hairy. From a leathern thong twisted about her waist there hung a clumsily made stone weapon, a celt, which in spite of its clumsiness was strongly hafted and useful for killing.

Miss Ogilvy wanted to shout aloud from a glorious sense of physical well-being, but instead she picked up a heavy, round stone which she hurled with great force at some distant rocks.

'Good! Strong!' she exclaimed. 'See how far it goes!'

'Yes, strong. There is no one so strong as you. You are surely the strongest man in our tribe,' replied her little companion.

Miss Ogilvy glanced at this little companion and rejoiced that they two were all alone together. The girl at her side had a smooth brownish skin, oblique black eyes and short, sturdy limbs. Miss Ogilvy marvelled because of her beauty. She also was wearing a single garment of pelts, new pelts, she had made it that morning. She had stitched at it diligently for hours with short lengths of gut and her best bone needle. A strand of black hair hung over her bosom, and this she was constantly stroking and fondling; then she lifted the strand and examined her hair.

'Pretty,' she remarked with childish complacence.

'Pretty,' echoed the young man at her side.

'For you,' she told him, 'all of me is for you and none other. For you this body has ripened.'

He shook back his own coarse hair from his eyes; he had sad brown eyes like those of a monkey. For the rest he was lean and steel-strong of loin, broad of chest, and with features not too uncomely. His prominent cheekbones were set rather high, his nose was blunt, his jaw somewhat bestial; but his mouth, though full-lipped, contradicted his jaw, being very gentle and sweet in expression. And now he smiled, showing big, square, white teeth.

'You . . . woman,' he murmured contentedly, and the sound seemed to come from the depths of his being.

His speech was slow and lacking in words when it came to expressing a vital emotion, so one word must suffice and this he now spoke, and the word that he spoke had a number of meanings. It meant: 'Little spring of exceedingly pure water.' It meant: 'Hut of peace for a man after battle.' It meant: 'Ripe red berry sweet to the taste.' It meant: 'Happy small home of future generations.' All these things he must try to express by a word, and because of their loving she understood him.

They paused, and lifting her up he kissed her. Then he rubbed his large shaggy head on her shoulder; and when he released her she knelt at his feet.

'My master; blood of my body,' she whispered. For with her it was different, love had taught her love's speech, so that she might turn her heart into sounds that her primitive tongue could utter.

After she had pressed her lips to his hands, and her cheek to his hairy and powerful forearm, she stood up and they gazed at the setting sun, but with bowed heads, gazing under their lids, because this was very sacred.

A couple of mating bears padded toward them from a thicket, and the female rose to her haunches. But the man drew his celt and menaced the beast, so that she dropped down noiselessly and fled, and her mate also fled, for here was the power that few dared to withstand by day or by night, on the uplands or in the forests. And now from across to the left where a river would presently lose itself in the marshes, came a rhythmical thudding, as a herd of red deer with wide nostrils and starting eyes thundered past, disturbed in their drinking by the bears.

After this the evening returned to its silence, and the spell of its silence descended on the lovers, so that each felt very much alone, yet withal more closely united to the other. But the man became restless under that spell, and he suddenly laughed; then grasping the woman he tossed her above his head and caught her. This he did many times for his own amusement and because he knew that his strength gave her joy. In this manner they played together for a while, he with his strength and she with her weakness. And they cried out, and made many guttural sounds which were meaningless save only to themselves. And the tunic of pelts slipped down from her breasts, and her two little breasts were pear-shaped.

Presently, he grew tired of their playing, and he pointed toward a cluster of huts and earthworks that lay to the eastward. The smoke from these huts rose in thick straight lines, bending neither to right nor left in its rising, and the thought of sweet burning rushes and brushwood touched his consciousness, making him feel sentimental.

'Smoke,' he said.

And she answered: 'Blue smoke.'

He nodded: 'Yes, blue smoke – home.'

Then she said: 'I have ground much corn since the full moon. My stones are too smooth. You make me new stones.'

'All you have need of, I make,' he told her.

She stole closer to him, taking his hand: 'My father is still a black cloud full of thunder. He thinks that you wish to be head of our tribe in his place, because he is now very old. He must not hear of these meetings of ours, if he did I think he would beat me!'

So he asked her: 'Are you unhappy, small berry?'

But at this she smiled: 'What is being unhappy? I do not know what that means any more.'

'I do not either,' he answered.

Then as though some invisible force had drawn him, his body swung around and he stared at the forests where they lay and darkened, fold upon fold; and his eyes dilated with wonder and terror, and he moved his head quickly from side to side as a wild thing will do that is held between bars and whose mind is pitifully bewildered.

'Water!' he cried hoarsely, 'great water – look, look! Over there. This land is surrounded by water!'

'What water?' she questioned.

He answered: 'The sea.' And he covered his face with his hands.

'Not so,' she consoled, 'big forests, good hunting. Big forests in which you hunt boar and aurochs. No sea over there but only the trees.'

He took his trembling hands from his face: 'You are right . . . only trees,' he said dully.

But now his face had grown heavy and brooding and he started to speak of a thing that oppressed him: 'The Roundheaded-ones, they are devils,' he growled, while his bushy black brows met over his eyes, and when this happened it changed his expression which became a little subhuman.

'No matter,' she protested, for she saw that he forgot her and she wished him to think and talk only of love. 'No matter. My father laughs at your fears. Are we not friends with the Roundheaded-ones? We are friends, so why should we fear them?'

'Our forts, very old, very weak,' he went on, 'and the Roundheaded-ones have terrible weapons. Their weapons are not made of good stone like ours, but of some dark, devilish substance.'

'What of that?' she said lightly. 'They would fight on our side, so why need we trouble about their weapons?'

But he looked away, not appearing to hear her. 'We must barter all, all for their celts and arrows and spears, and then we must learn their secret. They lust after our women, they lust after our lands. We must barter all, all for their sly brown celts.'

'Me . . . bartered?' she queried, very sure of his answer, otherwise she had not dared to say this.

'The Roundheaded-ones may destroy my tribe and yet I will not part with you,' he told her. Then he spoke very gravely: 'But I think they desire to slay us, and me they will try to slay first because they well know how much I mistrust them – they have seen my eyes fixed many times on their camps.'

She cried: 'I will bite out the throats of these people if they so much as scratch your skin!'

And at this his mood changed and he roared with amusement: 'You . . . woman!' he roared. 'Little foolish white teeth. Your teeth were made for nibbling wild cherries, not for tearing the throats of the Roundheaded-ones!'

'Thoughts of war always make me afraid,' she whimpered, still wishing him to talk about love.

He turned his sorrowful eyes upon her, the eyes that were sad even when he was merry, and although his mind was often obtuse, yet he clearly perceived how it was with her then. And his blood caught fire from the flame in her blood, so that he strained her against his body.

'You . . . mine . . .' he stammered.

'Love,' she said, trembling, 'this is love.'

And he answered: 'Love.'

Then their faces grew melancholy for a moment, because dimly, very dimly in their dawning souls, they were conscious of a longing for something more vast than their earthly passion could compass.

Presently, he lifted her like a child and carried her quickly southward and westward till they came to a place where a gentle descent led down to a marshy valley. Far away, at the line where the marshes ended, they discerned the misty line of the sea; but the sea and the marshes were become as one substance, merging, blending, folding together; and since they were lovers they also would be one, even as the sea and the marshes.

And now they reached the mouth of a cave that was set in the quiet hillside. There was bright green verdure beside the cave, and a number of small, pink, thick-stemmed flowers that when they were crushed smelt of spices. And within the cave there was bracken newly gathered and heaped together for a bed; while beyond, from some rocks, came a low liquid sound as a spring dripped out through a crevice. Abruptly, he set the girl on her feet, and she knew that the days of her innocence were over. And she thought of the anxious virgin soil that was rent and sown to bring forth fruit in season, and she gave a quick little gasp of fear:

'No . . . no . . .' she gasped. For, divining his need, she was weak with the longing to be possessed, yet the terror of love lay heavy upon her. 'No . . . no . . .' she gasped.

But he caught her wrist and she felt the great strength of his rough, gnarled fingers, the great strength of the urge that leapt in his loins, and again she must give the quick gasp of fear, the while she clung close to him lest he should spare her.

The twilight was engulfed and possessed by darkness, which in turn was transfigured by the moonrise, which in turn was fulfilled and consumed by dawn. A mighty eagle soared up from his eyrie, cleaving the air with his masterful wings, and beneath him from the rushes that harboured their nests, rose other great birds, crying loudly. Then the heavy-horned elks appeared on the uplands, bending their burdened heads to the sod; while beyond in the forests the fierce wild aurochs stamped as they bellowed their love songs.

But within the dim cave the lord of these creatures had put by his weapon and his instinct for slaying. And he lay there defenceless with tenderness, thinking no longer of death but of life as he murmured the word that had so many meanings. That meant: 'Little spring of exceedingly pure water.' That meant: 'Hut of peace for a man after battle.' That meant: 'Ripe red berry sweet to the taste.' That meant: 'Happy small home of future generations.'

VII

They found Miss Ogilvy the next morning; the fisherman saw her and climbed to the ledge. She was sitting at the mouth of the cave. She was dead, with her hands thrust deep into her pockets.

•

EDITH WHARTON
My Little Girl
(1935)

The following fragment was found amongst Edith Wharton's papers after her death in 1937. Her diaries and notes indicate that she had been planning a novella called Beatrice Palmato, *a dramatic story climaxing with the suicide of the heroine after she berates her husband for kissing their small daughter. Beatrice, it would have been revealed at the end, had been the victim of the incestuous attentions of her own father.*

The story was never begun, and the existing passage could have formed no part of the final narrative, for as Wharton's biographer R.W.B. Lewis notes: 'It does not really accord with the outline (which planned to conceal the incest until the last page), and in any event, no respectable magazine in the world would have published it. This makes it all the more intriguing . . .'

To discover such highly explicit words from the otherwise genteel pen of the author of The House of Mirth *(1897) and* The Age of Innocence *(1921) is as astonishing as it is intriguing. There is some evidence that the story was inspired by Alfred de Musset's erotic novel* Gamiani, *which was loosely based on the life of Edith Wharton's own favourite, George Sand, and which circulated in a privately printed edition in New York around 1926. Whatever the source, most critics take the view that Wharton wrote this passage for her own private use, to have the dark secret of* Beatrice Palmato *before her as she unfolded her story.*

The room was warm, and softly lit by one or two pink-shaded lamps. A little fire sparkled on the hearth, and a lustrous black bearskin rug, on which a few purple velvet cushions had been flung, was spread out before it.

'And now, darling,' Mr Palmato said, drawing her to the deep divan, 'let me show you what only you and I have the right to show each other.' He caught her wrists as he spoke, and looking straight into her eyes, repeated in a penetrating whisper: 'Only you and I.' But his touch had never been tenderer. Already she felt every fibre vibrating under it, as of old, only now with the more passionate eagerness bred of privation, and of the dull misery of her marriage. She let herself sink backward among the pillows, and already Mr Palmato was on his knees at her side, his face close to hers. Again her burning lips were parted by his tongue, and she felt it insinuate itself between her teeth, and plunge into the depths of her mouth in a long searching caress, while at the same moment his hands softly parted the thin folds of her wrapper.

One by one they gained her bosom, and she felt her two breasts pointing up to them, the nipples hard as coral, but sensitive as lips to his approaching touch. And now his warm palms were holding each breast as in a cup, clasping it, modelling it, softly kneading it, as he whispered to her, 'like the bread of the angels'.

An instant more, and his tongue had left her fainting mouth, and was twisting like a soft pink snake about each breast in turn, passing from one to the other till his lips closed on the nipples, sucking them with a tender gluttony.

Then suddenly he drew back her wrapper entirely, whispered: 'I want you all, so that my eyes can see all that my lips can't cover,' and in a moment she was free, lying before him in her fresh young nakedness, and feeling that indeed his eyes were covering it with fiery kisses. But Mr Palmato was never idle, and while this sensation flashed through her one of his arms had slipped under her back and wound itself around her so that his hand again enclosed her left breast. At the same moment the other hand softly separated her legs, and began to slip up the old path it had so often travelled in darkness. But now it was light, she was uncovered, and looking downward, beyond his dark silver-sprinkled head, she could see her own parted knees, and outstretched ankles and feet. Suddenly she remembered Austin's rough advances, and shuddered.

The mounting hand paused, the dark head was instantly raised. 'What is it, my own?'

'I was – remembering – last week –' she faltered, below her breath.

'Yes, darling. That experience is a cruel one – but it has to come once in all women's lives. Now we shall reap its fruit.'

But she hardly heard him, for the old swooning sweetness was creeping over her. As his hand stole higher she felt the secret bud of her body swelling, yearning, quivering hotly to burst into bloom. Ah, here was his subtle forefinger pressing it, forcing its tight petals softly apart, and laying on their sensitive edges a circular touch so soft and yet so fiery that already lightnings of heat shot from that palpitating centre all over her surrendered body, to the tips of her fingers, and the ends of her loosened hair.

The sensation was so exquisite that she could have asked to have it indefinitely prolonged; but suddenly his head bent lower, and with a deeper thrill she felt his lips pressed upon that quivering invisible bud, and then the delicate firm thrust of his tongue, so full and yet so infinitely subtle, pressing apart the close petals, and forcing itself in deeper and deeper through the passage that glowed and seemed to become illumined at its approach . . .

'Ah –' she gasped, pressing her hands against her sharp nipples, and flinging her legs apart.

Instantly one of her hands was caught, and while Mr Palmato, rising, bent over her, his lips on hers again, she felt his fingers pressing into her hand that strong fiery muscle that they used, in their old joke, to call his third hand.

'My little girl,' he breathed, sinking down beside her, his muscular trunk bare, and the third hand quivering and thrusting upward between them, a drop of moisture pearling at its tip.

She instantly understood the reminder that his words conveyed, letting herself downward along the divan until her head was in a line with his middle she flung herself upon the swelling member, and began to caress it insinuatingly with her tongue. It was the first time she had ever seen it actually exposed to her eyes, and her heart swelled excitedly: to have her touch confirmed by sight enriched the sensation that was communicating itself through her ardent twisting tongue. With panting breath she wound her caress deeper and deeper into the thick firm folds, till at length the member, thrusting her lips open, held her gasping, as if at its mercy; then, in a trice, it was withdrawn, her knees were pressed apart, and she saw it before her, above her, like a crimson flash, and at last, sinking backward into new abysses of bliss, felt it descend on her, press open the secret gates, and plunge into the deepest depths of her thirsting body . . .

•

SIMONE DE BEAUVOIR

Marcelle

(1942)

Simone de Beauvoir was born in Paris in 1908. After graduating in philosophy she embarked on a lifelong relationship with Jean-Paul Sartre and became a prominent figure in the Existentialist movement. Her earlier novels feature an existential anti-heroine who appears as Elizabeth in L'Invitée *(1943), as Denise in* Le Sang des autres *(1944) and as Paule in* Les Mandarins *(1954), which won the Prix Goncourt.*

De Beauvoir was also a distinguished writer of essays and autobiographical works, and her extended essay Le Deuxième Sexe *(1949), an analysis of women's secondary status in society, has been described as 'perhaps the century's most influential theoretical inquiry into women's condition'. 'Marcelle' is one of her earliest stories, of which she wrote: 'I had fun drawing a picture of piety gradually shading off into shameless appetite.'*

Marcelle Drouffe was a dreamy, precocious little girl: as early as the age of ten months she gave signs of being extraordinarily sensitive. 'When you hurt yourself, it wasn't the pain that made you cry,' her mother told her later. 'It was because you felt the world had betrayed you.'

Her parents cherished her, and she was so good that they never scolded her at all; but early in life she knew the taste of tears. As dusk fell she would slip under her father's desk or behind the heavy drawing-room curtains and let sadness and the night flow into her. She would think of the poor children and the orphans she had read about in story-books with gilt covers; she reflected that one day she would be a grown-up and that her mother would no longer take her on to her lap; or she imagined that her parents were dead and that she was alone in the world. Then the tears would roll down her cheeks and she would feel her body swoon away into a delicious void.

She liked crying in churches best: on holidays Mme Drouffe took her to admire the wax Infant Jesuses in their cradles or to breathe in the scent of the shrines. Through the shining haze round the candle-flames Marcelle would see wonderful visions. Her heart melted within her and, sobbing, she offered a young fair-haired God the sacrifice of her life. She had seen him once, at the cinema: in bed, at night, she told him her secrets and went to sleep snuggled in Jesus' bosom: she dreamed of wiping soft bare feet with her long hair.

One of Marcelle's great-aunts had a reading-room in the rue Saint-Suplice: she was an old lady with a croaking voice, and she always wore a ribbon round her throat. Marcelle's greatest pleasure was spending a day at Mlle Olivier's. She would choose among the works intended for the young (they had a Y after their titles in the catalogue) and then she would go and sit at a little table in a dark passage lined with books in black uniforms: there, by the light of a candle, she devoured Schmidt's tales, Reynes Montlaur's novels, or historical memoirs as bowdlerized by Mme Carette. Customers were not allowed into the corridors and the only person who occasionally stole through the gloom was an assistant in a high-necked blouse; she would climb a ladder, encumbered by her long skirt, and shine a torch along the shelves. When this happened Marcelle knew that another customer had just come in and had sat in silence on one of the leather chairs; looking curiously into the main room she usually saw old ladies and priests. Mlle Olivier, perched on a kind of rostrum, supervised the room with an austere expression; a large register, green and black, lay open before her, and before giving the customers their books – a red label on the back for novels, yellow for serious works – she wrote the title and the author's name in a round hand.

Some of the library's regular visitors aroused a passionate interest in Marcelle: middle-aged men with a pensive gaze, their faces matured and refined by thought. In their handsome greying hair, their overcoats, and their white hands she discerned an exalted elegance that seemed to come from the soul. Perhaps they were writers, poets: they certainly belonged to that intellectual élite that M. Drouffe often spoke about with a mysterious air. Marcelle gazed devoutly upon them. She ardently longed for one of them to notice her some day and to say in velvety tones, 'What serious books that pretty little girl does read, to be sure!' He would ask her questions and he would be astonished by her replies: then he would take her to a beautiful house full of books and pictures and he would talk to her as though she were a grown-up.

Marcelle could not wait to be older; she wanted to be a well-known writer and to have high-minded conversations with great men. Nothing pained her more than being treated as a child; she always remained in the drawing-room when her parents had visitors, and she liked being with these middle-aged men and women with their soft smiles, grave voices and restrained gestures. When M. Drouffe read them the tales and poems Marcelle wrote for her little brother Pascal, she felt rather shy but very happy. She was never unsociable except in the company of children of her own age: their loud laughter, their shouts and their wild, disorderly games filled her with horror. Mme Drouffe would have liked to send her to a private school, but Marcelle was so sensitive it scarcely seemed right to cross her and she was allowed to have lessons with an elderly spinster; her father, who taught grammar, undertook her literary education, correcting her stylistic exercises and reading her the great classics in the evening.

Yet when Mme Drouffe took Marcelle to the Tuileries or the Luxembourg Gardens she did not let her stay sitting there at her side. 'Go and play with your little friends,' she would say firmly: it was the only point on which she displayed authority. Marcelle obeyed, but she thought there was nothing so stupid as running about and pulling and pushing one another. She was not an agile child and she dragged along, hating the whole thing.

Later she often thought tenderly of those times, calling up the picture of that thoughtful little girl who hid in the window recesses when Christmas trees were lit up and when they danced in a ring under the drawing-room lights: the other children were too busy stuffing themselves with chocolate éclairs or putting on paper hats to bother about her, and far from their red faces and noisy laughter she escaped into an imaginary world.

Mlle Olivier, who had taken such pains with her catalogue of books for the young, would have been astonished to learn the kind of sustenance that her niece's dreaming drew from certain harmless stories and from Canon Schmidt's improving tales. Bluebeard's cruelty, the trials imposed upon the gentle Griselda by her suspicious husband, the Duke of Brabant's meeting with the unfortunate Geneviève, stark naked under her long hair – all these perturbed and excited Marcelle to a remarkable degree. The story of a woman, cruelly and harshly treated by an arrogant master, who eventually wins his heart by her submissiveness and her love was one that never failed to delight her. She identified herself with this heroine, sometimes imagining her innocent and misunderstood, but more often guilty of some grave offence, for she was fond of quivering with repentance at the feet of a sinless, beautiful and terrible man. He had the right of life and death over her, and she called him 'Lord': he made her strip herself naked before him, and he used her body as a step when he mounted his splendidly decked charger. With a sensuous delight she drew out this moment of feeling the harsh spur flay her servile back as she knelt there, her head bowed, her heart full of adoration and passionate humility. And when the stern-eyed avenger, vanquished by pity and by love, laid his hand on her head as a sign of forgiveness she clasped his knees in an exquisite swoon.

She was thirteen when she happened to see a *Petit Parisien* serial in a public lavatory – a man covering an alabaster breast with eager kisses. Marcelle could not put the picture out of her mind all day long, and that night, when she was in bed, she gave way to it without resistance, her cheeks on fire. From then on every night, when she was half asleep in her warm bed, she offered her bosom to searching, greedy lips: insistent gentle hands ran over her flesh, a warm body pressed against her own. In the morning she was ashamed of these thoughts, but with the fading of the light she became impatient for her heated phantasms to come back. She did not go to sleep for a long while: her dry throat and lips were painful and sometimes she had shivering fits and cold sweats. After about a year her nights grew calm again: she stopped indulging in fanciful imaginings and began looking forward, looking anxiously forward, to a future that should prove worthy of her.

Her heart was too exacting to be satisfied with the common-place affections of her everyday life at home. Mme Drouffe was passionately devoted to Marcelle, but she was neither very clever nor very highly cultivated; Marcelle adored her, of course, but she felt very much alone when she was with her mother and often she could not prevent herself from giving a cross answer. She had hoped that as she grew older she would become her father's friend, a friend he would confide in; but M. Drouffe was just as interested in Pascal, who was beginning to learn Latin, and in the little Marguerite as he was in Marcelle. Indeed, he would frequently tease his elder daughter about her shyness and the fact that her hands were big and that she did not know what to do with them. Marcelle was cruelly disappointed. Often and sadly she whispered 'Who will ever be capable of loving me?' One evening, when she came back from a party where no one had asked her to dance and her father reproved her for looking glum, she burst into tears, ran to her bedroom and locked herself in. Several times Mme Drouffe came and tapped softly on the door, but Marcelle would not open it; she lay there on the bed in the darkness, staring at the ceiling, lit from time to time by the glow of a passing tram: she was immeasurably sorry for herself. She never would be like those frivolous thick-witted girls that people in general thought more attractive: she never would consent to smother her soul.

'I am different from the others,' she said to herself passionately. She got up, opened the shutters and stepped out on to the balcony: Paris was covered with a sky as mauve as a field of autumn crocus and the night was so soft and mild that Marcelle's heart began to beat faster. She thought of Mme de Staël, of George Eliot, of the Comtesse de Noailles; and it was then, all of a sudden, that she had the wonderful revelation of her destiny. 'I shall live with a man of genius: I shall be his companion,' she said, in an ecstatic whisper.

The winter after war was declared she thought she had met him: he was a lieutenant, and he read Epictetus in the trenches. Marcelle wanted to be worthy of him. She was too young to be a nurse, but she made mounds of lint out of her old skirts and she tirelessly knitted Balaclava helmets; she also collected funds for the Red Cross in the Champs-Elysées. Mme Drouffe took to making her drink an infusion of orange-flowers every evening so that she should not dream of the poor wounded soldiers and the little refugees from the north all night: and it was at this time that Marcelle began to use powder because she wept over the horrors of the war so very often and so very much that she was always afraid of having red eyes and a swollen nose. She stopped believing in God: with the immensity of human suffering before her, she felt quite sure that Providence did not exist.

Those were terrible years for Marcelle, and in later times it often surprised her that she came through the crisis unbroken. She missed the presence of God; and men betrayed her. The heroic young lieutenant married one of her cousins. Every day the world grew more hostile, human contacts more disappointing. Marcelle longed to escape, to go a great way off. If she had not been afraid of hurting her mother she would have gone to nurse lepers in Madagascar. She went for long, long walks, and in the Bois de Boulogne she kissed the trunks of trees, rubbing a loving cheek against the rough bark of these living beings that would let themselves be loved without wounding her.

She was twenty when her father died, not long after the war. Pascal was working for his baccalauréat, his university entrance examination. Marguerite had just been moved up to the fifth form at school, among the twelve- and thirteen-year-olds. Paying her a modest sum, Mme Drouffe took over Mlle Olivier's reading-room, which brought in quite a considerable profit. Marcelle did not wish to be a burden on her mother and she wanted to give her life a meaning: she made up her mind to take a job. It had to be work that would appeal to her heart, and after two years of preparation she found a place as a social assistant at a welfare centre in the rue de Ménilmontant.

The Centre was run by a gentle, sensitive woman of forty whom life had treated cruelly: from their first meeting she was charmed by Marcelle's youth, the vivid life and eagerness in her voice and look; and Marcelle experienced the delights of friendship. Germaine Masson knitted filmy scarves for her and almost every Sunday she invited her to tea. Marcelle told Germaine about her childhood, and, speaking confidentially, about her hopes, her disappointments, and the peculiarities of her character. Germaine conceived a positively servile affection for her. But Marcelle did not find her work as rewarding as she had hoped: the Centre was concerned with distributing material help to the local poor, finding work for the unemployed young, and looking after sick or ill-treated children; it also provided medical consultations and free treatment, either at the Centre or at home. The nurses were competent, conscientious women, but they looked upon their calling merely as a means of earning a living; and during her inquiries Marcelle never heard a word of anything but worries about health and money. Never did she come into contact with a single soul.

In the evening, as she went home in the crowded Métro, Marcelle wondered sadly whether the emptiness in her heart would ever be filled: she gazed despairingly at the horny-handed men and the sickly-looking women – eyes that never showed the least gleam of an ideal. They had been toiling all day long and now they were going to eat: no beautiful memories there, no hopes, not even a sweetly running line of poetry to soothe their unhappiness. Lives as dark and subterranean as the tunnels into which the train kept plunging. In the foul-smelling carriages the atmosphere was stifling. Marcelle felt a wave of intense pity, and it seemed to her that she bore all the sufferings of the world on her shoulders; she would have liked to talk to these unfortunate people about beauty, about love, and about the meaning of pain and sorrow, speaking so convincingly that their lives would be transformed. She could do nothing for them: as well as the uselessness of her charity there was the physical distress caused by the smell of human sweat; and contact with coarse, rough bodies made her feel so sick that she was often compelled to get out and finish the journey on foot. At home once more she gazed a long while at her face in the mirror: the skin beneath her soulful eyes was somewhat worn, transparent and flecked with reddish-brown, like the throat of a foxglove. This pathetic face deserved the love of a hero.

'Oh beloved,' she whispered.

Marcelle had been working at the rue de Ménilmontant for a year before she had a chance to spend her unused treasures of strength and charity at last.

It was a morning in April: she was in her office, busy with accounts. 'To be strong, and to wear oneself out in base, unworthy occupations,' she muttered as she checked the totals. The concierge knocked on the door and gave her two visiting-cards: Maurice Perdrières, Director of 'Social Contact', and Paul Desroches, Government Civil Engineer, names unknown to her. A moment later she was in the company of two men of about twenty-five with intelligent faces and cheerful expressions: they seemed almost to be related to each other. Without wasting time on preliminaries they told Marcelle that they had come to ask her to collaborate with them, and they did so in a blunt, straightforward, trusting fashion that pleased her.

The idea of 'Social Contact' had arisen from the war: Perdrières and his friend Desroches had spent a year at the front, and, where others had seen only mud and slaughter, they had discovered that wonderful thing called brotherhood. When they went back to their books and their studies in 1919 they were at a loss: the purely intellectual life that had once satisfied them now seemed dry and sterile and they retained a longing for the fraternity of the war. Perdrières and Desroches decided to revive the deep, simple comradeship of the trenches – to revive it between the classes. Enthusiasm and goodwill vanquished all obstacles, and soon they had won over a large number of eager young people. Groups were set up: they were called teams, and in the evenings they travelled to the outlying districts to give lectures attended by apprentices and young workmen and to gain their friendship. The movement did not have the least political attachment, and, although Christian in its origins, it did not undertake any religious proselytism: disinterested exchange was the goal, and nothing else. The students brought the young workers the spiritual nourishment which alone gives man an inner dignity; in return they were quickened and invigorated by the blaze of generosity, good humour and courage which burns in the heart of the common people.

'We have been more successful than we hoped,' said Perdrières, 'and material difficulties are all that hold us up, particularly the question of premises: the meetings often have to take place in bistros.' He smiled. 'A bistro is fine, but it costs money, and after all one is not in one's own place. If you could give us some kind of a shelter, that would help us enormously.'

Leaning her chin on her hand, Marcelle gazed at Perdrières with the greatest interest: these men were quite outside the common run. 'Social questions concern me very deeply indeed,' she said. 'I am entirely at your service. Here we only look after people's bodies and it has often grieved me: man does not live by bread alone.'

'You could do a great deal for us,' said Desroches. 'You know this district's needs and its resources. Your help would be invaluable for setting up a team here.'

Marcelle gave her wholehearted agreement and asked them to dinner in two days' time so that they could look into the question more thoroughly. When she was alone again, an immense happiness flooded into her: at last she was going to be able to show what she was made of! She opened the window and leant out over the garden: thousands of sticky little leaves twinkled in the sun and all springtime murmured in her bosom – the inner wealth accumulated in solitude was yearning to blossom into action. Ecstatically, Marcelle greeted the renewal of her heart as the dawn of the renewal of the world itself.

The dinner took place in the Centre's dining-room; Germaine was not there. Marcelle had ordered a pleasant little meal, and she had covered the table with an embroidered cloth belonging to her mother. Perdrières and Desroches did not seem to pay any attention to their food; they talked all the time, with great eagerness, about social questions, pure poetry, and the fate of mankind. Marcelle had never heard such interesting conversation. They explained that what had to be done was to bring the people up to culture, not to bring culture down to the people, and Perdrières quoted the instance of a young printer who understood Valéry better than the professors at the Sorbonne. With dessert Marcelle gave them Benedictine, and she drank a finger herself. It was agreed that Perdrières should take charge of a study group every Thursday: between them Desroches and another member of the team would give lessons in English, bookkeeping and French. These lessons were intended for the young only. 'It is the young who must change the world,' said Perdrières. But to enter into contact with their families there would be lectures on subjects of general interest once a month in the hall to which members could bring their friends and relations. Perdrières also intended there to be group excursions, for he believed that picnics, marching in step, and songs with everyone joining in the chorus were of use in restoring the people's sense of spiritual values. As the Centre was empty after six o'clock, Marcelle proposed setting up a kind of club-room at that time; she would undertake the supervision until eight, and would see to it that there were books, magazines and a billiard-table.

The suggestion was eagerly adopted and Desroches spoke with great enthusiasm of the splendid way the rue de Ménilmontant team was going to spread and grow, thanks to Marcelle's brilliant ideas. While he was talking, Marcelle noticed that he had a little scratch at the corner of his mouth; she also noticed that Perdrières did not wear sock-suspenders and that when he crossed his legs his calves could be seen: this touched her heart. These exceptional beings were also men, big awkward children like all other men. She would have liked to tidy their rooms, arrange the knot of their tie and sew on their buttons, as she did for Pascal. A motherly affection blended with her admiration for them.

For some time now Germaine's soft, demanding friendship had been wearisome to her; Germaine was always wanting to find parallels between Marcelle's experiences and her own, and between their two characters; she badgered Marcelle with questions and she monopolized all her spare time: she was almost an old woman and she fed on her friend's youth and zest for life like a vampire. Contact with her was depressing. Friendly contact with men, on the other hand, greatly increased one's strength of will and one's spirit: it was direct, open and straightforward.

'In a way I am very feminine,' said Marcelle to Desroches one day, 'and yet I can only get on with men.'

She stopped seeing Germaine so often. When Marcelle had telephoned to cry off on Sunday, on Monday Germaine's eyes would be full of silent reproach: and at this Marcelle felt with pride that her untamable spirit could never submit to the bondage of Germaine's affection.

Marcelle gave the team all her free time. Many youths joined 'Social Contact'; but there were few who came out of a genuine wish to improve their minds and Marcelle nourished no illusions about their membership. They came to be among friends, and because nothing was asked of them, and because they could not afford to go to the café every evening. Some of them, reflecting that one day they might need a job or medical advice, wanted to be in favour with the Centre, which was looked upon as a power in the neighbourhood; their parents encouraged them to go to the hall – it might one day prove useful. Germaine, with her embittered, sceptical cast of mind, did not fail to point out these interested motives; but Marcelle looked upon all ways of getting members as justified. She carried out active propaganda with the families and the young people she knew through the medical side of the Centre or its employment agency; and gradually they brought in others.

The hall was very large: Marcelle settled discreetly at the far end and pretended to be absorbed in some sort of work; the young men played at cards or billiards, read the papers and talked among themselves. Marcelle had arranged with the head of a people's library that books should be available and she took advantage of their borrowing or returning them to enter into conversation. They spoke about the last study group or the next lecture; and sometimes the talk took a personal turn. Marcelle felt that in order to acquire an influence over these children she should in the first place be a friend, a comrade; presently she grew more familiar, leaning over their shoulders to see what they were reading and sometimes unceremoniously sitting on the table as she spoke to them. She liked this warm, youthful atmosphere: when she was joking with a young mechanic or a shop assistant it was perfectly obvious to her that the barriers between classes were brought into being by hatred and prejudice alone; and she did not look upon their reserve towards her as the evidence of a social difference but rather as a discreet and flattering tribute. Most of the team members were well behaved young people with serious tastes, belonging to respectable families; but as the movement spread, more dubious elements found their way into the group – even Communists and downright undesirables appeared. The best part of Marcelle's affection was kept for these lost souls: she undertook the task of awakening their moral sense and of pulling them out of their corrupted environment. On warm evenings, when they sat on the sills of the open window in their shirtsleeves, looking like graceful animals, Marcelle felt an overwhelming longing to grasp them in a motherly fashion and press their heads against her bosom.

There was one in particular, one whom Marcelle would have liked to hold in her arms to keep him from evil ways for ever. Fradin was his name: his features were irregular, his eyes velvety, his mouth childish and sensual; his open shirt shamelessly displayed a sunburnt chest and his sweat smelt of mint; it was said that he lived off women. Marcelle often asked him to stay after the others to help her tidy the room a little: he agreed in a good-natured way, but she never managed to make him talk. As soon as he had done he took his cap and in a guttersnipe voice bade Marcelle good-night.

She watched him go off to his own amusements with intense anxiety. Presently, in some low dancehall, girls covered with make-up would cling tight to him and smell his scent, resting their heads against the opening of his shirt: sitting on his knee, one of them would stroke his hair and then his neck, her hand slipping gently under his collar. Marcelle almost felt the touch of the warm, satiny skin under her palm. She quivered. How should one set about teaching these young creatures purity? The idea of the risks that Fradin was running – the risks to his soul and body – quite overcame her. Although her calling had brought her into contact with the harsh facts of life the words vice, syphilis, and venereal disease still filled Marcelle with disgust and fear.

For a moment she stood there in the empty room, sad at heart: they had all gone off, respectful and uncaring, leaving her to her purity and her loneliness. She put out the lights and walked down to the Ménilmontant station. She thought about Vigny's 'Moïse', and 'Christ on the Mount of Olives'. 'I give, I give, and who will give to me?' she whispered when she was back in her bedroom with its pale green wallpaper: sadly she brushed her lips over the cool petals of the flowers – there was always a bouquet on her table. She liked talking to things that had no life, and caressing them: they required nothing of her and they never refused themselves. Often, in the gentle glow of her lamp, she wept in spite of the scent of the roses.

Neither Perdrières nor Desroches had any inkling of these tears. They were men and they believed that ideas were enough to transform the world: their social theories interested Marcelle at first, and then they wearied her. In the company of these intellectuals she felt rich with a mysterious femininity, and lonely once again. They valued her because she was energetic, intelligent, calm. But who would ever be capable of understanding her and loving her weakness? 'The touching weakness of the strong,' she jotted down in a notebook; and she promised herself to write a poem ending with those words.

Marcelle got on better with Desroches than with Perdrières; there was greater subtlety in his character and he was more under-standing; although his culture and his mind were somewhat un-sophisticated and his sensitivity still childish, he was capable of melancholy and tenderness, and he had an inner life. As she was afraid of evil tongues if she were to see him often at her office, Marcelle sometimes met him away from the Centre. They went to lectures and concerts and they had tea together. She was not at all flirtatious with him: she looked upon flirting as a lack of candour, as something contemptible; but she did want him to know what she was really like, and as he was not very quick-witted she was obliged to emphasize certain aspects of her character. One day she welcomed him very soberly and spoke about the tragic state of the humble in such a feeling way that he had tears in his eyes when he left her: the next day he found an idle, frivolous woman who made fun of serious remarks. As they left a moving talk given by Claudel, instead of seeming touched, she mocked the poet's fatness and his thick spectacles: Desroches looked so taken aback that Marcelle burst out laughing. 'There's more than one woman in me,' she said.

In the early days Desroches always talked about 'Social Contact', the duties of the élite and the Christian's attitude towards economic and political questions – he was a practising Catholic. Marcelle was more interested in people than ideas, and for her friendship was not an exchange of viewpoints but a deep communication between souls: she questioned Desroches about his childhood and she told him some secrets of her own. They became more and more intimate. Desroches grew bold enough to give her violets from time to time, and he tried to define the precise shade of her beautiful hair.

'You are not only a superior woman,' he said to her one day in an earnest voice, 'you are also quite simply just a woman.'

'Yes,' said Marcelle tenderly, 'a woman.'

She did not find that Desroches had an outstanding personality, but she did like being understood and revered. When he asked her to marry him she accepted. Desroches did not want to be married until he had a position that would allow Marcelle to stop working, but to avoid any gossip they announced their engagement right away. There was a cheerful party at the Centre, and Perdrières, proposing the toasts, made a very successful speech.

A little while after this Marcelle spent a month in the country with her mother and she had time to appreciate and relish the full extent of her happiness: she sent Desroches and Germaine letters like welling springs. 'I spend my days lying on the grass in the meadows, drunk with sun like a young animal,' she wrote. 'I do not regret the weary years that I spent alone, without love: my joy would not be so splendid if I had not waited for it in tears. How wonderful it is, Germaine, to give myself up to the wafting air of a great love at last, after having borne the weight of my useless heart like a burden for so long.'

Marcelle was not one of those who are made selfish by happiness: once she was back in Paris she organized a women's team and took charge of the study circle. Every Saturday she gave talks on Claudel, Péguy, women's social mission and the meaning of pain to an admiring audience. In order to spread the movement she also persuaded Germaine to give a monthly dance, at which the young people belonging to the Centre could indulge in the pleasures suitable to their age. The first evening passed off very well indeed. Marcelle danced with Desroches: she also danced with Fradin and Linières. Every time their arms diffidently went round her waist she felt the beauty of this fraternization so intensely that her heart beat high and fast. When she left the dance she was too uplifted to want to sleep; she asked Desroches to see her home on foot, and they walked cheerfully along the deserted streets.

'An evening like this really makes one feel that bringing the classes together is merely a question of goodwill!' cried Desroches eagerly. Marcelle thoroughly agreed. But then all at once it occurred to her that men of goodwill were very rare; sadness overcame her and shivering she pressed herself against her fiancé. He put his arm round her and for a moment they stood there, linked in a silent communion: Marcelle closed her eyes: Desroches' arm round her shoulders burnt exquisitely: she turned her face to his.

Desroches hesitated a moment: then Marcelle felt two hot lips against her own: she returned his kiss passionately, in an ecstasy of tenderness and surrender. Almost at once he gently freed himself and walked on by her side without touching her. He seemed embarrassed, and Marcelle could no longer think of anything to say to him. All her happiness had vanished: now, after these hours in which she had spent herself so generously she had a sudden revelation of the vanity of all action, the vanity of all love. It appeared to her that even happiness itself was too small a matter for great souls.

Marcelle remained in low spirits and on edge during the days that followed. She wished she still believed in God so that she could go and cry in a church as she had done when she was a child: human things always left her deeply unsatisfied. She had imagined love as a wonderful fulfilment; but no doubt there would never be peace on earth for her troubled, restless heart. When she was away from Desroches she longed for his coming so intensely that her dry throat and her burning lips were really painful: when he was there she found his presence stifling. Desroches always had stories to tell her and ideas to impart and he never stopped smiling. While he talked Marcelle gazed despairingly at that stranger's body within which a soul was hidden, precious and inaccessible: she was so weary of herself that she would have liked to be lost in him for ever. But two beings who love one another and who sit side by side are still two separate, solitary entities: Desroches did not seem to have any notion of this tragedy. Yet one Sunday afternoon Marcelle was so gloomy that eventually he became concerned: half-sitting, half-lying on the divan in her pale-green room, she answered only in monosyllables; she saw the delicate harmonies of the carpet and the walls through a grey mist; the outlines of the things in the room seemed blurred and the daylight dull; her own body was as heavy as lead.

'What's the matter, darling?' asked Desroches, leaning over her.

She gave a faint smile: she was by no means sure what the sorrow was that needed soothing. 'Sit there, close to me,' she said. He sat down, taking her hand rather awkwardly: she laid her head on his shoulder. 'Oh, the world is too horrible,' she said, with tears in her eyes. He pressed her close. 'Let's stay like this,' she said. 'It's so comfortable.' With her cheek against the roughness of his jacket, the warmth of his body flooding into her and his strong arms about her, she forgot the inadequacy of happiness. The moment was heavy with a melancholy sweetness that words could not express: it was by a kiss alone that Desroches could have gathered the heart she was offering. He did not kiss her: he stroked her hair and then stood up. When he had gone, Marcelle lay there for a long while, exhausted, with no strength, no desire: she would have liked to vanish, to dissolve into nothingness. When she came out of this painful torpor she could not bear her own company and she went out: for two hours she walked wherever her feet happened to lead her along the streets, shaken by sobs, she could not tell why; sometimes she felt that she was going to faint and she had to lean against a wall.

Some days later she had a long talk with Desroches: he told her how much the restraints he imposed upon himself made him suffer and how often he had a violent longing to take her in his arms. But he was of the opinion that a Christian should not experience carnal joys before their sanctification by the sacrament of marriage; and even then, he thought, the degree to which these pleasures were allowable presented a serious moral problem.

'The sacrament of marriage is not a glorification of the body,' he said. 'It is the acceptance of our animal nature. But at the same time it insists that this aspect must remain under the control of our will and reason: we must not allow it an independent existence. Yielding to merely physical drives is the denial of our human dignity.'

Marcelle thoroughly agreed. She felt that the act of love should not be the brutish satisfaction of an appetite: it had to be freely granted on both sides and as it were rendered spiritual by an intention of kindness and affection. 'But it is no unworthy pleasure that we expect from kisses and embraces,' she said. 'Often there is no other language that allows hearts to speak to one another.'

Desroches eagerly replied that he saw the matter in just the same light. Only their engagement had to be long: and so that their wedding night might retain all its touching solemnity they should take care that their bodies did not grow used to each other, even through the most chaste of caresses.

Marcelle thought it admirable that an engaged couple should be able to talk about such things with no false shame, and she told Desroches how much she appreciated his delicacy. Yet afterwards it grieved her to see how easily he obeyed the rules he had set himself. His was neither a passionate nor a troubled nature.

'I do not blame him in any way,' she said sadly to Germaine. 'But there you are: I was looking for giants, and there are only men.'

Marcelle met with cruel disappointments at 'Social Contact' as well. Although, in his articles and lectures, Perdrières asserted that uncultivated spirits were the best suited for enjoying the everlasting masterpieces of the human mind, the working girls and shop assistants of the team were not very interested in Racine, nor in Baudelaire. They could not understand why a married woman should give up her job to look after the house. And Marcelle's fine lectures on resignation and self-sacrifice did not move them at all. When she left the Centre she was completely worn out from giving the best of herself, and all in vain. In the spring she had serious difficulties with the women's section: the young men and the girls who had been meeting regularly at the dances took to seeing one another in secret: on Sundays they would often tell their parents that they were going out in a group, some with Marcelle, others with Perdrières, when in fact they went off together without the least supervision. When this was discovered it caused a minor scandal in the neighbourhood. The dances had to be stopped, and from then on great care was taken to avoid all contact between the sexes.

Marcelle took to hating the team, the Centre, and the rue de Ménilmontant: when there was a lecture and all the members, their relatives and their friends gathered in the long building smelling of rotten wood, the atmosphere was so oppressive that Marcelle felt despair overcome her. The girls never stopped their silly tittering; their mothers' eyes rested on Marcelle with distrust, sometimes with dislike; the students and the learned men who came to talk about Péguy, the United States, or prehistoric man, according to their speciality, were all most disappointingly commonplace. Looking over the grey mass of the audience, Marcelle gazed at the sheets of oiled paper that served as window-panes and she reflected that her youth was being frittered away uselessly. The evening Perdrières introduced Denis Charval to her she was agreeably surprised; he was different from the other lecturers – an elegant, offhand young man with a lock of black hair falling over his forehead.

'Is he a friend of yours?' she asked Perdrières as Charval sat down at the green-covered table.

'He's the friend of a friend's brother,' said Perdrières. 'It seems that he has published some very remarkable verse. Do you think a talk on Rimbaud can amount to much?'

'Why not?' said Marcelle. She directed an interested stare at the young poet: his green eyes gave one the impression of an artless, capricious spirit, given to extremes. Marcelle felt that in speaking of Rimbaud he would present a picture of himself.

Charval spoke with feeling, and he spoke skilfully. He described Rimbaud as a man who had refused to stifle his thirst for the infinite, and as one who had turned down all the commonplace advantages and benefits that delude others – affection, family, love, fame, and even his own genius. When he spoke of the beauty of this refusal, Charval's voice assumed a tone so grave and tender that Marcelle felt she could see his heart laid bare and interpret it. 'We admire Rimbaud for the matchless harmony of his poetry and his prose,' he ended. 'But the reason why we love him like a brother, like a pure and terrible angel, is because he refused even that beauty which delights us: it is because of all the sublime pages he never wrote.'

There was a certain amount of applause: Perdrières leant towards Marcelle. 'I think we made a mistake,' he said in an anxious voice. Marcelle shrugged. 'Obviously Rimbaud can't serve as an example for this herd.' She pushed back her chair and went up to Charval to thank him in the team's name and to tell him how much she had admired his lecture. Charval modestly disclaimed all merit and then invited Marcelle, Perdrières and Desroches to have a drink with him. Marcelle had never set foot in a café: when she passed through the door of one of the big Montmartre establishments she felt that she had suddenly been transported into the middle of a fantastic dream: she had observed that the taximeter showed twenty francs, she reckoned that the white cashmere scarf that went so well with Charval's greatcoat must have cost over a hundred francs, and all this splendour dazzled her, though at the same time she found it slightly shocking. She would have liked to know Charval better: his mouth was rather like young Fradin's, and it had a disillusioned line at the corner; comparing these features with those of Desroches, which were devoid of mystery, she felt that Charval had already seen a great deal of life.

The conversation was less interesting than it might have been because Perdrières kept talking about the people and about culture. With real vexation Marcelle thought that Charval was going to vanish from her life before he had been able to appreciate her. 'Life

is already quite good enough at condemning people to loneliness,'
she reflected. 'We ought not to turn ourselves into its accomplices.'
She told Charval that she would very much like to read his poems
and she asked him to tea the next Sunday.

It was a wonderful encounter. From the very beginning Marcelle
gave their conversation an intimate, personal turn: she confessed
that she no longer believed in action and Charval told her confidentially that for his part he had never believed in it. Nor did either of
them believe in friendship any more. Marcelle said that her dreams
and the poetic essays she sometimes confided to her notebooks
were her only refuge and she was overwhelmed when she learnt
that for Charval even poetry often seemed a useless amusement or a
falsehood: he lived for a few pure, precious impressions that he
could not translate into words without betraying them. Marcelle
protested: in a voice trembling with emotion she told Charval
about the poet's mission and she begged him to believe in himself.
She would have liked to take his handsome, bitter face between her
hands and transfuse some of her own faith and ardour into him.

Charval was too young and too shy to court her friendship, but
Marcelle generously set the pace: she perceived that she had a part
to play in this sad child's life. Together they went to the new show
at the Vieux Colombier, to a Picasso exhibition, to the Studio des
Ursulines – they saw one another almost every day. Charval questioned Marcelle about her job, her pursuits, her family: he told her
about the entrancing sadness that drifted through the bars, saloons
and night-spots after dark, about modern aesthetics and the
absurdity of life. Marcelle wanted to know his friends: sometimes
she went with him to cafés where he talked about cubism, dadaism,
Cocteau's latest poems, and the fourth dimension with writers and
poets dressed in light-coloured suits and soft shirts; it was not easy
to follow the conversation, because it skipped from one subject to
another, interrupted by jokes and allusions comprehensible only to
the initiated, but Marcelle was delighted at being transported at last
into the only atmosphere in which she had ever wanted to live – in
this very strange and subtle world, surrounded by young geniuses,
she could at last come into bloom. Of all these chosen beings,
Denis was the handsomest, the youngest and the most elegant; his
voice was the most caressing, his eyes the dreamiest. On no other
face did Marcelle see such heart-stirring promise. His opinions were

often paradoxical and she listened to them indulgently: if she ever gained any influence over Charval she would bring him back to a sounder way of thinking. But she loved his careless, offhand phrases and their delightful, unpredictable turns.

It was scarcely three weeks after their first meeting that Denis asked Marcelle to dine with him at a restaurant on the banks of the Marne. It was a beautiful summer evening and Marcelle was wearing a wide-brimmed straw hat and a green print dress with puffed sleeves: she looked at the pale sky, she looked at Charval's smooth cheeks; and she hesitated because Desroches was invited to dinner that evening at the Drouffes'. A week before, Marcelle had had a violent scene with her fiancé: she had accused him of being timid, obtuse, insensitive; she had told him that she was sick of his tender care and his unfailing good humour, and since then their relationship had been strained; but Marcelle did not wish to do anything grossly uncivil.

'Telephone your home. Make something up: it doesn't matter what,' said Charval in a sulky, peremptory tone. Marcelle smiled: it was a curiously pleasant experience, giving way to the whims of this child. 'One can't refuse you anything,' she said.

They ate fried potatoes and a matelote of eels in the open air: Marcelle was not very fond of wine, but she drank nearly half a bottle. After the meal they lay on the grass, side by side, on the river bank. Paris was a great way off; the rue de Ménilmontant, 'Social Contact' and Desroches had ceased to exist; it seemed to Marcelle that she was being carried along like an obedient toy by a fate that was quite out of her control. She was no longer aware of anything but the beating of her heart and of the warm breath close, very close to her face. Something was going to happen, and she would not do anything to prevent it: motionless and passive she acquiesced. For years she had filled the role of a strong, affectionate, anxious woman and now she yearned to give it all up, if only for a moment, and think of nothing, wish for nothing.

At first it was a shower of urgent kisses on her eyes, the corner of her mouth, then the warmth of a body against her own and a long deep kiss full on her mouth: she let herself go – there was nothing in her but well-being and weakness, and lying there in Denis's arms she discovered the sweet experience of communicating with the void.

All at once fear shot through her like a lightning flash; her muscles stiffened and with both hands she thrust at the man whose weight was upon her. This was how seducers enticed girls far out into the deserted countryside to betray them. 'Let me go,' she said in a choking voice. 'You are out of your mind.'

Charval drew back. 'Forgive me,' he said, 'I let myself be carried away . . .' She had stood up and he put his hand on her shoulder. 'I preferred relying on kisses rather than words; you mustn't hold it against me, Marcelle – I'm shy with you.' He looked uncomfortable, awkward, and charming. 'I love you – extraordinary creature.' He took her in his arms again and pressed her close: now that she was out of danger she let him fondle her breasts and the back of her neck without resisting.

They walked by the river most of the night. Marcelle thought of the future that lay in wait for Charval if a loving woman did not devote herself to him, and she pictured it with horror; he was sceptical, disillusioned and wounded, and he would waste his precious gifts – he would sink into a facile life, perhaps into vice. She alone could save him: she had never dreamt of a finer destiny than being the inspiration of a brilliant man, brilliant but weak. Desroches did not need her to be able to live: on the contrary, it was she who had sought refuge with him, a contemptible piece of cowardice in her – she was not made to receive but to give. When she got home she wrote to Desroches, breaking off the engagement.

Neither Mme Drouffe nor Pascal made any comment: they always approved Marcelle's decisions. Germaine hid her surprise as well as she could; and with a kind of pride Marcelle put up with the nurses' ill-natured astonishment when she told them of her forthcoming marriage to Charval. There was not the least reason for a long engagement: Charval had neither private means nor a job, but he could live with Marcelle until he found something. He explained that up until now he had managed on the money his family sent him: the family no doubt looked upon the marriage with an unfavourable eye, for it gave no sign of life.

Mme Drouffe was very anxious that her daughter should be married in white, and although Marcelle had often expressed her horror of official ceremonies she did not want to deprive her mother of this pleasure. She ordered a very simple dress that could easily be made suitable for small dinner-parties: everyone agreed that with her tulle veil she looked like a Madonna. The wedding was very quiet; Marguerite wore a shot-taffeta dress that did not become her, but Pascal looked very fine in his dark suit; and as he led his sister to the altar he seemed deeply moved. In the vestry Germaine burst into sobs, and Marcelle herself could not keep back a few tears. Nevertheless the modest reception that Mme Drouffe gave after the Mass was very cheerful: Denis displayed great resources of amiability and he was thought infinitely charming.

The young couple had decided not to leave for Brittany until the next day. Having publicly told the chauffeur to drive them to the Gare Montparnasse, on the way Denis gave him the address of an hotel where they booked a room for the night. They went to drink a glass of port in one of the big cafés on the boulevards and then Denis took Marcelle to have a particularly good dinner at Weber's. She was rather surprised to see how much he enjoyed the excellent food: for her part she was so overwrought that the mouthfuls stuck in her throat and she scarcely touched the meal. She was so impatient for the night that shivers ran through her; yet at the same time she was afraid. She had certainly heard that for women of her age losing one's virginity was not painful; but that did not entirely reassure her.

As they went up the hotel staircase her knees gave way beneath her: she wanted to sit by Denis and take his hands, and for both of them to talk soberly about the solemn act that they were going to carry out. By means of their bodies' imperfect union their souls would try to reach one another, perhaps in vain: Marcelle would have liked to weep over the touching splendour of this attempt, cuddled there in Denis's arms, and then to pass gently from tears to caresses.

But Denis did not seem aware of the gravity of the moment: in a perfectly natural tone he said he was dropping with sleep, and he went to undress in the bathroom. Marcelle was already in bed when he knocked; she was wearing a pale-green lacy nightgown, and her heart was beating fast.

Lying there beside her, Denis talked about unimportant things for a little while and then, in no particular hurry, began to kiss her. As he did so Marcelle felt the blood flow to her temples and swell her lips and breasts. 'Now he is going to put out the light,' she thought. 'Is he going to hurt me much?'

Denis slipped the pale green nightgown over Marcelle's head and did not put out the light: then, as he kissed her bosom and her belly, she closed her eyes and began to tremble; the idea that a man's eyes were delighting in her nakedness made her whole being quiver with a shame whose stab was sweeter than the sweetest caress.

Denis drew her close and she felt the warmth, the tender suppleness of a naked body against her own: and a mysterious, quivering, hard flesh throbbed against her belly. But even more than by this animal contact, Marcelle was stirred by the skilful hands that fondled her; it was not only a delightful stroking of her skin, for these hands had an awareness and a will of their own; they were shameless and masterful, they compelled the coming of her pleasure; and it was their tyranny that made Marcelle faint with sensual delight.

She opened her eyes: Denis's face appeared before her, changed with desire, intensely eager, almost unrecognizable: he looked capable of beating her, torturing her, and the sight filled Marcelle with so piercing a pleasure that she began to groan. 'I'm at his mercy,' she said to herself and she was engulfed by an ecstasy in which shame and fear and joy were all intermingled. She groaned so loudly that Denis had to put his hand over her mouth: she kissed the hand – she would have liked to call out to Denis that she was his thing, his slave: and tears ran down her cheeks. All at once he penetrated her: she did not exactly feel pleasure, but this violation of her most secret flesh made her gasp with gratitude and humility. She took every one of Denis's piercing thrusts with passionate submission, and to make his possession of her the more complete she let her consciousness glide away into the night.

When she woke up Denis's face had its usual look once more, and he was smiling; this embarrassed her and she pulled the sheet up to her chin. She would have liked to speak, but she found nothing to say. 'Happy?' he murmured. 'Of course,' she said with a little laugh. In that instant she utterly hated him: angrily she remembered that she had groaned in his arms and that he had known how very deeply she was moved. She blushed for shame and this time there was no pleasure mingled with her confusion.

There was an awkward silence; then with an air of spontaneity she said, 'How funny it is, being in Paris and staying in an hotel.

Don't you think it would be lovely not to know Paris, and to come for one's honeymoon?'

Denis agreed. He was very, very fond of Paris: indeed, for him Paris was the only place on earth where it was worth living. The charms of nature, on the other hand, hardly meant anything to him. Enthusiastically Marcelle began to list these charms: she told him how happy she was at the idea that presently she would see the shores of Mont-Saint-Michel and the moors of Brittany, which were, she thought, an exact equivalent of her own internal land-scape. Having listened politely for a while Denis cut her short, taking her in his arms and seeking her mouth.

Marcelle stiffened in his grasp: once more the blood came flooding to her lips, but this time she knew: she knew that these eager hands wanted to make her sink down into a bottomless pit of abjection. This man was an enemy, one who would laugh at her fall; she felt the horror of such a humiliation so strongly that she began to tremble with desire and in a jet of passion she bit Denis's shoulder. He started; his hands gripped her body harder and he nibbled the quivering flesh; Marcelle clung to him ecstatically, drunk with shame. 'I'm his thing, his slave,' she murmured to herself; and aloud, 'I adore you.' Abruptly he turned her on her belly and made her kneel. 'Stay like that,' he whispered. 'It's more fun.' She trembled: a man, a being endowed with a conscience, wanted her to join him in an unclean act. He was bending her into this ridiculous position and relishing its ignominy. 'On all fours, like animals,' she thought: the idea made her head spin and he had to tense all his muscles to keep her in this degrading posture – she was like one of those victims the executioners force to dance under the whip. 'He's enjoying me, he's enjoying me,' she said to herself in a paroxysm of sensual delight. When Denis drew away she fell gasping on the bed, almost fainting.

She heard him moving about the room: when he came back and lay beside her she kept her eyes shut: at all costs she had to stay deep down in this drowsiness where shame turns into physical pleasure – she must never wake up again – it was impossible to face that half-affectionate, half-mocking look, impossible to allow a clear recollection of the caresses she had undergone. Yet Marcelle felt, and felt with a dreadful anguish, that in spite of all she could do the gentle mist was slowly, ineluctably fading: the nervous tension became so great that her teeth started to chatter.

The chattering was only slight at first and she could have stopped it by opening her eyes; but they remained tightly closed. Gradually the sound grew louder and louder. With a kind of relief Marcelle listened to the sound of clashing bone resonating in her head: it took up all her attention, her awareness, and defended her against recollection. Sobs ran the length of her body, making her shoulders shake convulsively: from time to time she clenched her teeth, but a violent trembling instantly followed this exhausting effort – she had lost all control. Yet she felt that the spell could be broken; all she had to do was to stop believing in it for a moment. But she took pleasure in thinking that she was possessed by unknown forces, and that stiffening her muscles was no use, since they did not obey her. Tears ran down her cheeks: Denis began stroking her hair and talking in an anxious, very irritated voice. 'It's nerves,' she stammered. 'Leave me alone. Let me go to sleep.' She could not bear being face to face with him again. She pulled the blankets over her and turned towards the wall.

The next day they set off for their honeymoon: Marcelle was disappointed by Mont-Saint-Michel, and once more she perceived that life always fell short of dreams. She did find Chateaubriand's grave as imposing as she had hoped it would be, but she liked Chateaubriand less than she had when she was young; and, indeed, she laughed heartily when Denis made disrespectful fun of romanticism. As he often did when he was talking to her, he spoke about the new aesthetic that France had to be provided with. For her part she would have liked to tell him memories of her childhood, but it was not a subject that he found very interesting. Sometimes their conversation tended to die away: Denis would then kiss her neck, stroking her breasts. She loathed those brief caresses. At the slightest contact her body prepared itself for a great yielding, a complete surrender, and since she had to regain possession of herself right away she remained all on edge until the evening. She could not prevent herself from being impatient for night to come, and this made her resent Denis – almost hate him.

At the end of a week Denis suggested going back to Paris: Marcelle had counted on spending her fortnight's holiday in Brittany, but she readily agreed to make this sacrifice for him. Denis was very grateful to her, and he was particularly kind and attentive on the train. They talked about the life that was waiting for them in

Paris, and Denis confessed how much it grieved him to be obliged to be dependent on her. At this time the Drouffes were very comfortably off: Pascal had left the École des Chartes and he had been given a grant for research. He was supervising an edition of medieval texts and, having made some quite good contacts in literary circles, he might prove a very valuable ally for Denis. For the moment Marcelle and Pascal had decided to leave the young writer all the free time he needed to finish his apprenticeship.

'You'll soon manage to get a name for yourself, you see if you don't,' said Marcelle. With much feeling Denis kissed her hands and promised to show himself worthy of such unselfishness: but he had so terribly little confidence in himself. 'I'm so bad at living, so awkward, so ill-adapted, my poor darling,' he said, and his look darkened. 'I can only bring care and anxiety to those who love me.' Marcelle's eyes filled with tears and rapturously she said that she believed in him. 'I shouldn't have married you if I hadn't been perfectly certain you were an exceptional being,' she said; and then smiling, 'I still remember the evening my fate was revealed to me, a completely mauve evening. I had been crying for a long while because the world was so ordinary and commonplace and I wanted to die. And then all at once I knew that one day you would come.' He listened to her with deep emotion, taking her hand: the blaze of genius shone in his gold-flecked eyes. 'I never stopped waiting for you,' she said.

The young couple settled in Mme Drouffe's apartment, taking over a room separated from the rest by a long corridor. Marcelle went through a period of frivolity: even after she had returned to her work at the Centre she went out with Denis almost every evening, going to the theatre, the cinema, the Lapin Agile, the Noctambules, and sometimes having supper in Montparnasse or Montmartre. On Sundays they stayed in bed until noon. Marcelle gave up her voluntary work at 'Social Contact' for good.

'The only thing I believe in now,' she told Germaine, 'is individual action. Influencing the masses may seem more spectacular, but if you want to accomplish anything of real value it is better to give yourself up entirely to one single worthwhile person.'

Germaine was in complete agreement: she had quite seen that Marcelle's generous giving of her best to the team had not been rewarded. Marcelle confessed that her sense that those beings she cared for so wholeheartedly were so remote from her had been a positive torment, and that in her bedroom at night she had often wept with despair. After this talk it occurred to Marcelle that perhaps she had been slightly unfair to Germaine, and she inwardly promised to overlook her little failings: Marcelle often asked her advice, and the renewal of their friendship made Germaine very happy.

As a wedding present Germaine had given her friend a sum of money that Marcelle, accustomed to a modest way of life, thought quite considerable; and shortly after her return to Paris she was disagreeably surprised to find that she had frittered away more than half of it. 'I'm letting myself be carried away by a whirlwind,' she said to herself.

She would have to speak to Denis. Long before this Marcelle had observed that he did not understand the value of money: he wore silk shirts and at the theatre he took seats in the stalls. He seemed to float above all vulgar realities, and for several days Marcelle could not bring herself to talk to him about a question that seemed to her shabby and mean. It was one evening at a nightclub that her duty became perfectly clear. Ever since she had calculated what it cost, this going out had lost its charm for Marcelle, but she had no excuse for refusing: on this particular evening, after a certain amount of pressing, Marcelle had put on her wedding-dress (a little dressmaker had altered it very prettily so that it would do to wear in the evening), put on lipstick and wrapped herself in a Spanish shawl that belonged to her mother. Denis gave her a queer kind of a look, and when they were sitting down with two sherry cobblers in front of them he asked her why she did not have her hair cut short. Marcelle answered curtly that her hair was an integral part of her personality: it was black and lustrous, and everyone had always acknowledged that it was very beautiful.

Denis did not dwell on the subject: he seemed to enjoy listening to the bawling music of the jazz band and watching the women with dyed hair – they all laughed with the same ingratiating laugh, rubbing themselves against the men. Marcelle shivered and drew the shawl over her shoulders. Sorrowfully she called to mind the dreamy, thoughtful child who had fled from the tawdry glitter of balls: she remembered her exacting youth, her proud sufferings and the wealth of her inner life. She must react against this current of frivolity that was sweeping her along: it was her duty to show Denis how to lead a life filled with serious, sober joys, with work and with lofty thoughts. She turned to him. 'I wonder what we are doing here,' she said.

He looked at her with a rather obstinate expression on his face and said, 'It's a pleasant spot for dancing.'

She sighed. Sometimes he quite took her aback: the Denis who was so understanding and sensitive, the Denis who had the outlook of a poet, would now and then utter gross or cynical opinions for the fun of it. She would make him confess that he found these expensive, futile amusements depressing. 'We have given in to the insidious temptation of happiness – given in only too much,' she said to herself thoughtfully. She decided to speak to Denis right away. 'What shall we have gained intellectually or spiritually when this evening is over, Denis?' she asked. 'Listen, since we came back we have been satisfied with easy shows and easy music, and we no longer draw anything from ourselves. We are letting our happiness lull us to sleep – it's understandable in a way; but we are confusing pleasure and happiness.'

He looked at her attentively, with an ironical expression on his face. 'As far as I'm concerned, it's a delightful life,' he said. He did not seem to be taking Marcelle at all seriously.

'In any case it's not a life than we can go on leading any more,' she said curtly. 'We can no longer afford it.'

Denis's face hardened. 'Ah? We're broke? You should have said so right away.'

Marcelle gave an impatient shrug. 'But that's only a secondary issue, Denis,' she said. 'Just think how you are wasting your wonderful gifts in idleness. You must set yourself to work. Besides, we can perfectly well go out once or twice a week, you know.'

'Once a week, on Saturdays!' He smiled unpleasantly, and then in an offhand tone he said, 'Oh well, I suppose you're right. Tomorrow I'll start that article on Lautréamont I was talking to Pascal about. It will surely bring me in a little pocket money.'

'Denis,' said Marcelle in a reproachful voice, blushing violently. Denis's attitude wounded her: he forgot that it was she who earned the money he threw away so readily, but she could not remind him of the fact without looking mean. It was vexing.

Denis was ill-humoured during the days that followed and the atmosphere at home grew stormy. Pascal was perfectly tactful and discreet, but Mme Drouffe was not very fond of Denis; he was often rude to her and sometimes they quarrelled violently. Marguerite admired Denis, and she took his side with a zeal that did nothing to lessen the animosity. As far as Marcelle herself was concerned, Denis changed: he remained polite, but he was irritable and on edge and he made a point of avoiding serious conversations. It was only at night, when he took her in his arms, that Marcelle's faith in him and in his love came back: to see this child she watched over like a mother during the day change into an imperious young male overwhelmed her and she yielded to his whims with intense pleasure. He always went to sleep first: with her body voluptuously relaxed she gazed at his calm features and uttered the loving promise, 'You will never wear out my patience.' She would no doubt have a great deal to suffer, but she would accept these sufferings with joy; and one day, when he was fully mature and at the height of his fame, he would look back over the past and understand.

Yet Denis could hardly be said to be taking the road to fame, and presently Marcelle grew anxious. When she came unexpectedly into the room, she found him lolling on the bed, smoking or reading detective stories: she thought it her duty to make disapproving remarks, and these he did not like at all. 'You can't write a poem as though it were a thesis,' he said irritably. As for the articles that Pascal had suggested placing for him, it was no good – he had never been able to turn his ideas into money. He spoke with such contempt that Marcelle shed tears. The lack of understanding that great men usually met with from those around them had often made her feel indignant, and she had thought she would be an ideal companion for a superior mind: but genius is always disconcerting – Marcelle was horribly afraid that she had inflicted a vulgar scene on Denis and that she had not fully appreciated the rights of poetry. For the whole of one night she had anxiously wondered how she ought to behave. There were child prodigies who never fulfilled themselves, and dreamers who could be made to produce masterpieces only by compulsion. A perfect understanding and acceptance of the weaknesses and even perversities that were the price of genius did not mean that one must not struggle against them. Marcelle bravely assumed the thankless role that fell to her: she insisted that every evening Denis should show her what he had written during the day: she resolutely checked him for his idleness, she patiently put up with his bad moods. And one day he would kiss her eyelids, his heart torn with remorse, and she would smile and say, 'Everything you brought me made me happy.'

This idea kept her going for a while: at night she stroked Denis's hair, filled with gentle, sweet thoughts of all the sacrifices she had made for him and of those she was still prepared to make; and her eyes filled with tears. But even these moments became more and more rare. Although she carefully rationed his pocket money, Denis took to spending his days in cafés and to going out in the evening without his wife: when he came and lay down at Marcelle's side he scarcely seemed to notice that she was there – in an absent-minded way he accepted her kisses and then went straight to sleep. Marcelle was obliged to speak to him firmly: she described his life in unflattering terms and stated that she would not pay his debts. In return Denis made unsparing fun of her bourgeois carefulness and mocked the yearning for the ideal that tormented her. His cruel and unfair words wounded Marcelle's heart: she repeated them to herself during the sleepless nights that she spent by Denis's peaceful, relaxed body; she remembered their earlier embraces and she trembled with disgust and longing. She grew very highly strung, and particularly at those times of the month when she was unwell she was incapable of keeping back the insulting words that rose to her lips. By way of response Denis assumed an insolent, arrogant manner; and he was insufferably offhand with Mme Drouffe and Pascal. The only person he was kind to was Marguerite, who was in open-mouthed admiration of all he did. Mme Drouffe thought he had a thoroughly bad influence on her younger daughter, and she held it against him: there were frequent scenes between Marguerite and her mother.

At dinner one day Marguerite asked Denis what was meant exactly by an 'American bar': he readily told her, ending, 'If you would like to see one, it's perfectly easy. I'll take you this very evening.'

'It's no place for a girl,' said Mme Drouffe sharply.

Marguerite shrugged. 'No place for a girl! That makes no sense. What do you imagine could happen to me?'

'I don't want you to go out this evening,' said Mme Drouffe.

'Why not this evening? What difference does it make?'

'Don't start arguing again,' said Marcelle. 'Mama doesn't want you to go out, and that's all. You really might give way sometimes, Marguerite.'

Marguerite's lips trembled with anger. 'I'm absolutely determined to go out with Denis,' she said in an unsteady voice.

Denis began to laugh and made her a sign not to go on. Nothing further arose until they reached coffee. When he had drunk his cup Denis stood up and said calmly, 'Well, Marguerite, are you coming?'

'You know perfectly well Mama is against it,' said Marcelle in a furious voice. 'Your behaviour is indecent.'

Marguerite hesitated for a moment, then she walked towards the door.

'I absolutely forbid you to go,' said Mme Drouffe, growing very red.

'Good-night, everybody,' said Denis. He pushed Marguerite by the shoulder and they ran down the stairs laughing.

It was the first time Marguerite had ever so deliberately disobeyed her mother. Mme Drouffe burst into tears. Pascal and Marcelle soothed her and persuaded her to go to bed. Marcelle undertook to wait up for Marguerite and Denis.

She talked to Pascal for a few moments and then she too went to her bedroom: it was not so much the sadness of her lot that overwhelmed Marcelle as the injustice. She had always foreseen that life would make her suffer, because one does not prefer heroism and beauty to pleasure without having to pay for it; but she had never doubted that by her refusal of easy pleasures she was making herself worthy of those joys which are the reward of great souls. Now her faith wavered. Maybe there was something rotten in the world: maybe she had saved herself for a promised land that did not exist.

To while away the time Marcelle looked for a book; but she was incapable of reading. The street noises had stopped: the silence was almost oppressive. Marcelle was extremely afraid of the dark, and the slightest creaking made her start. She walked up and down the room for a while; then she sat down at Denis's desk and leafed through the untidy papers. He had scarcely written two or three pages, and even those were all crossed out: she had staked everything on him and she had lost.

Without thinking what she was doing, Marcelle opened one of the drawers: a little heap of letters lay at the bottom, perhaps a dozen of them. With a certain dread she took the letters and spread them out before her. There were a few trifling notes – appointments with friends, requests for money. Marcelle glanced through one of the letters: 'You tell me that your freedom is the most precious of those golden bowls that we sometimes have to throw into the sea, like the King of Thule, so as to weep for them afterwards,' wrote a man called André on the occasion of his friend's marriage. 'But what will become of me while you sit sadly watching the rings on the water? Without you, shall we still play the dangerous game you taught us – play it wholeheartedly? I am afraid of forgetting how to live.' Marcelle also found a poem by this André and she was about to read it when a blue letter caught her eye: it was a letter from a woman, dated two days earlier. The address, engraved in dark blue at the top of the sheet, was 12 rue du Ranelagh: the woman signed herself Marie-Ange and it was obvious that she was Denis's mistress. At this Marcelle started searching the bedroom without the least scruple. In a coat pocket she found another blue letter dated three months before and signed M. A. Lamblin. The lady asked Denis to come to tea: she wanted him to meet some interesting people. At this time she was still calling him *vous* rather than the intimate *tu*. Denis must have locked away the rest of their correspondence, because Marcelle's search uncovered nothing more.

'He's betrayed me,' she reflected. Denis had married her because he had nothing to live on and because he disliked the idea of working: but now that he was the lover of a no doubt very wealthy woman, he no longer bothered to treat her decently. For two hours and more Marcelle was prostrated: she wept over all those days lost in devotion and tears; and these present tears were no longer the restoring promise of a brilliant future but a sterile bitterness of mind. She was no longer young; she was physically weary; she had committed her life for good and all: presently she would be a useless old woman, one who had never known happiness. She thought of Denis with a cold hatred.

Three was striking when she got up and put the letters back in their place. She compelled herself to spend a long time getting ready for bed: she wanted to regain full control of herself and she wanted to take her revenge on Denis. With a calm, dignified sadness she would make him thoroughly aware of his wrongdoing; she would crush him with her scorn; she would not speak of the letters.

Marguerite and Denis came back an hour later: Marcelle stared at her half-drunk sister in silence and then turned to her husband. 'It seems to me we had better have it out,' she said.

'Do you really think so?' said Denis, following her into their room: he sat down on the bed to take off his shoes. Marcelle folded her arms and looked at him steadily.

'I do not blame you for no longer having any love for me, nor even any respect,' she said. 'But what I should like to know is why, under such circumstances, you married me?'

Denis hesitated. 'Perhaps I was wrong,' he said. 'I thought that with you I should find the peaceful atmosphere I needed – a happy, well-balanced life. I ought to have preferred my freedom to peace.'

'You admit that you never loved me?'

Denis smiled and began to untie his tie. 'What is love?' he said.

'I've sacrificed everything for you,' said Marcelle in a trembling voice.

'I know,' he said quickly. 'I eat the bread you earn by the sweat of your brow: but I do assure you it's very bitter bread.'

This took Marcelle's breath away. 'Oh,' she cried. 'This is too much. You think it perfectly normal to exploit us and then you dare to come and complain!'

He looked at her gravely and there was a deep contempt in his eyes. 'It's true that for you people these questions of money count enormously. You must forgive me, but I've never been able to get used to that turn of mind.'

Marcelle reddened: no insult could have wounded her more. She bitterly regretted her clumsy words. 'I devoted myself to you body and soul,' she said.

'For my part I thought you rather liked it,' said Denis insolently. 'But now, if it no longer satisfies you, there's a very easy answer – we only have to part.'

'Part!' cried Marcelle: the blood left her cheeks and she sank into a chair. She had seen the appalling fate of living with Denis without love and without hope, but never for a moment had she thought of leaving him.

'I can't change myself,' said Denis, 'and you can't accept me as I am. The best thing is a clean break.'

He was young and he was loved; he would be happy away from her and she would be alone. Little did she care now whether she had her revenge or not: she could not bear the idea of sleeping alone for ever, of never feeling a warm, strong body's weight again.

'Would you spoil my life without any remorse at all?'

'Since you're not happy with me . . .'

Marcelle stood up, took Denis's shoulders and looked deep into his eyes. 'You're only a child,' she said slowly, 'a cruel child. But I love you, Denis: I shall always love you, in spite of everything.'

He freed himself, slightly embarrassed. 'I'm not a brute, Marcelle,' he said in a rather unsure voice. 'Believe me, I've a great deal of affection for you.' He smiled. 'Only I'm just not made for family life.'

Denis said nothing more about parting: Marcelle had been so afraid of losing her husband that she decided to put up with anything at all to keep him. If only he stayed it did not matter if he never became a genius or if he loved other women. 'True love forgives all,' she reflected.

Marcelle spent some unhappy, painful days: instead of being grateful for such a degree of abnegation, Denis took advantage of it to throw off all restraint. During the hours she spent waiting for him to come back at night, Marcelle sadly remembered the free and peaceful time of her girlhood, when her life ran to the rhythm of melodious verse, when she was surrounded by poets and heroes, brotherly figures always ready to respond to her call, and when she thought about the books she would write in the vague future, about the delicate impressions she had gathered during the day, about happiness, death and fate. Now this calm meditation was denied her: now her daily lot was anxiously listening to the footsteps in the street, evoking the picture of Denis with a woman in his arms, hating him, longing for his caresses. Sometimes she had the despairing thought that her passion for Denis was laying waste a spirit which had been meant for a great destiny, and she found herself wishing for no matter what kind of release.

One Saturday, when she came back from the Centre, she found a letter on her bed. She knew at once what had happened.

'Do not think of me too unkindly,' wrote Denis. 'No doubt I shall never find another love like yours; but my poor dear Marcelle there are some beings who refuse even love. Do you know that in Thule there was a king who threw his golden bowl into the sea so that he might watch the rings on the water and sigh. No doubt one day I shall bitterly miss this happiness I am giving up: may you, for your part, find consolation very soon. I do not dare to hope for your forgiveness.'

The wardrobe and drawers were empty. 'He has got hold of some money,' thought Marcelle. 'It's that woman.' Her eyes remained dry. 'My life is finished,' she said under her breath.

She took off her hat and coat and automatically smoothed her black hair as she stood in front of the wardrobe mirror. A strange peace flooded into her. 'My life is finished,' she said again, with a kind of indifference. She was no longer thinking about Denis: she gazed at the reflection of a woman with a broad forehead and soulful eyes, a woman who was still young and who no longer looked forward to anything at all. She lay down on the divan: from the far end of the corridor small noises reached her bedroom – the closing of a door, footsteps, the metallic sound of forks. Unconscious of the tragedy, Mme Drouffe was laying the table: Pascal was running through his index cards.

'All I have left is myself,' said Marcelle. She closed her eyes: it seemed to her that she was coming back to her real self, as if from a long banishment. Once more she thought of the sad, precocious child, crouching behind heavy curtains that separated her from the world or hiding in the shadows of a book-lined corridor. She saw herself as an adolescent, enthusiastic and misunderstood, confiding her sorrow to a mauve night sky; she saw her lonely youth, full of pride and high, uncompromising demands. This road, so painfully traversed, had brought her back to solitude; and never again would she be tempted to escape from herself. A great exaltation filled her; she stood up and walked over to the window, drawing the curtains back with a sudden jerk. She was not to look beyond herself for the meaning of her life; she was set free from love, from hope, and from that stifling presence that had taken up all her strength and her time for more than a year. Everything was fine.

Marcelle leaned her forehead against the cool window-pane: in rejecting commonplace pleasures, playthings, finery, social success and easy flirtation she had always saved herself for some splendid happiness. Yet it was not happiness that had been granted to her: it was suffering. But perhaps it was only suffering that could satisfy her heart at last. 'Higher than happiness,' she whispered. This great bitter thing was her lot on earth and she would know how to receive it; she would know how to transform it into beauty; and one day strangers, brothers, would understand her disincarnate soul, and they would cherish it. Higher than happiness. Tears came into her eyes: she could already feel the dawn of sublime poems quivering within her.

For the second time she had the wonderful revelation of her fate. 'I am a woman of genius,' she decided.

Translated by Patrick O'Brian

•

CLAIRE RABE
Sicily Enough
(1963)

The Olympia Press was founded by Maurice Girodias in Paris in 1953 following the model of his father's Obelisk Press, which had published controversial works by writers as diverse as James Joyce and Henry Miller. Under the new Olympia imprint appeared works such as Lolita *and* The Ginger Man, *as well as many more frankly pornographic titles. Girodias was constantly beset with legal and financial difficulties, but that did not deter him from launching* Olympia *magazine in 1962.*

It ran for just four issues and the quality of the contents varied enormously, but like the Olympia Press it occasionally featured female writers like 'Harriet Daimler' (a pseudonym of Iris Owens) with The Woman Thing, *and the present writer, Claire Rabe. 'Sicily Enough' is described as being by 'a young American widow' – and that, apart from the photograph of her face on the cover of the magazine, is all that is known of this author. Her sensuous writing has an authenticity mostly lacking in the other contributions to* Olympia, *and it seems unlikely that this could have been her only work.*

Taormina is an island on a mountain. A female, rising and falling town. I sucked away at it for over a year because I wanted everything.

Dogshadow thin I arrive, carrying my third child like a weapon through this old town, while the only thing I feel is my hair tight, hurting where the baby holds on. A fierce clock, she reminds my vague shocked self that I must function. We kiss and I inhale her breath like food, warm as the milk I flowed into her some months ago.

October in Sicily, and there is the first volcano I have ever seen. Cool mountain, lambent with snow on its mouth; how can it be so hot inside?

I buy grapes, wash them in the fountain while broody dark men watch me bending over. I suddenly feel well-fleshed, and the skin of grapes slides agreeably over my tongue. The baby has fun spitting with them. I buy a great deal more to bring to the other children waiting at home.

It will be easy to eat in this country.

Long walks, up and down steps, going from view to view, the town spread around in broken architecture, painted in tired colour that was once red. Walls better than current art, moonpitted, incredibly dry. What a sun has made all this happen! Centuries of summer, centuries of cats and dogs breeding under Roman arches.

Women who still wear black, faces yellow, a smear of bad flesh under the eyes that arouses me and suggests a hundred perversities. Every woman has breasts and thighs and hair in her armpits; I see them as black curling flowers. Their legs are strong and hairy, men do not force them to shave; here they do not alter animals or their passions.

This directness, this use of the body attracts me at once to the Sicilians and makes me feel warm. There is no subtle sex here, no American sex, but coupling itself. The day for a Sicilian has happened if he has made love. It seems empty to sleep unless it is post-coital; it's lonely.

I long for a lover here as I have longed for dogs to sleep with in my virtuous days. I want warm animals so near me that they are inside.

*

Desire grows on me. I see it reflected in the men who stare at me,
their lust is an approval of my fattening body. I eat so much now,
just to look at the vegetables is to feel nourished. A kind of
cauliflower that grows almost nowhere else is in season. The whole
top of it is painted deep purple, formidable as the colour runs off
into the cooking water till finally eaten, white again, drenched in
pungent olive oil.

My children are so well here. They break rough bread and dunk
it in sauce, they eat garlic and tomatoes; our cuisine is the maid's,
who makes lentil soup with pasta, broccoli with rice. We seem to
be in a farmer's kitchen. My house is a good smell, while in the
garden pomegranates burst on trees and oranges hang like lanterns.

Everything here becomes hazed over by sun and abundance. If
something terrible has happened to me I no longer remember it so
harshly. I feel as though I have a million senses now, held together
by brain and guts. All I have known and suffered and longed for
come together for me in Sicily. Good and bad, hard and soft, there
is everything in those four words, any combination of them means
something. Good soft bad hard or good hard bad soft or. If I am to
go on living, and I must, since I have six black eyes looking at me,
since my children are happy and do not understand that someone
has died, then I shall become part of this landscape. I will grow
into these trees, into these hills, and wait and stare and hope for the
volcano to erupt.

There he is, small angry-faced man. As he stands up to greet me a
ray of sun slanting through the window grabs his eyes. They glare at
me in the agate yellow of certain birds, the pupils pinned on me. I have
seen that yellow in the amber I found on the beaches of the Baltic,
where I played as a child. I have seen that yellow in the eyes of Clarita
when she lusted for me. She was rapacious, like the watching bird, her
eyes cold yellow pointed exactly to the centre of me. As his are now.

'You are American?'

'You speak English.'

'Not very well.'

'Oh, too well. I want to learn Italian.'

'You will have a Sicilian accent if you learn from me.'

'I want to.'

This will be my first lover. I must prepare myself as for the first
time ever.

My hair needs to be cut, no more pins in it. I examine my fine
skin and bathe it carefully. I polish my children as one does
beautiful apples. My walks have a direction now. I go to his bar
where he stands in the doorway waiting, sure of me. I had no idea
that he is the richest young man in town, the most beautiful. It is
his eyes I look for.

We work slowly, he is patient, always teaching, so aware that I
am getting ready for him.

We go for many drives, I admire the countryside, and he takes
me as far as the snow of the mountain.

How magical the preparation for love.

In the café I meet his Sicilian friends. There, every woman who
passes is judged. When they approve, '*buona*' is uttered with a
hoarse gusto, and I picture at once an entwining of genitals like the
display of entrails in a butcher shop.

The face of the woman is looked at last. She must simply not be
ugly. A robust body with abundant breast and rear and a fattish
face is a fine '*cavallo*' or '*vaca*'. The inspection is continuous, noisy
with smacks and hisses, an obvious need to make each opinion
public, to share. They tell each other exactly how they feel and how
they would treat each case.

I have learned quickly to know what they say if only by their
gestures. Beautiful in the way of mutes, hands weave away at the
meaning of their talk. Hands measure intensity of meaning, but a
small downward motion of the mouth destroys an entire argument.

My mother had this way of destroying me. Her mouth is thin
and the slightest doubt is immediately visible in the downward arch
of her lips – and there is a real shock in me as I know that she is
against me. Her mouth curves at me like a snake, her face changes
so much there is no chance for the girl to impress this judge.
Everything has been smudged over. Is it then that I begin to lie?
Or do I just begin to sneak? Sometimes I try again to tell her what
I feel and again she makes this unbearable face. More and more I
hide what I feel and soon am such an expert that I even cease to
feel.

The seduction of my mother failed. She will not marvel at me.
As did Clarita when she caressed my young body with her old
appreciation, the yellow glowing in her eyes. My mother made me

cold. I slept with a million blankets and no heat came; my body was sealed off in a cold young coffin.

And here is a country without music, books, painting, only certain lusts. Of course I must live here; this is why I came to this quicksand where there is no space for sadness, only quick frantic sucking motion, up, down.

Night. Palm trees staring straight up, sky soft around stars, clouds moving through the heads of trees. Olive, cypress and palm, their different foliage hard in the black distance, trees so separate from one another that one cannot imagine a forest. Palm, cypress, olive; leaf, shape, size, everything unique, blowing up into the sky all at once, the night dark, glowing with such ornament, waiting for its own end.

In the cemetery night pushes against what was, while the cypress rises and small birds rest.

Sound of mandolins in the tavern, sweet and liquid, played by two ugly men, drifting around Roberto like a habit, he hears none of it, just stares at my thighs. The first music I've been able to listen to in a long time, it does not frighten me into the past.

Red wine, fresh from the slopes of the mountain, cheap and delicious like penny candy, I drink it fast, it seems to improve my Italian. The room, square and low, underlit, with a skinny dog asleep on one of the chairs. The owner dedicates a song to me about the torment of love, smiling at the 'nuova coppia' that has the town talking.

I feel pleasant, involved with everything and everyone there. A ditchdigger I have seen working along the streets, dark and beautiful, now dressed in a marvellous velveteen jacket that shines like a chestnut, nods to me but I do not answer. I resent his trying to make real my flirtation with him. I only like to watch him working, to dream about his strength and simplicity, I really wish he would not confuse his reality with my fantasy. 'Don't speak,' I think, 'don't let me hear your voice, just be there and let me dream about you. I don't want to touch you, I just want the idea of you. That's my man there, that handsome creature lounging by my side, more elegant than you, an offspring of Greeks and Moors with the body Michelangelo had adored.'

Yes, my eyes roam the men with ease for I am safe among them, coupled to Roberto whose loins are making me happen.

'*Quanto sei bello,*' I whisper. He grins but has to answer: 'A man is *simpatico* not beautiful.'

'I don't speak Italian well, make mistakes, but don't teach me too much.'

'*Va bene, va bene,*' he nods, his eyes iridescent, picking up all the light there is in the room.

The piazza where we meet every morning. He in his kingdom, that bar where he strides about like a small emperor.

'You are my empress now,' he says lovingly, so proud.

'No, just your mistress,' I answer in a coy way, new to me. His courtship of me has gotten into my bones. I feel all woman, organ deep as I glisten around him, my breasts full.

Walking down the corso, thighs heavy against my sex on this Sicilian street where I pass several times a day, where nothing changes except the flimsiest detail, where I am on parade. They all know what has happened. *La Americana, amante de Roberto.* I have fallen into a certain status, condemned yet full of prestige because my lover is rich. Besides, it's not often that a woman with three children has any vitality left here. The women are jealous of my strong body, the men wonder about me. 'She must be very good,' I overhear. '*Che buona.*'

There is a ritual as I enter through the arch into the wide incredible piazza, more beautiful than the shell in Siena. I go to the railing that overlooks the sea, trees falling down the view to the sea, the earth dark and dry green. To the right glares Etna. I look there first, no, I behold it. Nearly a perfect cone, it rises strong at the sky, the snow hard and clean, whiter than a nun's eye.

The piazza, bounded by curving, crumbling churches on two sides, with Roberto's bar in between, hypnotizes me. I sit for hours at a table, trying every drink ever brought to Italy, looking endlessly at the pure view of space and sky hanging over the piazza where emptiness is broken only by seven trees and the people strolling. Seven oleander trees that never cease to bloom, white, pink and red flowers.

Five miles along the coast, gigantic over the cold sea, rises the town of Forza d'Agro. Lazy in medieval poverty, it waits to be looked at. Roberto and I are spring coming into those black, sunless streets. Shops are tombs for food showing porkfat, tripe, enormous loaves of bread. Awful old people stare at me, disapprove of my tight trousers and the way I hold Roberto's hand. He is clean among them, so young.

Passing a stable I desire him and pull him quickly into the warm smell of manure.

'Let's make love here,' I say, but he laughs and worries. I take off my shoes and push my feet into the texture of dung. I suppose I am going too far, but I feel different here, not vicarious but in the actual sway of history. The age of this town has pulled off a certain veneer.

Roberto looks very uncomfortable and tries to get me out. '*Questa pazza!*' he exclaims. But I do not feel crazy, I simply feel less civilized and wish he would go along with me in my sudden involvement with the twelfth century.

However, his embarrassment has spoiled my mood and I follow him. He wants to show me the town and its silly monuments. While he gapes at a church I smell bread baking. There is the oven, teeming with fire. A donkey stands patiently by the door, so heavily laden with wild rosemary that it resembles a solid halo. 'Look,' I say, but he hardly knows what I mean. Certainly the church is lovely and I am tempted to steal from it. How I should like one of those wooden candelabras, golden and flaky where worms have been.

Down below in Naxos, the first town built by the Greeks in Sicily, eating prehistoric octopus, while my eyes drift over the splendid view of my island above.

Worn, fabulous landslide of a view, green as black jagging to that sea where lava still lies exposed as it has lain for centuries.

Not thinking of the view; it has been sown into me. His body planted in me, I feel a tree. How shocking in the mirror, how very secret and deep it looks from the outside, while inside there is a wet intensity even deeper than what the mirror shows, and that's very deep. How cataclysmic to be penetrated, those thighs opening wide to let him in.

From a dusty fig tree I take a bursting fruit. It must be splitting to be good. As I am at my full opening, ripe and glad to have this pleasure made known to me. How many women are allowed this as they plough through years of intimacy that are never catastrophic.

Perhaps I am losing my mind in this fleshbath, perhaps I shall lose everything, even my children. I forget them so often now. I have only this spastic, one-dimensional affair, but oh, it goes deep.

I know I do not live in order to remember; at the end memory will be as nothing. To say I really had it, how might it be if in the dry years I would have to say where was it? I do know that what I experience now is important, the future might only matter if I had lacked this.

With or without regret life ends and it makes no difference to me how it will end, only that it will end. It doesn't matter how things turn out; they change anyway. How can I provide for the future, even my children's! What is perfectly clear is that I adore them now and am in touch with life itself three times a day: eating, sleeping and fornicating – there is no other tenderness.

Fatigue pulls me on the bed. I should sleep and become strong for the rash sun tomorrow. It's always too bright in the morning. The day begins fast with the running sounds of children as they continue the day before. For them sleep has been a simple interruption. 'Oh, children, your noise is my reality!'

My heart has gone dim in the huddle with night, spread under him like a stain of red wine on a white cloth. I put on dark glasses to protect me from this sun and the size of the mountain growing whiter each day.

How well we know each other, if knowledge has anything to do with these odd gropings over a foreign bed in a foreign country. The man caresses me in Italian: 'You are my bread,' he says and eats away at me, mushing my body into this incredible fatigue, his weight on me like stones I have helped put there. What am I doing? What is this strange excess?

When he sleeps everything is over, he is merely beautiful – not someone I care for. Why doesn't he leave? I don't need his shut face lying there, his body so still that he might as well be dead.

His sleeping wakes me and I rush to see my children in their beds, afraid they will look dead as well. Oh no, sleep lies on them lightly, on their round breathing faces life is growing.

*

My mother's thin face over the lush, soft body, this sense of being her all over again. My face is what I saw in her when she was thirty and I needed her most and was lonely for the generous droop of breast that Roberto loves so and uses as though I were his mother.

All dimensions gone here. Just the way the cocks crow in the night as nowhere else. What disturbs them so? Dark night with roosters screaming, wind pouring from the sky in a dry rain; I do not grow older but deeper.

But the weight of my children is a monkey on my back. Impossible to neglect them with ease. Coming home late, so late, I go into their rooms to stare at those simple yielding bodies. One of them coughs and I feel destroyed.

My passion with Roberto is a labyrinth where I hump along from angle to curve, free for a very short time, the white thread of my children wrapping me into a knot instead of leading me out. I go deeper into the maze, dragging them with me while I long to be childless, thoughtless, immune to all former feeling. Often now I lie so still under him, afraid that one more move will make me swoon, blot me out.

In a dark museum where his body is the only statue, more splendid than David, perfect because it's also warm. How well I understand a torso murder for love of each limb. I hack away at him with appalling want. And he, how he spreads himself for me in his self love. He would exhibit his anus without compunction, aware that every part of him is appropriate. I feel like one of those insane collectors who will do anything to acquire a Michelangelo. I am insane till I lie down alone again, pale from greed, sex-rotten.

I know so well that I should leave here. It's the crazy people who make me sure. That one, all dressed in black, a male widow, shouting to the children behind him. I see my own son, angered I pull him away and force him to be sad. 'But I wasn't laughing,' he says.

The madman stops in the piazza, stands in the centre, a fountain yelling. Everyone laughs. I myself worry. What's wrong with me? For these people sanity is real and insanity is a spectacle not to be taken seriously; the crazy man is a clown. I am considered a sentimental fool. What's to be done in this red and white country?

Every time I leave my villa, lying slightly above the town, I walk slowly down the steps towards the sound below. A kind of welcoming hell swells towards me from the corso where the entire town is walking hard, talking hard, hungry, agitated.

Listen to the noise, it's the only music of the place. There is a strong and evident rhythm; one can tell the time of day by the amount of it, strongest in the evening about seven, before dinner.

I walk through them, only listening, not enchanted by their mess. I crave monotony, don't want anything more to happen, still haven't understood what has happened.

Winter here is a few weeks of rain, hard wind at night that empties the streets. I walk along the corso feeling free and clean.

In the café idle men huddle around the fireplace. Roberto sits with me in a corner, worried about business, constantly interrupting me as I try to read a book. I'm sick of his banal problems, how boring he is out of bed. Should he bring prices down, is it going to be a good carnival so that he'll make up for these bad few weeks? I don't care, watch instead his pretty mouth, the nice way he slumps in the chair. I long for a deaf mute.

My house is soaking from all the rain, clothes don't dry, the maid complains, children irritable from staying in so much.

Three weeks of this, the town looks lonely, unprepared as every year for anything but sun. These Sicilians don't realize that it must rain and be cold sometimes. Their houses poorly equipped, they press around puny charcoal fires, old women hide them under long skirts. Several of them die every year from the fumes.

'*Cattivo tempo*,' is all they say, stacking black umbrellas around the rooms where the rain is really in.

Roberto is worried about me, aware of my boredom.

'You'll feel better when the sun shines. I know this place is dull for you like this.'

He takes me with him when he buys lemons for the bar. This interests me because we drive through dreary, sick villages, the heart of this country. Such places, all the poverty spilled in the streets, rags of children everywhere while the mothers sit and sew or pee! Whatever vegetable is in season. That's the diet, a plate of fried greens or tomatoes, on good days a rind of meat. Sad looking people, unprotesting, much too used to this.

In the lemon factory it's warm. There are special heated canteens that turn green lemons yellow in a hurry. Women grade the fruit according to size and colour, wrapping the best ones in little papers that makes the crate look festive.

How they stare at me, anxious to know what country I come from. I have soft, friendly talks with these swift-handed women who work ten hours to earn less than a dollar. One of them cuts a thick-fleshed lemon and teaches me to eat it with salt. Roberto watches with delight, glad I'm not bored, pleased when they refer to me as his wife.

The sound of rain is becoming intolerable; it's washing away the glamour of Sicily. These dull people are wearing me down. Roberto seems puny and always thinking about money. When there are no girls to look at the town idlers have long, stupid talks about the government. The only thing they ever read is some sort of reactionary newspaper that makes more ado about the killings than politics. Amazing, dreary murders happen every day in this last country, always involving hatchets or other farm implements. The Taormina citizens are proud of their clean record. Of course they have the Greek theatre that brings them slews of tourists every year. But what is there to look at in a town like Giarre except mean faces, people who are deep down hungry and call it love.

Roberto and I quarrel often about all this.

'Yes, you're right,' he says, 'but it takes time.'

What he is really thinking is how he would be better off in Rome where the real money is. When I get angry he shrugs his shoulders, lapses into dialect full of vowel sounds like Arabic, and tells me how I excite him, how he would rather go to bed.

'You don't really care about politics, *bella*, you need me. I will soothe you.'

All right, I slither off with him. He is right but sometimes making love is going off to be slaughtered. Pigs, cows, what a base animal I've become.

Sullen, avoiding the centre of the steps where water runs steadily, cursing the mob of cats sitting trance-like against sodden walls, bored by the prospect of going to meet my inferior lover – awful wet world.

The corso is a tunnel where I clatter along in the grim light of the afternoon. My butcher is busy stuffing sausages, a hot water-bottle stuck in his belt to keep him warm. His hands are terrible pushing pork and anis seeds into shiny membranes. In the grocery Don Vincente is spraying Flit. Some of his cats are walking on the counter going after ricotta, some bits of mortadella left in the slicer. He doesn't chase them off, not till the customers come in anyway. I wish I had some appetite, it's such good food when the sun is shining.

'*Signora Americana, buona sera,*' he calls to me. I wish they wouldn't keep greeting me all the time. Can't walk down this street without being saluted twice a day. '*Buon giorno*' in the morning when I least feel like talking, but one has to answer, '*buon passegio*' in the afternoon, they wish you well for everything. '*Buona niente,*' I mumble back, ashamed of myself.

I suppose I am the first person in town to know the sun is back since I do not close my shutters at night. Going to bed is a preparation to enter a tomb. How many times I've avoided Roberto because he can't sleep unless everything is shut tight so that I feel anonymous. In such total darkness there is no telling who is next to you. But an open window is forbidden, one will get a stiff neck or catch a cold. Fresh air belongs outside, so does light. Anyway, how else can you keep out the flies and mosquitoes. Sicily is really the darkest place at night. Bombs have fallen here but windowscreens are unheard of.

Sun. At last.

My maid brings up a plate of strange spiny fruit in celebration. 'Be careful,' she says when my son grabs one. Too late, his palm is full of little thorns that will take hours to get out with pincers and some of them will stay in and fester. Concertina opens the prickly pear with three precise gashes and offers me the startling red fruit inside.

'This is practically what we lived on during the war,' she explains. 'It's full of nourishment but you must be careful not to eat too many. In the war, when there was so little bread, we ate many of these. Sometimes we couldn't defecate for days after.'

She shows me how to lift it out of the skin without getting any *spina*, and to swallow the seed without chewing. Juicy and cool inside, the rain has been good for them.

Later in the day I watch some boys getting this difficult harvest. They tie a tin can to a long stick, cup the tin over the fruit growing out of a large cactus, and snap it off into a bucket. It seems a nervous procedure, especially after all this rain. No matter, the fruit is good, winter is over.

The sight of him wobbles my groin. Desire flares inside me as the sun on my back. Hot as hell and deep like that; red in all my corners, the thick smell of sex everywhere.

We make love like religion. He lets out my name with his sperm and I feel adored in a way that no virgin has ever been prayed to.

Lapped in waves of good feeling, free and solid my body rises for him. So profound is our contact, today I have forgotten my children. A holiday of the flesh, essential breathing flesh, connective tissue between day and night, before and after love, it's all a rhythm going towards and coming away from actual love which is intercourse.

That in me which can be touched responds only to him. My response is sudden gushes, my inside mucous flesh seems to detach itself from tough walls in an unbelievably painless wave. His very fingerprint is a profound mark on me. Like patterns in the desert that are, after all, the only sign of anything there, it doesn't matter how lasting. If the wind did not stir the sand the desert would have no movement at all.

Thus I lie under this hot Sicilian sun, sweating at last, waiting for more swells and rills.

For weeks cats have disturbed me. Their baby-voiced pain sends me hunting for a child; I think it is my baby screaming.

There are more cats here than people, thinner, wilder, hungrier. At night they rush around in packs, knocking over garbage cans, eating away at anything. They are stronger, more organized in their hunt than the dogs that pad after them. Also in their love-making, for dogs look stupid then, as though caught up in something they had nothing to do with. Cats in heat make such a special noise that nights flare into a new season; sleep is given over to the sound of their lust.

*

Oddly enough, when I finally succeed in watching two cats mate, it is before noon on a hot, clear day. At night they always disappear into corners I cannot find.

There they are, as unaware of the world as I would like to be, deep in an act so mutual it stuns me. Jealous, I wonder about my own sex; surely it is less profound, copulating with Roberto, a fragment of the passion visible here.

The male is much younger and smaller. He has yellow fur, lion crouched on the old female he holds her nape in his teeth, growling moistly, she underneath him all silent, completely held.

He works a long time. My baby tugs at me, wants something. Some women stop and go on quickly, clearly disapproving of my standing there, so openly watching.

'*Disgraziata*,' they say to the cats, certainly to me. For happening there, in front of that American and her child is an act of night, of hiding. I feel very much their hostility, sorry about it, but not enough to stop watching. I like to see animals coupling. It eases memories of my mother and father on sad-sounding beds, sighs dangling into my thin sleep like broken arms. I used to lie in my little room, in my little body, afraid that nothing else existed except that sound and myself listening to it.

The small yellow male jumps off the old female and they both lie down opposite one another, begin to lick and suck and scratch at the wet they have produced.

Down to the beach to feel movement, the fast tough drive down, the sight of water pushing and pulling.

Up in Taormina one never hears the sea, although it is everywhere visible as a remote view pretty and undisturbing. It has no sound at all. Taormina so still, so permanent.

Here at the beach the sea makes noise. The sea here is immediate, contingent on itself. It is change. I watch the tough water, so soft from far away, such a dream of water when you look down at it from that eternal town above.

And here – look how water grows into a killer!

The red flag is run up. A bad current suddenly makes my children struggle in the water. Rocks the size of a child's fist are pulling out from under my feet. Roberto yells to get out of there, keeps on dressing himself.

The waves come in hard and yellow, flat with mud. I grab the children and run up the beach, clutching them like stolen flowers.

Then I take each one for a rest. Lying on top of me, the youngest first, how different they are, how varied their clinging to me. My breasts hurt under their weight but I ask of them an impossible tenderness, pushing them against me this hard is useless, children cannot comfort the mother.

This is my real loneliness – lying on top of me.

We float in a huge grotto, the boat threatened by rocks growing like thorns out of the sea. Black, unwelcoming, the cave goes deep, bats live at the back. But the water is brilliant, looking at it I feel upside down, as if it were sky. So blue that swimming in it would surely leave colour on the skin. But I am afraid to jump in, too radical a place to enter.

Roberto keeps looking at me, watching my nervous face. I keep very still, make my face hard, don't want to show him anything. Why should he know any more about me; this is a private thing winding among rock thorns, I don't want his comments nor his looks.

'How nervous you are,' he says, seeming to like it very much and this makes me feel cold and like his mother. He should not be with me.

I do jump off the boat into that infernal blue, a kind of bravado I detest takes hold of me, forces me towards the end of the grotto where black is waiting. A sudden swell on the water, a motorboat must have passed outside, and I see how far away he is, watching for me, strain showing on his chest where he pushes the oar to steady the boat. I'd better go back, he doesn't swim well enough to save me, would he even try?

My feet scrape on the side of the cave as I turn fast, more afraid than ever now that I sense what a coward he must be. The rock here is purple like a medusa. My son once caught a medusa. Trapped in an empty carton it quivered, really mauve, dangerously beautiful. The afterbirth that oozed out of my body rapidly, I wanted to eat it. It looked more significant than the son just born. The doctor was shocked but he did let me touch it. I was stunned by the look of this glassy, soft flesh that had just left my womb.

The medusa cannot be touched nor eaten and I have warned my son.

*

There is my son lying flat on the sand, his legs crossed and swaying. He holds a bar of ice cream high over his head, brings it down for the lick, fans it above his head again, looks at it as it melts and drips in the sun.

He eats that ice cream with the complete concentration available to him at six. At this moment I see my son as he would make love and find him beautiful, as though I had already aged to the time when there would be no more envy, nor any more desire to make him my lover. My fantasy is fabulous. I'm able to imagine the most forbidden. Surely I am a good mother since I know so well when I am not.

The sight of his body reminds me that I can never really touch him. To eat him is to eat Roberto. Is my lover the son made possible, returned to me, put back in short blasting thrills, without that pain I bore so well?

Roberto has driven into me like a corkscrew; I cannot disengage myself without losing essential pieces. In these hot patches of afternoon, light and heat gather into direct touch. He becomes light and heat itself, welling around me in absolute contact. Myself turned inside out spills away at him. I am the beach where he ebbs and tides. Windless days moving only in my belly.

Yet nothing gets finished. Sick grows my lust. I feel afraid but it's only here, buried inside this Sicilian tomb, that I can conceive of death, perhaps accept it as the only dignified craving.

Hot light of the Sicilian sun hits me like a rock. Through the window I see the woman next door washing her endless sheets. An ugly creature who screams her way into my life every morning so that I hate right away. No way to wake up except hating noise and light and the things in the room that I can't see clearly because of my bastard eyesight.

She is threatening; her bulk a black hole in the sky. I pull up the blanket to cover that red hole I've become.

All this terror because of my eyes, hysterical vision, blurred, every small light an immense fire, her sheets ride at me in flags, pointing to the prostitute sleeping late.

In the bathroom I look closely at what she might have seen. A frightened, nostalgic search for the gaudy object of the night before; the mirror returns an ugly result of a thin, strained face with spider dreaming eyes, so magnificent at night when she paints herself for the part. Black light not caused by drugs as her friends suspect. Caused by what then? All her fevers.

Yes, Regina of the night, a huge flower nearly a foot in diameter, blooming only in the night. Profoundly open, showing a vast white depth, as I show black in my deep myopic eyes. Startling to wind around dark streets and find this giant growing, opening. By day a wilted mess of long hanging, worn petals.

That bitch over there, scrubbing her virtue while a tense Sicilian song screams out of her, going past me to the neighbours waiting for her message like savages.

Swimming today was unpleasant, the water too warm.

Scooping my hands through the soft wet, of a sudden I held a medusa. Frantically I let go, shaking away the feel of it. Then I looked down at the vague rocks below, hating my weak eyes. I would always be afraid of it down there. Why not, I couldn't see it. A low pressure feeling made my body heavy, swimming was hard, a tunnel to be dug.

Roberto spread on the sand in an odd, passive position. '*Molto pederaste*,' I tease, standing over him, stealing light.

'Why do you put shadows in front of me,' he complains, sliding away in the luxuriant way of a man who pleasures deeply in sex, gives his man milk freely. A passive gladiator, knowing himself to be potent at will.

'Oh, *bella*, what could be better?' he asks.

'All that which isn't,' I answer him.

For him there is nothing casual about sex, it is an absolute and absorbing experience. How it tires and thrills me. I sit inside this rainbow of sensations like a supersensitive doll, lost but watching. I feel that I control him, that our copulating is an art exercised by me. I need only to use certain gestures and he swoons. My effect on him makes me swoon.

Then I forget him and listen to the termites eating the bed that holds us.

Summer is a violent presence. Too hot now to drive to the beach. I scold my children into the cool house, annoyed by their energy. My son kills flies while the baby pokes at ants. Her milk sours in the glass.

The streets are quiet, a fierce glare on the pavement. In the distance Etna looks ordinary without snow.

The maid uses her umbrella to go shopping. I worry what will please the children. So hard to eat anything in this heat except fruit and vegetables. The best thing is melon, a huge speckled kind with a ruby centre. We are all thinner from this diet. Only way to tolerate this weather is to sleep all day and sit in the café evenings. Then the piazza is alive again with frantic children. There's no use putting them to bed before eleven, much too hot. My maid wets down the pillow under her head.

'This is nothing,' she sighs, 'wait till the scirocco blows.'

I wish I had the energy to leave here.

Scirocco wraps me in a humid trance. The fish on the beach called Molla, at first I thought it was the fin of a great fish but there it lay, being all of it, really small and dead and grey. Touching it was such a mistake, all slime, with the most sticky smell. I kept digging my fingers into the sand, trying to scrape off the smell, the matter.

Just so is the scirocco fast on me. I sit in space padded by that kind of slime the fish had, the muck that jellyfish are made of.

I look at it all. The sea, the rocks, people; just objects. I'm afraid I will sit like this in another country waiting for a sense of importance, lying, manipulating, to bring back a sense of life. There is no sense leaving here for there is always that formidable silence, that sitting so still that I do better than anyone else, while inside me is movement. I think and think, my hands paralysed, eyes gone far, staring blind at the horizon.

I have sat like this a long time, in a fever of silence. Inside my face is hard, aching tension. All my life stirs in me, pushing at me, begging to be let out.

This seems to be my new madness.

I need this piazza with its lack of view, only sky against which trees hold still and the lanterns flare into several moons. There is only that, and myself on the other side of it.

Now the heat and the mountain are together, fire and size closing up my view. The sky is thick with scirocco and never blue.

As Clarita loved blue with her sapphire ring and the blue, man-tailored suits and blue eyes that I wanted to eat as I have eaten the eyes of carp my mother cooked for me. Who watched me eat the head of the fish and there was no disgust only approval of my taste. The tongue of the fish milky soft, the eyes gelatin soft, soft heads of fish, my mother's eyes love soft on her happy-eating child.

As I wish now to lick the eyes of Roberto because there is nothing disgusting about him. Clarita spoiled my pleasure when she watched me eat the head of the carp. She felt disgust and gave it to me. But Roberto has renewed my desire to eat eyes. I want his. The appetite more important than the eating and thus I know that I am not yet mad. The head of a fish and the head of a man – I still know the difference.

As there is no separation here between sky and water and mountain; it's all together in a humid blur, put before me on this piazza where those few trees still stupidly produce florist-size flowers, dropping into coffee cups. Those trees will never be a forest, will never know the difference.

I realize now how lonely the metaphor; when Roberto was inside me I said, 'You are a tree inside me.'

For days the air has been too heavy. In cool countries it's this way before a storm but there is no rain for Sicily in August.

Roberto keeps checking the mountain. 'That's where it's coming from,' he says thoughtfully. 'You'll see something happen very soon,' he adds, as though he is planning a special gift for me.

And it does. Etna goes into full eruption. A sudden, dull boom calls for attention. There, in a dark moonless sky, twenty kilometres away, the volcano pours and roars out the fire inside it. Hundreds of feet in the air the flames shoot straight up, red as forever.

The town is awake, this hasn't happened in years, not this strong. The air is better now, some of the pressure gone.

I show my children what they have never seen before.

'Are we all going to burn, Mama?'

'No,' I answer softly, 'it's too far away.'

But inside me there is a great fear along with terrific excitement; my body is very hot as though it were a huge erection.

I am so confused by this erupting landscape, I rush towards Roberto who receives me proudly as though he has made this happen. I look for some sense of order, everything appears hot and smolten together. What is male or female any more? What am I doing with an erection? Oh yes, it's his! But I feel the potent one.

Etna continues to erupt. News of it is in all the papers of the world. Relatives send me telegrams to see if we are all right. Of course we are at this distance, but I feel troubled. The sight of lava boiling down a mountainside, even miles away, is not simple.

My love-making is affected. Some nights I only want to be kissed; it's everything to me. In a kiss there is no finishing, only constant hunger and constant eating. Making love is finite; somebody, some organ tires. But in my mouth is every desire and I feel the juice and the teeth and the deep smell of the person I kiss and whose longing for me I suck into me.

Roberto is bewildered yet he follows the contours of my temperament as though I were the mountain we are both excited by.

I begin to despise his lack of protest. His tolerance of me is flaccid, I cannot respect a man who will permit me every caprice. Kissing is not enough, he should know that, should rape me.

After many days of intense, pointed heat the eruption subsides. The climate is radically changed; summer seems over. I long for clean empty cold, so necessary to my burdened self. But winter from here is a rare feat, even in my imagination.

Fretting away time, swinging on people's talk, grasping their faces like fruit falling; a poor harvest, nothing like the appetite inside me.

A blind man passes, blowing on a flute, making sounds so high, hurting, but really music. My breathing slops along with his; together we go to the same high, thrilling place.

But the six o'clock light in the piazza is toneless, not blue. Seven oleander trees sticking out, dusty, always quiet trees, I never see them move. Wrought-iron trees, they might as well be the same species as the lanterns near them.

I put some money in his hand and beg him to play on. He does, his Sicilian face bent over complicated sounds, his face down dragged, trying to please me. But it's difficult to breathe, all the dull green, old, non-moving growth of Sicily is here in this piazza, in these seven trees. Sound becomes just that and I am no longer interested.

I walk away, out of town, towards the low hills stretched out like a chain of cemeteries. The dead green colour; no real green, just shades of black, especially the cypresses, black ties of mourning worn by men, the priest-coloured trees.

How annoyed I am, sensing my own fatigue in the tired presence of this ancient country. With those women staring at me, ill shadowed faces pressed against the window of the door, the only source of light. Fat, pale women, engorged from bad food, a bland short-lived look in their eyes. Visions of their dusty organs that will some day dry up and peel away from them like the paint on their decayed houses.

They sit alone or in smudged groups, sewing on their dowries of gorgeous bedsheets. This is the only passion allowed them before marriage, the linen they will bring to the eventual husband must be the finest, scrolled with such tiny stitches that it takes a month just to embroider the edges.

Nearly all wear mourning, their sex gored by black dresses making the curves of them look empty, all wrong. Barbaric religion with its loud, dime-store rites, at the innumerable fiestas these camouflaged women carry wooden saints like lovers, fireworks blasting away the little money earned, on their faces the bang bang joy of childish sacrifice.

Immense boredom that forces me into the manufacture of intrigue, of false sentiment. Grabbing the looks of strangers, finding here a nose, there a mouth that pleases. And the women looked at by me, the sudden man. That lovely Italian girl. I said she is the pillow of a bed and had to explain that it meant the softest, the best part of the bed, of lying down. A woman's face like a soft sigh of relief.

Roberto sitting alongside me in this fog of sex. We do nothing but invent each other's perversities. I am dutifully degenerate, but my face is false; not passionate with desire, but passionate with a desire to feel. Yet there is this thickness, this awareness of sexual importance. The mountain hovers, girls pass, each one appraised and filed away by both of us in a special safety vault of flesh.

This theatrical doom, this smear of a landscape so tired of living, of reproducing itself, having lost all vital organs. Only some desire left and that old, antiquely worn, a patina of what was. A tired stage with pointless drama. Scrub, flowers, no real trees just the worn spears of cypresses.

And yet I feel important here. I have a role, my mirror is

Roberto who values all that in me which he cannot name but finds in my bed where I give him, because I can still do that, so much loveliness. Inside me there is something sensitive with many feelers like an octopus, nervous star of the sea.

What happened today except that I laid my head on the legs of Pino.

I had just been swimming, felt a great energy in the water like a bird flying. The water a deep, dangerous sky. Outside the bay the water incredibly cold, made my urine come hot and slow and I lay still to let it happen.

A feeling of rest afterwards, lying against him on the beach, pebbles on my thighs sticking hard, creating ugly toad skin in marvellous colours. I was sure nothing else would happen to me that day; it had all gone in the water.

Roberto up in town, working. He is certainly not jealous of Pino, a homosexual. 'You need friends,' he says, making pitifully clear his limited function in my life.

I spend hours with Pino. Meeting him is seeing a real shape in a cloud and then watching it disperse. He looks like a man, I cannot believe him when he talks about men, it must all be a trap to make me love his soul. For there is love between us but we touch only with words and certain concentrated looks. I feel a special fear lying on a part of him that belongs to his body. One of us is virgin; I cannot afford to long for him, there is something so deep and erotic between us that any contact can only magnify its impossible dimensions.

Talking with him makes me feel large, round, swollen with white light. 'Tonight at two o'clock the moon will be full. Try and get away from him.' He says this, he who has the moon inside him in big flat circles.

There is my baby twirling her white towel around her in a moon circle. She doesn't know how much I watch her. Thinking about Pino I absorb her complete sanity and am grateful, I think also of Roberto standing so concretely somewhere in his bar. I certainly love those two simple creatures, experience them in the same way.

But Pino with his insistent intellect draws me to him. 'You're just using Roberto,' he says. 'You don't love him.'

'I can love many people all at the same time.'

'Perhaps, but your love is in pieces, broken into three.'

Of course I know what he means but he is only waiting for me to lose my sex while I wait to see his. In the meanwhile he's revolting. All his physical processes annoy me in small definite beats; just the way he is sucking an orange, juice dribbling on his hairless chest. I recall Roberto on whose body hair grows like experience.

This queer, with his snaky mouth enveloping food, his toenails are enormous, his arms too short. Touching him would be grey as brain skin.

And yet, what must he feel in my presence, he who is so much more delicate than I am. Of course he is homosexual, it's spilled on him like wine, enhancing but also sour. I long for one straightforward person. Really only children please me now. I am becoming saturated with sex. I shall need a retreat soon.

When the moon is full I visit Pino in his room. He looks so destroyed, lying on a bed, dressed in ugly clothes which make him look washed up. He does so want to be picked up and put together again. In his body, by me.

As I find him there, strewn on that bed, I worry, afraid he'll make a move towards me. I cannot desire him because he is manwoman and I only want simple loving, shape of tulip, penis flower.

'You want everything,' he says, as though this is wrong of me. But surely he says this because he can give me so little, that pervert.

Like the eruption of Etna, when I saw too much light, I feel affected by him, confused.

'You're my first Eve,' he continues, and I feel disgust at a confession he should make to his mirror since he is his own woman. Pino is every gender put into one body, badly twisted, depressing because of its complex shape. A body should be plain. Being with him makes me swollen in an unnatural way, not at all like being pregnant, my body then a great rich avocado.

Even his mouth is in sections, long snaking over words, and kissing him is kissing parts. Shame rises in me now in the clearest fashion, shame not desire forces me into this impossible pose. I lie crumpled on his bed, part of the particular debris around him. Not a place for sleep here, full too full of books and terrible ripped pages of poetry, where has he gotten all those? Everyone who has ever written lies on his bed, he knows too much, reads to me while the moon hovers dangerously near the window. I know nothing compared to him but he does not know it's shame over my poor exploited body that keeps me from him. I can only think of the perfect athletes he is used to while his head longs for me. But if I am to be his first woman love then I must be perfect and I am not. Thoughts of Roberto who sucks even my toes and becomes potent with the sight of my soft, tired breasts, my mother scars. Fairies only know love in the front or love in the back. Pino fouls my idea of myself. Lousy queer, young and childless, without anything, just the idea of me in his head.

Finally we touch somewhere. He fingertips across my hair which goes limp under his hand. I wonder whether he desires me now or whether he just wants to see how I am made.

Vaguely aggressive his odourless body near me is a thorn spread out as he lays himself flat against me. I follow his position and we are two people in the same coffin.

'I must go.'

'You're so incomplete,' he accuses, but I do get up, nauseated by this long evening. Later on I will push my face into Roberto, glad to get his smell. His sweat is something good coming at me, his very exudations are appetizing, just as my children's bodies are completely edible, my appetite for the four of them never diminishes.

Now just the face of Pino is left, full sad before me as I prepare to leave, exposed as for a death-mask. He has the air of someone in constant preparation for suicide. But I have enough of him, must leave. His head is separate from his body; he is in pieces and I will not help him. Loving cannot be talked about. He is wrong about everything below his head and his body went away from him a long time ago.

Electric light busts the leaves and palm trees split the sky while we sit in this garden and talk. He is a bottomless pit, graining the landscape. The garden full of ignored flowers in oppressive abundance. No smell at all, only appearance. Field and country unknown here, wailing with cats and dogs in each of which I see my own peculiar disfigurement, depending on the degrees of sadness that makes me either shrug or cry.

With Pino I am frankly sad, allow my face to ugly away. My hair is tight in brain-pulling hurt; I confront with him open suffering. Which he does not believe in. Or does not find sufficient.

'Do you ever tell the truth, or rather do you ever feel the truth?' he asks, his black milk eyes staring into me and I am glad that he does not have as many eyes as the limbs of an octopus. Yet he sucks at me in the same way and I become fish caught, human eaten.

Oh this garden, with that face exposed like an over-ripe melon. Clarita, when she tired of me, threw me away from her like rotten fruit.

Pino is quiet, looking down, deep lines frame his snake mouth. In his swamp of thought he waits for me but my body is right, my mother was a peasant, once she was thick and blood fresh. I saw her working in another garden, a long time down, her animal health leg-spread over the hot growth she tended. It doesn't matter now about her change, the smell of nasturtiums still puts me in a swoon of remembrance.

Here in Sicily I eat the flower itself and come that much closer to the smell of it and I chew at the memories of other beaches where I gathered pieces of amber to save for ever but have lost.

I grab at the flowers, at my mother who took care of me then on the white sweet sand. I roll in the smell of her orange love, thick inside the dear flesh of her palms that curve me round with bliss.

Now my own children are the face I wanted to be and I wait for their deep sleeping when I thieve away at those round open faces, finding my mother's love in giving to them. Do finally get full, in feeding I am fed.

Day hazes into night. The flesh trap opens and I fall under Roberto's body. The hair on his chest is so many sculpted flowers. My hand traverses a forest, indescribably mine. I suck at his nipples as at a female fountain held up by a phallus. 'I'll split you open with my penis,' he says, a passion in his voice that heats me and makes me obey.

When will this end? The pleasure I find with Roberto is wrong, he is not my peer. My talks with Pino have brought me back somewhat; I have loved a better person. But I want Roberto's body, worried over wanting an animal. Never have I gone so against my grain. Why can't I love the right man with all my red flesh? This little man with the delicious skin, I would so much like to respect him. And do not. And continue to sleep with him.

'Your sex is an illusion,' says Pino, and I don't know any more, he has blurred me. Who will save me? will bring me the word? Who will tell me that making love is honest? I do love Roberto if love means everything, including disgrace. His body and mine together are love concrete. Before and after we are dogs and cats, vulgarity and boredom. I do not esteem him.

But the trap shuts hard, banging at me a message that says only this moment, this movement is the truth.

'Stop seeing so much of Pino.'

'You said I need friends.'

'People are talking.'

'Everyone knows he is queer.'

'He is still a man.'

'You flatter me.'

'Bitch, don't play with me!' and Roberto slaps me in the face. 'You know I've been patient with you. But don't make me appear a *cornuto* in front of my friends.'

'So that's your problem, not whether I'm faithful to you, but whether your friends think so.'

'You can't understand us. You are a foreigner.'

'I'm glad. I don't want your problems. You have stupid problems, you think everything is sex.'

'Without sex there is nothing.'

My face burns. Really quite pleasant. He looks beautiful, anger comes straight at me like an arrow from a bow. A terrific flush of desire takes me to the nearest wall where I spread myself out as his target.

Goodbye to Pino.

I offered him my hand in the most furtive, fleeting way. He had no time at all to say anything. I did not want him to speak; everything had ended for us. The rest could only be sentiment and lecture.

I cannot forget the startled eyes, the clear pain staring at me, at my cowardly farewell. The fool I'd made of him in loving me.

I left him abruptly as I had done so many times in his house. But this was the last and he knew it and ached from it; I only felt impressed by the expression in his eyes.

*

There sit the two brothers in front of me. Made of the same flesh, one more beautiful, both with thick graceful skin that I want to bite. I wish to have them both lust for me and put me in bed between them. Imagine two brothers bursting over the same woman!

This perversity is clearly confined to my imagination. If Roberto knew that I even thought about his brother he would probably beat me. A woman belongs only to one man in his country. His brother hardly ever speaks to me for fear of arousing any suspicion. If he cares for me at all, and I think he does, his every intention is to leave his brother's woman alone. Some day I hope to meet him in another country.

Sicily, old, with a tough sense of order. A story in the paper of a woman whose husband was killed. She knew the killer but would not tell the police. She merely pointed to her belly, swollen with child, and said: 'He knows, and will attend to it some day.'

Vendetta. When I am bad with Roberto he just stretches out his hand, bobs it up and down lightly. The gestures carries a gentle but very precise warning.

Yet I happen only here in the place I resent. Sicily manures me into being. If I could only respect the fruit of me. Rotten, complicated bloom of sex, exaggerated as the flower of a cactus.

Tired, all juiced out. I'm thinner, very fatigued. The doctor recommends an analysis of my blood. But it's all this fornicating that's draining me. Nothing else is any good, or good enough, only with him can I stop thinking. I don't even dare sleep; my dreams are weary reminders that I have no other recourse.

My mother an octopus. Many arms coming out of the very centre, all grabbing me to her soft parts where she may, I permit it, chew me, use me up. I am now the octopus, mucus, held together by soft moist membrane, suckering everywhere. Dreams of unending hunger, interrupted by sleep. I have many mouths and only in the suck-feel attachment of my tentacles do I feel in contact, my reach is long and bizarre. I shudder at the cold touch of many arms that I never wanted to grow but only to have around me from another source.

I find myself like pressed flowers in an old book, dry and faded, an ugly trace of what was once wild and juicy. I look for water to fill me, I drink and swim, Japanese flowers that grow in water and become something. I dive as deep as I can but come up dehydrated.

There is that glossy sun again, open above me like a naked body, while in this Sicily those secret pubic hills keep on and on, hiding from me. Are they attics and cellars I crept around in with my schoolfriends as we jabbed and scratched into our child bodies looking for hair and holes and black sex. My inside felt exhausted, the dull worn green of Sicilian earth, not growing any more – only there.

How long is desire when given time enough, Sicily enough?

I wait for an end to this degrading passion. I wish he did not exist, while the sight of him, his teeth, his glittering eyes, grapes spit out, fish bones, his urine, all that is produced by his body excites me.

There are moments of hatred between us, we drift into a mean way, I've reduced him to an exasperated state. He slaps me around, spits. And I need this humiliation in order to feel. Only crisis provokes me.

What will happen to him when I am gone? For I shall get out of this. I am complex, capable of many excitements, a sensual intellectual, and he has also made me beautiful. Never have I looked so well, surely this is the last ripening, my flower fall, myself a ripe fruit in fall. Where to land, where to conceive further?

And he will be left behind to idle away his life in stupid innocence, unwilling to grant me evil, believing that my usage of him has been love. Yet now, while I am here, I am committed to him; a witch ensnared by a fool.

Exposed to myself as that small beach where we wait for a tide that is never high enough. The filth of the Mediterranean remains, more obvious now because of the clean edge.

Roberto is deep in thought and does not feel the wave that spreads over his feet making them shine.

Earlier we argued; he saw me flirting with some tall Swede. I do it on purpose; his jealousy excites me for I am at that point where any effort is an interruption in the blank day, that *vuoto* where nothing happens except when it is beaten into me. I've become the big lax mouth and even ugly food is chewed at; disgust itself becomes something felt, more interesting than ordinary pleasure, pushed down my throat so there is no choice.

'Suck me here,' he says and I do, pleased by the command, the actual revulsion layered over by months of effort to be sexually enormous.

'Lick me,' and I, aware of my lying face, cannot avoid my duty because I too can see my passionate face in the pupils of his love-frantic eyes. I have conned this boy with my liar charm – I suck and lick and sigh while he is truly involved with a woman he has never expected to love. Small animal that he is, smaller than his emotions, laid across her in tiring ceremony.

'Are you satisfied now, do you still need some one else?'

'Maybe tomorrow,' I taunt.

He rolls away from me and goes to sleep. The small beach is dull. I look at the terraced hump of fields behind, a chewed out skyline. Eyes pale in my head; I am not curious.

Ruin of a castle, built by the Saracens, it decays above the town in toothy outline. Not splendid any more, just a good place to take the children where we play hide and seek.

'Where are you, Mama,' yells the middle one, a girl who looks like a happy version of me. What a disgusting woman I am behind the mother she loves.

I bury myself in the shadows of the castle, wanting to delay her discovery of me. To the west lies Etna, no longer active, nothing but a shadow now, as thin as the dark I'm hiding in. 'If only you'd keep on blowing up,' I think, 'it would keep me moving, anything is better than this dry burden of myself.'

It's cold leaning against that dark wall. I'm tired of this game. Why doesn't she find me or is it save me? Yes, my children will save me, they are my only weapon.

How long it seems till she comes, her voice screams closer, 'Mama, I'll get you, wait, wait . . .' breaks off in laughter at the sight of me. Her hand is warm pulling me into the sun, her trophy.

One cloud in the whole sky, exactly like wet cotton. There is no wind and that white blob stays there, nearly inside the mouth of

Etna. I am determined to sit it out, surely the cloud will move on, nothing up there should be so still, large as a nightmare when the vomit kept heaving up from the bottom of me.

Alone in the night of my mother's garden, my suffering real, visible in spit and bile and tears. She's not there to wipe it off, gone the soft cotton of her breasts. Agony looking at that sky with the stinking stars, burning down to me the first knowledge of infinity. Everything small and close and warm gone; my mother an abstraction.

I see her in the mountains of Sicily, a face in the dry tough hills where olive trees shrug off indecently small fruit. The age of these trees darker than the Greek ruins spread about here like ordinary facts; history is a carpet to walk on, marble columns are flowers I ignore. My lament is not general – I want only my mother.

The cloud hangs over me. I watch it hopelessly like a mystic fixed on the wrong object. A false symbol as is false my love with Roberto. But I want everything now, my greed established from the very beginning, the mark on my forehead pressed deep by my mother's blundering, blameless hand.

Lusting for a red split mountain but this is not a mountain of a man. He is caving in, his soft parts eroded from my excessive want. 'Let me rest a while, it will come back,' he sighs, useless next to me.

I go to the bathroom and try, with very cold water, to wash away my affliction. Downstairs some child is coughing in his sleep but I don't have the energy to go see who it is. I'm the one in trouble.

When I am back in bed he puts his head on my breasts where I allow him to remain. He clings to me in the passive way of a helpless child who already dislikes his mother.

'I'm sorry,' he mumbles, 'As soon as I'm rested I'll go home.'

'Don't worry,' I answer politely, feeling free of him. If he were suddenly dead it wouldn't matter to me.

'Do you think I should see a doctor?'

'Why don't you wait and see if it happens again.'

'Yes, that's true, it's only the first time.'

He gets up, dresses with excessive care. 'My impotent dandy,' I think, 'I use you like flowers in a room, distracting from the white wall.'

He stands by the window, taller now in his shoes. He says, 'You have a beautiful view of my country,' his voice too loud in my empty room.

'Hurry up, I want to see the children.'

'But they're asleep, they don't need you.'

Intensely nervous I snarl, 'What do you know about their dreams?'

'I'll see you tomorrow when you feel better,' and he tiptoes out, in his exit all the cowardice I've suspected in him.

Etna erupts again, but it's a stale event, I've seen it before. Seen by day the fire is weak, a dull red. Let the tourists gape at it, I think, and remain in the café where parts of strangers' faces rock me in the maze of my past.

I sit in this cooling land. Summer is over, my passionate swimming gone dry. Dogs I no longer love straggle across the piazza.

This is a ride on a badly lit bus taking me from an unhappy place to an indifferent one. Going home from school was like this, not really sad, just pale, lifeless. I felt like the other passengers looked. We were all poorly made statues coming alive at stops and starts, disliking one another.

A certain sleep is riding me, a doze like the underlit bus I've known.

Roberto noses at me with regained confidence. He bullies me into feeling something, but it's flat, my body responds to a habit. He bores me, the town bores me; I've understood everything. This idolatry of a human body – where does magic begin any more?

The bed is soft, too soft; the covers heavy on me, too warm – but warm. Outside the air is a hostile mass, inside this bed the heat I crave is mixed with his particular flesh. Has no one ever loved me like this? Is that the clue? He wants to give me his blood; I will let him.

Again he is a gorgeous statue all mine, lost in me. I am absorbed by the hard penis and the soft red wet of his mouth. How difficult it would be to lie alone in the wind outside . . . He does mean something to me after all, he is my deepest physical sense, the one I least understand, or least satisfy, or most – I don't know even this any more.

*

Sloppy drunk, the corso yawns ahead like a tunnel, I push on, the hell with walls, I just want to get through.

'*Guarda l'americana*,' I hear in the shops. My condition is obvious and I don't care, I wipe my hands along the windows just for spite.

I feel bad, crippled, the sky a near dampness in my bones. I ache; wrong colour on the walls, the narrow street is one big stone.

Finally the arch that opens to the piazza. I need coffee, Italian coffee stuck into me like an injection of energy.

There's Roberto, my little horse, sitting all tight and vanished in himself, waiting among the bad sounds, his voice harsh in greeting: '*Ubriaca*, sit down before you fall.'

That voice, low, of a small man, bent against pedlar songs more powerful than his. The fish dart of vulgar speech drones at me: '*Cativa*,' he hisses, and pulls me into a chair. People are staring. 'Your children should see you now.'

I've heard that. Now I sit still, in false dignity, on the auction block of this market where I have sold myself to undignified pleasure. He fills my vagina as I fill time, waiting for an end.

So it's possible to adore legs and shoulders, the place where teeth are set. Look at him, what a passionate ornament he is. Anger and frustration have coloured him into a man. He's holding on to my arm as though it were his. Having lost respect for all else, what remains? Only parts of the body. What a limited cult. Here I am on my knees in filth, praying over a groin.

Can one survive without killing? I need his death as I need health.

The real disgrace is in the drink poured down during the act of disgracement.

'Look at you, you haven't even washed your feet for me.'

'Get me a drink.'

'Wash your feet.'

'Spit on them.'

I drag out of bed, wipe up his saliva, my body naked as a cross.

'What a beautiful back you have anyway,' he says in a forgiving way.

A long pull at the bottle to help swallow this *merda*. Then a pill, enzyme to digest the *merda*, colour of dirty tongue licking away at my self-esteem, whatever that was, I can't remember. There are only traces of something I recall and which continue to feel heavy. But lick, suck, squeeze away loneliness; hate is better than an empty bed.

After such love – oh mother, forgive me – my body lies in a crazy heap. Head splitting, eyes breaking open, afraid to look. But also afraid to lose this mad pattern, it does interest me, it does eat time. Pour down more drink, another pill, avoid health for it may mean death. Certainly someone will have to be eliminated.

Oh my fantastic affliction, are you feeling weak? What can I give you now, or what will you take away from me? Who will I be when you leave, and where are you going?

To my children?

I hate you. I shall destroy you, not Roberto.

Oh children, do not open the door if I am not your mother.

I send my maid away for a few days, hoping that work will put a straitjacket around me.

She will visit her family in a hill-town close by where the harvest is on. 'Come on Sunday with the children, I'll show you how we press the wine.'

'Yes, I want to see that, want to see new things.'

'But where is she going, Mama, who will take care of us?'

'I will, of course.'

'Oh you're always tired, or visiting friends.'

I look at them, aghast at how far things have gone.

'Well, I was tired for a while, now I'm OK and we'll have fun.'

They still believe in me. Together we set the house in order, go shopping. I feel well protected walking down the very street where I stumbled so recently. 'I'll make you pancakes for supper just like in America.'

We buy strawberry jam and lots of apples, hard and yellow, grown on the slopes of Etna. Don Vincente gives each of the children a candy.

We scatter on down the corso, nothing seems to get in the way. Through the arch and into the big golden piazza where I lose them like balloons.

I rest on the steps of the cathedral and watch them play. Across the street I see Roberto working over the cash register. He beckons to me but I gesture no, no, too busy with the children.

He comes over with some cakes for each of them. My son declines, 'Yeah, I know, now you'll just talk to him and we won't have any fun.'

'Don't be silly,' I answer. 'Take the cake and let's go on to the *giardino pubblico*.'

Safe among them in the public garden. It's a formal tropical garden like a painting by Rousseau. All kinds of flowers, even daisies lushed out into trees. Nothing is small, hibiscus the size of a hand, trumpet flowers, flesh-thick, grown to man-eating size, with a smell so deep. They say if you sleep under them you can never wake up.

The sun is digging at me, tiring and complicating my view of this Sicilian growth repulsive with overproduction. Never dying but also never beginning, it's a still place where I have seen hills retain the same colour for nearly a year, a dreadful green, lacking all vitality.

In the middle of it all stands Etna, the top of her black, bare as a bone. 'Look at the mountain,' my daughter says. 'It must be very thirsty.'

Sunday morning we drive to Granite, a town built on the rock it's named for. A bleached succession of stone huts blending into the background like rubble.

Concertina, very clean and glad to see us. Her mother and father shake my hand in a formal way. He's old and small, a tough remnant of a man. He leads us into the house, and we all sit down at a large table. The mother cuts some rude bread. We drink a toast with wine that's almost blue it's so strong.

Then it's quiet. A lot of flies gather around us. The old woman scatters them away from the bread. I am shocked by the many creases in the palm of her hand, as though she's cut herself too often.

Concertina shows us the house, steps leading to the plain room where she was born. She opens a wooden trunk and counts through the linen she has prepared for a dowry. 'What a lucky husband you will have,' I say to show my appreciation. It's pleasant to be here; these are kind people who see no evil in me and so I have none.

We talk about America, look at pictures of relatives who live there. The mother has me describe the subway, 'Yes, yes, just like our bus when it goes through a tunnel.' She shivers, 'It's so cold then.'

I look around at their belongings. So little else except the beds, the table. The kitchen is merely a recess in the main room, with charcoal fire and some water in a pitcher. One large, highly coloured religious scene is the ornament on the wall, which is painted a pale cold blue. These people could move out of here with very little fuss. On this quiet Sunday poverty seems an attractive state.

Later we all walk down the miserly street to the tavern. In the back room, on a platform, some boys are stamping on a pile of grapes with bare feet. It's very damp and cold, their feet are blue, toenails black from the stain of grapes.

The juice runs off the platform into a barrel from where it will be strained and poured into bottles. The smell is terrific, fresh and sour at the same time.

In the gloom of this cavern the boys treading look like prisoners. They are young unhealthy creatures, they make the sunlight we've come from a memory.

My children are restless. I buy some tepid Coca Cola to drink in the bright street. My son drops his bottle and some dogs rush over to lap at the mess.

'Let's go to the oil press,' Concertina suggests.

We continue down the street, dogs following, in each doorway some people are staring at us.

Another cave with a large wooden press with more boys turning it. I wonder what happened to the men in this town. I feel ill from the rancid odour, the viscous product looks dreadful.

'We must be getting back,' I tell the maid. 'You'd better get ready.'

'But my mother has a meal for you.'

'Good, the children must be very hungry.'

We go back to the house and I try to eat the pasta heavy with oil and tomatoes. 'I'm sorry, Signora, my stomach is not good today, forgive me if I don't finish.'

'You must make your lady some camomile tea when you get home, Concertina.'

The maid looks at me strangely.

On the way back, the baby falls asleep in her arms. I feel sad and jealous, wish I were going back without the maid so the baby would have just me again.

I drive too fast, want to get finished with this dreary ride. Approaching Taormina, the lights of the town glow like pearls in the dusk, a necklace of wealth awaits us up there.

The piazza is lush with people in Sunday clothes. The church door is wide open, an elegant light streaming out as from the lobby of a great hotel.

The café is full of Sicilians from Messina. They always come on Sunday night to have a treat, to look at tourists. As I enter the terrace, pushing my way through ample families eating ice cream, drinking sodas, I feel a hundred curious eyes on me. Fortunately I've put on a skirt and some high heels, it just won't do to wear pants and sandals on these nights, it makes me more of an oddity than I already am with my straight hair and pale lips. Anyway, a woman is not considered '*elegante*' unless she is dressed the way they are. I've not been able to convince Roberto that to be casual is to be chic, he'll approve of my costume tonight, I'm sure.

Finally I see him, way in the back, watching over the waiters as they carry trays out of the kitchen.

He looks nasty and busy; I suppose I ought to come back later when there's less work but I want to be near him. The sight of him makes me feel heavy, not in a good way but complex, too full of something.

'So you're back for more,' he mocks, not standing up to greet me. My excitement falls apart like a badly wrapped package. There's nothing inside me now except the awareness of fraud. I feel ugly as he looks me up and down.

'You look very tired from all your hard work, maybe you'd better sit down here,' he adds in a bland voice.

I realize then that he is play-acting, he is trying to hide his pleasure at having me back. But who can pay the price for this tawdry bit of theatre except myself?

That night I watch his eyes go flat, absolutely under my reign, while his body over me is sodden with joy at mounting me again.

I have a squalid sense of victory. I do not desire him, all this now is patience on my part, an animal loneliness and also a kind of whoredom. Next, thinks a whore; next, think I.

Clearly the fever in this unlovely affair is in the vulgarity. Truce, calm found only in bed after the act. A bad calm, full of knowledge that this sweet exhaustion is momentary, that in the daytime our ugly tempers will muck all that went before. But the fight is unfair; I am superior even though I seem to lose. I allow him to win as soon as I feel his stark, desperate love. For I am sure that the only tender moments in his life are with me. Underneath his dreadful breeding, inside the heart of this merchant there is a soft man, seen only by me, his first love.

I am his bread in a starved country where he was taught to distrust gentleness. 'Only a *ciuca*, a fool, gives to a beggar what he himself might use some day.'

He says this and shows me trunks of clothes he can no longer wear, stacks of junk that he can't throw away because some of it might be useful some day. 'Some day,' this is the slogan of Sicily, decrepit from centuries of vengeance, where fear of the Mafia is greater than the fear of God.

This flesh bath is growing tepid. I begin to smell him. Horrid pre-occupation with new details of him, smells, gestures. Even as I use him night after night the judgement of him continues. The decline brings nastiness but I savour it; survival is an ugly struggle. Success is in one more tentacle to make me more fit in this complicated world. I am an octopus swimming off in a new direction, quickly, so that my arms will not pull me to pieces inside the trap.

Watching him eat, I really must leave the table. Terrible mixing of foods in his mouth, eating with such concentration. That which makes him exciting in bed oddly enough makes him intolerable in common life. Real gluttony. How vulgar this insistence on doing only what he is doing, as though he has killed the rest of life. He gorges himself, is made nervous and sick by his appetite. He cannot accept more than what he can hear or touch. There is so much more, but he is afraid.

He washes, washes before and after love, keeping busy, shutting out the afterward, which is for me the only reality. What I do with him, what he considers the real present, I think of as a lapse in me, a jump towards earth in a dubious parachute, longing for the solid creaking plane above me ploughing through an abstract beautiful sky, arriving nowhere – but having been everywhere.

It's true that I needed him to fill the blank present. But to love him could never hurt me because I never valued him. My investment was small, worth a piece of skin only organ deep. I can cut him out as one can cut the genitals of a man – as one can never cut off the real, slow sadness of thought.

My past is a train that he has boarded and it is here that I sever myself from him. As we sit under the same motion, while I think, he picks his feet and reads the paper. Nearly everything passes by him. He does not sink into the gloom produced by motion which must be felt if one is more than animal. He knows only that life is inconvenient while for me the train keeps on, the view moves and I am moved.

There he sits, irritating me. Just the sound of pages turning, his cough, are reminders of my disgrace when my sex deceived me and tried to be all of me.

Wretchedly, graph clear, the downward curve races on. This hot confused affair, once a complicated maze in a formal garden, becomes a simple descent. I've worn him down, he scratches in an effort to caress. And what is left for me except occasional wet drunk explosions into emotion more remembered than felt, a phony tenderness as I accept and also resent the ending which is happening.

He tries to beat me back to the original time and chills at my passivity where once I hit back, aroused by any kind of touch, excited by his very fingerprint.

The long season is over, it ends clearly as these November days sharpen and widen in view. Scirocco has left; the sky is blue by day and blue by night. The moon is strong seen, no mist. The mountain is so lucid that it seems smaller.

My humid trance is over.

With terrible logic my sense of nausea has become actual; I vomit in the morning for a whole week till I finally suspect, no accept, that I am pregnant.

Disgust, nausea, irritation, exactly these three; they are my lover. And I?

Split, torn, sobbing self. An octopus born in the twin month. But my suffering is not divided. There is no doubt in me. I will not carry this man's child.

I see my three children and there is no dilemma. To love them means to hate this foreign object inside me. To conceive a new life one must respect it, and I despise Roberto whose tool I've used, turned against me now as a boomerang.

When the pygmies kill a female elephant the best of the hunters climbs into her womb and then cuts his way out in fierce celebration.

Oh no, the problem is not what to do but how to go about doing it. I want a very brief ritual.

Concertina is not surprised. 'I've worried about you for some time, the way you don't eat. But anyway, what do you expect the way you've been carrying on.'

'Don't judge me, just help me.'

'What about him, what does he say?'

'He doesn't know. I don't want him involved in this.'

'You Americans are crazy. He's had his fun with you, why shouldn't he pay for it?'

'Because it's not his fault.'

'Well he did it, didn't he?'

'No. I let it happen. Now enough of this. Tell me where to go and then be quiet.'

She stares at me: the line between servant and master is thin.

'This is a bad country for women, Signora. There's not a priest who would help you now. They get fat from our sins.'

'I know. That's why I'm counting on you.'

'But I've no right to help you.'

'Do you want to, Concertina?'

'I guess so. I don't know, I'm scared.'

'I'm pregnant.'

A long silence between us. We're sitting in the kitchen, two women alone. Her simple face looks as sad as any I've ever seen.

She gets up and draws a glass of water, drinks and offers the same glass to me.

'Go and see old Maria, she knows a lot.'

Her voice absolves me; the servant has set the master free.

I find Maria's house in the poorest part of town, where there are no streets only vague steps leading down. Steps so narrow, I stumble and feel blind, find the way again, hooked to the last light of afternoon. It will be easier going back.

Rabbit skins nailed to the wall, outside, inside. The yard is gorged with live rabbits, nasty red-eyed animals, much too soft.

She kills them expertly, one neat pull severs the head from the spine. A gash, and the animal is turned inside out.

'One must work for a living,' she says, her face so calm and so old that I instantly believe in her.

'Wait till I finish, the butcher is waiting.'

In her hands the transition between life and death is so smooth that it's hardly worth watching. I smoke some cigarettes, while she goes on killing, cutting, nailing.

'So you've heard about me?'

'Yes, they say you know the truth.'

'Why not, why only talk about good things. I am not a gypsy.'

'Will you do it?'

'As you can see, I do everything, just as you want everything.'

Black eyes fever into me. My hand in hers is a quivering rabbit. Her vision spurts at me like blood; I am the creature wounded.

'Lie down and let me have a look.'

She pushes up her sleeves and goes to the faucet, begins to wash her hands with a green lump of soap. My sigh interrupts her. I lean against a soft wall where the fur of dead animals is nailed in rough squares.

'Don't be afraid, it's only a little pain.'

There's no use arguing with a witch, I just leave.

Going up the steps I take a last look down at this wrong place. I need a bigger country.

The first snow has laid a cool glove on the mountain. Soothed, I am able to breathe again, my loneliness is clear fresh air.

That meal is over. Having truly eaten him, I must now rid myself of him. Only a doctor can help me. What difference now another pain, another killing. How true that it becomes easier to live this evil, cutting life. The aborting knife will disinvolve me; a cool clean instrument will erase this last remnant of the humanity that *was* present in those long repeated moments of red forgetting.

•

LAILA BAALABAKI
A Spaceship of Tenderness to the Moon
(*c.* 1964)

Born in Lebanon into a Shi'ite family in 1936, Laila Baalabaki gave up her education to work in the Lebanese parliament, and made a deep impression with her first novel, I Live, *an honest account of a woman's life in a patriarchal society. 'A Spaceship of Tenderness to the Moon', from her short-story collection of the same title, explores an Arab couple's erotic relationship with an outspokenness so unusual in that culture in modern times that it was the subject of an investigation by the authorities.*

Baalabaki is regarded as a pioneer of the Arabian women's liberation movement in Beirut, which has been continued by such writers as Ghada Samman and Hanan Shaykh, and which shows more Western influence than parallel movements in other Arabian countries.

When I closed my eyes I was able to see everything around me, the long settee which fills one vast wall in the room from corner to corner; the shelves on the remaining walls; the small table; the coloured cushions on the carpet; the white lamp, in the shape of a large kerosene one, that dangled from a hole in the wall and rested on the tiled floor. Even the windows we had left curtainless. In the second room was a wide sofa; a table supporting a mirror; a wall-cupboard and two chairs upholstered in velvet. Since our marriage we hadn't changed a thing in the little house, and I refused to remove anything from it.

I opened my eyelids a little as I heard my husband mumble, 'It's light and we alone are awake in the city.' I saw him rising up in front of the window as the silver light of dawn spread over his face and naked body. I love his naked body.

Once again I closed my eyes; I was able to see every little bit of him, every minute hidden detail: his soft hair, his forehead, nose, chin, the veins of his neck, the hair on his chest, his stomach, his feet, his nails. I called to him to come back and stretch out beside me, that I wanted to kiss him. He didn't move and I knew, from the way he had withdrawn from me and stood far off, that he was preparing himself to say something important. In this way he becomes cruel and stubborn, capable of taking and carrying through decisions. I am the exact opposite: in order to talk things over with him I must take hold of his hand or touch his clothes. I therefore opened my eyes, threw aside the cushion I was hugging and seized hold of his shirt, spreading it across my chest. Fixing my gaze on the ceiling I asked him if he saw the sea.

'I see the sea,' he answered.

I asked him what colour it was.

'Dark blue on one side,' he said, 'and on the other a greyish white.'

I asked him if the cypress trees were still there.

'They are still there among the houses that cling close together,' he answered, 'and there's water lying on the roofs of the buildings.'

I said I loved the solitary date-palm which looked, from where we were, as though it had been planted in the sea and that the cypress trees put me in mind of white cemeteries.

For a long while he was silent and I remained staring up at the ceiling. Then he said, 'The cocks are calling,' and I quickly told him I didn't like chickens because they couldn't fly and that when I was a child I used to carry them up to the roof of our home and throw them out into space in an attempt to teach them to fly, and both cocks and hens would always land in a motionless heap on the ground.

Again he was silent for a while, after which he said that he saw a light come on at the window of a building opposite. I said that even so we were still the only two people awake in the city, the only two who had spent the night entwined in each other's arms. He said that he had drunk too much last night. I quickly interrupted him by saying I hated that phrase – I drank too much – as though he regretted the yearning frenzy with which he had made love to me. Sensing that I was beginning to get annoyed he changed the subject, saying: 'The city looks like a mound of sparkling precious stones of all colours and sizes.'

I answered that I now imagined the city as coloured cardboard boxes which would fall down if you blew on them; our house alone, with its two rooms, was suspended from a cloud and rode in space. He said that his mouth was dry and he wanted an orange. I concluded what I had been saying by stating that though I had never lived in any other city, I hated this one and that had I not dreamt that I would one day meet a man who would take me far far away from it I would have died of dejection long long ago. Pretending that he had not heard my last remark he repeated: 'I want an orange, my throat's dry'. I disregarded his request and went on to say that with him I paid no heed to where I was: the earth with its trees, its mountains, rivers, animals and human beings just vanished. Unable to wait further, he burst out at me, 'Why do you refuse to have children?'

I was sad, my heart was wrung, the tears welled up into my eyes, but I didn't open my mouth.

'How long is it since we married?' he asked. I uttered not a word as I followed him round with my eyes. He stiffened and continued, 'It's a year and several months since we married and you've been refusing and refusing, though you were crazy about children before we married; you were dying for them.'

He swerved and struck the settee with his hands as he burst out, 'Hey chair, don't you remember her entreaties? And you lamp, didn't you hear the sound of her wailing? And you cushions, did she not make of you tiny bodies that she hugged to herself and snuggled up to as she slept? Speak, o things inanimate. Speak. Give back to her her voice which is sunk into you.'

Quietly I said that inanimate things don't feel, don't talk, don't move. Angrily he inquired: 'How do you know they're dead?' I replied that things weren't dead, but that they drew their pulse beats from people. He interrupted me by saying that he wouldn't argue about things now and wouldn't allow me to escape solving the problem as I always did. Absent-mindedly I explained to him that the things around me, these very things – this settee, this carpet, this wall, this lamp, this vase, the shelves and the ceiling – are all a vast mirror that reflects for me the outside world: the houses, the sea, the trees, the sky, the sun, the stars and the clouds. In them I see my past with him, the hours of misery and dejection, the moments of meeting and of tenderness, of bliss and of happiness, and from them I now deduce the shapes of the days to come. I would not give them up.

He became angry and shouted, 'We're back again with things. I want to understand here and now why you refuse to have children.' No longer able to bear it, I shouted that he too at one time refused to have them. He was silent for a while, then he said, 'I refused before we were married, when it would have been foolish to have had one.' Sarcastically I told him that he was afraid of them, those others, those buffoons in the city. He used to beg for their assent, their blessing, their agreement, so that he might see me and I him, so that he might embrace me and I him, so that we might each drown the other in our love. They used to determine for us our places of meeting, the number of steps to be taken to get there, the time, the degree to which our voices could be raised, the number of breaths we took. And I would watch them as they secretly scoffed at us, shamelessly slept with the bodies they loved, ate three meals a day, smoked cigarettes with the cups of coffee and carafes of arak, and guffawed as they vulgarly chewed over stories about us and thought up patterns of behaviour for us to put into effect the following day. His voice was choked as he mumbled: 'I don't pay attention to others. I was tied to another woman.'

Ah, how can I bear all this torture, all this passionate love for him? He used to be incapable of confessing the bitter truth to her, that he didn't love her, wouldn't love her. Choking, he said that it wasn't easy, he wasn't callous enough to be able to stare into another human being's face and say to her, after nine years of getting up each and every day and finding her there, 'Now the show's over,' and turn his back and walk off. I told him to look at my right hand and asked him if my blood was still dripping from it hot on to the floor? 'You were mad,' he mumbled, 'mad when you carried out the idea. I opened this door, entered this room and saw you stretched out on this settee, the veins of your hand slashed, your fingers trailing in a sea of blood. You were mad. I might have lost you.' I smiled sadly as I pulled the shirt up to my chest, my face breathing in the smell of it. I said that my part in the play required that I should take myself off at the end, and the form of absence possible for me, the form I could accept and bear, was a quick death rather than a slow, cruel crawling, like that of the turtle in the film *Mondo Cane* that lost its way in the sands, held in the sun's disc, as it searched for the river-bank. He repeated sadly that he didn't know I was serious about him. I asked him sarcastically whether he was waiting for me to kill myself in order to be sure that I was telling the truth. I told him that I had lost myself in my love for him; oblivious to all else, I slipped unseen, like a gust of wind, through people's fingers, scorching their faces as I passed through the street. All I was conscious of was the weight of bodies, the height of buildings and of his hands. I asked him to draw closer and give me his hand which I craved to hold. He remained standing far off, inflexible, and at once accused me that after all that misery and triumph I was refusing to become pregnant from him, had refused again and again and again, and that from my refusal he understood I no longer loved him.

What? I cried out that he could never accuse me of that. Only yesterday I was stretched out beside him and he gave himself up to deep sleep while I was open-eyed, rubbing my cheeks against his chin, kissing his chest, snuggling up under his arm, searching in vain for sleep. I told him frankly that I was upset by the speed with which he got to sleep, and by my being left alone and awake at his side. He hastened to deny this, saying that he had never been aware of my having remained sleepless. He believed that I dozed off the moment he did. I revealed maliciously that it wasn't the first time he had left me alone. I then related in full yesterday's incident, telling of how he had been asleep breathing quietly, with me stretched close up against him smoking a cigarette, when suddenly in the emptiness of the room through the smoke, I had seen a foot fleeing from under the sheets. I moved my own but it didn't move and a coldness ran through the whole of my body. I moved it but it didn't move. It occurred to me to shout. I moved it but it didn't move. I hurriedly hid my face in his hair. I was afraid. He moved and the foot moved. I cried silently. I had imagined, had felt, had been unable to tell the difference between his foot and mine. In a faint voice he said: 'In this age people don't die of love.' Quickly seizing the opportunity I said that in this age people didn't beget children. In olden times they knew where the child would be born, who it would be likely to resemble, whether it would be male or female; they would knit it woollen vests and socks, would embroider the hems, pockets and collars of its dresses with coloured birds and flowers. They would amass presents of gold crucifixes for it and medallions with 'Allah bless him' on them, opened palms studded with blue stones, and pendants with its name engraved on them. They would reserve a midwife for it, would fix the day of the delivery, and the child would launch out from the darkness and be flung into the light at the precise time estimated. They would register a piece of land in the child's name, would rent it a house, choose companions for it, decide which school it would be sent to, the profession it would study for, the person it could love and to whom it could bind its destiny. That was a long, long time ago, in the time of your father and my father. He asked, 'Do you believe that twenty years ago was such an age away? What has changed since? What has changed? Can't you and can't I provide everything that is required for a child?' To soften the blow I explained that before I married I was like a child that lies down on its back in front of the window, gazes up at the stars and stretches out its tiny arm in a desire to pluck them. I used to amuse myself with this dream, with this impossibility, would cling to it and wish it would happen. He asked me: 'Then you were deceiving me?'

Discovering he had changed the conversation into an attack on me so as to win the battle, I quickly told him that only the woman who is unfulfilled with her man eagerly demands a child so that she can withdraw, enjoy being with her child and so be freed. He quickly interrupted me: 'And were you unsatisfied?' I answered him that we had been afraid, had not travelled to the last sweet unexplored regions of experience; we had trembled in terror, had continually bumped against the faces of others and listened to their voices. For his sake, for my own, I had defied death in order to live. He was wrong, wrong, to doubt my being madly in love with him.

'I'm at a loss. I don't understand you,' he muttered. I attacked him by saying that was just it, that he also wouldn't understand me if I told him I didn't dare become pregnant, that I would not perpetrate such a mistake.

'Mistake?' he shrieked. 'Mistake?' I clung closer to his shirt, deriving strength from it, and slowly, in a low voice, I told him how scared I was about the fate of any child we might cast into this world. How could I imagine a child of mine, a being nourished on my blood, embraced within my entrails, sharing my breathing, the pulsations of my heart and my daily food, a being to whom I give my features and the earth, how can I bear the thought that in the future he will leave me and go off in a rocket to settle on the moon? And who knows whether or not he'll be happy there. I imagine my child with white ribbons, his fresh face flushed; I imagine him strapped to a chair inside a glass ball fixed to the top of a long shaft of khaki-coloured metal ending in folds resembling the skirt of my Charleston dress. He presses the button, a cloud of dust rises up and an arrow hurls itself into space. No, I can't face it. I can't face it.

He was silent a long, long time while the light of dawn crept in by his face to the corners of the room, his face absent-minded and searching in the sky for an arrow and a child's face. The vein between his eyebrows was knotted; perplexity and strain showed in his mouth. I, too, remained silent and closed my eyes.

When he was near me, standing like a massive tower at a rocket-firing station, my heart throbbed and I muttered to him that I adored his naked body. When he puts on his clothes, especially when he ties his tie, I feel he's some stranger come to pay a visit to the head of the house. He opened his arms and leaned over me. I rushed into his embrace, mumbling crazily: 'I love you, I love you, I love you, I love you, I love you.' He whispered into my hair: 'You're my pearl.' Then he spread the palm of his hand over my lips, drawing me to him with the other hand, and ordered: 'Let us take off, you and I, for the moon.'

Translated by Denys Johnson-Davies

•

SIV HOLM
I, a Woman
(1965)

Siv Holm's semi-autobiographical novel, originally published in Denmark in 1965 and translated into English as I, a Woman *in 1967, was a scandalous bestseller in its day and was made into a film starring Essy Pearson. Telling the story of a young woman who frees herself from her family and small-town background, the book shocked because its heroine wanted – and found – sex without fretting too much about marriage or long-term relationships, as the following episode shows.*

This was the dawn of the so-called permissive society, when such attitudes were still unacceptable in many quarters, and I, a Woman *no doubt contributed to Scandinavia's reputation for sexual licence, whether deserved or not.*

Siv is again sitting at home in the evening. She has put a record of Tchaikovsky on the record player, has opened up a new pack of cigarettes. She has gone to the library the previous day and taken out a whole pile of books. They are mostly books about travel. One day she is going to travel and see the whole world. Go to Egypt and see the pyramids, look up into the face of the unfathomable Sphinx, go to Africa and rumple the dark curly hair of a little Negro boy, go to China and curtsey low for an honourable mandarin.

For a while she forgets about her uneasy loneliness, smokes and reads.

What time is it now? Only nine?

She stretches herself and notices a tingling uneasiness in her body. It is very strange; is this how one lives in a big city where there are lots of people?

She looks at her divan and smiles ironically to herself: She had thought that she would be able to find a man very quickly in Copenhagen, a man for her, one who would think it wonderful to visit her place and her divan, one who would lift her up into the seventh heaven and leave her with a smile and a thank you. That must be a delightful arrangement for a man, don't you think? A girl who does not want to get married and does not ask for promises, but just wants to swing in time with him as long as it lasts.

Heinz, you are far away up there on your high peak of experience. What would you make of all this? Am I still delightful? Why can't I find anybody – a man? Do I long for you? Yes, I do. I long to tell you about this and hear your explanation. I long for a person to love me. It is cowardice, I know. Now, I am all by myself, just as I wanted to be, and I have to discover everything on my own.

She puts on her jacket and decides to go for a walk.

Not a single evening goes by in which Siv does not go for a walk. It becomes a desperate vice for her to take a walk late at night. She walks up and down the streets, around corners, over roads and squares.

She encounters many men on these evening walks of hers. They look at her with interest as she passes them. She looks quickly at them – and walks on. What else can she do? But couldn't it happen that there are other people walking the streets for the same reason? Someone who is just as lonely and starving?

And couldn't it be possible that one of these is meant for her?

But if a man speaks to her, he is usually drunk or looks stupid and speaks with a slow, ugly accent.

Young men shout, whistle and act silly and they do not interest her. They invite her to dances, the movies or restaurants. They will tell their stupid jokes and shyly kiss her goodbye at her street door, while they agree upon another date. Then there are the soldiers. They are just not to be tolerated, because they are not normal human beings when they walk along gathered into a flock, wearing the same uniform on their bodies.

There are small, fat men, with narrow, satiated eyes. Tall, thin men with sway backs and wretched coats. They look sickly at her and give up before they have thought the thought.

Then there are the gay businessmen who come out of warm, well-lit places, with their coats unbuttoned and their hats on a slant, smoking cigars.

They look at her with pleasure as they pass her, say something to a colleague and walk on, filled with cognac and solid business deals: a sweet tart, something you enjoy looking at, but you haven't time for more.

There are also men who get nervous when they look at her. Their eyes fly out of control: This girl is too demanding.

Siv pulls her jacket around her. No, it must be stupid to have the idea that you can find a man in the streets. She walks quickly home, puts her key in the door and lets her body into the warm room. How can she be so foolish? To throw away an entire evening wandering around looking for something which cannot be found *there*.

It is one o'clock at night. She has to hurry to bed. She has to be at work at seven in the morning. She crawls under her blanket and feels very stupid.

She tosses and turns, cannot sleep, lights a cigarette, and bitter, angry thoughts begin to tumble around in her head.

*

Civilization has stuck cotton in men's ears, made their eyes polite and frightened, paralysed their tongues and their hands.

They stand along the streets with taut, strained bulges in their pants. They look at the girls, from the front, from behind. They imagine themselves already inside them, imagine that they move their feet to pursue, raise their hands to stop the object of their desire.

But they just sigh and remain standing where they are.

The woman sees their eyes as she walks past them. For a short moment both of them shiver a little, then she walks on, feeling the man's eyes on her back. Her body sways a little, straightens up, gets a conscious rocking movement.

Does anything happen? Does anything happen? Does anything happen?

No. No. Nothing happens.

Because they are all well-bred people, they are civilized.

It is the man's duty just to look with admiration, it is the girl's duty to walk on, quickly and nervously. What if he should speak to her? What if his desire overcame his politeness? Then she is supposed to close her eyes, shake her head and rush away. She has to go home and say that some disgusting and shabby man had embarrassed her with a dirty proposition.

Oh, how lovely it is to hide yourself in a cloak of annoyance when you do not have to listen and do what nature incites you to do.

Just go on and cry, you little, confused girl and all of you big, polite men.

Couldn't you have approached that woman? Perhaps she had an engagement.

Maybe, but then, couldn't she just smile and say 'No, thanks'?

No, things don't work out that way; you know very well that that is not how she would react. She would think 'What an idiotic man this man must be; perhaps he is also drunk.' Something could be wrong with him – and he could also make her pregnant, couldn't he?

Or else: If she says yes – or even maybe – what wouldn't he think of her later? He would not consider her to be of much worth, nothing more than a slut.

And you don't want to be considered a slut. You want to be considered a civilized human being.

Yes, that is how things are. The Christian Bible says that there is
a place called hell, an awful, heart-rending hell. A place where there
is an endless Mardi Gras with masks, closed eyes and smiles.
Behind the masks lie soft, vulnerable flesh, warm blood, fearful
lusts, unutterable dreams and a bad conscience.

Behind the masks, yes, behind the masks.

But no one ever looks behind the masks, because they can never
be taken off. They are glued on with the thick, sticky glue of fear.
They make the thin skin underneath bleed. But they cannot, must
not be removed.

Because what would we see then? A naked face, which is
shocking because it is *human*.

This hell makes life incomprehensible.

Siv fusses with her cigarette in the ashtray, slowly and emphatically.
Something must be done about this civilization, with its mistakes
and incomprehensible things which create untieable knots in men's
minds. But how?

Siv suddenly sits up in bed, lights a new cigarette with shaking
fingers: Now she knows – you could *write* about it. You could
write about people, as they are – and not as they want to be. Yes,
you could do that. But how do you get started? With yourself? She
winces a bit. Yes, you will have to start with yourself and your own
desires. That is probably the safest and the most honest way of
going about it.

She begins to speculate as to how much a typewriter costs; it can
also be bought on the instalment plan, can't it? She puts out the
next cigarette, turns resolutely over on her side, because the decision
has been made: Tomorrow she is going to go down to buy a
typewriter, teach herself to type – you can surely buy instruction
manuals. Then she will have something to occupy herself with
during the long nights. She will no longer walk the streets searching
for something. She will not search at all. One day it will surely
come to her, all the wonderful things she longs for. And in the
meantime, she will write. It must be easy to write, if you write in
the same way that you think. But could she get it published?

Ha! She jumps up in bed. If she has a book published some day,
she will send it to Heinz. Perhaps she will also write to him and tell
him that she has started to write. He'll be proud that he has known

her. He'll say to himself, 'I knew it. I understood it the first time I saw Siv – she's not an ordinary woman; she's an artist.'

Siv snuggles down into her pillow, bends her legs in excited expectation, already feels herself standing on a peak of fame and admiration.

But she is going to write because she wants to help mankind get around the sharp, cutting corners of civilization, isn't she? Yes, of course, she hasn't forgotten – but it would also be nice if she could become famous at the same time.

She can understand much better why she has had such an awful time, is so lonely and misunderstood. Artists have always had an awful time; if they don't, then they are not really artists.

Siv falls asleep with a happy smile on her lips.

The next day, when Siv is finished with her work, she goes out to buy a typewriter. She wants to test it in the store.

A very natural thing to do, isn't it?

She sits at a little table with a burning redness in her cheeks, then she quickly gets up. 'I have to learn how to type first, so I would like to have an instruction manual, if you have any.'

The man smiles – is he just smiling, or is he laughing? Siv tries to stand proudly. There is nothing shameful in her not being able to type. There are many people who can't. She just entered the store in the wrong way, wrapped in a golden fog of dreams, like a famous and discriminating author who could only type on the very best machine.

She tumbles out of the store with the brown case, holding it by the handle. She turns and smiles an embarrassed farewell. The man stands behind the window-pane looking smilingly at her with both hands in his pockets. Why did he stand there with his hands in his pockets? He looked so mocking and superior, didn't he?

He was probably just happy to have sold something. Siv forgets her painful blushes. She rushes home, locks her door, sets the case on the table and carefully takes the machine out, very carefully, as if it were a little child.

There it is, black, shiny and very promising.

Siv feels a shiver go down her spine. She runs her fingers over the keys, steps back a little and looks at it. She has also bought paper. She unpacks this and with great difficulty manages to insert

a sheet of paper into the machine, pulls over a chair, sits down –
and stops cold. She remembers that she cannot type.

She begins slowly, with one finger: 'I am now going to write a
book about what kind of a person I am and what I think other
people are like.'

It takes a long, long time to write just these few words.

She takes out her instruction manual and begins to practice with
ten resisting fingers. After half an hour, she gets up, stretches,
laughs at the machine, grates her teeth, raises her eyebrows and
looks steadily and threateningly at it. 'I'll learn how to type. Yes,
you all can rest assured' (she says this to the collected peoples of the
world) 'that I'll learn how to type. You'll see, some day I'm going
to write a book that will explode – with all that I want to say.'

She leaves the room and fixes herself some food, has suddenly
become ravenously hungry, singing as she cooks.

Life has again been given a purpose, because here she stands, the
newly hatched author dreaming herself into authorship.

One evening Siv has typed for four hours. It is nine o'clock, and,
feeling heaviness in her head, she decides she needs some fresh air.
She puts on her coat and goes out for a walk.

Half an hour later she is sitting in a sidewalk café in the square
facing the City Hall. She has ordered a beer, has drunk it and now
sits rolling the empty glass between her hands, looking out at the
delightful square with all its neon signs and its talkative mass of
people. She deliberates as to whether she wants another glass or
not. Should she pay, get up and go home and try to type some
more? She can also go to bed. It is a pleasure to write, but it is a
lonely pleasure. She looks down at her hand holding the glass: It is
cold and empty, this glass, it is dead. She longs for something
warm to hold.

She suddenly hears a rustling noise at the side of her table. She
turns abruptly; there is a man standing in front of her. He has put a
hand on her table, bows a little, smiles. Her eyes glance quickly
over his entire body. He is probably thirty years old, strong, solid
and well-built, his skin is tanned and weatherbeaten, clean as only
the sun and the sea can make it. And he is smiling at Siv with a
crooked, foxy smile, a bit embarrassed. He raises one of his
eyebrows in an amusing arch. 'My name is Lars Thompsen. May I
offer you a drink?'

She nods with a smile: Of course, if he wants to.

He pulls over a chair and sits down in front of her, waves for the waiter, orders and, afterwards, folds his hands upon the tablecloth as if he wanted to say: That's *that*. He smiles and looks at her with pleasure and contentment.

And Siv laughs. She does not really know why she laughs, but she feels a warm, chuckling joy in her body which has to come out one way or another.

He stretches his hand across the table and grabs hers. 'I'm a sailor, but I'm not sailing at the moment.' He wrinkles his brow and quickly explains that certain family problems make it necessary for him to be at home for a while.

So the formalities are over. Siv has told him her name. They have shaken hands, and his hand remains on top of hers on the table.

A pair of hands are much better than words, much better. Her hand flutters like a baby bird inside this new warmth. She looks at him, looks down again, smiles a trembling smile which ripples the corners of her mouth: Thank God, she does not look like a lady this evening.

He has a tattoo on the back of his hand, a ship with an anchor.

An unknown man with a song in his body.

She does not know him, but he is warm and close and *her type*.

They drink up and walk over to the Tivoli amusement park. They knock down dishes and ride the roller-coaster; Siv howls and lets him put his arms protectingly around her. At midnight they watch the fireworks.

He has such a funny, crooked eyebrow, this Lars. Siv has looked at it so often that he finally touches it with his finger and explains, 'It was scarred once when I was in a fistfight. Therefore I always look as if I'm winking at all the girls.'

She laughs. 'And you probably do, too.'

'Only if they are pretty.' He looks at her, bites his lips together for joy over his catch. His suntanned face is warm and honest.

When they come out of the gates, he stops, puts a hand on her neck. 'You'll come home with me, won't you?'

She hesitates, because that is what you are supposed to do. He fans his fingers out and lets them run through her hair, tries to capture her eyes, does not repeat his question.

She still does not answer, but, then, she does not have to.

They walk silently through the city side by side.

Lars has a nice place. Large, comfortable easy chairs, many unique things from strange countries – rugs, pillows, figurines – and everything smells of dust, tobacco, newspapers – and man. Lars rushes about. 'What will you have, straight whisky or a cocktail?' Siv tells him. She sinks down into a deep easy chair and enjoys the active man in the plaid shirt with the rolled-up sleeves. Do you think he is just as brown, has just as many strong muscles over the rest of his body?

He walks toward a door. 'Where are you going?' 'Just a minute – it will only take a minute. I'll be right back.' He disappears into the kitchen – and returns a while later with a large tray. 'Help yourself, dear lady. I hope that you're hungry.' She sniffs at the tray: thick slices of French bread, liver paste, an opened can of shrimps, warm, bursting sausages.

Oh, yes, she is hungry, ravenously hungry and happy, gay as a lass of sixteen who is about to experience something exciting for the first time. She gobbles the food, talks, drinks, laughs at the man who sits across from her, warm and full of expectation. She has forgotten her loneliness, forgotten all her long walks to try to find the right man, because here he is, right in front of her. He drinks with her, and his grey eyes sparkle with warm curiosity. She throws her legs over the arm of the chair, lets her sandals fall to the floor, sinking down into a quiet happiness with a cigarette and a piece of chocolate.

'Tell me, are you always so well supplied? You must be used to walking the streets picking up poor, lonely, hungry girls and taking them home.'

He becomes serious, looks questioningly at her. 'Do you really have no boyfriend?' She shakes her head, her mouth full of chocolate.

'You see – you understand –' It comes out hesitantly, somewhat embarrassed, 'I don't want to get in anybody's way.' Siv cringes a little. 'No, I'm free for the time being.' She has become serious, is about to begin remembering.

He discovers her seriousness, stands up, throws out his hands, looks at her with a big smile. 'Shall we play a game? We are the only people left in the world, and we are stranded on a deserted island.' He wrinkles his eyebrows. 'And what in hell does a sailor do when he is stranded on a deserted island with a delightful girl?'

He has walked over to the other end of the room. 'Come here to me!'

Siv looks at him with annoyance. Is it going to take such a long time, be postponed still more, this delightful thing which is about to happen? 'I can't. I've drowned here in this chair.'

'Oh, yes, you can. Come on. Come on!'

He snaps his fingers, calling on her like a little dog. 'Come on. Come on!'

'Well, I guess I'll have to try.'

She breathes heavily and groans, makes a lot of needless movements and finally manages to draw her body up out of the chair.

She then stands a few yards from him, in her stockings and mussed-up hair. She raises her eyes up to him without raising her head. 'Shall we meet halfway?'

'No, come on!' He stands there laughing with joy. 'Closer. Closer.' He puts his hands on his hips, taps his foot on the floor. 'You can still come much closer.'

Siv walks right up to him, puts her chin against his chest, grinds her nose into his body and bites him through his thin shirt.

'What the hell!' He throws his arms around her, crushing her to him, shakes her head back so that her thick, black hair flies away from her face. Looks down into her half-serious, half-smiling flushed face.

Then he picks her up and walks around with her as if she were a little child, carries her into another room, holds her high over the bed and lets her fall. He sits down beside her, puts his hands around her hips, strokes his lips over her neck, whispers with a voice smothered by her mussed hair, 'How silly you were to come home with me, because now I'm going to eat you up.'

She sits in the middle of the bed, with her arms around his knees and her chin resting on them. She is smoking and amuses herself by blowing streams of smoke over his stomach. The smoke breaks up into strange waves and disappears among the curly hair on his chest. Oh, how nice he is. She had been sure of it, she guessed it when he stood in front of her in the restaurant – his entire body is brown, clean and muscular.

He puts his arms under her neck and looks smilingly at her. 'You always ought to be naked. You are natural that way. You should never do anything other than love and be loved.'

She laughs a little. 'Then I would be worn out too soon. No one can last like that.'

But she thinks with relief that he likes her – just like that, just as she is. She throws herself on his stomach and looks at this man lying stretched out in contentment. It is a pure animal pleasure to lie close to this man.

She strokes his smooth, tanned body with her hand, slides her hand in under his balls, puts her face against his stomach, biting gently with her lips. And she groans with pleasure. She lets her mouth glide up over his chest, tugging the fragrant hair with her teeth, on up to his arm, putting her teeth into his trembling muscles.

He lies very still, trembling, looking wonderingly at her. She laughs a little, knowing very well what he is thinking. 'It's very seldom that a man is caressed like this by a girl, isn't it?'

'Yes, but how do you know that?'

'Oh, I just do.'

'But, then, you are not a girl. You are the greatest, most wonderful, devilish lover of all time.' His face is creased with pleasure. He raises his torso and pulls her up against him. 'Where have you learned to act like this?'

'I have never really learned it – I just like it.'

And she lets him pull her across his stomach, and he glides tightly and firmly into her. She bends forward, stroking her breasts caressingly against him, stretches herself backwards so that she fastens her arms around his bended knees, laughs loudly, howls aloud, from pleasure and her lust for love. Because he is wonderful, this lover of hers, and she knows that she also is wonderful, feels it in her taut body which is bubbling over with lust and pride:

What a ride of love!

A little later she jumps out of the bed. 'Where is the toilet?'

'In the courtyard.'

'In the courtyard? Ugh!'

He is amused by this frightened, naked girl. 'Look, here is a dressing-gown.'

A beautiful Japanese silk kimono appears out of a drawer. Siv

stands in front of the mirror, wraps the soft silk cloth around her.
He has hopped back into bed, lies there and looks at her, and his
voice is husky when he says, 'You can keep it. It's yours. It fits
you, you little doll.'

She looks quickly at him and looks away again. 'Thanks a lot,
but I'll just borrow it, okay?' She begs him with her eyes to
understand. He must not be disappointed, because things are so
good as they stand between them now. She cannot accept his gift.
They do not owe each other anything and must not come to do so.

He nods. 'As you wish. But put it on and get it over with.'

The night is beautiful. Siv stands quietly in the middle of the
courtyard. She breathes the air in deeply. And the truth dawns on
her, not heavily and commanding, but with a trembling bird's call
at dawn: God is pleased – and the angels laugh when they watch
the happy love of people.

Translated by J. W. Brown

•

CAROL EMSHWILLER
Sex and/or Mr Morrison
(1967)

*'Easily the strangest sex story ever written,' said Harlan Ellison, introducing
'Sex and/or Mr Morrison' in his ground-breaking 1967 anthology* Dangerous Visions. *'It would be nice,' added the author of the story, 'to live in a
society where the genitals were really considered Beauty. It seems to me that
any other way of seeing them is obscene. After all, there they are. Why not
like them?'*

*Carol Emshwiller's writing – mostly in the short-story form – employs
poetic and experimental forms with scrupulous care: hers is a distinctive
voice that shines out of the US science-fiction scene in which most of her
work has appeared. She is also the author of the surrealist fantasy novel*
Carmen Dog *(1988).*

I can set my clock by Mr Morrison's step upon the stairs, not that
he is that accurate, but accurate enough for me. 8.30 thereabouts.

(My clock runs fast anyway.) Each day he comes clumping down and I set it back ten minutes, or eight minutes or seven. I suppose I could just as well do it without him but it seems a shame to waste all that heavy treading and those puffs and sighs of expending energy on only getting downstairs, so I have timed my life to this morning beat. Funereal tempo, one might well call it, but it is funereal only because Mr Morrison is fat and therefore slow. Actually he's a very nice man as men go. He always smiles.

I wait downstairs sometimes looking up and sometimes holding my alarm clock. I smile a smile I hope is not as wistful as his. Mr Morrison's moonface has something of the Mona Lisa to it. Certainly he must have secrets.

'I'm setting my clock by you, Mr M.'

'Heh, heh . . . my, my,' grunt, breath. 'Well,' heave the stomach to the right, 'I hope . . .'

'Oh, you're on time enough for *me*.'

'Heh, heh. Oh. Oh yes.' The weight of the world is certainly upon him or perhaps he's crushed and flattened by a hundred miles of air. How many pounds per square inch weighing him down? He hasn't the inner energy to push back. All his muscles spread like jelly under his skin.

'No time to talk,' he says. (He never has time.) Off he goes. I like him and his clipped little Boston accent, but I know he's too proud ever to be friendly. Proud is the wrong word, so is shy. Well, I'll leave it at that.

He turns back, pouting, and then winks at me as a kind of softening of it. Perhaps it's just a twitch. He thinks, if he thinks of me at all: What can she say and what can I say talking to her? What can she possibly know that I don't know already? And so he duck-walks, knock-kneed, out the door.

And now the day begins.

There are really quite a number of things that I can do. I often spend time in the park. Sometimes I rent a boat there and row myself about and feed the ducks. I love museums and there are all those free art galleries and there's window-shopping and, if I'm very careful with my budget, now and then I can squeeze in a matinee. But I don't like to be out after Mr Morrison comes back. I wonder if he keeps his room locked while he's off at work?

His room is directly over mine and he's too big to be a quiet man. The house groans with him and settles when he steps out of bed. The floor creaks under his feet. Even the walls rustle and the wallpaper clicks its dried paste. But don't think I'm complaining of the noise. I keep track of him this way. Sometimes, here underneath, I ape his movements, bed to dresser, step, clump, dresser to closet and back again. I imagine him there, flat-footed. Imagine him. Just imagine those great legs sliding into pants, their godlike width (for no mere man could have legs like that), those Thor-legs into pants holes wide as caves. Imagine those two landscapes, sparsely fuzzed in a faint, wheat-coloured brush finding their way blindly into the waist-wide skirt-things of brown wool that are still damp from yesterday. Ooo. Ugh. Up go the suspenders. I think I can hear him breathe from here.

I can comb my hair three times to his once and I can be out and waiting at the bottom step by the time he opens his door.

'I'm setting my clock by you, Mr M.'

'No time. No time. I'm off. Well . . .' and he shuts the front door so gently one would think he is afraid of his own fat hands.

And so, as I said, the day begins.

The question is (and perhaps it is the question for today): Who is he really, one of the Normals or one of the Others? It's not going to be so easy to find out with someone so fat. I wonder if I'm up to it. Still, I'm willing to go to certain lengths and I'm nimble yet. All that rowing and all that walking up and down and then, recently, I've spent all night huddled under a bush in Central Park and twice I've crawled out on the fire escape and climbed to the roof and back again (but I haven't seen much and I can't be sure of the Others yet).

I don't think the closet will do because there's no keyhole, though I could open the door a crack and maybe wedge my shoe there. (It's double A.) He might not notice it. Or there's the bed to get under. While it's true that I am thin and small, almost child-sized, one might say, still it will not be so easy, but then neither has it been easy to look for lovers on the roof.

Sometimes I wish I were a little, fast-moving lizard, dull green or a yellowish brown. I could scamper in under his stomach when he opened the door and he'd never see me, though his eyes are as quick as his feet are clumsy. Still I would be quicker. I would skitter off behind the bookcase or back of his desk or maybe even just lie very still in a corner, for surely he does not see the floor so much. His room is no larger than mine and his presence must fill it, or rather his stomach fills it and his giant legs. He sees the ceiling and the pictures on the wall, the surfaces of night table, desk and bureau, but the floor and the lower halves of everything would be safe for me. No, I won't even have to regret not being a lizard, except for getting in. But if he doesn't lock his room it will be no problem and I can spend all day scouting out my hiding-places. I'd best take a snack with me too if I decide this is the night for it. No crackers and no nuts, but noiseless things like cheese and fig newtons.

It seems to me, now that I think about it, that I was rather saving Mr Morrison for last, as a child saves the frosting of the cake to eat after the cake part is finished. But I see that I have been foolish, for, since he is really one of the most likely prospects, he should have been first.

And so today the day begins with a gathering of supplies and an exploratory trip upstairs.

The room is cluttered. There is no bookcase but there are books and magazines by the hundreds. I check behind the piles. I check the closet, full of drooping, giant suit coats I can easily hide in. Just see how the shoulders extend over the ordinary hangers. I check under the bed and the kneehole of the desk. I squat under the night table. I nestle among the dirty shirts and socks tossed in the corner. Oh, it's better than Central Park for hiding-places. I decide to use them all.

There's something very nice about being here, for I do like Mr Morrison. Even just his size is comforting; he's big enough to be everybody's father. His room reassures with all his father-sized things in it. I feel lazy and young here.

I eat a few fig newtons while I sit on his shoes in the closet, soft, wide shoes with their edges all collapsed and all of them shaped more like cushions than shoes. Then I take a nap in the dirty shirts. It looks like fifteen or so but there are only seven and some socks. After that I hunch down in the kneehole of the desk, hugging my knees, and I wait and I begin to have doubts. That pendulous stomach, I can already tell, will be larger than all my expectations. There will certainly be nothing it cannot overshadow or conceal, so why do I crouch here clicking my fingernails against the desk leg when I might be out feeding pigeons? Leave now, I tell myself. Are you actually going to spend the whole day, and maybe night too, cramped and confined in here? Yet haven't I done it plenty of times lately and always for nothing too? Why not one more try? For Mr Morrison is surely the most promising of all. His eyes, the way the fat pushes up his cheeks under them, look almost Chinese. His nose is Roman and in an ordinary face it would be overpowering, but here it is lost. Dwarfed. 'Save me,' cries the nose, 'I'm sinking.' I would try, but I will have other more important duties, after Mr Morrison comes back. Duty it is, too, for the good of all and I do mean *all*, but do not think that I am the least bit prejudiced in this.

You see, I did go to a matinee a few weeks ago. I saw the Royal Ballet dance *The Rite of Spring* and it occurred to me then . . . Well, what would *you* think if you saw them wearing their suits that were supposed to be bare skin? Naked suits, I called them. And all those well-dressed, cultured people clapping at them, accepting even though they knew perfectly well . . . like a sort of Emperor's New Clothes in reverse. Now just think, there are only two sexes and every one of us *is* one of those and certainly, presumably that is, knows something of the other. But then that may be where I have been making my mistake. You'd think . . . why, just what I *did* start thinking: that there must be Others among us.

But it is not out of fear or disgust that I am looking for them. I am open and unprejudiced. You can see that I am when I say that I've never seen (and doesn't this seem strange?) the very organs of my own conception, neither my father nor my mother. Goodness knows what *they* were and what this might make me?

So I wait here, tapping my toes inside my slippers and chewing hangnails off my fingers. I contemplate the unvarnished underside of the desk top. I ridge it with my thumbnail. I eat more cookies and think whether I should make his bed for him or not but decided not to. I suck my arm until it is red in the soft crook opposite the elbow. Time jerks ahead as slowly as a school clock, and I crawl across the floor and stretch out behind the books and magazines. I read first paragraphs of dozens of them. What with the dust back here and lying in the shirts and socks before, I'm getting a certain smell and a sort of grey, animal fuzz that makes me feel safer, as though I really did belong in this room and could actually creep around and not be noticed by Mr Morrison at all except perhaps for a pat on the head as I pass him.

Thump . . . pause. Clump . . . pause. One can't miss his step. The house shouts his presence. The floors wake up squeaking and lean towards the stairway. The banister slides away from his slippery ham-hands. The wallpaper seems suddenly full of bugs. He must think: Well, this time she isn't peeking out of her doorway at me. A relief. I can concentrate completely on climbing up. Lift the legs against the pressure. Ooo. Ump. Pause and seem to be looking at the picture on the wall.

I skitter back under the desk.

It's strange that the first thing he does is to put his newspaper on the desk and sit down with his knees next to my nose, regular walls, furnaces of knees, exuding heat and dampness, throwing off a miasma delicately scented of wet wool and sweat. What a wide roundness they have to them, those knees. Mother's breasts pressing towards me. Probably as soft. Why can't I put my cheek against them? Observe how he can sit so still with no toe tapping, no rhythmic tensing of the thigh. He's not like the rest of us, but could a man like this do *little* things?

How the circumstantial evidence piles up, but that is all I've had so far and it is time for something concrete. One thing, just one fact, is all I need.

He reads and adjusts the clothing at his crotch and reads again. He breathes out winds of sausages and garlic and I remember that it is after supper and I take out my cheese and eat it as slowly as possible in little rabbit bites. I make a little piece last a half an hour.

At last he goes down the hall to the bathroom and I shift back under the shirts and socks and stretch my legs. What if he undresses like my grandmother did, under a nightgown? Under, for him, some giant, double-bed-sized thing?

But he doesn't. He hangs his coat on the little hanger and his tie on the closet doorknob. I receive his shirt and have to make myself another spy hole. Then off with the shoes, then socks. Off come the huge pants with slow, unseeing effort (he stares out the window). He begins on his yellowed undershorts, scratching himself first behind and starting earthquakes across his buttocks.

Where could he have bought those elephantine undershorts? In what store were they once folded on the shelf? In what factory did women sit at sewing-machines and put out one after another after another of those other-worldly items? Mars? Venus? Saturn more

likely. Or perhaps, instead, a tiny place, some moon of Jupiter with
less air per square inch upon the skin and less gravity, where Mr
Morrison can take the stairs three at a time and jump the fences (for
surely he's not particularly old) and dance all night with girls his
own size.

He squints his oriental eyes towards the ceiling light and takes
off the shorts, lets them fall loosely to the floor. I see Alleghenies
of thigh and buttock. How does a man like that stand naked even
before a small-sized mirror? I lose myself, hypnotized. Impossible
to tell the colour of his skin, just as it is with blue-grey eyes or the
ocean. How tan, pink, olive and red and sometimes a bruised
elephant-grey. His eyes must be used to multiplicities like this, and
to plethoras, conglomerations, to an opulence of self, to an intemper-
ant exuberance, to the universal, the astronomical.

I find myself completely tamed. I lie in my cocoon of shirts not
even shivering. My eyes do not take in what they see. He is utterly
beyond my comprehension. Can you imagine how thin my wrists
must seem to him? He is thinking (if he thinks of me at all), he
thinks: She might be from another world. How alien her ankles and
leg bones. How her eyes do stand out. How green her complexion
in the shadows at the edges of her face. (For I must admit that
perhaps I may be as far along the scale at my end of humanity as he
is at his.)

Suddenly I feel like singing. My breath purrs in my throat in
hymns as slow as Mr Morrison himself would sing. Can this be
love, I wonder? My first *real* love? But haven't I always been
passionately interested in people? Or rather in those who caught
my fancy? But isn't this feeling different? Can love really have come
to me this late in life? (La, la, lee la from whom all blessings flow.)
I shut my eyes and duck my head into the shirts. I grin into the
dirty socks. Can you imagine *him* making love to *me*!

Well below his abstracted, ceilingward gazes, I crawl on elbows
and knees back behind the old books. A safer place to shake out the
silliness. Why, I'm old enough for him to be (had I ever married)
my youngest son of all. Yet if he were a son of mine, how he
would have grown beyond me. I see that I cannot ever follow him
(as with all sons). I must love him as a mouse might love the hand
that cleans the cage, and as uncomprehendingly too, for surely I see
only a part of him here. I sense more. I sense deeper largenesses. I

sense excesses of bulk I cannot yet imagine. Rounded after-images linger on my eyeballs. There seems to be a mysterious darkness in the corners of the room and his shadow covers, at the same time, the window on one wall and the mirror on the other. Certainly he is like an iceberg, seven eighths submerged.

But now he has turned towards me. I peep from the books holding a magazine over my head as one does when it rains. I do so more to shield myself from too much of him all at once than to hide.

And there we are, confronting each other eye to eye. We stare and he cannot seem to comprehend me any more than I can comprehend him, and yet usually his mind is ahead of mine, jumping away on unfinished phrases. His eyes are not even wistful and not yet surprised. But his belly button, that is another story. Here is the eye of God at last. It nestles in a vast, bland sky like a sun on the curve of the universe flashing me a wink of heat, a benign, fat wink. The stomach eye accepts and understands. The stomach eye recognizes me and looks at me as I've always wished to be looked at. (Yea, though I walk through the valley of the shadow of death.) I see you now.

But I see him now. The skin hangs in loose, plastic folds just there, and there is a little copper-coloured circle like a fifty-cent piece made out of pennies. There's a hole in the centre and it is corroded green at the edges. This must be a kind of 'naked suit' and whatever the sex organs may be, they are hidden behind this hot, pocked and pitted imitation skin.

I look up into those girlish eyes of his and they are as blank as though the eyeballs were all whites, as blank as having no sex at all, eggs without yolks, like being built like a boy-doll with a round hole for the water to empty out.

God, I think. I am not religious but I think, My God, and then I stand up and somehow, in a limping run, I get out of there and down the stairs as though I fly. I slam the door of my room and slide in under my bed. The most obvious of hiding-places, but after I am there I can't bear to move out. I lie and listen for his thunder on the stairs, the roar of his feet splintering the steps, his hand tossing away the banister.

I know what I'll say. 'I accept, I accept,' I'll say. 'I will love, I love already, whatever you are.'

I lie listening, watching the hanging edges of my bedspread in the absolute silence of the house. Can there be anyone here at all in such a strange quietness? Must I doubt even my own existence?

'Goodness knows,' I'll say, 'if I'm normal myself.' (How is one to know such things when everything is hidden?) 'Tell all of them that we accept. Tell them it's the naked suits that are ugly. Your dingles, your dangles, wrinkles, ruts, bumps and humps we accept whatever there is. Your loops, strings, worms, buttons, figs, cherries, flower petals, your soft little toad-shapes, warty and greenish, your cat's tongues or rat's tails, your oysters, one-eyed between your legs, garter snakes, snails, we accept. We think the truth is lovable.'

But what a long silence this is. Where is he? For he must (mustn't he?) come after me for what I saw. But where has he gone? Perhaps he thinks I've locked my door, but I haven't. I haven't.

Why doesn't he come?

•

ALIFA RIFAAT
My World of the Unknown
(*c*.1971)

Working exclusively inside Arabian culture – she has apparently read no Western literature apart from occasional translations – the Egyptian writer Alifa Rifaat expresses in her stories a form of dissatisfaction very different from that of more Western-influenced authors like Laila Baalabaki.

In Rifaat's work the traditional structure of Muslim society, with its Qur'anic precept that 'men are in charge of women' and where adultery is simply a Sin, is not challenged; her questions concern women's rights within this structure – including the right to sexual fulfilment. In this early story, 'My World of the Unknown', the woman's thoughts as she lies beside her indifferent husband are not of satisfaction with another man, but turn to fantasies of another, altogether stranger kind.

There are many mysteries in life, unseen powers in the universe, worlds other than our own, hidden links and radiations that draw creatures together and whose effect is interacting. They may merge or be incompatible, and perhaps the day will come when science will find a method for connecting up these worlds in the same way as it has made it possible to voyage to other planets. Who knows?

Yet one of these other worlds I have explored; I have lived in it and been linked with its creatures through the bond of love. I used to pass with amazing speed between this tangible world of ours and another invisible earth, mixing in the two worlds on one and the same day, as though living it twice over.

When entering into the world of my love, and being summoned and yielding to its call, no one around me would be aware of what was happening to me. All that occurred was that I would be overcome by something resembling a state of languor and would go off into a semi-sleep. Nothing about me would change except that I would become very silent and withdrawn, though I am normally a person who is talkative and eager to go out into the world of people. I would yearn to be on my own, would long for the moment of surrender as I prepared myself for answering the call.

Love had its beginning when an order came through for my husband to be transferred to a quiet country town and, being too busy with his work, delegated to me the task of going to this town to choose suitable accommodation prior to his taking up the new appointment. He cabled one of his subordinates named Kamil and asked him to meet me at the station and to assist me.

I took the early morning train. The images of a dream I had had that night came to me as I looked out at the vast fields and gauged the distances between the towns through which the train passed and reckoned how far it was between the new town in which we were fated to live and beloved Cairo.

The images of the dream kept reappearing to me, forcing themselves upon my mind: images of a small white house surrounded by a garden with bushes bearing yellow flowers, a house lying on the edge of a broad canal in which were swans and tall sailing boats. I kept on wondering at my dream and trying to analyse it. Perhaps it was some secret wish I had had, or maybe the echo of some image that my unconscious had stored up and was chewing over.

As the train arrived at its destination, I awoke from my thoughts. I found Kamil awaiting me. We set out in his car, passing through the local souk. I gazed at the mounds of fruit with delight, chatting away happily with Kamil. When we emerged from the souk we found ourselves on the bank of the Mansoura canal, a canal on which swans swam and sailing boats moved to and fro. I kept staring at them with uneasy longing. Kamil directed the driver to the residential buildings the governorate had put up for housing government employees. While gazing at the opposite bank a large boat with a great fluttering sail glided past. Behind it could be seen a white house that had a garden with trees with yellow flowers and that lay on its own amidst vast fields. I shouted out in confusion, overcome by the feeling that I had been here before.

'Go to that house,' I called to the driver. Kamil leapt up, objecting vehemently: 'No, no – no one lives in that house. The best thing is to go to the employees' buildings.'

I shouted insistently, like someone hypnotized: 'I must have a look at that house.' 'All right,' he said. 'You won't like it, though – it's old and needs repairing.' Giving in to my wish, he ordered the driver to make his way there.

At the garden door we found a young woman, spare and of fair complexion. A fat child with ragged clothes encircled her neck with his burly legs. In a strange silence, she stood as though nailed to the ground, barring the door with her hands and looking at us with doltish inquiry.

I took a sweet from my bag and handed it to the boy. He snatched it eagerly, tightening his grip on her neck with his podgy, mud-bespattered feet so that her face became flushed from his high-spirited embrace. A half-smile showed on her tightly closed lips. Taking courage, I addressed her in a friendly tone: 'I'd like to see over this house.' She braced her hands resolutely against the door. 'No,' she said quite simply. I turned helplessly to Kamil, who went up to her and pushed her violently in the chest so that she staggered back. 'Don't you realize,' he shouted at her, 'that this is the director's wife? Off with you!'

Lowering her head so that the child all but slipped from her, she walked off dejectedly to the canal bank where she lay down on the ground, put the child on her lap, and rested her head in her hands in silent submission.

Moved by pity, I remonstrated: 'There's no reason to be so

rough, Mr Kamil. Who is the woman?' 'Some mad woman,' he said with a shrug of his shoulders, 'who's a stranger to the town. Out of kindness the owner of this house put her in charge of it until someone should come along to live in it.'

With increased interest I said: 'Will he be asking a high rent for it?' 'Not at all,' he said with an enigmatic smile. 'He'd welcome anyone taking it over. There are no restrictions and the rent is modest – no more than four pounds.'

I was beside myself with joy. Who in these days can find somewhere to live for such an amount? I rushed through the door into the house with Kamil behind me and went over the rooms: five spacious rooms with wooden floors, with a pleasant hall, modern lavatory, and a beautifully roomy kitchen with a large veranda overlooking vast pistachio-green fields of generously watered rice. A breeze, limpid and cool, blew, playing with the tips of the crop and making the delicate leaves move in continuous dancing waves.

I went back to the first room with its spacious balcony overlooking the road and revealing the other bank of the canal where, along its strand, extended the houses of the town. Kamil pointed out to me a building facing the house on the other side. 'That's where we work,' he said, 'and behind it is where the children's schools are.'

'Thanks be to God,' I said joyfully. 'It means that everything is within easy reach of this house – and the souk's near by too.' 'Yes,' he said, 'and the fishermen will knock at your door to show you the fresh fish they've caught in their nets. But the house needs painting and redoing, also there are all sorts of rumours about it – the people around here believe in djinn and spirits.'

'This house is going to be my home,' I said with determination. 'Its low rent will make up for whatever we may have to spend on redoing it. You'll see what this house will look like when I get the garden arranged. As for the story about djinn and spirits, just leave them to us – we're more spirited than them.'

We laughed at my joke as we left the house. On my way to the station we agreed about the repairs that needed doing to the house. Directly I reached Cairo I cabled my husband to send the furniture from the town we had been living in, specifying a suitable date to fit in with the completion of the repairs and the house being ready for occupation.

*

On the date fixed I once again set off and found that all my wishes had been carried out and that the house was pleasantly spruce with its rooms painted a cheerful orange tinge, the floors well polished and the garden tidied up and made into small flowerbeds.

I took possession of the keys and Kamil went off to attend to his business, having put a chair on the front balcony for me to sit on while I awaited the arrival of the furniture van. I stretched out contentedly in the chair and gazed at the two banks with their towering trees like two rows of guards between which passed the boats with their lofty sails, while around them glided a male swan heading a flotilla of females. Halfway across the canal he turned and flirted with them, one after the other, like a sultan amidst his harem.

Relaxed, I closed my eyes. I projected myself into the future and pictured to myself the enjoyment I would have in this house after it had been put in order and the garden fixed up. I awoke to the touch of clammy fingers shaking me by the shoulders.

I started and found myself staring at the fair-complexioned woman with her child squatting on her shoulders as she stood erect in front of me staring at me in silence. 'What do you want?' I said to her sharply. 'How did you get in?' 'I got in with this,' she said simply, revealing a key between her fingers.

I snatched the key from her hand as I loudly rebuked her: 'Give it here. We have rented the house and you have no right to come into it like this.' 'I have a lot of other keys,' she answered briefly. 'And what,' I said to her, 'do you want of this house?' 'I want to stay on in it and for you to go,' she said. I laughed in amazement at her words as I asked myself: Is she really mad? Finally I said impatiently: 'Listen here, I'm not leaving here and you're not entering this house unless I wish it. My husband is coming with the children, and the furniture is on the way. He'll be arriving in a little while and we'll be living here for such period of time as my husband is required to work in this town.'

She looked at me in a daze. For a long time she was silent, then she said: 'All right, your husband will stay with me and you can go.' Despite my utter astonishment I felt pity for her. 'I'll allow you to stay on with us for the little boy's sake,' I said to her gently, 'until you find yourself another place. If you'd like to help me with the housework I'll pay you what you ask.'

Shaking her head, she said with strange emphasis: 'I'm not a servant. I'm Aneesa.' 'You're not staying here,' I said to her coldly, rising to my feet. Collecting all my courage and emulating Kamil's determination when he rebuked her, I began pushing her in the chest as I caught hold of the young boy's hand. 'Get out of here and don't come near this house,' I shouted at her. 'Let me have all the keys. I'll not let go of your child till you've given them all to me.'

With a set face that did not flicker she put her hand to her bosom and took out a ring on which were several keys, which she dropped into my hand. I released my grip on the young boy. Supporting him on her shoulders, she started to leave. Regretting my harshness, I took out several piastres from my bag and placed them in the boy's hand. With the same silence and stiffness she wrested the piastres from the boy's hand and gave them back to me. Then she went straight out. Bolting the door this time, I sat down, tense and upset, to wait.

My husband arrived, then the furniture, and for several days I occupied myself with putting the house in order. My husband was busy with his work and the children occupied themselves with making new friends and I completely forgot about Aneesa, that is until my husband returned one night wringing his hands with fury: 'This woman Aneesa, can you imagine that since we came to live in this house she's been hanging around it every night. Tonight she was so crazy she blocked my way and suggested I should send you off so that she might live with me. The woman's gone completely off her head about this house and I'm afraid she might do something to the children or assault you.'

Joking with him and masking the jealousy that raged within me, I said: 'And what is there for you to get angry about? She's a fair and attractive enough woman – a blessing brought to your very doorstep!' With a sneer he took up the telephone, muttering: 'May God look after her!'

He contacted the police and asked them to come and take her away. When I heard the sound of the police van coming I ran to the window and saw them taking her off. The poor woman did not resist, did not object, but submitted with a gentle sadness that as usual with her aroused one's pity. Yet, when she saw me standing in tears and watching her, she turned to me and, pointing to the wall of the house, called out: 'I'll leave her to you.' 'Who?' I shouted. 'Who, Aneesa?' Once again pointing at the bottom of the house, she said: 'Her.'

The van took her off and I spent a sleepless night. No sooner did day come than I hurried to the garden to examine my plants and to walk round the house and carefully inspect its walls. All I found were some cracks, the house being old, and I laughed at the frivolous thought that came to me: Could, for example, there be jewels buried here, as told in fairy tales?

Who could 'she' be? What was the secret of this house? Who was Aneesa and was she really mad? Where were she and her son living? So great did my concern for Aneesa become that I began pressing my husband with questions until he brought me news of her. The police had learnt that she was the wife of a well-to-do teacher living in a nearby town. One night he had caught her in an act of infidelity, and in fear she had fled with her son and had settled here, no one knowing why she had betaken herself to this particular house. However, the owner of the house had been good enough to allow her to put up in it until someone should come to live in it, while some kind person had intervened on her behalf to have her name included among those receiving monthly allowances from the Ministry of Social Affairs. There were many rumours that cast doubt upon her conduct: people passing by her house at night would hear her conversing with unknown persons. Her madness took the form of a predilection for silence and isolation from people during the daytime as she wandered about in a dream world. After the police had persuaded them to take her in to safeguard the good repute of her family, she was returned to her relatives.

The days passed and the story of Aneesa was lost in oblivion. Winter came and with it heavy downpours of rain. The vegetation in my garden flourished though the castor-oil plants withered and their yellow flowers fell. I came to find pleasure in sitting out on the kitchen balcony looking at my flowers and vegetables and enjoying the belts of sunbeams that lay between the clouds and lavished my balcony with warmth and light.

One sunny morning my attention was drawn to the limb of a nearby tree whose branches curved up gracefully despite its having dried up and its dark bark being cracked. My gaze was attracted by something twisting and turning along the tip of a branch: bands of yellow and others of red, intermingled with bands of black, were creeping forward. It was a long, smooth tube, at its end a small striped head with two bright, wary eyes.

The snake curled round on itself in spiral rings, then tautened its body and moved forward. The sight gripped me; I felt terror turning my blood cold and freezing my limbs.

My senses were numbed, my soul intoxicated with a strange elation at the exciting beauty of the snake. I was rooted to the spot, wavering between two thoughts that contended in my mind at one and the same time: should I snatch up some implement from the kitchen and kill the snake, or should I enjoy the rare moment of beauty that had been afforded me?

As though the snake had read what was passing through my mind, it raised its head, tilting it to right and left in thrilling coquetry. Then, by means of two tiny fangs like pearls, and a golden tongue like a twig of *arak* wood, it smiled at me and fastened its eyes on mine in one fleeting, commanding glance. The thought of killing left me. I felt a current, a radiation from its eyes that penetrated to my heart ordering me to stay where I was. A warning against continuing to sit out there in front of it surged inside me, but my attraction to it paralysed my limbs and I did not move. I kept on watching it, utterly entranced and captivated. Like a bashful virgin being lavished with compliments, it tried to conceal its pride in its beauty, and, having made certain of captivating its lover, the snake coyly twisted round and gently, gracefully glided away until swallowed up by a crack in the wall. Could the snake be the 'she' that Aneesa had referred to on the day of her departure?

At last I rose from my place, overwhelmed by the feeling that I was on the brink of a new world, a new destiny, or rather, if you wish, the threshold of a new love. I threw myself on to the bed in a dreamlike state, unaware of the passage of time. No sooner, though, did I hear my husband's voice and the children with their clatter as they returned at noon than I regained my sense of being a human being, wary and frightened about itself, determined about the existence and continuance of its species. Without intending to I called out: 'A snake – there's a snake in the house.'

My husband took up the telephone and some men came and

searched the house. I pointed out to them the crack into which the snake had disappeared, though racked with a feeling of remorse at being guilty of betrayal. For here I was denouncing the beloved, inviting people against it after it had felt safe with me.

The men found no trace of the snake. They burned some wormwood and fumigated the hole but without result. Then my husband summoned Sheikh Farid, Sheikh of the Rifa'iyya order in the town, who went on chanting verses from the Qur'an as he tapped the ground with his stick. He then asked to speak to me alone and said:

'Madam, the sovereign of the house has sought you out and what you saw is no snake, rather it is one of the monarchs of the earth – may God make your words pleasant to them – who has appeared to you in the form of a snake. Here in this house there are many holes of snakes, but they are of the non-poisonous kind. They inhabit houses and go and come as they please. What you saw, though, is something else.'

'I don't believe a word of it,' I said, stupefied. 'This is nonsense. I know that the djinn are creatures that actually exist, but they are not in touch with our world, there is no contact between them and the world of humans.'

With an enigmatic smile he said: 'My child, the Prophet went out to them and read the Qur'an to them in their country. Some of them are virtuous and some of them are Muslims, and how do you know there is no contact between us and them? Let your prayer be "O Lord, increase me in knowledge" and do not be nervous. Your purity of spirit, your translucence of soul have opened to you doors that will take you to other worlds known only to their Creator. Do not be afraid. Even if you should find her one night sleeping in your bed, do not be alarmed but talk to her with all politeness and friendliness.'

'That's enough of all that, Sheikh Farid. Thank you,' I said, alarmed, and he left us.

We went on discussing the matter. 'Let's be practical,' suggested my husband, 'and stop all the cracks at the bottom of the outside walls and put wire mesh over the windows, also paint wormwood all round the garden fence.'

We set about putting into effect what we had agreed. I, though, no longer dared to go out on to the balconies. I neglected my garden and stopped wandering about in it. Generally I would spend my free time in bed. I changed to being someone who liked to sit around lazily and was disinclined to mix with people; those diversions and recreations that previously used to tempt me no longer gave me any pleasure. All I wanted was to stretch myself out and drowse. In bewilderment I asked myself: Could it be that I was in love? But how could I love a snake? Or could she really be one of the daughters of the monarchs of the djinn? I would awake from my musings to find that I had been wandering in my thoughts and recalling to mind how magnificent she was. And what is the secret of her beauty? I would ask myself. Was it that I was fascinated by her multi-coloured, supple body? Or was it that I had been dazzled by that intelligent, commanding way she had of looking at me? Or could it be the sleek way she had of gliding along, so excitingly dangerous, that had captivated me?

Excitingly dangerous! No doubt it was this excitement that had stirred my feelings and awakened my love, for did they not make films to excite and frighten? There was no doubt but that the secret of my passion for her, my preoccupation with her, was due to the excitement that had aroused, through intense fear, desire within myself; an excitement that was sufficiently strong to drive the blood hotly through my veins whenever the memory of her came to me, thrusting the blood in bursts that made my heart beat wildly, my limbs limp. And so, throwing myself down in a pleasurable state of torpor, my craving for her would be awakened and I would wish for her coil-like touch, her graceful gliding motion.

And yet I fell to wondering how union could come about, how craving be quenched, the delights of the body be realized, between a woman and a snake. And did she, I wondered, love me and want me as I loved her? An idea would obtrude itself upon me sometimes: did Cleopatra, the very legend of love, have sexual intercourse with her serpent after having given up sleeping with men, having wearied of amorous adventures with them so that her sated instincts were no longer moved other than by the excitement of fear, her senses no longer aroused other than by bites from a snake? And the last of her lovers had been a viper that had destroyed her.

I came to live in a state of continuous torment, for a strange feeling of longing scorched my body and rent my senses, while my circumstances obliged me to carry out the duties and responsibilities that had been placed on me as the wife of a man who occupied an important position in the small town, he and his family being objects of attention and his house a Kaaba for those seeking favours; also as a mother who must look after her children and concern herself with every detail of their lives so as to exercise control over them; there was also the house and its chores, this house that was inhabited by the mysterious lover who lived in a world other than mine. How, I wondered, was union between us to be achieved? Was wishing for this love a sin or was there nothing to reproach myself about?

And as my self-questioning increased so did my yearning, my curiosity, my desire. Was the snake from the world of reptiles or from the djinn? When would the meeting be? Was she, I wondered, aware of me and would she return out of pity for my consuming passion? One stormy morning with the rain pouring down so hard that I could hear the drops rattling on the window-pane, I lit the stove and lay down in bed between the covers seeking refuge from an agonizing trembling that racked my yearning body which, ablaze with unquenchable desire, called out for relief.

I heard a faint rustling sound coming from the corner of the wall right beside my bed. I looked down and kept my eyes fixed on one of the holes in the wall, which I found was slowly, very slowly, expanding. Closing my eyes, my heart raced with joy and my body throbbed with mounting desire as there dawned in me the hope of an encounter. I lay back in submission to what was to be. No longer did I care whether love was coming from the world of reptiles or from that of the djinn, sovereigns of the world. Even were this love to mean my destruction, my desire for it was greater.

I heard a hissing noise that drew nearer, then it changed to a gentle whispering in my ear, calling to me: 'I am love, O enchantress. I showed you my home in your sleep; I called you to my kingdom when your soul was dozing on the horizon of dreams, so come, my sweet beloved, come and let us explore the depths of the azure sea of pleasure. There, in the chamber of coral, amidst cool, shady rocks where reigns deep, restful silence lies our bed, lined with soft, bright green damask, inlaid with pearls newly wrenched from their shells. Come, let me sleep with you as I have slept with beautiful women and have given them bliss. Come, let me prise out your pearl from its shell that I may polish it and bring forth its splendour. Come to where no one will find us, where no one will see us, for the eyes of swimming creatures are innocent and will not heed what we do nor understand what we say. Down there lies repose, lies a cure for all your yearnings and ills. Come, without fear or dread, for no creature will reach us in our hidden world, and only the eye of God alone will see us; He alone will know what we are about and He will watch over us.'

I began to be intoxicated by the soft musical whisperings. I felt her cool and soft and smooth, her coldness producing a painful convulsion in my body and hurting me to the point of terror. I felt her as she slipped between the covers, then her two tiny fangs, like two pearls, began to caress my body; arriving at my thighs, the golden tongue, like an *arak* twig, inserted its pronged tip between them and began sipping and exhaling; sipping the poisons of my desire and exhaling the nectar of my ecstasy, till my whole body tingled and started to shake in sharp, painful, rapturous spasms – and all the while the tenderest of words were whispered to me as I confided to her all my longings.

At last the cool touch withdrew, leaving me exhausted. I went into a deep slumber to awake at noon full of energy, all of me a joyful burgeoning to life. Curiosity and a desire to know who it was seized me again. I looked at the corner of the wall and found that the hole was wide open. Once again I was overcome by fear. I pointed out the crack to my husband, unable to utter, although terror had once again awakened in me passionate desire. My husband filled up the crack with cement and went to sleep.

Morning came and everyone went out. I finished my housework and began roaming around the rooms in boredom, battling against the desire to surrender myself to sleep. I sat in the hallway and suddenly she appeared before me, gentle as an angel, white as day, softly undulating and flexing herself, calling to me in her bewitching whisper: 'Bride of mine, I called you and brought you to my home. I have wedded you, so there is no sin in our love, nothing to reproach yourself about. I am the guardian of the house, and I hold sway over the snakes and vipers that inhabit it, so come and I shall show you where they live. Have no fear so long as we are together. You and I are in accord. Bring a container with water and I shall place my fingers over your hand and we shall recite together some verses from the Qur'an, then we shall sprinkle it in the places from which they emerge and shall thus close the doors on them, and it shall be a pact between us that your hands will not do harm to them.'

'Then you are one of the monarchs of the djinn?' I asked eagerly. 'Why do you not bring me treasures and riches as we hear about in fables when a human takes as sister her companion among the djinn?'

She laughed at my words, shaking her golden hair that was like dazzling threads of light. She whispered to me, coquettishly: 'How greedy is mankind! Are not the pleasures of the body enough? Were I to come to you with wealth we would both die consumed by fire.'

'No, no,' I called out in alarm. 'God forbid that I should ask for unlawful wealth. I merely asked it of you as a test, that it might be positive proof that I am not imagining things and living in dreams.'

She said: 'And do intelligent humans have to have something tangible as evidence? By God, do you not believe in His ability to create worlds and living beings? Do you not know that you have an existence in worlds other than that of matter and the transitory? Fine, since you ask for proof, come close to me and my caresses will put vitality back into your limbs. You will retain your youth. I shall give you abiding youth and the delights of love – and they are more precious than wealth in the world of man. How many fortunes have women spent in quest of them? As for me I shall feed from the poisons of your desire, the exhalations of your burning passion, for that is my nourishment and through it I live.'

'I thought that your union with me was for love, not for nourishment and the perpetuation of youth and vigour,' I said in amazement.

'And is sex anything but food for the body and an interaction in union and love?' she said. 'Is it not this that makes human beings happy and is the secret of feeling joy and elation?'

She stretched out her radiant hand to my body, passing over it like the sun's rays and discharging into it warmth and a sensation of languor.

'I am ill,' I said. 'I am ill. I am ill,' I kept on repeating. When he heard me my husband brought the doctor, who said: 'High blood pressure, heart trouble, nervous depression.' Having prescribed various medicaments he left. The stupidity of doctors! My doctor did not know that he was describing the symptoms of love, did not even know it was from love I was suffering. Yet I knew my illness and the secret of my cure. I showed my husband the enlarged hole in the wall and once again he stopped it up. We then carried the bed to another corner.

After some days had passed I found another hole alongside my bed. My beloved came and whispered to me: 'Why are you so coy and flee from me, my bride? Is it fear of your being rebuffed or is it from aversion? Are you not happy with our being together? Why do you want for us to be apart?'

'I am in agony,' I whispered back. 'Your love is so intense and the desire to enjoy you so consuming. I am frightened I shall feel that I am tumbling down into a bottomless pit and being destroyed.'

'My beloved,' she said. 'I shall only appear to you in beauty's most immaculate form.'

'But it is natural for you to be a man,' I said in a precipitate outburst, 'seeing that you are so determined to have a love affair with me.'

'Perfect beauty is to be found only in woman,' she said, 'so yield to me and I shall let you taste undreamed of happiness; I shall guide you to worlds possessed of such beauty as you have never imagined.'

She stretched out her fingers to caress me, while her delicate mouth sucked in the poisons of my desire and exhaled the nectar of my ecstasy, carrying me off into a trance of delicious happiness.

After that we began the most pleasurable of love affairs, wandering together in worlds and living on horizons of dazzling beauty, a world fashioned of jewels, a world whose every moment was radiant with light and formed a thousand shapes, a thousand colours.

As for the opening in the wall, I no longer took any notice. I no longer complained of feeling ill, in fact there burned within me abounding vitality. Sometimes I would bring a handful of wormwood and, by way of jest, would stop up the crack, just as the beloved teases her lover and closes the window in his face that, ablaze with desire for her, he may hasten to the door. After that I would sit for a long time and enjoy watching the wormwood powder being scattered in spiral rings by unseen puffs of wind. Then I would throw myself down on the bed and wait.

For months I immersed myself in my world, no longer calculating time or counting the days, until one morning my husband went out on the balcony lying behind our favoured wall alongside the bed. After a while I heard him utter a cry of alarm. We all hurried out to find him holding a stick, with a black, ugly snake almost two metres long, lying at his feet.

I cried out with a sorrow whose claws clutched at my heart so that it began to beat wildly. With crazed fury I shouted at my husband: 'Why have you broken the pact and killed it? What harm has it done?' How cruel is man! He lets no creature live in peace.

I spent the night sorrowful and apprehensive. My lover came to me and embraced me more passionately then ever. I whispered to her imploringly: 'Be kind, beloved. Are you angry with me or sad because of me?'

'It is farewell,' she said. 'You have broken the pact and have betrayed one of my subjects, so you must both depart from this house, for only love lives in it.'

In the morning I packed up so that we might move to one of the employees' buildings, leaving the house in which I had learnt of love and enjoyed incomparable pleasures.

I still live in memory and in hope. I crave for the house and miss my secret love. Who knows, perhaps one day my beloved will call me. Who really knows?

Translated by Denys Johnson-Davies

•

ANGELA CARTER
Flesh and the Mirror

(*c.* 1972)

Angela Carter's fiction has been described as both 'neo-Gothic' and 'magic realism'. From her first novel, The Magic Toyshop *(1967) to later works such as* The Bloody Chamber *(1979) and* Nights at the Circus *(1984), her work displays an extraordinary talent, which tackles the most challenging issues of female sexuality (and much else besides) provocatively and very entertainingly.*

From working-class origins in the north of England, she worked first as a journalist and later as an academic and writer in Britain, the USA and Japan, where 'Flesh and the Mirror' is set. Amongst her non-fiction works are The Sadean Woman *(1979) and* Nothing Sacred *(1982). She also co-wrote the screenplay for* The Company of Wolves, *which was based on one of her stories.*

She died in 1992 at the age of fifty-two.

It was midnight – I chose my times and set my scenes with the precision of the born artiste. Hadn't I gone eight thousand miles to find a climate with enough anguish and hysteria in it to satisfy me? I had arrived back in Yokohama that evening from a visit to England and nobody met me, although I expected him. So I took the train to Tokyo, half an hour's journey. First, I was angry; but the poignancy of my own situation overcame me and then I was sad. To return to the one you love and find him absent! My heart used to jump like Pavlov's dogs at the prospect of such a treat; I positively salivated at the suggestion of un-pleasure, I was sure that *that* was real life. I'm told I always look lonely when I'm alone; that is because, when I was an intolerable adolescent, I learned to sit with my coat collar turned up in a lonely way, so that people would talk to me. And I can't drop the habit even now, though, now, it's only a habit and, I realize, a predatory habit.

It was midnight and I was crying bitterly as I walked under the artificial cherry blossom with which they decorate the lamp standards from April to September. They do that so the pleasure quarters will have the look of a continuous carnival, no matter what ripples of agitation disturb the never-ceasing, endlessly circulating, quiet, gentle, melancholy crowds who throng the wet web of alleys under a false ceiling of umbrellas. All looked as desolate as Mardi Gras. I was searching among a multitude of unknown faces for the face of the one I loved while the warm, thick, heavy rain of summer greased the dark surfaces of the streets until, after a while, they began to gleam like sleek fur of seals just risen from the bottom of the sea.

The crowds lapped round me like waves full of eyes until I felt that I was walking through an ocean whose speechless and gesticulating inhabitants, like those with whom medieval philosophers peopled the countries of the deep, were methodical inversions or mirror images of the dwellers on dry land. And I moved through these expressionist perspectives in my black dress as though I was the creator of all and of myself, too, in a black dress, in love, crying, walking through the city in the third person singular, my own heroine, as though the world stretched out from my eye like spokes from a sensitized hub that galvanized all to life when I looked at it.

I think I know, now, what I was trying to do. I was trying to subdue the city by turning it into a projection of my own growing pains. What solipsistic arrogance! The city, the largest city in the world, the city designed to suit not one of my European expectations, this city presents the foreigner with a mode of life that seems to him to have the enigmatic transparency, the indecipherable clarity, of dream. And it is a dream he could, himself, never have dreamed. The stranger, the foreigner, thinks he is in control; but he has been precipitated into somebody else's dream.

You never know what will happen in Tokyo. Anything can happen.

I had been attracted to the city first because I suspected it contained enormous histrionic resources. I was always rummaging in the dressing-up box of the heart for suitable appearances to adopt in the city. That was the way I maintained my defences for, at that time, I always used to suffer a great deal if I let myself get too close to reality since the definitive world of the everyday with its hard edges and harsh light did not have enough resonance to echo the demands I made upon experience. It was as if I never experienced experience *as* experience. Living never lived up to the expectations I had of it – the Bovary syndrome. I was always imagining other things that could have been happening, instead, and so I always felt cheated, always dissatisfied.

Always dissatisfied, even if, like a perfect heroine, I wandered, weeping, on a forlorn quest for a lost lover through the aromatic labyrinth of alleys. And wasn't I in Asia? Asia! But, even though I lived there, it always seemed far away from me. It was as if there were glass between me and the world. But I could see myself perfectly well on the other side of the glass. There I was, walking up and down, eating meals, having conversations, in love, indifferent, and so on. But all the time I was pulling the strings of my own puppet; it was this puppet who was moving about on the other side of the glass. And I eyed the most marvellous adventures with the bored eye of the agent with the cigar watching another audition. I tapped out the ash and asked of events: 'What else can you do?'

So I attempted to rebuild the city according to the blueprint in my imagination as a backdrop to the plays in my puppet theatre, but it sternly refused to be so rebuilt; I was only imagining it had been so rebuilt. On the night I came back to it, however hard I looked for the one I loved, she could not find him anywhere and the city delivered her into the hands of a perfect stranger who fell into step beside her and asked why she was crying. She went with him to an unambiguous hotel with a mirror on the ceiling and lascivious black lace draped round a palpably illicit bed. His eyes were shaped like sequins. All night long, a thin, pale, sickle moon with a single star pendant at its nether tip floated upon the rain that pitter-pattered against the windows and there was a clockwork whirring of cicadas. From time to time, the windbell dangling from the eaves let out an exquisitely mournful tinkle.

None of the lyrical eroticism of this sweet, sad, moon night of summer rain had been within my expectations; I had half expected he would strangle me. My sensibility wilted under the burden of response. My sensibility foundered under the assault on my senses.

My imagination had been pre-empted.

The room was a box of oiled paper full of the echoes of the rain. After the light was out, as we lay together, I could still see the single shape of our embrace in the mirror above me, a marvellously unexpected conjunction cast at random by the enigmatic kaleido-scope of the city. Our pelts were stippled with the fretted shadows of the lace curtains as if our skins were a mysterious uniform provided by the management in order to render all those who made love in that hotel anonymous. The mirror annihilated time, place and person; at the consecration of this house, the mirror had been dedicated to the reflection of chance embraces. Therefore it treated flesh in an exemplary fashion, with charity and indifference.

The mirror distilled the essence of all the encounters of strangers whose perceptions of one another existed only in the medium of the chance embrace, the accidental. During the durationless time we spent making love, we were not ourselves, whoever that might have been, but in some sense the ghosts of ourselves. But the selves we were not, the selves of our own habitual perceptions of ourselves, had a far more insubstantial substance than the reflections we were. The magic mirror presented me with a hitherto unconsidered notion of myself as I. Without any intention of mine, I had been defined by the action reflected in the mirror. I beset me. I was the subject of the sentence written on the mirror. I was not watching it. There was nothing whatsoever beyond the surface of the glass. Nothing kept me from the fact, the act; I had been precipitated into knowledge of the real conditions of living.

Mirrors are ambiguous things. The bureaucracy of the mirror issues me with a passport to the world; it shows me my appearance. But what use is a passport to an armchair traveller? Women and mirrors are in complicity with one another to evade the action I/she performs that she/I cannot watch, the action with which I break out of the mirror, with which I assume my appearance. But *this* mirror refused to conspire with me; it was like the first mirror I'd ever seen. It reflected the embrace beneath it without the least guile. All it showed was inevitable. But I myself could never have dreamed it.

I saw the flesh and the mirror but I could not come to terms with the sight. My immediate response to it was to feel I'd acted out of character. The fancy-dress disguise I'd put on to suit the city had betrayed me to a room and a bed and a modification of myself that had no business at all in my life, not in the life I had watched myself performing.

Therefore I evaded the mirror. I scrambled out of its arms and sat on the edge of the bed and lit a fresh cigarette from the butt of the old one. The rain beat down. My demonstration of perturbation was perfect in every detail, just like the movies. I applauded it. I was gratified the mirror had not seduced me into behaving in a way I would have felt inappropriate – that is, shrugging and sleeping, as though my infidelity was not of the least importance. I now shook with the disturbing presentiment that he with his sequin eyes who'd been kind to me was an ironic substitute for the other one, the one I loved, as if the arbitrary carnival of the streets had gratuitously offered me this young man to find out if I *could* act out of character and then projected our intersection upon the mirror, as an objective lesson in the nature of things.

Therefore I dressed rapidly and ran away as soon as it was light outside, that mysterious, colourless light of dawn when the hooded crows flap out of the temple groves to perch on the telegraph poles, cawing a baleful dawn chorus to the echoing boulevards empty, now, of all the pleasure-seekers. The rain had stopped. It was an overcast morning so hot that I broke out into a sweat at the slightest movement. The bewildering electrographics of the city at night were all switched off. All the perspectives were pale, gritty grey, the air was full of dust. I never knew such a banal morning.

The morning before the night before, the morning before this oppressive morning, I woke up in the cabin of a boat. All the previous day, as we rounded the coast in bright weather, I dreamed of the reunion before me, a lovers' meeting refreshed by the three months I'd been gone, returning home due to a death in the family. I will come back as soon as I can – I'll write. Will you meet me at the pier? Of course, of course he will. But he was not at the pier; where was he?

So I went at once to the city and began my desolate tour of the pleasure quarters, looking for him in all the bars he used. He was nowhere to be found. I did not know his address, of course; he moved from rented room to rented room with the agility of the feckless and we had corresponded through accommodation addresses, coffee shops, poste restante, etc. Besides, there had been a displacement of mail reminiscent of the excesses of the nineteenth-century novel, such as it is difficult to believe and could only have been caused by a desperate emotional necessity to cause as much confusion as possible. Both of us prided ourselves on our passionate sensibilities, of course. That was *one* thing we had in common! So, although I thought I was the most romantic spectacle imaginable as I wandered weeping down the alleys, I was in reality at risk – I had fallen through one of the holes life leaves in it; these peculiar holes are the entrances to the counters at which you pay the price of the way you live.

Random chance operates in relation to these existential lacunae; one tumbles down them when, for the time being, due to hunger, despair, sleeplessness, hallucination or those accidental-on-purpose misreadings of train timetables and airline schedules that produce margins of empty time, one is lost. One is at the mercy of events. That is why I like to be a foreigner; I only travel for the insecurity. But I did not know that, then.

I found my self-imposed fate, my beloved, quite early that

morning but we quarrelled immediately. We quarrelled the day away assiduously and, when I tried to pull the strings of my self and so take control of the situation, I was astonished to find the situation I wanted was disaster, shipwreck. I saw his face as though it were in ruins, although it was the sight in the world I knew best and, the first time I saw it, had not seemed to me a face I did not know. It had seemed, in some way, to correspond to my idea of my own face. It had seemed a face long known and well remembered, a face that had always been imminent in my consciousness as an idea that now found its first visual expression.

So I suppose I do not know how he really looked and, in fact, I suppose I shall never know, now, for he was plainly an object created in the mode of fantasy. His image was already present somewhere in my head and I was seeking to discover it in actuality, looking at every face I met in case it was the right face – that is, the face which corresponded to my notion of the unseen face of the one I should love, a face created parthenogenetically by the rage to love which consumed me. So his self, and, by his self, I mean the thing he was to himself, was quite unknown to me. I created him solely in relation to myself, like a work of romantic art, an object corresponding to the ghost inside me. When I'd first loved him, I wanted to take him apart, as a child dismembers a clockwork toy, to comprehend the inscrutable mechanics of its interior. I wanted to see him far more naked than he was with his clothes off. It was easy enough to strip him bare and then I picked up my scalpel and set to work. But, since I was so absolutely in charge of the dissection, I only discovered what I was able to recognize already, from past experience, inside him. If ever I found anything new to me, I steadfastly ignored it. I was so absorbed in this work it never occurred to me to wonder if it hurt him.

In order to create the loved object in this way and to issue it with its certificate of authentication, as beloved, I had also to labour at the idea of myself in love. I watched myself closely for all the signs and, precisely upon cue, here they were! Longing, desire, self-abnegation, etc. I was racked by all the symptoms. Even so, in spite of this fugue of feeling, I had felt nothing but pleasure when the young man who picked me up inserted his sex inside me in the blue-movie bedroom. I only grew guilty later, when I realized I had not felt in the least guilty at the time. And was I in character when

I felt guilty or in character when I did not? I was perplexed. I no longer understood the logic of my own performance. My script had been scrambled behind my back. The cameraman was drunk. The director had had a *crise de nerfs* and been taken away to a sanatorium. And my co-star had picked himself up off the operating table and painfully cobbled himself together again according to his own design! All this had taken place while I was looking at the mirror.

Imagine my affront.

We quarrelled until night fell and, still quarrelling, found our way to another hotel but this hotel, and this night, was in every respect a parody of the previous night. (That's more like it! Squalor and humiliation! Ah!) Here, there were no lace drapes nor windbells nor moonlight nor any moist whisper of lugubriously seductive rain; this place was bleak, mean and cheerless and the sheets on the mattress they threw down on the floor for us were blotched with dirt although, at first, we did not notice that because it was necessary to pretend the urgent passion we always used to feel in one another's presence even if we felt it no longer, as if to act out the feeling with sufficient intensity would re-create it by sleight of hand, although our skins (which knew us better than we knew ourselves) told us the period of reciprocation was over. It was a mean room and the windows overlooked a parking lot with a freeway beyond it, so that the paper walls shuddered with the reverberations of the infernal clamour of the traffic. There was a sluggish electric fan with dead flies caught in the spokes and a single strip of neon overhead lit us and everything up with a scarcely tolerable, quite remorseless light. A slatternly woman in a filthy apron brought us glasses of thin, cold, brown tea made from barley and then she shut the door on us. I would not let him kiss me between the thighs because I was afraid he would taste the traces of last night's adventure, a little touch of paranoia in *that* delusion.

I don't know how much guilt had to do with the choice of this decor. But I felt it was perfectly appropriate.

The air was thicker than tea that's stewed on the hob all day and cockroaches were running over the ceiling, I remember. I cried all the first part of the night, I cried until I was exhausted but he turned on his side and slept – he saw through that ruse, though I did not since I did not know that I was lying. But I could not sleep because of the rattling of the walls and the noise of traffic. We had turned off the glaring lamp; when I saw a shaft of light fall across his face, I thought: "Surely it's too early for the dawn." But it was another person silently sliding open the unlocked door; in this disreputable hotel, anything can happen. I screamed and the intruder vanished. Wakened by a scream, my lover thought I'd gone mad and instantly trapped me in a stranglehold, in case I murdered him.

We were both old enough to have known better, too.

When I turned on the lamp to see what time it was, I noticed, to my surprise, that his features were blurring, like the underwriting on a palimpsest. It wasn't long before we parted. Only a few days. You can't keep *that* pace up for long.

Then the city vanished; it ceased, almost immediately, to be a magic and appalling place. I woke up one morning and found it had become home. Though I still turn up my coat collar in a lonely way and am always looking at myself in mirrors, they're only habits and give no clue at all to my character, whatever that is.

The most difficult performance in the world is acting naturally, isn't it? Everything else is artful.

•

JOANNA RUSS
An Old-fashioned Girl
(1974)

'*Sex* per se *is impossible to write about directly. Like fatigue, or hunger, or pain (or any kind of physical pleasure), it's a primary experience, and the best you can do with those is either name them or indicate the effect they have on the minds of your characters – i.e. treat them by metaphor.*'

So wrote Joanna Russ in her original note on this story, and since then in novels like The Female Man *(1975), the linked narratives of* Extra-(Ordinary) People *(1984) and the various adventures of* Alyx *she has explored gender roles and sexuality with an intelligence and cool wit that is unusual within the fantasy/s.f. genre.*

She is also an academic and the author of such challenging critical works as How to Suppress Women's Writing *(1983) and* Magic Mommas, Trembling Sisters, Puritans and Perverts *(1985). Her 1972 story 'When It*

*Changed', about the appearance of male astronauts in a happy and productive
world of females, has acquired classic status and is frequently anthologized.
Of the present story, Russ said: '. . . what I really wanted was a role-
reversal – the* Playboy *Bunny with testicles, so to speak.'*

I woke up in a Vermont autumn morning, taking my guests home
inside the glass cab while all around us the maples and sugar maples
wheel slowly out of the fog. Only this part of the world can
produce such colour. We whispered at a walking pace through wet
fires. Electric vehicles are quiet, too; we heard the drip of water
from the leaves. When the house saw us, my old round lollipop-on-
a-stick, it lit up from floor to top, and as we came nearer, broadcast
the Second Brandenburg through the black, wet tree trunks and the
fiery leaves, a delicate attention I allow myself and my guests from
time to time. Shouting brilliantly through the wet woods – I prefer
the unearthly purity of the electronic scoring.

One approaches the house from the side, where it looks almost
flat on its central column – only a little convex, really – it doesn't
squat down for you on chicken legs like Baba Yaga's hut, but lets
down from above a great, coiling, metal-mesh road like a tongue
(or so it seems; in reality it's only a winding staircase). Inside, you
find yourself a corridor away from the main room; no use wasting
heat.

Davy was there. The most beautiful man in the world. Our
approach had given him time to make drinks for us, which my
guests took from his tray, staring at him. But he wasn't embarrassed
– curled up most un-waiter-like at my feet, with his hands around
his knees and proceeding to laugh at the right places in the
conversation (he takes his cues from my face).

The main room is panelled in yellow wood with a carpet you can
sleep on (brown) and a long, glassed-in porch from which we
watch the blizzards sweep by five months out of the year. I like
purely visual weather. It's warm enough for Davy to go around
naked most of the time, my ice lad, in a cloud of gold hair and
nudity, never so much part of my home as when he sits on the rug
with his back against a russet or vermilion chair (we mimic autumn
here), his drowned blue eyes fixed on the sunset outside, his hair
turned to ash, the muscles of his back and thighs stirring a little.
The house hangs oddments from the ceiling: found objects, mobiles,

can-openers, red balls, bunches of wild grass. Davy plays with them.

I showed the guests around – calm Elinor, nervous Priss, pushy Kay. There were the books, the microfilm viewer in the library in touch with our regional library miles away, the storage spaces in the walls, the various staircases, the bathrooms moulded of glass fibre and put together from two pieces, the mattresses stored in the walls of the guest rooms, and the conservatory (near the central core, to make use of the heat), where Davy comes and mimics wonder, watching the lights shine on my orchids, my palmettos, my bougainvillaea, my whole little mess of tropical plants. I even have a glassed-in space for cacti. There are outside plantings where in season you can find mountain laurel, a tangled maze of rhododendron, scattered irises that look like an expensive, antique cross between insects and lingerie – but these will be under snow in a few weeks. I even have an electrified fence, inherited from the previous owner, that encloses the whole estate to keep out the deer and occasionally kills trees which take the mild climate around the house a little too much for granted.

I let my friends peep into the kitchen, which is an armchair with controls like a 707's, but not the place where I store my tools and from which I have access to the central core when House has indigestion. That's dirty, and you need to know what you're doing. I showed them Screen, which keeps me in touch with my neighbours, the nearest of whom is ten miles away; Telephone, who is my long-distance back-up line; and Phonograph, where I store my music.

Priss said she didn't like her drink; it wasn't sweet enough. So I had Davy dial her another.

Do you want dinner? (I said)

And she blushed.

I woke later that day. Davy sleeps near by. You've heard about blue-eyed blonds, haven't you? I passed into his room barefoot and watched him curled in sleep, unconscious, the golden veils of his eyelashes shadowing his cheeks, one arm thrown out into the streak of light falling on to him from the hall. It takes a lot to wake him (you can almost mount Davy in his sleep) but I was too sleepy to start right away and only squatted down by the mattress he sleeps on, tracing with my fingertips the patterns the hair made on his chest: broad high up, over the muscles, then narrowing toward his delicate belly (which rose and fell with his breathing), the line of hair to below the navel, and that suddenly stiff blossoming of the pubic hair in which his relaxed genitals nestled gently, like a rosebud.

I'm an old-fashioned girl.

I caressed his dry, velvety-skinned organ until it stirred in my hand, then ran my fingernails lightly down his sides to wake him up; I did the same – though very lightly – to the insides of his arms.

He opened his eyes and smiled starrily at me.

It's very pleasant to follow Davy's hairline around his neck with your tongue or nuzzle all the hollows of his long-muscled, swimmer's body; inside the elbows, the forearms, the places where the back tapers inward under the ribs, the backs of the knees. A naked man is a cross, the juncture elaborated in vulnerable and delicate flesh like the blossom on a banana tree, that place that's given me so much pleasure.

I nudged him gently and he shivered a little, bringing his legs together and spreading his arms flat; with my forefinger I made a transient white line on his neck. Little Davy was half-filled by now, which is a sign that Davy wants to be knelt over. I obliged, sitting across his thighs, and bending over him without touching his body, kissed him again and again on the mouth, the neck, the face, the shoulders. He is very, very exciting. He's very beautiful. Putting one arm under his shoulders to lift him up, I rubbed my nipples over his mouth, first one and then the other, which is nice for us both, and as he held on to my upper arms and let his head fall back, I pulled him to me, kneading his back muscles, kneading his buttocks, sliding down to the mattress with him. Little Davy is entirely filled out now.

So lovely: Davy with his head thrown to one side, eyes closed, his strong fingers clenching and unclenching. He began to arch his back, and his sleepiness made him a little too quick for me. I pressed Small Davy between thumb and forefinger just enough to slow him down and then – when I felt like it – playfully started to mount him, rubbing the tip of him, nipping him a little on the neck. His breathing in my ear, fingers convulsively closing on mine.

I played with him a little more, tantalizing him, then swallowed him whole like a water-melon seed – so fine inside! with Davy moaning, his tongue inside my mouth, his blue gaze shattered, his whole body uncontrollably arched, all his sensation concentrated in the place where I held him.

I don't do this often, but that time I made him come by slipping a finger in his anus: convulsions, fires, crying in no words as the sensation was pulled out of him. If I had let him take more time, I would have climaxed with him, but he's stiff for quite a while after he comes, and I prefer that; I like the after-tremors and the after-hardness, slipperier and more pliable than before; Davy has an eerie malleability at those times. I grasped him internally, I pressed down on him, enjoying in one act his muscular throat, the hair under his arms, his knees, the strength of his back and buttocks, his beautiful face, the fine skin on the inside of his thighs. Kneaded and bruised him, hiccoughing inside with all my architecture: little buried rod, swollen lips, and grabby sphincter, the flexing half-moon under the pubic bone. And everything else in the vicinity, no doubt.

I'd had him. Davy was mine. Sprawled blissfully over him – I was discharged down to my fingertips but still quietly throbbing – it had really been a good one. His body so wet under me and inside me.

And looked up to see –

Priss. Elinor. Kay.

'For Heaven's sakes, is *that* all!' said Elinor to Priss.

I got up, tickled him with the edge of a fingernail, and joined them at the door. 'Stay, Davy.' This is one of the key words that the house 'understands'; the central computer will transmit a pattern of signals to the implants in his brain and he will stretch out obediently on his mattress; when I say to the main computer 'Sleep', Davy will sleep. He's a lovely limb of the house. The original germ-plasm was chimpanzee, I think, but none of the behaviour is organically controlled any more. True, he does have his minimal actions which he pursues without me – he eats, eliminates, sleeps, and climbs in and out of his exercise box – but even these are caused by a standing computer pattern. And I take precedence, of course.

It is theoretically possible that Davy has (tucked away in some nook of his cerebrum) consciousness of a kind that may never even touch his active life – is Davy a poet in his own peculiar way? – but I prefer to believe not. His consciousness – such as it is, and I am willing to grant it for the sake of argument – is nothing but the permanent possibility of sensation, a mere intellectual abstraction, a nothing, a picturesque collocation of words. It is experientially quite empty, and above all, it is nothing that need concern you and me. Davy's soul lies somewhere else; it's an outside soul. Davy's soul is in Davy's beauty.

'Leucotomized,' said Kay, her voice heavy with outrage. 'Lobotomized! Kidnapped in childhood!'

'Nonsense,' said Elinor. 'They're extinct. Have been for decades. What is it?' So I told them. Elinor put her arm around Kay – I think I told you I was an old-fashioned girl – and explained serenely to Kay that there was a popular misconception that in the past men had had Janies as I had a Davy, that women had been to men what Davy was to me, but that was a legend. That was utter nonsense. 'Popular ignorance,' said Elinor. She would tell us the real story some other time.

Priss was staring and staring. 'Is he expensive?' she said (and blushed). I let her borrow him – we had to modify some of his programming, of course – so we tiptoed out and left them; it was the first time, Priss said, she had ever seen such soul in a creature's eyes.

And she's right. She's right, you know. Davy's soul is in Davy's beauty; it's poignant that Davy himself can never experience his own soul. Beauty is all that matters in him, and Beauty is always empty, always on the outside.

Isn't it?

•

VERENA STEFAN
State of Emergency
(1975)

Born in Switzerland, where she remained until her schooling was complete, Verena Stefan went to Berlin to train in physiotherapy and sociology. She began to write while working with the women's group Bread & Roses, and during her seven years in Berlin completed her first novel Häutungen, *which was originally issued in 1975 by the Munich feminist publishing house Frauenoffensive.*

A journey of exploration detailing a woman's ordinary experiences and the discarding of traditional roles, with all the pain that it may entail, the book was a huge critical and commercial success in West Germany, and it has since been published in many other countries – in English as Shedding.

'It is easier for me to talk to women than to men,' a women friend tells me. 'It is easier to live with women, easier to get along with them, I feel more comfortable around them than around men . . .'

'But why,' I ask her. 'Why do you have a relationship with a man, when it is easier for you to *talk*, *live* and *get along* with women?'

'Approval . . .' she says. 'And it is . . . sexual . . . I mean – I haven't had much experience with women, but maybe that was because it wasn't . . . any better than with a man . . .'

'I know what you mean,' I say. 'Fenna and I had problems too. Not because we wanted men's approval, but because we didn't know how to create a new, unique kind of passion – there is a kind of solidarity between women, one in which compassion, eroticism . . . sincerity and security are wrapped up together. Many of the feelings which often prove disastrous in relationships with men, are at the same time . . . a reserve of strength which we can draw on for mutual support. Women's emotional resources are greater. With a man, emotional atrophy usually sets in so early that somewhere along the way he becomes incapable of having humane relationships . . . he can hold his own only as long as we are there to render him bodily and emotional . . . support . . .'

'But men are victims of conditioning, too!' she interrupts. 'You can't blame them for . . .'

'I'm not!' I say. 'I don't blame them for having learned that kind of destructive behaviour expected of men . . . but on the other hand, I *do* expect them to want to change – but I don't see any sign of that happening . . . not even with men who in terms of their work, lifestyle, intellect would seem capable of changing, not even with men who claim that they would like to shed their masculine skin . . .'

'But they aren't all like that . . . sometimes it is possible to have

... a humane relationship with a man ... even sexually ... a humane sexuality ...'

'It is possible to have a humane sexual relationship with a woman,' I counter.

'Even women try to control each other,' she says. 'Exclusivity has not been overcome, you still see jealousy, dramatic scenes, calamities ...'

'It's such an easy way out to say that women haven't got all the answers either,' I reply. 'It goes back to the idea that women are supposed to be model human beings – simply because they are women ... It is hard to be humane. When women get together, they are still just groups of human beings who have been deformed by society. They have certain basic things in common – their sex is the colour of their skin. They share a common cultural, historical, sexist ... past and still live in the same sexist society ... among themselves they can cast off the traditional roles if they really want to – and here, it seems to me, the fundamental issue is one of a woman coming to terms with her self, whether or not she ever slept with another woman is not the important thing ...'

'I agree,' she says. 'It is simply not true that it is necessarily better with women ...'

'You're missing the point,' I retort. 'First of all it is a question of wanting to *fundamentally* change relationships between people, and this would imply, among other things ... foregoing traditional relationships which are based on stereotypes. It is a question of woman realizing that she doesn't need another person to feel like a complete human being. But whether or not she will succeed depends upon the kind of work she does, her children, upon all the demands that are made on her – where can she find the strength to break free? The strength to become abnormal? To me it seems more and more unnatural, I really do mean *unnatural*, to have had access only to people of one sex. For the last twenty-six years for example, I had to live without another woman's breast ... how could I ever have known what it is like to bury my head in someone's breasts? When I am together with another woman I learn something about my self. With a man I learn only that I am different and that my body is supposed to be there for him, I don't really learn about my body or about my self ...'

'But the electricity, the attraction ... something is missing ...'

'Do you mean that which is usually termed "sexual arousal"?' I ask. 'Doesn't anything happen when you're together with a woman? You don't feel anything in the pit of your stomach, you sit across from her, feeling a bit awkward perhaps . . .'

'Exactly,' she says. 'That's exactly how I feel!'

'Of course,' I say, 'but that's just it, then why do you still want to sleep with her? You feel this closeness to her, you have finally met up with that which you've always been giving to men, for the first time it is not only you who is paying attention, offering support and compassion, you are, instead, also the recipient, you sense another woman evoking in you a feeling of . . . longing, when up to now only men had found that women evoked feelings of longing in them . . . the man himself cannot evoke longing in you. Isn't it really the case that your sense of longing is the desire to evoke desire in him? . . . It isn't our body we learned to love . . . it is merely the desire that our body arouses in a man . . . do we love the male body or . . . do we love being desired? The period when the male body could evoke longings in us . . . belongs to the past – what is it you are really longing for, when you long for that body?'

'But what about . . . approval . . .' she says hesitantly. 'Can you get along without men's approval?'

'What is it they should approve of? Is it important that they accept me, that in their eyes I conform to the image of what a woman should be? In fact it's the eyes that really get to me, I mean literally these eyes which reflect the distorted bodies of women in rightist and leftist magazines. It is this distorted perspective . . . that we are supposed to measure up to, these eyes reduce me to an object . . . and whether or not I feel whole, they dismember me, they focus on my breasts . . . this also happens with friends and acquaintances and not only with strangers on the street. I always get that uncomfortable feeling . . . that a man wants something from me. He invariably demands that I lavish my undivided attention on him as soon as he appears on the scene – because he is a man and I am a woman. He expects me to notice him, to be interested in him because he is a man and I am a woman – for no other reason! He naturally assumes that the woman who is graced with his approving stare is at his disposal . . . I feel less inhibited among women . . .'

'But you are being just as one-sided,' she says, 'that's not any different . . .'

'But it is,' I say, 'it *is* different. I admit that it is one-sided, but that's not the issue, what is important to me is whether I am getting hurt, whether I am being weakened or strengthened . . . severed relationships can't be mended from one day to the next! . . . and why should women do that all by themselves? They provide the impetus, men have to take it from there. I cannot, for example, ignore the fact that during all the thousands of years of male domination, the penis, just like all other implements . . . has become a weapon, and the attitude towards everything living has become correspondingly sadistic and destructive. The experiences most women have had with intercourse are ghastly enough without even mentioning abortions and torture.'

'Everything has gotten so complicated!' she says. 'But it must be possible to find one man somewhere with whom one could have a humane relationship . . . I don't want to exclude him from my life, but I am no longer going to be there just for him alone, women are part of my life too . . .'

'I know, a man sometimes will sit there in the room without budging when he knows damn well that his woman wants to have a private conversation with other women!' We both start to laugh.

'This how-can-you-do-this-to-me look,' she says, 'because I am no longer there alone next to him! It didn't use to make any difference to him what I did – he had his work, his football buddies, his political group and me – but now that I have a women's group . . . what's going on with him? Sometimes a woman does arouse a new kind of feeling in me, a different kind of attraction . . . one which can, for a few seconds, be so intense that it carries over into the following day. It is also an erotic sensation and it is fulfilling – it is not only the signal of some dubious need for 'more' . . . I used to believe I was content all day after having slept with him, whether or not I had an orgasm, simply because I was with him – but now I feel empty when we sleep with each other, even though I do enjoy it, I do like having sex with him . . . I do get aroused . . .'

'Do you really?' I ask, 'or are you saying that only because the idea is so engrained in your mind, and because you can rationalize intercourse that way. Don't we usually sleep with a man because of social pressures rather than because we . . . feel secure? Don't we often take a man in because that gives us the feeling of being needed? And if copulation is unpleasant or humiliating, we still have ample opportunity to remain somewhat detached – what goes on in the far reaches between penis and vagina doesn't really have to concern us. The penis is too . . . alien to be able to really reach us – this sort of schizophrenia has become incredibly complex and multifaceted! We need it for self-protection – in order to survive . . . we fake enjoyment in order to come up to expectations, in order to be left alone – can you talk to him about sexuality?'

'Hardly!' she says. 'He gets scared, feels hurt, has guilt feelings – how am I supposed to tell him that I feel unfulfilled with sleeping with him . . . that I don't feel close to him, that weeks go by when I don't want to go to bed with him . . . perhaps things would improve if the intervals between intercourse were longer, if we would spend more time talking to each other. Can you talk to Fenna? Did you two have sexual problems?'

'Yes,' I say. 'It took a long time before we felt we could be open with each other, before we could talk about what each of us wanted. Even with her it took a long time before I believed that she actually found my body beautiful. It was of course different, hearing it from her than from a man, but I still didn't trust myself . . . I noticed, too, that with a man, the real sense of touch usually gets lost in the myriad of prescribed stimuli and responses . . .'

'Yes, that's how it seems to me, too. But how does this new way of touching become . . . different and yet exciting?'

'It takes time,' I say. 'Time played a really important role in building an intimate relationship. Now a new sense of longing, of excitement, of devotion has come into being – but it is devotion which stems from affection rather than from submission and brute force. This male society has gotten under our skin. It takes all the strength we can muster just to keep from perpetuating it, through conditioned gestures, wishes, activities, and reactions . . . why, for instance, do you put on make-up when you go out to meet a man, even though you don't wear any at home?'

'I want to look good, want him to find me attractive . . .'

'Do you go out to dinner with women too? Do you find that exciting, fascinating, do you look forward to that or does it seem less interesting than going out with a man? Don't women have anything to report about the big wide world out there, do you feel that only men, at least for a moment, can help you overcome the feeling of being closed in?'

'It is true that women's experiences out in the world are limited, but that isn't the problem. I'm more interested in women than in men, their history, their lives are more interesting than men's, it's easier to talk to them. But when we are ready to leave ... even if we walk home together ... I just don't know where to go from there ...'

The winter after my return from America is mild. In December we can go for walks in the gardens of the Charlottenburg Palace. Here and there crocuses are blooming. Fenna and I walk along with our coats unbuttoned. She stops, lifts her face towards the sun and slowly says, I would like to be passionately in love again – I am not really interested in becoming involved, yet I'd like to experience that passion again, with a woman, I want to feel that special excitement as soon as I walk in the door ... I don't believe we are capable of that any more.

I nod. Yes, I say, I feel the same way. But I still need time to recuperate. Recovering from the wounds inflicted over the past ten years is taking longer than I thought it would. I have no sexual needs. I want only peace and quiet, time to write. What do we really mean by passion, excitement?

A year ago, shortly before I left for America, the venture with Fenna began to take shape. We came upon regions of human affection which had lain fallow until then. We were not in love at the start, and we warily watched our moves. For a long time we were equipped with nothing but the knowledge that we wanted to have something to do with each other – we even had to learn how to speak. We were at one and the same time helpless and grateful in barren, unmapped territory.

> I am quite sure
> that you used to dwell in trees
> as I in lakes and rivers.
> In my glittering hair of moss
> solar energy erupted.

Your strands of hair fanned down
along the roots through the ground.
They still store up memories
of life within the mantle of bark
each of the dark tendons
is taut with the strength
of survival in the forest. The gnarls
on the trunks, these too
you have brought along with you.

Your hands coarse and damp
the moment I want to live
with you, not just survive. An unreal
leafy green. You take
refuge in a corner of the blanket
to dry your hands, but also
to keep me out
of your life
and to hide so far away
that only the forest eyes can be seen and
the tiny roots of hair on your forehead.

Life in the water now long past
emerged
on to a barren rock. Surrounded by
perilous swamp, no end
in sight. The rock
no room for two
not yet enough ground broken
for a life outside the water
a bit of mossy hair,
in the sun.

You run lost through the woods, uprooted
hair, most women
long since expelled
or atrophied
crippled and brittle.
Only a few broke free
in time.

Many

individually

> we hatch the world anew
> we stir up time
> we shed our shadow skin
> fire breaks out

I cannot remember any more,
how many nights there were during that winter which is almost two years hence, nights when Fenna and I lay down together in the same bed – back to back – and warmed each other before curling up to sleep.

The matter-of-fact way in which we got undressed and crawled under the covers was comforting. Perhaps we murmured this or that to each other, lit a candle or two, when my feet got too cold I warmed them on her legs before we rolled over and snuggled up ... we treated each other kindly and with great care. The weeks passed peacefully, yet awkwardly. Since we did not know how to approach each other, we refrained from touching. Since we did not know how to view each other's bodies, we refrained from looking.

In the meantime I had become aware of my need to throw open my door after finishing my work and go to Fenna, placing one foot in front of the other as I went. A renewed desire to speak another language after work was done, a new language of skin words, laughing, bubbling billowing sounds had surfaced within me.

I was treading water.

I could not think of any way to get things going between Fenna and me. The sincerity between us was so profound that I couldn't possibly be wily and underhanded. It seemed impossible to break down the reserve that Fenna had displayed when she helped me through my period of withdrawal from sexuality. It seemed that my intimacy with Nadjenka should have made it easier, but there was no comparison. Nadjenka and I were cut from much the same cloth. It was not difficult for us to touch each other. We soon found that we shared a common need, and we could immerse ourselves in it. This was the way it had always been for me. If I didn't feel a certain immediate inexplicable attraction towards the other person, I couldn't make love happen.

This time, though, eroticism developed only gradually. Hesitantly, timorously, it dissipated as soon as we drew back from each other. It lacked vital energy at first.

But there was at least this sense of having the reins in one's own hand for the first time, of not being drawn into a preconceived pattern, of not being led by incomprehensible series of actions and reactions. One had the sense of spinning the threads of one's own fate wittingly.

From time to time we spent a whole day together taking long walks. It was on one of those occasions that we went to Fenna's house afterwards to listen to music. Sitting there, we cuddled up to each other. Our eyes met in agreement, our faces began to draw closer and stopped just before touching. I could submerge myself in the shadowy crescents beneath her eyes. The rim of her iris glimmered green in the last few rays of sun streaming through the window-panes. The green emitted light grey beams flecked with amber which converged upon the pupil. The smiling lashes descended slowly and interlaced with those below.

We could hardly draw apart, sighing, laughing, 'why haven't we ever . . .' – the obstacles seemed to have been overcome. But as time went on they imposed themselves between us again and again.

Although we went away shortly thereafter and spent a whole week together on a farm, we did not go to bed with each other.

Only the nocturnal hours could have brought us closer, since we were not alone. Besides, Fenna needed the daylight hours for painting. We wanted to make use of the time and peace and quiet and we did not want to neglect our work in favour of sexuality.

Was that really it?

Wasn't it really the fear of losing one's head, the possibility of our lives becoming too entangled, the uncertainty as to whether we were indeed capable of remaining individuals while carrying so much of each other within us?

We vacillated because we had both grown used to being alone, we knew that, in some ways at least, it was simpler to face problems alone.

> Piece by piece, dear sister
> life by life
> fossil by fossil
> history by history

fingertip by fingertip
approach by approach
smile by smile
word upon word
skin upon skin
affection upon affection
Oh, sister dear
You'll be amazed at what mountains we build!

Strange things happened that week on the farm. On top of all the difficulties we created for ourselves, there were also external circumstances which kept us from getting together. It did not take much to keep us at a distance.

Just after our lips had taken up from where our last kiss had ended, we were interrupted by cats yowling beneath our window. Our hearts stopped beating, we sat bolt upright in bed. Wasn't that the shadow of a man? Was it really just the wind rustling through the trees? Sobered and wide awake we lay next to each other, apart once again.

'Cats,' murmured Fenna, drifting off to sleep, 'it would have to be cats that disturb us!'

Another night, as we embraced in spite of suffering from sunburn and chills, we heard a strange scratching sound behind us: a tiny mouse was sitting on the pillow. One leap and we were both standing in the middle of the room. The mouse disappeared into a hidden crevice. We lay down again and agreed that though we weren't really afraid of mice, we didn't especially like for one to crawl over us. I could not sleep. I kept hearing the scratching every so often, at four in the morning I actually found the mouse sitting next to my head again.

A group of us women had gone together to a vacation spot at the ocean. The castle we were living in was huge, a labyrinthine building with many entrance-ways.

In the village there was a small old bathhouse, a relic of bygone days. It even had a sauna. We had arranged to meet the old village woman there. Fenna planned to make love to her with all of us there looking on. It was a ritual, no one thought it strange.

The old one was wizened and withered and clothed all in rags.

One almost expected her to reek of cod-liver oil. She hobbled about in shoes made of animal skins. She spoke not a word but was very friendly, serene, she had made her peace with the world.

We sat there in the bathhouse and waited for her to arrive. After she came in, she sat down on the floor and began to take off her stockings, very slowly and ceremoniously. I was sitting next to her. Her heavy grey cotton stockings covered enormously hefty legs bulging with varicose veins. We were awed by her ugliness for we knew that this was what awaited women at the end of their lives. We wanted to rid ourselves of the aesthetic prejudices we still carried within us, wanted to begin to revere the ancient misshapen old ones like her.

It all took too long to suit me, I left. Later on, the others told me that the ritual had not taken place after all, why, I don't know.

How could Fenna and I overcome our shyness and fear? How were we to learn to touch, kiss, confront the lips between our legs?

Is it this image which shocks people into reacting so defensively when the subject of lesbian love is broached? One allows one's own hand, a man's hand, a penis, a man's mouth to do that which is forbidden between women.

We have learned to kiss the penis, and yet are afraid of the
lips between our own legs.
The hand on its way to the clitoris
of another woman
traverses centuries.
It can get lost a thousand times.
It fights its way through fragments of civilization.
And in addition, the route it takes
leads to a place which has no name:
I have no clitoris.
I have no vagina. No vulva. No pussy.
No bust, no nipples.
My body is corporeal. There are no places on my body which correspond to these incorporeal and brutal designations. Clitoris has nothing in common with this part of my body which is called clitoris. In order to find new words I will have to live differently for as many years as I have lived believing in the meaning of these terms.

This part of my body which is called clitoris is not my focal point, my life does not revolve around it. It is not that I want to minimize its importance, it is just that I do not want to be limited again to only one part of my body.

I am beginning to see myself for what I really am.

I assemble the separate parts to make one whole body. I have breasts and a pelvis.

My legs run together to form curves, folds, lips. I glide and fall with Fenna through meadows of blossoming labella (only a man could have named one of these erotic feminine flowers *snapdragon*).

From now on we'll just call them vulva flowers, Fenna decides.

I set the scene: Hello, I'd like a bunch of vulva flowers . . .

What do you want? Get out of here!

Fenna and I convulse with laughter.

That's not right, I interrupt, having a vulva is nothing to be ashamed of. I take a good look at myself, become immersed in the hues, the shadings, the variegations of skin. The lips of my vulva are wrinkled folds. They really do look like rolled-up flower petals, reddish-brown and bright pink when I gently unfurl them. How many different unknown shades of colours to be discovered on my body! We create ourselves anew by touching, looking, talking. My breasts pendulate before her body, they begin to laugh, to vibrate with novel sensations. Gently I place a breast on her eye. How apropos that in German men say 'it fits like a fist in the eye' . . .

– It looks nice

                    Um hm, purplish –

– Couldn't you go on any longer?

                    No, I'd lost you –

– Yeah, it really is difficult sometimes . . .

Bubbles of laughter fill the room. Genital solemnity, where is your sting?

'I still can't quite deal with our relationship,' said Fenna in the last conversation before I left for America. 'I can't fit us into my life. I don't even know whether I want to – my painting is still the most important thing to me.' I felt rejected. 'What we have between us hasn't helped me up to now. I am still afraid of being taken over,' she went on.

She was sitting way over on the other side of the bed. I reached over my hand, an emissary.

'Don't,' she said. 'Don't touch me. I have to talk first.'

'We can talk and touch,' I countered.

She refused. 'I can't do both.'

The initial difficulties we encountered in linking one life to the other surfaced again and again. They did not seem to diminish as time passed. They were still able to overpower us. We constantly expressed our doubts as to whether or not we even wanted to let another person become so important to us. We felt too threatened by the possibility that our feelings would lead to uncontrollable passion, pain, peril. Where does one draw that thin line between seeing each other only seldom and remaining total strangers, between intimacy and addiction? Our encounters were few and far between. There always seemed so little for us to build upon. Our trust in each other did not seem to be increasing, nor did our reticence readily wane. At each encounter it took a while to re-establish our ties.

Talking still exhausted me. It was hard labour for me to learn to speak. After two hours I was totally worn out.

We could never take refuge in sexuality, for us it could never serve as a substitute language for things left unsaid, undone, it could never be used to camouflage problems. Being together demanded a great deal of time. Our intimacies were circumspect. In the time it took for us to exchange a single kiss, I would in the past have already had intercourse and found myself standing there fully clothed and ready to depart.

Today I am leaving for America, I said to myself the following morning as I wandered home through the empty streets. I had to laugh. The word America did not mean anything to me. I knew only that I would be away for three months. There was nothing left for me to do in Berlin, nor was I looking to find anything. It was enough to glide naked through space for a time, covered only by Fenna's warm dry lizard-skin.

In Frankfurt I made one last call to Nadjenka. Her voice still echoed in my ears long after I had arrived in New York.

I am worried about you, she says.

Wanting to reassure her, I say, Nothing is going to happen to me.

I always worry about you, she says, you don't need to go to America for that.

I had not seen her for a long time. I saw her at a women's conference in spring but we didn't really have a chance to talk. She had driven in with a friend in order to see me. But I was all involved in special meetings. She caught me on the run between workshops, plenary sessions and discussions with other women, I was terribly busy, I was all wrapped up, I had no time to sit down and have a private chat with her. Politics was the issue of the moment.

Could our conference have any meaning for Nadjenka, any impact on her, on her daughter, her husband, her household, her life in the suburbs?

I felt a pang when I saw her. Why didn't we have any projects in common? Was my work with these women really irrelevant to her life? Why didn't *she* undertake anything? She attempted to laugh on the wing. Her fair hair still fluttered about her face. She stood there next to the woman she had come with, who also had a child. They seemed able to give each other mutual support, they were thinking of going on vacation together.

Her life is changing, I thought.

She will get along without me.

When had I ever offered her help?

Would it really have helped if I had shared my life with her?

I was not willing to take the risk of restructuring my own life, of beginning a new life with her. We had only talked about *her* venturing the new beginning, the leap into the unknown, the break with the past, she was supposed to be the one to finally pull herself together and raze her former dwelling . . . at that time I had not realized how much I was asking of her. I only saw how uncomplicated my life was in Berlin, how easy it was to make contact with the many groups, I was young, I had time, time enough to ask Nadjenka to come and join me in Berlin.

She felt old and all worn out, thirty, feared the unknown . . . the leftists didn't impress her. How could I, myself a ghetto dweller, have countered her objections? She watched me moving from one commune to the next, running through group after group, humanizing man after man.

Seeing you again at the women's conference was very painful for me, wrote Nadjenka. I got the feeling that we didn't really mean that much to each other any more, that our relationship had lost that special something. Something had come between us. You parcel out your affection equally to everybody – I get my share too, of course, but there is nothing special about it.

Her voice reaches me through the telephone: I'm worried about losing you.

Don't be ridiculous, Nadjenka, how could that possibly happen?

Another woman could make it happen, she says. Only another woman can come between us. I was never afraid of losing you before, a man was never a threat to what we had.

Not even another woman could break up our relationship, I say. It isn't Fenna that you fear, it is the strength I draw from the women's movement, my close ties to those women, the importance I attach to my work with women . . . I do relate to you differently now than I used to when on the rebound from a man . . . but that doesn't mean that you're not still someone very special to me – no, I repeat, it isn't Fenna. It is that your life is so different from mine while Fenna's and mine are so alike – both of us are single, neither of us has children, we're both involved with 'Bread & Roses' . . . for more than two years we have been helping shape that group and give it new direction.

For months Nadjenka kept me at arm's length, nothing changed until she came to visit me at the beginning of the following year. She didn't want me to be a part of her life any more, she shut me out only to take me back in again, she weighed the situation, pondered. She tried to examine the strands of her life, tried to untangle those hard knotted strands. I didn't hear from her all the while I was gone, she doggedly remained silent.

'There were times when I really missed you while you were in America,' said Fenna as we walked through the gardens of the Charlottenburg Palace. 'I can't tell you exactly what it was, but it seemed to be more difficult to cope with things. Conflicts were harder to resolve, once when I had my period I just broke down – not that I necessarily wanted to spend more time with you, it was more . . . the idea that I could discuss my problems with you . . . I longed for your . . . emotional support.'

The summer had passed us by. The warmth would have favoured our attempts to get together, I thought. Now we will have to bundle ourselves up again in two or three layers of clothes, coats caps scarves and gloves.

Brussels, a telephone booth. My head spinning, the first thing I did upon arriving was to change some money.

Hello? Fenna's voice on the other end.

It's me, I finally say.

Veruschka! Where are you?

In Brussels.

If I leave right away, she says slowly, I can meet you in Frankfurt and we can still drive back tonight.

I steady myself on the wall of the phone booth. You mean you're really going to come pick me up?

She laughs. What do you think I meant?

'This bond between us . . .' I said, as we continued our walk through the gardens, 'I think it has something to do with that nebulous notion of "motherliness", That term is so ambivalent, so ambiguous . . . how can we attain immediate, direct access to "motherliness"? For too long we have been thought of as nothing but furrows for sowing seeds – the issue here isn't . . . the woman who gave birth to each of us . . . it's not the blood ties, the guilt feelings, the silence that we want, it . . . isn't a question of making amends, of "motherliness" only towards her, the issue is the power of motherliness, motherliness as a shared human characteristic . . .'

Two days before Easter it is snowing, sodden and ugly. When I had taken a walk in the park at Christmas, the forsythia were blooming.

I curse as I put on my heavy winter coat, hurry to the subway and immerse myself in a book. I'm *already* snowed in, lost to the world. Last night I was taught to swim like a fish, to cleave through the waters, to part the seas, to furrow them. Mightier than the oceans!

After treating my private patient I return to the apartment, swearing a blue streak. Some nice soup will come to my rescue, you can always depend on cauliflower. I wash the dishes in order to warm my hands. I would like nothing better than to refill the sink with fresh hot water for each and every dish.

My head, charged with bolts of lightning from the ride on the subway, is ready to burst, the soup is steaming next to the typewriter, it tastes like cardboard and like the grey walls in front of my window, its warmth only skin deep. Soon there will be ice water flowing through my veins. I take refuge in the kitchen, turn on all three gas burners and let the blue flames flare; I want to put on some water for tea, pour it into me by the gallon until I am thawed out. I let the laundry run through the machine two, three, five, ten times, hotter than blazes!

The washing-machine is sizzling, the plastic is melting, the kitchen is steaming, my hair is standing on end, my head explodes. Cold sweat, with clammy fingers I turn off the gas flames, the washing-machine.

I'm getting my period.

The uterus lies cramped between the pelvic bones. The lining of the inner walls is saturated with blood. Dark brown spots for three days now, traces of bright red on the tampon. The lining stubbornly refuses to detach itself. It is taking unusually long this time, it's a nuisance. My head is spinning and this waiting weighs upon me like oppressive weather. The skin on my abdomen is more taut than usual, stretched tightly over the contracting uterus, the pelvic musculature has become too tense, it tugs downward. In previous months the pain had been sudden and acute. Almost the whole lining had been expelled the first day, dark clots. But immediate relief had followed, my tummy warm and relaxed, a premonition of what a period could be like.

Nadjenka came to see me. It can only have been two weeks ago, yet it seems as if she has been gone for ever. The long weekend was much too short; afterwards I was filled with an emptiness as never before, I could hardly warm up again. At night her life preyed upon me, tore at my breast.

The pain radiating, sometimes I have to stop in my tracks. To have your period on the weekend, of all times, the two days without interruption from the outside world. Monday is shot, private patients in the morning, and the afternoon spent at the clinic where I work part time. Just looking at the typewriter gives me a backache. (My back is killing me, says a patient, I have the curse.) The muscles contract again and again in order to loosen the lining. Nadjenka's spasmodic sobs still cling to me, she is choking, her life is strangling her. I rock her gently, tell me what's wrong . . .

Never had a choice. Became a secretary because there was no
money for anything else, married to get away from home, to finally
have a home, had a child, after many years finally a child, in order
to . . .

'What'll happen to you, if anything happens to her?'

Nadjenka becomes faceless. Impossible to imagine. 'It's simple,'
she says then, slowly. 'Either I'll go on living without her or I
won't.'

'Perhaps.'

What a burden for a mother to bear, right from the very moment
of conception, this anticipation of being abandoned. Is life to be
reduced to the attempt to overcome loneliness?

'Berlin wouldn't have been the answer, I know that for sure
now,' she says. 'I needed someone to take me by the hand, and you
couldn't have done that. You can't imagine the shape I would have
been in, how dependent I would have been on you, at least for
quite some time.'

Each of us had had a man at our side at that time, later our lives
took decidedly different courses. Perhaps our getting together
would have destroyed everything?

She is my alter ego. When I encounter her, I encounter a part of
my self as well. No shared projects, outside interests, hardly a
common history. Yet the intimacy lingers, no matter how seldom
we see each other. If we were together, would we discover that
much was lacking? Is this intimacy really a basis or is it ultimately
only that which we cannot – or only with great difficulty – achieve
with other people? Someone approaches me the same way I approach others – does that make her my alter ego, is Nadjenka a
mirror image, or are we mistaken, but if so, about what . . . why
shouldn't we believe each other, why shouldn't we be able to
shelter each other, be close to each other despite spatial distance?

Perhaps my period is all loused up this time, maybe everything is
blocked up. I get the speculum and take a look. The mouth of the
cervix appears from the depths, stands out glistening, brilliant
between the coral walls enclosing it.

Out of the circular opening a drop of bright red blood, more of
them gather, run down from the vault of the cervix, the confluence
of the red river. I can't help smiling, the flashlight illuminates more
than the cervix. The darkness of the past fifteen years pales. For

fifteen years, every month, red days. I have *my* period, it belongs to me. Having my period was my only chance to belong to my self.

I remember back to the days in school when the girls who were menstruating had to bring a note from their mothers to be excused from gym. Each girl was terribly proud the first time she could present this note, it made her a member of the secret society, it gave her a certain feeling of power. Once in a while, just for the fun of it, all of us would appear before the gym teacher with forged excuses, disconcerted, he would mutter: But – you can't – all – at the same time ... how could he prove the contrary? So we were free to leave, as soon as he came, we took off. Menstruation was a collective event. The cramps, clenched teeth during class, fleeting conversations in the bathroom – all of that met with an understanding smile, a knowing glance.

The traces on the tampon are bright red for one more day. But then the cramps grow stronger, they radiate out from the uterus, I get diarrhoea. I lie down, toss and turn trying in vain to find a comfortable position. The warmth from the heating pad finally seems to help a bit, I drink hot tea with milk. It still hurts, I curl up into a ball, anything to keep from having to straighten my back now. The blood is rushing through my head as usual, I am sweating, all at once saliva collects in my mouth and I try to fight it off but finally stumble to the toilet and spit up the tea. My face is blotchy and contorted. I lie down again, it seems to have passed. Another day is ruined, perhaps by evening I'll be able to think clearly again.

State of Emergency

A woman travels through Germany
ten bleak hours through the chill of night.
Already at the signal of departure
her face shatters
penned in among the sultry vapours of the moving train
she rebels
to avoid being crushed by that fragment of life
at her disposal

Myself outside
before the icy window pane

my breasts sway
anxiously to and fro
a long night coming as the train rushes on
from the fibres of my lips
grow incredulous blossoms

into her abandonment. How far removed
from me she rests
with the deep folds between her legs
from which she brought forth
a daughter, to avoid remaining
alone in that fragment of life
at her disposal.

At the first light of dawn
my anxious breasts must yield.
Lost blossoms wander to and fro
unfathomable between us
to and fro.

Now the red stream is flowing strong, one tampon can dam it for
no more than two hours. My breasts don't hurt any more, but the
web of veins is bluer than usual. I am restless, overwrought, I sleep
fitfully, am worn out when I get up, by hand I write words and
lines which I constantly rearrange. In the afternoon I get tired and
try to sleep for an hour. The merry-go-round inside my head keeps
me cold and tense, my body remains suspended an inch above the
bed, only gradually does it yield, sinking, the pillow meets me
halfway, I can finally rest my head. The cries of the children
playing in the yard fade away, their ball rolls out of earshot. My
toes make my stockings cold. I glide into darker interstages, the
walls of the room disappear. My racing heartbeat brings me back, I
bury my head in the sleep-enticing folds of the pillow, but it's no
use.

   At night I walk with other women along a southern coast. The
cliff drops sharply to the dark blue turquoise-mottled sea below.
We have to fight our way against a wall of wind, but while the
others move on forward, I am caught up in a funnelling draft of air
and slung in spirals towards the sky. Flying! I spread my arms.
Above me an incandescent seagull floating with me in the same

ethereal stream. In gentle waves we glide through the luminous heavens.

This year I had enough time to spend five weeks in the north of Germany. My need for space, for room to breathe, was satisfied in a new way, space gave way to other space. The unsettling vastness of far-away places, the disquieting expanse of foreign lands, the stimulating space of the cities – all these needs were not yet satisfied, yet I did not long for those other places.

Vastness

in which the sun still shone brightly, pouring its balmy light across the sky. The yarrow growing wild at the bottom of the field was so high that I disappeared in it whenever I waded towards the fence to gaze across the meadow. High above in the blue streaked with white, an airplane left its trail every evening at the same time. Oddly enough, I didn't sense the usual pang of take-me-along.

Sitting there behind the house and watching the sinking sun I began to remember that about two years ago this longing for trees, sky, space had last surfaced in me. But since then I hadn't been aware of it or if it had arisen for a moment, I hadn't taken it seriously. It was two years ago, when returning from a trip to Switzerland after spring vacation and landing at the airport in Berlin, that I noticed that the exhilaration of being home was missing. That hadn't happened in five years. Even on the long bus ride home, the usual excitement of being home again was absent. I knew where I was, swayed nonchalantly past familiar buildings and shop windows. I must be exhausted, I decided. I have to get up at six tomorrow, there won't be any time to think until the weekend.

When I reached the apartment I was sharing with the other women, I landed right in the middle of a group meeting. I felt a strong sense of aversion. The naked bulb hanging down in the living-room burned brightly, inhospitable as always; I could only make out the silhouettes of the various women. I wanted peace and quiet, wanted to be home at last. Something was pulsating in my head, dark green shadows. The floodwaters of the Aare River, which had impressed me so, rose inside me for a moment as I put down my bags in my dark room. The walks along the lush overgrown banks, pleasantly light and sunny – I'd done nothing but take walks and look around.

Hours later, when I slipped between the smooth sheets, the green shadows of the darkness began to grow, they overran my bed, a rustling filled the room: There were forests, whole forest regions reflected in the train windows from Bern to Zurich.

I'm getting old, I thought to myself that night on the farm as I drifted off to sleep. At least the landscape of Switzerland doesn't disturb me any more.

I am a slow brooder. I walk around for days without finding any words, or can't choose between the words I do find. They are all inadequate. It wouldn't be so bad if all I had to do was choose the words and then arrange them in a certain order, construct the phrases and arrange them in a certain pattern, and, having done this, find that everything I wanted to say would be there in black and white. But I must create new words, must be selective, write differently, use concepts in a different way. Every so often a word breaks out of my walled-in brain. In the morning I often awaken in the middle of a sentence, at night agitated, I jump out of my warm nest, a word, an image, paper, pencil! Quick, before the landslide in my head begins, before I can clack away at the typewriter until my arms fall off. I let them lie there. The skin on my forehead is cool from the beads of icy sweat. I am full and empty.

There is lightning in the courtyard. The stagnant heat has paralysed me for days. With arms folded I stand at my window. If only it would start to pour! The bleak light tries to peel away the heat from the walls of the building, but it tenaciously refuses to yield. Across the adjoining parking lot bits of paper whirl about in the breeze. An arid wind begins to blow between the buildings, the gusts becoming stronger and stronger.

The light reminds me of the fallow horses Fenna and I had once seen in the country, the tiny foals nestling up against the bellies of the mares.

A door slams shut. I leave the window and walk through the almost empty apartment. Three of the women have gone on vacation. The wind has already scattered the papers lying about on their desks. Will I be able to breathe more freely in this apartment after the storm has blown over? Ever since I came back from the farm it has seemed stifling and cramped in here.

'I figured you would probably come back feeling somewhat alienated and out of touch,' said a woman I live with.

I close the windows. The high ceilings, the walls, everything is closing in on me. I feel like a mummy in this setting. I'd like to empty all six rooms with one fell swoop, throw open all the doors and windows. How could I ever have thought this apartment so large? I take all the pictures down from the walls of my room. Fenna brings me her painted clouds of the north German sky.

The light has turned sulphurous. The room grows dim, the wind has done its job. Now the rain begins to trickle down.

I stretch my hands out of the window. How they were filled with Fenna's full lush lips. They floated through my fingers. My hands a chalice, I search for imprints left behind, but only a calyx of fragrance remains.

Just now in the bathroom
I wanted to take a cold shower because I
felt faint
I noticed that I still
am a bit tan at least
the skin tone on my shoulders and neck
is different than
where my breasts begin
Fenna! and I write you a letter since I wonder
when you'll ever have the time and chance
to observe,
at length and in detail
as such observation demands, that
the skin tone on my shoulders and neck
is different than
where my breasts begin?

We constantly
come up against
limits in our explorations. The limits
of our own strength of available time of
economic resources, of our careers and
our longings. When can we
clarify what longings really are? How can we make
room for our sensual life? The new
emerges but slowly, shedding the old, patchwork.

Do you know this feeling in your abdomen
when the uterus for no apparent reason
contracts and sensations arise out of
fear of being tested, out of sexual desire and
menstrual pain? For years this feeling has now and
again surfaced even when I was under no
extraordinary pressures in the middle of the day
perhaps without apparent cause.

But if I think of
how I felt in the kitchen as a child,
I can retrace the faint trail –
relationships which have been severed
or damaged beyond repair.

Last night in my dreams I stood before a three-panelled mirror.
When I looked straight in I saw my face as it looks back at
me during the day or in recent photos, only my hair was still
long and piled atop my head. When I turned my head to the left
my face changed in that side of the mirror, it was my eyes which
were first transformed. Bruises appeared all around my eyes, dark
blue on my eyelids purplish along my cheekbones. My eyebrows
became bushy and black my skin wilted. My hair turned grey and
coarse.

It did not surprise me that my face had aged.

But it became the face of a total stranger. Not a single line was
familiar. If I turned straight ahead again I saw my real face. So the
old woman in the left half of the mirror must have something to do
with me. I was startled because the face seemed disfigured and I
moved closer to get a better look at the bruises. I discovered a
delicate pattern of veins in the purplish marks. I turned sideways to
the left portion of the mirror and looked at my shoulders, then my
back. A shawl was draped across my shoulders: a veil of twining
tendrils and flowers green blue and red. From above the aged face
peered down at me. Fenna,
I said, look, look how beautiful that is!
What's going on here? My face ages on my
body a new fabric. I finally realize
that I always thought my body unfashionable

out-of-date, and that thinking it
out-of-date actually spared me much.
If I hadn't complicated matters so much
carrying my body around a dead weight,
if I hadn't lugged it around as I did
I would have been more completely coopted by
everyday sexuality. My body itself kept that from
happening. It didn't measure up to
male expectations.
I can recognize fragments of my own past history
as well as that of all other women.
There is a trend which gives direction
to the future even in the present
there are multiple layers of processes going on at
different speeds rhythms and on
different levels.
There is no simultaneity to be found. The various
processes collide inside of me
at different points in time with varying degrees
of impact – this sense that life is sometimes
so *compacted*. Even though it is already a
thing of the past I often think of
what I felt on the flight back from New York.
I knelt on the floor and pressed my face against
the window as the plane took off. Far below
the coast disappeared, a white outline. When I
saw that it actually resembled the one
on the globe I had a fleeting image of
America and an idea of the contours of the globe
as a whole. Again I felt this urgent desire to
know the *world* as I flew back to Europe, back to
Berlin without knowing what I was still seeking there.
But in these last glimpses of the American coastline
I had a certain feeling, one which flared up only to
die down again, a feeling that I was not really
returning but rather moving on without ever
taking hold.
How casually this giant continent
coasts into the ocean!

It gave me such a lift, seemed so simple and
natural seeing it, the confines of my own body
could expand for a few moments.
Our being, on the other hand, is
boxed in on all sides.
Now that it seems that we are not smothering
each other even though the intimacy has grown
now that the perils of a love affair
while not completely ruled out
have so far at least been held in check . . .
now we notice that we can't do anything right.
A long time ago
we began with the vague desire
to have something to *do* with one another. Now that
it is really a serious matter, we find there are
so many obstacles to overcome. We must constantly
neglect something in favour of something else.
The job suffers because of political activities the
political activities because of the job
the job on the other hand doesn't bring in
enough money earning money takes time away from
our other important work.
We lose each other along the way. Constantly having
to decide
between us and our work – that too a
conflict – if we neglected our work the perils
of a love affair would mount. Painting and
writing to some extent offer tangible guidelines,
it is only because of these that we can survive,
that we can attempt to transcend
the tragically restrictive means of communication
open to us.
But we cannot rise above the fits of anger and despair.
Tomorrow morning I will ring your doorbell you
will open the latch I will drop these pages into
your mailbox, having compressed into a few lines
that which would require many hours
not perhaps to capture
our longings but to communicate them

not perhaps to live but to suspend
merely surviving
for a few hours.

Translated by Johanna Moore and Beth Weckmüller

•

BESSIE HEAD
The Collector of Treasures
(1977)

*Her Scottish mother was imprisoned for life in South Africa for becoming
pregnant by a Zulu stable worker. Taken from her at birth, Bessie Head
was brought up by a black foster-family before receiving secondary education
and teacher training at a mission orphanage in Durban. She soon became
active in African Nationalist affairs and fled to Botswana in 1964, where
she taught, wrote journalism for* Drum *and worked with other political
refugees.*

Her first novel, When Rain Clouds Gather *(1969), was an international
success and, like all her writing, it tackled racial, political and sexual issues
with tremendous impact. A* Question of Power *(1973) followed a massive
breakdown, and agonizingly evokes the mental anguish of the author at this
time. 'The Collector of Treasures', first published in* Ms *magazine, is one of
a number of Botswana stories and sketches that she wrote before her death
from hepatitis in 1986.*

The long-term central state prison in the south was a whole day's
journey away from the villages of the northern part of the country.
They had left the village of Puleng at about nine that morning and all
day long the police truck droned as it sped southwards on the wide,
dusty cross-country track-road. The everyday world of ploughed
fields, grazing cattle, and vast expanses of bush and forest seemed
indifferent to the hungry eyes of the prisoner who gazed out at them
through the wire mesh grating at the back of the police truck. At
some point during the journey, the prisoner seemed to strike at some
ultimate source of pain and loneliness within her being and, overcome
by it, she slowly crumpled forward in a wasted heap, oblivious to

everything but her pain. Sunset swept by, then dusk, then dark and still the truck droned on, impersonally, uncaring.

At first, faintly on the horizon, the orange glow of the city lights of the new independence town of Gaborone, appeared like an astonishing phantom in the overwhelming darkness of the bush, until the truck struck tarred roads, neon lights, shops and cinemas, and made the bush a phantom amidst a blaze of light. All this passed untimed, unwatched by the crumpled prisoner; she did not stir as the truck finally droned to a halt outside the prison gates. The torchlight struck the side of her face like an agonizing blow. Thinking she was asleep, the policeman called out briskly:

'You must awaken now. We have arrived.'

He struggled with the lock in the dark and pulled open the grating. She crawled painfully forward, in silence.

Together, they walked up a short flight of stairs and waited awhile as the man tapped lightly, several times, on the heavy iron prison door. The night-duty attendant opened the door a crack, peered out and then opened the door a little wider for them to enter. He quietly and casually led the way to a small office, looked at his colleague and asked: 'What do we have here?'

'It's the husband murder case from Puleng village,' the other replied, handing over a file.

The attendant took the file and sat down at a table on which lay open a large record book. In a big, bold scrawl he recorded the details: Dikeledi Mokopi. Charge: Man-slaughter. Sentence: Life. A night-duty wardress appeared and led the prisoner away to a side cubicle, where she was asked to undress.

'Have you any money on you?' the wardress queried, handing her a plain, green cotton dress, which was the prison uniform. The prisoner silently shook her head.

'So, you have killed your husband, have you?' the wardress remarked, with a flicker of humour. 'You'll be in good company. We have four other women here for the same crime. It's becoming the fashion these days. Come with me,' and she led the way along a corridor, turned left and stopped at an iron gate which she opened with a key, waited for the prisoner to walk in ahead of her and then locked it with the key again. They entered a small, immensely high-walled courtyard. On one side were toilets, showers, and a cupboard. On the other, an empty concrete quadrangle. The wardress walked to the cupboard, unlocked it and took out a thick roll of clean-smelling blankets, which she handed to the prisoner. At the lower end of the walled courtyard was a heavy iron door which led to the cell. The wardress walked up to this door, banged on it loudly and called out: 'I say, will you women in there light your candle?'

A voice within called out: 'All right,' and they could hear the scratch-scratch of a match. The wardress again inserted a key, opened the door and watched for a while as the prisoner spread out her blankets on the floor. The four women prisoners already confined in the cell sat up briefly, and stared silently at their new companion. As the door was locked, they all greeted her quietly and one of the women asked: 'Where do you come from?'

'Puleng', the newcomer replied, and seemingly satisfied with that, the light was blown out and the women lay down to continue their interrupted sleep. And as though she had reached the end of her destination, the new prisoner too fell into a deep sleep as soon as she had pulled her blankets about her.

The breakfast gong sounded at six the next morning. The women stirred themselves for their daily routine. They stood up, shook out their blankets and rolled them up into neat bundles. The day-duty wardress rattled the key in the lock and let them out into the small concrete courtyard so that they could perform their morning toilet. Then, with a loud clatter of pails and plates, two male prisoners appeared at the gate with breakfast. The men handed each woman a plate of porridge and a mug of black tea and they settled themselves on the concrete floor to eat. They turned and looked at their new companion and one of the women, a spokesman for the group, said kindly:

'You should take care. The tea has no sugar in it. What we usually do is scoop the sugar off the porridge and put it into the tea.'

The woman, Dikeledi, looked up and smiled. She had experienced such terror during the awaiting-trial period that she looked more like a skeleton than a human being. The skin creaked tautly over her cheeks. The other woman smiled, but after her own fashion. Her face permanently wore a look of cynical, whimsical humour. She had a full, plump figure. She introduced herself and her companions: 'My name is Kebonye. Then that's Otsetswe, Galeboe, and Monwana. What may your name be?'

'Dikeledi Mokopi.'

'How is it that you have such a tragic name,' Kebonye observed. 'Why did your parents have to name you *tears*?'

'My father passed away at that time and it is my mother's tears that I am named after,' Dikeledi said, then added: 'She herself passed away six years later and I was brought up by my uncle.'

Kebonye shook her head sympathetically, slowly raising a spoonful of porridge to her mouth. That swallowed, she asked next:

'And what may your crime be?'

'I have killed my husband.'

'We are all here for the same crime,' Kebonye said, then with her cynical smile asked: 'Do you feel any sorrow about the crime?'

'Not really,' the other woman replied.

'How did you kill him?'

'I cut off all his special parts with a knife,' Dikeledi said.

'I did it with a razor,' Kebonye said. She sighed and added: 'I have had a troubled life.'

A little silence followed while they all busied themselves with their food, then Kebonye continued musingly:

'Our men do not think that we need tenderness and care. You know, my husband used to kick me between the legs when he wanted that. I once aborted with a child, due to this treatment. I could see that there was no way to appeal to him if I felt ill, so I once said to him that if he liked he could keep some other woman as well because I couldn't manage to satisfy all his needs. Well, he was an education-officer and each year he used to suspend about seventeen male teachers for making schoolgirls pregnant, but he used to do the same. The last time it happened the parents of the girl were very angry and came to report the matter to me. I told them: "You leave it to me. I have seen enough." And so I killed him.'

They sat in silence and completed their meal, then they took their plates and cups to rinse them in the wash-room. The wardress produced some pails and a broom. Their sleeping quarters had to be flushed out with water; there was not a speck of dirt anywhere, but that was prison routine. All that was left was an inspection by the director of the prison. Here again Kebonye turned to the newcomer and warned:

'You must be careful when the chief comes to inspect. He is mad about one thing – attention! Stand up straight! Hands at your sides!

If this is not done you should see how he stands here and curses. He does not mind anything but that. He is mad about that.'

Inspection over, the women were taken through a number of gates to an open, sunny yard, fenced in by high barbed wire where they did their daily work. The prison was a rehabilitation centre where the prisoners produced goods which were sold in the prison store; the women produced garments of cloth and wool; the men did carpentry, shoe-making, brick-making, and vegetable production.

Dikeledi had a number of skills – she could knit, sew, and weave baskets. All the women at present were busy knitting woollen garments; some were learners and did their work slowly and painstakingly. They looked at Dikeledi with interest as she took a ball of wool and a pair of knitting needles and rapidly cast on stitches. She had soft, caressing, almost boneless, hands of strange power – work of a beautiful design grew from those hands. By mid-morning she had completed the front part of a jersey and they all stopped to admire the pattern she had invented in her own head.

'You are a gifted person,' Kebonye remarked, admiringly.

'All my friends say so,' Dikeledi replied smiling. 'You know, I am the woman whose thatch does not leak. Whenever my friends wanted to thatch their huts, I was there. They would never do it without me. I was always busy and employed because it was with these hands that I fed and reared my children. My husband left me after four years of marriage but I managed well enough to feed those mouths. If people did not pay me in money for my work, they paid me with gifts of food.'

'It's not so bad here,' Kebonye said. 'We get a little money saved for us out of the sale of our work, and if you work like that you can still produce money for your children. How many children do you have?'

'I have three sons.'

'Are they in good care?'

'Yes.'

'I like lunch,' Kebonye said, oddly turning the conversation. 'It is the best meal of the day. We get samp and meat and vegetables.'

So the day passed pleasantly enough with chatter and work and at sunset the women were once more taken back to the cell for lock-up time. They unrolled their blankets and prepared their beds, and with the candle lit continued to talk a while longer. Just as they were about to retire for the night, Dikeledi nodded to her new-found friend, Kebonye:

'Thank you for all your kindness to me,' she said, softly.

'We must help each other,' Kebonye replied, with her amused, cynical smile. 'This is a terrible world. There is only misery here.'

And so the woman Dikeledi began phase three of a life that had been ashen in its loneliness and unhappiness. And yet she had always found gold amidst the ash, deep loves that had joined her heart to the hearts of others. She smiled tenderly at Kebonye because she knew already that she had found another such love. She was the collector of such treasures.

There were really only two kinds of men in the society. The one kind created such misery and chaos that he could be broadly damned as evil. If one watched the village dogs chasing a bitch on heat, they usually moved around in packs of four or five. As the mating progressed one dog would attempt to gain dominance over the festivities and oust all the others from the bitch's vulva. The rest of the hapless dogs would stand around yapping and snapping in its face while the top dog indulged in a continuous spurt of orgasms, day and night until he was exhausted. No doubt, during that Herculean feat, the dog imagined he was the only penis in the world and that there had to be a scramble for it. That kind of man lived near the animal level and behaved just the same. Like the dogs and bulls and donkeys, he also accepted no responsibility for the young he procreated and like the dogs and bulls and donkeys, he also made females abort. Since that kind of man was in the majority in the society, he needed a little analysing as he was responsible for the complete breakdown of family life. He could be analysed over three time-spans. In the old days, before the colonial invasion of Africa, he was a man who lived by the traditions and taboos outlined for all the people by the forefathers of the tribe. He had little individual freedom to assess whether these traditions were compassionate or not – they demanded that he comply and obey the rules, without thought. But when the laws of the ancestors are examined, they appear on the whole to have been vast, external disciplines for the good of the society as a whole, with little attention given to individual preferences and needs. The ancestors made so many errors and one of the most bitter-making things was that they relegated to men a superior position in the tribe, while women were regarded, in a congenital sense, as being an inferior form of human life. To this day, women still suffered from all the calamities that befall an inferior form of human life. The colonial era and the period of migratory mining labour to South Africa was a further affliction visited on this man. It broke the hold of the ancestors. It broke the old, traditional form of family life and for long periods a man was separated from his wife and children while he worked for a pittance in another land in order to raise the money to pay his British Colonial poll-tax. British Colonialism scarcely enriched his life. He then became 'the boy' of the white man and a machine-tool of the South African mines. African independence seemed merely one more affliction on top of the afflictions that had visited this man's life. Independence suddenly and dramatically changed the pattern of colonial subservience. More jobs became available under the new government's localization programme and salaries sky-rocketed at the same time. It provided the first occasion for family life of a new order, above the childlike discipline of custom, the degradation of colonialism. Men and women, in order to survive, had to turn inwards to their own resources. It was the man who arrived at this turning-point, a broken wreck with no inner resources at all. It was as though he was hideous to himself and in an effort to flee his own inner emptiness, he spun away from himself in a dizzy kind of death dance of wild destruction and dissipation.

One such man was Garesego Mokopi, the husband of Dikeledi. For four years prior to independence, he had worked as a clerk in the district administration service, at a steady salary of R50.00 a month. Soon after independence his salary shot up to R200.00 per month. Even during his lean days he had had a taste for womanizing and drink; now he had the resources for a real spree. He was not seen at home again and lived and slept around the village, from woman to woman. He left his wife and three sons – Banabothe, the eldest, aged four; Inalame, aged three; and the youngest, Motsomi, aged one – to their own resources. Perhaps he did so because she was the boring, semi-literate traditional sort, and there were a lot of exciting new women around. Independence produced marvels indeed.

There was another kind of man in the society with the power to create himself anew. He turned all his resources, both emotional and material, towards his family life and he went on and on with his own quiet rhythm, like a river. He was a poem of tenderness.

One such man was Paul Thebolo and he and his wife, Kenalepe, and their three children, came to live in the village of Puleng in 1966, the year of independence. Paul Thebolo had been offered the principalship of a primary school in the village. They were allocated an empty field beside the yard of Dikeledi Mokopi for their new home.

Neighbours are the centre of the universe to each other. They help each other at all times and mutually loan each other's goods. Dikeledi Mokopi kept an interested eye on the yard of her new neighbours. At first, only the man appeared with some workmen to erect the fence, which was set up with incredible speed and efficiency. The man impressed her immediately when she went around to introduce herself and find out a little about the newcomers. He was tall, large-boned, slow-moving. He was so peaceful as a person that the sunlight and shadow played all kinds of tricks with his eyes, making it difficult to determine their exact colour. When he stood still and looked reflective, the sunlight liked to creep into his eyes and nestle there; so sometimes his eyes were the colour of shade, and sometimes light brown.

He turned and smiled at her in a friendly way when she introduced herself and explained that he and his wife were on transfer from the village of Bobonong. His wife and children were living with relatives in the village until the yard was prepared. He was in a hurry to settle down as the school term would start in a month's time. They were, he said, going to erect two mud huts first and later he intended setting up a small house of bricks. His wife would be coming around in a few days with some women to erect the mud walls of the huts.

'I would like to offer my help too,' Dikeledi said. 'If work always starts early in the morning and there are about six of us, we can get both walls erected in a week. If you want one of the huts done in woman's thatch, all my friends know that I am the woman whose thatch does not leak.'

The man smilingly replied that he would impart all this information to his wife, then he added charmingly that he thought she would like his wife when they met. His wife was a very friendly person; everyone liked her.

Dikeledi walked back to her own yard with a high heart. She had few callers. None of her relatives called for fear that since her husband had left her she would become dependent on them for many things. The people who called did business with her; they wanted her to make dresses for their children or knit jerseys for the winter time and at times when she had no orders at all she made baskets which she sold. In these ways she supported herself and the three children but she was lonely for true friends.

All turned out as the husband had said – he had a lovely wife. She was fairly tall and thin with a bright, vivacious manner. She made no effort to conceal that normally, and every day, she was a very happy person. And all turned out as Dikeledi had said. The work-party of six women erected the mud walls of the huts in one week; two weeks later, the thatch was complete. The Thebolo family moved into their new abode and Dikeledi Mokopi moved into one of the most prosperous and happy periods of her life. Her life took a big, wide upward curve. Her relationship with the Thebolo family was more than the usual friendly exchange of neighbours. It was rich and creative.

It was not long before the two women had going one of those deep, affectionate, sharing-everything kind of friendships that only women know how to have. It seemed that Kenalepe wanted endless amounts of dresses made for herself and her three little girls. Since Dikeledi would not accept cash for these services – she protested about the many benefits she received from her good neighbours – Paul Thebolo arranged that she be paid in household goods for these services so that for some years Dikeledi was always assured of her basic household needs – the full bag of corn, sugar, tea, powdered milk, and cooking oil. Kenalepe was also the kind of woman who made the whole world spin around her; her attractive personality attracted a whole range of women to her yard and also a whole range of customers for her dressmaking friend, Dikeledi. Eventually, Dikeledi became swamped with work, was forced to buy a second sewing-machine and employ a helper. The two women did everything together – they were forever together at weddings, funerals, and parties in the village. In their leisure hours they freely discussed all their intimate affairs with each other, so that each knew thoroughly the details of the other's life.

'You are a lucky someone,' Dikeledi remarked one day, wistfully. 'Not everyone has the gift of a husband like Paul.'

'Oh yes,' Kenalepe said happily. 'He is an honest somebody.' She knew a little of Dikeledi's list of woes and queried: 'But why did you marry a man like Garesego? I looked carefully at him when you pointed him out to me near the shops the other day and I could see at one glance that he is a butterfly.'

'I think I mostly wanted to get out of my uncle's yard,' Dikeledi replied. 'I never liked my uncle. Rich as he was, he was a hard man and very selfish. I was only a servant there and pushed about. I went there when I was six years old when my mother died, and it was not a happy life. All his children despised me because I was their servant. Uncle paid for my education for six years, then he said I must leave school. I longed for more because as you know, education opens up the world for one. Garesego was a friend of my uncle and he was the only man who proposed for me. They discussed it between themselves and then my uncle said: "You'd better marry Garesego because you're just hanging around here like a chain on my neck." I agreed, just to get away from that terrible man. Garesego said at that time that he'd rather be married to my sort than the educated kind because those women were stubborn and wanted to lay down the rules for men. Really, I did not ever protest when he started running about. You know what the other women do. They chase after the man from one hut to another and beat up the girlfriends. The man just runs into another hut, that's all. So you don't really win. I wasn't going to do anything like that. I am satisfied I have children. They are a blessing to me.'

'Oh, it isn't enough,' her friend said, shaking her head in deep sympathy. 'I am amazed at how life imparts its gifts. Some people get too much. Others get nothing at all. I have always been lucky in life. One day my parents will visit – they live in the south – and you'll see the fuss they make over me. Paul is just the same. He takes care of everything so that I never have a day of worry . . .'

The man Paul attracted as wide a range of male friends as his wife. They had guests every evening; illiterate men who wanted him to fill in tax forms or write letters for them, or his own colleagues who wanted to debate the political issues of the day – there was always something new happening every day now that the country had independence. The two women sat on the edge of these debates and listened with fascinated ears, but they never participated. The following day they would chew over the debates with wise, earnest expressions.

'Men's minds travel widely and boldly,' Kenalepe would comment. 'It makes me shiver the way they freely criticize our new government. Did you hear what Petros said last night? He said he knew all those bastards and they were just a lot of crooks who would pull a lot of dirty tricks. Oh dear! I shivered so much when he said that. The way they talk about the government makes you feel in your bones that this is not a safe world to be in, not like the old days when we didn't have governments. And Lentswe said that ten per cent of the population in England really control all the wealth of the country, while the rest live at starvation level. And he said communism would sort all this out. I gathered from the way they discussed this matter that our government is not in favour of communism. I trembled so much when this became clear to me . . .' She paused and laughed proudly. 'I've heard Paul say this several times: "The British only ruled us for eighty years." I wonder why Paul is so fond of saying that?'

And so a completely new world opened up for Dikeledi. It was so impossibly rich and happy that, as the days went by, she immersed herself more deeply in it and quite overlooked the barrenness of her own life. But it hung there like a nagging ache in the mind of her friend, Kenalepe.

'You ought to find another man,' she urged one day, when they had one of their personal discussions. 'It's not good for a woman to live alone.'

'And who would that be?' Dikeledi asked, disillusioned. 'I'd only be bringing trouble into my life whereas now it is all in order. I have my eldest son at school and I can manage to pay the school fees. That's all I really care about.'

'I mean,' said Kenalepe, 'we are also here to make love and enjoy it.'

'Oh I never really cared for it,' the other replied. 'When you experience the worst of it, it just puts you off altogether.'

'What do you mean by that?' Kenalepe asked, wide-eyed.

'I mean it was just jump on and jump off and I used to wonder what it was all about. I developed a dislike for it.'

'You mean Garesego was like that!' Kenalepe said, flabbergasted.

'Why, that's just like a cock hopping from hen to hen. I wonder what he is doing with all those women. I'm sure they are just after his money and so they flatter him . . .' She paused and then added earnestly: 'That's really all the more reason you should find another man. Oh, if you knew what it was really like, you would long for it, I can tell you! I sometimes think I enjoy that side of life far too much. Paul knows a lot about all that. And he always has some new trick with which to surprise me. He has a certain way of smiling when he has thought up something new and I shiver a little and say to myself: "Ha, what is Paul going to do tonight!"'

Kenalepe paused and smiled at her friend, slyly.

'I can loan Paul to you if you like,' she said, then raised one hand to block the protest on her friend's face. 'I would do it because I have never had a friend like you in my life before whom I trust so much. Paul had other girls you know, before he married me, so it's not such an uncommon thing to him. Besides, we used to make love long before we got married and I never got pregnant. He takes care of that side too. I wouldn't mind loaning him because I am expecting another child and I don't feel so well these days . . .'

Dikeledi stared at the ground for a long moment, then she looked up at her friend with tears in her eyes.

'I cannot accept such a gift from you,' she said, deeply moved. 'But if you are ill I will wash for you and cook for you.'

Not put off by her friend's refusal of her generous offer, Kenalepe mentioned the discussion to her husband that very night. He was so taken off-guard by the unexpectedness of the subject that at first he looked slightly astonished, and burst out into loud laughter and for such a lengthy time that he seemed unable to stop.

'Why are you laughing like that?' Kenalepe asked, surprised.

He laughed a bit more, then suddenly turned very serious and thoughtful and was lost in his own thoughts for some time. When she asked him what he was thinking he merely replied: 'I don't want to tell you everything. I want to keep some of my secrets to myself.'

The next day Kenalepe reported this to her friend.

'Now whatever does he mean by that? I want to keep some of my secrets to myself?'

'I think,' Dikeledi said smiling, 'I think he has a conceit about being a good man. Also, when someone loves someone too much, it hurts them to say so. They'd rather keep silent.'

Shortly after this Kenalepe had a miscarriage and had to be admitted to hospital for a minor operation. Dikeledi kept her promise 'to wash and cook' for her friend. She ran both their homes, fed the children and kept everything in order. Also, people complained about the poorness of the hospital diet and each day she scoured the village for eggs and chicken, cooked them, and took them to Kenalepe every day at the lunch-hour.

One evening Dikeledi ran into a snag with her routine. She had just dished up supper for the Thebolo children when a customer came around with an urgent request for an alteration on a wedding dress. The wedding was to take place the next day. She left the children seated around the fire eating and returned to her own home. An hour later, her own children asleep and settled, she thought she would check the Thebolo yard to see if all was well there. She entered the children's hut and noted that they had put themselves to bed and were fast asleep. Their supper plates lay scattered and unwashed around the fire. The hut which Paul and Kenalepe shared was in darkness. It meant that Paul had not yet returned from his usual evening visit to his wife. Dikeledi collected the plates and washed them, then poured the dirty dishwater on the still-glowing embers of the outdoor fire. She piled the plates one on top of the other and carried them to the third additional hut, which was used as a kitchen. Just then Paul Thebolo entered the yard, noted the lamp and movement in the kitchen hut and walked over to it. He paused at the open door.

'What are you doing now, Mma-Banabothe?' he asked, addressing her affectionately in the customary way by the name of her eldest son, Banabothe.

'I know quite well what I am doing,' Dikeledi replied happily. She turned around to say that it was not a good thing to leave dirty dishes standing overnight but her mouth flew open with surprise. Two soft pools of cool liquid light were in his eyes and something infinitely sweet passed between them; it was too beautiful to be love.

'You are a very good woman, Mma-Banabothe,' he said softly.

It was the truth and the gift was offered like a nugget of gold. Only men like Paul Thebolo could offer such gifts. She took it and stored another treasure in her heart. She bowed her knee in the traditional curtsey and walked quietly away to her own home.

*

Eight years passed for Dikeledi in a quiet rhythm of work and
friendship with the Thebolos. The crisis came with the eldest son,
Banabothe. He had to take his primary school leaving examination
at the end of the year. This serious event sobered him up consider-
ably as like all boys he was very fond of playtime. He brought his
books home and told his mother that he would like to study in the
evenings. He would like to pass with a Grade A to please her. With
a flushed and proud face Dikeledi mentioned this to her friend,
Kenalepe.

'Banabothe is studying every night now,' she said. 'He never
really cared for studies. I am so pleased about this that I bought
him a spare lamp and removed him from the children's hut to my
own hut where things will be peaceful for him. We both sit up late
at night now. I sew on buttons and fix hems and he does his
studies . . .'

She also opened a savings account at the post office in order to
have some standby money to pay the fees for his secondary education. They were rather high – R85.00. But in spite of all her
hoarding of odd cents, towards the end of the year, she was short
on R20.00 to cover the fees. Midway during the Christmas school
holidays the results were announced. Banabothe passed with a
Grade A. His mother was almost hysterical in her joy at his
achievement. But what to do? The two youngest sons had already
started primary school and she would never manage to cover all
their fees from her resources. She decided to remind Garesego
Mokopi that he was the father of the children. She had not seen
him in eight years except as a passer-by in the village. Sometimes he
waved but he had never talked to her or inquired about her life or
that of the children. It did not matter. She was a lower form of
human life. Then this unpleasant something turned up at his office
one day, just as he was about to leave for lunch. She had heard
from village gossip that he had eventually settled down with a
married woman who had a brood of children of her own. He had
ousted her husband, in a typical village sensation of brawls, curses,
and abuse. Most probably the husband did not care because there
were always arms outstretched towards a man, as long as he looked
like a man. The attraction of this particular woman for Garesego
Mokopi, so her former lovers said with a snicker, was that she went
in for heady forms of love-making like biting and scratching.

Garesego Mokopi walked out of his office and looked irritably at the ghost from his past, his wife. She obviously wanted to talk to him and he walked towards her, looking at his watch all the while. Like all the new 'success men', he had developed a paunch, his eyes were bloodshot, his face was bloated, and the odour of the beer and sex from the previous night clung faintly around him. He indicated with his eyes that they should move around to the back of the office block where they could talk in privacy.

'You must hurry with whatever you want to say,' he said impatiently. 'The lunch-hour is very short and I have to be back at the office by two.'

Not to him could she talk of the pride she felt in Banabothe's achievement, so she said simply and quietly: 'Garesego, I beg you to help me pay Banabothe's fees for secondary school. He has passed with a Grade A and as you know, the school fees must be produced on the first day of school or else he will be turned away. I have struggled to save money the whole year but I am short by R20.00.'

She handed him her post office savings book, which he took, glanced at and handed back to her. Then he smiled, a smirky know-all smile, and thought he was delivering her a blow in the face.

'Why don't you ask Paul Thebolo for the money?' he said. 'Everyone knows he's keeping two homes and that you are his spare. Everyone knows about that full bag of corn he delivers to your home every six months so why can't he pay the school fees as well?'

She neither denied this, nor confirmed it. The blow glanced off her face which she raised slightly, in pride. Then she walked away.

As was their habit, the two women got together that afternoon and Dikeledi reported this conversation with her husband to Kenal-epe who tossed back her head in anger and said fiercely: 'The filthy pig himself! He thinks every man is like him, does he? I shall report this matter to Paul, then he'll see something.'

And indeed Garesego did see something but it was just up his alley. He was a female prostitute in his innermost being and like all professional prostitutes, he enjoyed publicity and sensation — it promoted his cause. He smiled genially and expansively when a madly angry Paul Thebolo came up to the door of his house where he lived with *his* concubine. Garesego had been through a lot of these dramas over those eight years and he almost knew by rote the dialogue that would follow.

'You bastard!' Paul Thebolo spat out. 'Your wife isn't my concubine, do you hear?'

'Then why are you keeping her in food?' Garesego drawled. 'Men only do that for women they fuck! They never do it for nothing.'

Paul Thebolo rested one hand against the wall, half dizzy with anger, and he said tensely: 'You defile life, Garesego Mokopi. There's nothing else in your world but defilement. Mma-Banabothe makes clothes for my wife and children and she will never accept money from me so how else must I pay her?'

'It only proves the story both ways,' the other replied, vilely. 'Women do that for men who fuck them.'

Paul Thebolo shot out the other hand, punched him soundly in one grinning eye and walked away. Who could hide a livid, swollen eye? To every surprised inquiry, he replied with an injured air:

'It was done by my wife's lover, Paul Thebolo.'

It certainly brought the attention of the whole village upon him, which was all he really wanted. Those kinds of men were the bottom rung of government. They secretly hungered to be the President with all eyes on them. He worked up the sensation a little further. He announced that he would pay the school fees of the child of his concubine, who was also to enter secondary school, but not the school fees of his own child, Banabothe. People half liked the smear on Paul Thebolo; he was too good to be true. They delighted in making him a part of the general dirt of the village, so they turned on Garesego and scolded: 'Your wife might be getting things from Paul Thebolo but it's beyond the purse of any man to pay the school fees of his own children as well as the school fees of another man's children. Banabothe wouldn't be there had you not procreated him, Garesego, so it is your duty to care for him. Besides, it's your fault if your wife takes another man. You left her alone all these years.'

So that story was lived with for two weeks, mostly because people wanted to say that Paul Thebolo was a part of life too and as uncertain of his morals as they were. But the story took such a dramatic turn that it made all the men shudder with horror. It was some weeks before they could find the courage to go to bed with women; they preferred to do something else.

Garesego's obscene thought processes were his own undoing. He really believed that another man had a stake in his hen-pen and like any cock, his hair was up about it. He thought he'd walk in and re-establish his own claim to it and so, after two weeks, once the swelling in his eye had died down, he espied Banabothe in the village and asked him to take a note to his mother. He said the child should bring a reply. The note read: 'Dear Mother, I am coming home again so that we may settle our differences. Will you prepare a meal for me and some hot water that I might take a bath. Gare.'

Dikeledi took the note, read it and shook with rage. All its overtones were clear to her. He was coming home for some sex. They had had no differences. They had not even talked to each other.

'Banabothe,' she said. 'Will you play near by? I want to think a bit then I will send you to your father with the reply.'

Her thought processes were not very clear to her. There was something she could not immediately touch upon. Her life had become holy to her during all those years she had struggled to maintain herself and the children. She had filled her life with treasures of kindness and love she had gathered from others and it was all this that she wanted to protect from defilement by an evil man. Her first panic-stricken thought was to gather up the children and flee the village. But where to go? Garesego did not want a divorce, she had left him to approach her about the matter, she had desisted from taking any other man. She turned her thoughts this way and that and could find no way out except to face him. If she wrote back, don't you dare put foot in the yard I don't want to see you, he would ignore it. Black women didn't have that kind of power. A thoughtful, brooding look came over her face. At last, at peace with herself, she went into her hut and wrote a reply: 'Sir, I shall prepare everything as you have said. Dikeledi.'

It was about midday when Banabothe sped back with the reply to his father. All afternoon Dikeledi busied herself making preparations for the appearance of her husband at sunset. At one point Kenalepe approached the yard and looked around in amazement at the massive preparations, the large iron water pot full of water with a fire burning under it, the extra cooking pots on the fire. Only later Kenalepe brought the knife into focus. But it was only a vague blur, a large kitchen knife used to cut meat and Dikeledi knelt at a grinding-stone and sharpened it slowly and methodically. What was in focus then was the final and tragic expression on the upturned face of her friend. It threw her into confusion and blocked their usual free and easy feminine chatter. When Dikeledi said: 'I am making some preparations for Garesego. He is coming home tonight,' Kenalepe beat a hasty retreat to her own home terrified. They knew they were involved because when she mentioned this to Paul he was distracted and uneasy for the rest of the day. He kept on doing upside-down sort of things, not replying to questions, absent-mindedly leaving a cup of tea until it got quite cold, and every now and again he stood up and paced about, lost in his own thoughts. So deep was their sense of disturbance that towards evening they no longer made a pretence of talking. They just sat in silence in their hut. Then, at about nine o'clock, they heard those wild and agonized bellows. They both rushed out together to the yard of Dikeledi Mokopi.

He came home at sunset and found everything ready for him as he had requested, and he settled himself down to enjoy a man's life. He had brought a pack of beer along and sat outdoors slowly savouring it while every now and then his eye swept over the Thebolo yard. Only the woman and children moved about the yard. The man was out of sight. Garesego smiled to himself, pleased that he could crow as loud as he liked with no answering challenge.

A basin of warm water was placed before him to wash his hands and then Dikeledi served him his meal. At a separate distance she also served the children and then instructed them to wash and prepare for bed. She noted that Garesego displayed no interest in the children whatsoever. He was entirely wrapped up in himself and thought only of himself and his own comfort. Any tenderness he offered the children might have broken her and swerved her mind away from the deed she had carefully planned all that afternoon. She was beneath his regard and notice too for when she eventually brought her own plate of food and sat near him, he never once glanced at her face. He drank his beer and cast his glance every now and again at the Thebolo yard. Not once did the man of the yard appear until it became too dark to distinguish anything any more. He was completely satisfied with that. He could repeat the performance every day until he broke the mettle of the other cock again and forced him into angry abuse. He liked that sort of thing.

'Garesego, do you think you could help me with Banabothe's school fees?' Dikeledi asked at one point.

'Oh, I'll think about it,' he replied casually.

She stood up and carried buckets of water into the hut, which she poured into a large tin bath that he might bathe himself, then while he took his bath she busied herself tidying up and completing the last of the household chores. Those done, she entered the children's hut. They played hard during the day and they had already fallen asleep with exhaustion. She knelt down near their sleeping mats and stared at them for a long while, with an extremely tender expression. Then she blew out their lamp and walked to her own hut. Garesego lay sprawled across the bed in such a manner that indicated he only thought of himself and did not intend sharing the bed with anyone else. Satiated with food and drink, he had fallen into a deep, heavy sleep the moment his head touched the pillow. His concubine had no doubt taught him that the correct way for a man to go to bed, was naked. So he lay, unguarded and defenceless, sprawled across the bed on his back.

The bath made a loud clatter as Dikeledi removed it from the room, but still he slept on, lost to the world. She re-entered the hut and closed the door. Then she bent down and reached for the knife under the bed which she had merely concealed with a cloth. With the precision and skill of her hardworking hands, she grasped hold of his genitals and cut them off with one stroke. In doing so, she slit the main artery which ran on the inside of the groin. A massive spurt of blood arched its way across the bed. And Garesego bellowed. He bellowed his anguish. Then all was silent. She stood and watched his death anguish with an intent and brooding look, missing not one detail of it. A knock on the door stirred her out of her reverie. It was the boy, Banabothe. She opened the door and stared at him, speechless. He was trembling violently.

'Mother,' he said, in a terrified whisper. 'Didn't I hear father cry?'

'I have killed him,' she said, waving her hand in the air with a gesture that said – well, that's that. Then she added sharply: 'Banabothe, go and call the police.'

He turned and fled into the night. A second pair of footsteps followed hard on his heels. It was Kenalepe running back to her own yard, half out of her mind with fear. Out of the dark Paul Thebolo stepped towards the hut and entered it. He took in every detail and then he turned and looked at Dikeledi with such a tortured expression that for a time words failed him. At last he said: 'You don't have to worry about the children, Mma-Banabothe. I'll take them as my own and give them all a secondary school education.'

•

NICOLE WARD JOUVE
Black and White
(1977)

After graduating in English literature in Paris in 1958, Jouve spent a year at Cambridge University and married the British novelist Anthony Ward. She has since lectured in Canada, Britain and France. Her critical work, Baudelaire: a Fire to Conquer Darkness, *was published in 1980; she has also written many articles and papers for learned journals, and translated works by various French writers (including Colette) into English.*

The story below is from her first fiction collection, Shades of Grey, *which was published to great acclaim in France in 1977. The women in these stories lead lives 'neither black nor white, but only shades of grey', their inner thoughts at odds with their external circumstances – as are the thoughts of the pregnant heroine of 'Black and White'.*

She has read LeRoy Jones, Eldridge Cleaver, James Baldwin, Richard Wright's complete works and Sartre's introduction to *The Wretched of the Earth*. On she goes, the great White Whore, beating her guilty breast, swinging on her crutches, at times resting the rubber heel of her plaster on the pavements of Paris. She spots the Negroes in the crowd on the Boulevard Saint-Michel, mysterious ebony columns erect among the leprous white, sprung from the depths of Africa, from the triangular slave trade, their blood shrieking for revenge for raped mothers and lynched fathers. White blood, her blood, says here I am, I am guilty. Or rather, from the

Freudian depths of her own triangular trade, your whitefucker words excite me, sacrifice me on your nocturnal altars. Priests of the black sun, draw out your long knives.

But the grey crowd, dotted with black, opens and closes. And the only curiosity which assails her is roused not by her seething cunt but, casually, by her plaster. 'Did you do it skiing?' And the throbbing of her desire, measured by the forward strides of the clicking crutches, is misread from the outside, only a hopping woman, a picturesque sight, soon forgotten. Traffic jams on a Friday night, the price of those damn ski-lifts gone up again, children drunk with sun and fatigue nodding off at their school desks on Monday mornings, that's the best inverted image this limping female can hope to cast on the mental retina of the pedestrians. What good would it do to shatter their cosy cliché with her prosaic truth? 'I ran out one morning to buy some matches, there was black ice on the front-door step.'

She plants her crutches into cracks in the pavement, skips on her one white bootee, lands. She sizzles with sweat under her sheepskin jacket and polo-necked pullover, and her hurried breath steams in the acrid morning air. Since she's arrived in Paris, such a rich sin mine, in search of some modest adulterous seam, those grey accostings to which she has been subjected, around Pigalle or Porte de Versailles, have only soured her. A fire shimmers on ebony pectorals, streaming with a water that comes to mingle, fresh, with the tricklings from her armpits and loins. Her dripping body, exhausted with pacing up and down left bank and right bank, *quaerens quem devoret*, has become fertile, it breeds all about her leaping shapes, black as naked trees. And the black racism dancing in her head draws her desire as unswervingly as the spire a thunderbolt.

It was in the coach from Orléans that her flesh began to brew, to be the place where brewings took place. Before, there had been the broken leg. Cancelled, perhaps, that holiday she had so looked forward to at the outset of a depression she had only shaken off with pills and self-love. For months now things hadn't been going well with her and her husband, she white and dry as paper. And he had been the one to say, 'You need a break, go to Paris. Go and resurrect our marriage.' On top of that this leg, sticking up, grotesquely twisted, in the icy morning fog, and she staring at it in disgust, moaning, 'I won't be able to go to Paris, I won't be able to go to Paris', there, prostrate, the arc of that leg with its laddered stocking and the ridiculous little red shoe at the end, there she was, teeth chattering, cowed, until a kindly motorist, brakes on, and an ambulance. And the hours-long wait in the corridor where nurses nonchalantly gossiped, pain drowning her head, choking her hopes, lips bitten holding back the moans, until, at last, nearly evening, an anaesthetist, awaited like a messiah, vacuumed her dry of pain.

On a break in the bus journey when everyone got off, she had stayed alone, hobbled as far as the door, and listened to the morning: a whole battery of falling drops, rhythmic, rolling down roofs and trees and gates to the ground, light fingers tapping drums. Later, forehead glued to the window where rain coursed down, in the smooth rolling of the coach she had caught, deep inside her, the first signs of an answering thaw. Against the iron-grey sky, in the nervy lace of the elms, crows' nests stood out like knots, parasitic as mistletoe. Heat rose up her legs from under the seat. A Libyan sat next to her. He was talking about this FLN* killer, a friend of his, a professional who couldn't adjust after the war. He had murdered fifty people, his own uncle among them. Since he could not stop killing, the only thing he was good at, when the war was over he had enlisted as a mercenary. The violence had passed into her, sitting there shoulder to shoulder with that descendant of the Numids in his European overcoat, with his dilated nostrils and his proud mouth. Browing erectile memories in her. Big black Ben hounded by the police on the Chicago roof tops, the murder of 'Dutchman', the lynch mobs of the Mississippi, black potency. There was a hot space inside her, shaped to the Libyan's member, knowing his size, calling for him, an imperious intake. She tried to utter words concealing subterranean bargainings, but he had lost interest. After a while, he got up to move to another seat. Was she repulsive? Did desire actually smell, had that smell disgusted him? Did he despise her? She felt ashamed, and her heart was singing.

But black powers were conspiring to enslave her desires. The very air was loud with their whisperings. In the foyer of the hotel

* FLN – the National Liberation Front in Algeria during the Algerian war.

where she was spending her second night, looking over the papers to kill time before her film, she was interrupted by a Negro whose beauty left her breathless. Tall. Sarcastic. His chest, slender in a deep pink shirt, vividly contrasting with the skin: sunset over night.

'You're pretending to read, but I know you're listening to me telling you that I've had enough. Things would be ridiculous if they weren't so awful. It gives you a pain too, doesn't it, lady?'

Leaning towards her over the newspaper, the iris in his eyes coal-black in the bluey cornea. Couldn't care less about the effect he's having. Reckless, violent. From his armchair opposite, an older gentleman, briefcase-glasses-scarf-grey-overcoat, intervenes, uneasy, benevolent, 'Come come you must admit that the government . . .'

The Negro has gone back to him, and they argue, engrossed, the Negro sometimes appealing to her, 'don't you agree, lady? you at least are on my side, aren't you?' as though to an accomplice whose presence allows him to threaten the gentleman – with what? With a scene? Or is he making fun of me, and cheap at the price? Or does he reckon that she, obviously bourgeois with her sheepskin-jacket and butter-wouldn't-melt-in-her-mouth look, is shocked at being involved in their argument? Her presence at any rate works as a distraction in the dialogue, she is drawn into that world – *which* former colony is he so distressed about? But the gentleman is on his feet, 'we'll be late for dinner, come on let yourself be treated' and she is without resources to join them. And the silhouette, tall and supple, head tipped slightly backwards, hands dangling or dancing in turns, vanishes through the revolving doors.

Leaving ravages in its wake. Belly, *quaerens quem devoret*. Another black man enters, hands in the pockets of his leather jacket. 'Monsieur Vincent, please.'

Bustlings, real or fictitious, on the part of the receptionist. 'Already gone out, sir.'

Monsieur Vincent. Saint Vincent de Paul, bestowing on the poor-in-pleasure the black and pink alms of his presence. Throughout the film, a chaste study of the agrarian revolution in Hungary, a black head rises from the furrows in the fields, nodding or dancing; or from behind the old man who bares his great wizened torso to the village committee, 'all my flesh is invested in my earth and you want to sunder me'. And she hopes that out of darkness, on the seat next to hers, there will suddenly materialize the long body which had so memorably furrowed her evening. The seat is still empty.

He wasn't wearing an overcoat, must be staying at the hotel, the gentleman must have come to collect him. Her plaster resting on the edge of the bath, she arches then relaxes her back, slowly rocking herself up and down in the water; and when she surfaces, traces of water soon gone from the islands of her breasts and the curved beach of her belly, her flesh, she sees, in all the white all the shimmering, is truly luminous. Thinks he is going to knock she will meet him on the landing. Goes under again. But all that milky that dripping white, lying in wait there among the neon and the enamel, fails to ensnare the darkness.

Later still.

Lying legs open between the smooth sheets. Though the lead on her right ankle drags at her. She wanders through this mine. Vast, where you penetrate deeper and deeper. When she thinks of herself, closing her eyes, she can get inside herself. A corridor endlessly bending to the right with a slight continuous drop, arching walls soft as down, and the curve which makes the horizon an ever-drifting obstacle is textured like an ear. She is hollow like the sky. The whole city, she soars above it, indecently enters her. Chimneys spurting their vaporous seed, plane trees scattering to the winds their feathery spume, telegraph poles erected at regular intervals, even the obscene tip of the colonne Vendôme and the dome of the Sacré Coeur, the whole city strains towards the sky, her sky, drills roaring and the revving of cars endlessly escalated. In the bowels of the earth, the tube train hammers away through the tiled vaults, curving over adrift like the funnel of an ear. Ticket barriers, arcades, triumphal arches, are crossed. In the cafés, doors swinging to and fro like auricles rhythmically pumped open and shut by blood, liquids flow down throats, bending the uvula as they pass. She is the source of the universal pulsation, the place where it all happens. She falls asleep, rocked by the nocturnal trembling which the laths of the shutters impart to her.

Against the iron-grey sky, in the nervy lace of the elms, crows' nests stand out like knots, parasitic as mistletoe.

Her hand clenches the handle of the telephone. Tibia in a dog's jaw. Janus tibia, a face of peace for the ear, a face of war for the mouth. Must plug the panic circuit of her brain-heart into it. Anything rather than do it. For instance, the texture of the plaster, so rough by contrast with the smooth plasticity of the handle, for a moment interrupts. Who will he take me for, who I want to be, but what am I going to say to him, what they say in such situations, in films, in novels, can I see you again, are you free today, I'd like to know more about. The lot. Your duty, I'll despise you for ever if you funk it. Clinging to the handle as though to a handle in the tube to steady herself against the rolling, 'could I speak to Mr Vincent please, yes yes, he's staying at the hotel'. Black shimmers between her and the window-latch, 'must must must must'. A gallery of echoes gapes and reverberates on the threshold of her right ear, '*café complet* for number twenty-nine, no, *twen*-ty-nine, yes, sir, nine-fifty exactly.' 'I'm sorry madam you must have made a mistake. There's nobody of that name staying at the hotel. Of course madam, I've checked. Quite certain.'

Rhea, when Chronos or was it Uranos buried her children inside her bowels. Cunt must swallow back its desire, or choke on it. Sap soured.

And the last evening comes.

She surfaces from the underground at the end of a calvary climb, panting from having patiently forced her way backwards through so many brutal doors, eyes barred with pain from staring too long, each time the crutches went down, at the metal ridge of the steps. Layer upon layer, the grey exhalation of the traffic winding anticlockwise round the Arc de Triomphe, thickens the chalky sky. Passers-by again gape at, or rather down, her plaster. Stupid bastards. Then she notices that the bandage which covered the tip of her toes has dropped off, probably as she was heaving herself up those stairs. Foul bluey-black, her toes jut out of the already soiled plaster. Come along ladies and gentlemen let me introduce you to the new *Femme fatale* the matrix in which Paris is fermenting. That other night she felt as if she was pure space. Tonight, shamed, she shrinks down to five bruises.

Tract sellers surround her and stuff pamphlets into her pockets. 'No need to carry them, look, they balance in your pockets, five francs.' Five francs, five toes. I'm always being had. Had by life.

She feels herself sweating with failure. In the crowd, hounds sniff, ready to snatch their bite from the prey. She hobbles on her three legs, wishing herself invisible, hating the curious stares she attracts, in front of the Drugstore, streaming with tourists, neon lights and trinkets, past the Publicis cinema queue. The universal stooge, grotesque, defeated from the start. Get yourself run over and forget all about it. You sweat with your stink of failure. Flesh for vultures. She skirts close to the shop-windows, her back to the crowd, trying to look absorbed, beauty parlours, insurance companies, travel agencies, anything not to feel looked at. Not a hole to crawl into. She hates it all, the jacket stretching with the heavy pamphlets, the sweater sticking to her armpits, the rhythmic pressure of the crutches, and above all, the dead weight on her right side which the rest of her body has to drag around. She stops and looks for a long time at a miniature Concorde, ripped open from end to end, her eyes full of tears fixed on the tiny sitting figures, hoping that her dull passivity will weary the persistent gent in the loose overcoat who for a while now, hands buried in his pockets, has been following her. She attracts perverts like a dead donkey buzzards. What acrobatic delights can he be concocting, there, appraising her intently? But he draws nearer, stands close to her, he is chewing mint chewing-gum and the hand which brushes against her is covered with red hairs; and she strides angrily away reaching out with her crutches. But he gets wind of her panic and he follows her, keeping a few steps behind, calmly, sure of his catch. At my age. To be had like a kid. Hands bound by her crutches like her leg by the plaster, a cinema a café he'll sit near her an underground station he'll corner her there. He has all the time in the night, the dank gloomy night, and her panic on his side. He is tracking her by the musk of her fear, she who wished to be hunted by the scent of her desire. Each time she dives forward on her mechanical legs the pavement rolls. And there is nothing she can hurl forward before she hurls herself to try and reassure herself that the rolling, the gaping, are imaginary; that it is concrete she is pitching towards and not the unnameable deep horror of some well.

'Can I help you missis?'

Joy. Tears of joy. O deliverance, grace descending into the sinner's parched soul. Tall and slender. Hands horizontally pushed into pockets of leather jacket. Free as the embodiment of night himself, of a night neither dank nor gloomy but warm, but full of whispers. And a voice in which the whole of America is singing.

'That is very kind of you. Yes please.'

'Come on. Let's get across.'

He's guiding her, with a gentle touch on her elbow. Rather as you would an old lady, perhaps, but he's inserted himself between her and her follower, between her and the fall, with his tall nonchalance. And she, she is letting herself be led on, docile with gratitude, towards the pavement across the road where the cafés line the pavement; where she can, thus escorted thus normalized, become an integral part of the crowd.

'Shall we have a drink?'

'What a good idea.'

He orders a beer, and she, who hates beer, orders the same. One elbow each on the round table, facing the crowd, crutches laid against a spare chair, they are a couple like any other. Only, other girls must be envying her for being with such a good-looking man. He is an airline pilot, he comes from Florida, he wanders from country to country as he pleases, his brother, a pilot too, is married to a German girl, he loves Paris, he is called neither Sam nor Richard nor LeRoy but Hermann, and his hair, curly like the fleece of those black lambs that girls in mountain villages once had to procure as a dowry for their husbands, frames a forehead curved at the temples. Frames. Like the curtains in the Grand Trianon castle windows, with a curved dip at the centre of the pelmet.

They're going down the Champs-Elysées again, Elysian Fields now, and he is dancing all round her so prolific seem his movements alongside her own metallic progress. The supple leaves entwine the rigid stem, and they proliferate, a living caduceus. Talking, laughing. Now that the beer is going to her head, making it swim, she feels her crutches as an extension of her arms, organic, like the front legs of a praying mantis.

'Let's have another drink.'

Two more beers. This time they are inside a long curved window, and the seats are covered with red plush velvet. The atmosphere is old-worldish and select, the waiter, who knows Hermann, jokes tactfully with him. He must leave good tips.

He talks. She listens, all his. He explains that what impelled him towards her is Christian love, not the other kind. 'We're all brothers, what does it matter if you're white and I'm black, I love you. Like a sister. With a brother's love. Not a lover's. You understand what I'm saying to you when I say that I love you? You're my sister.

'I have no prejudices against white girls. Besides, they never refuse to go out with me. At London airport there was an airhostess. So blond, so beautiful. She dropped her papers on the floor. I went down on my knees to pick them up. The legs she had. The legs of a goddess. I stayed there, down on the floor, looking at her legs. What I would not have done to those legs. What I haven't done to those legs. Just to her legs.'

Melancholy, she stares at her plaster. Laid across a chair.

'All brothers. We must help one another like brothers. If we did that, the world wouldn't be in such a bad way. You could be green, blue, colour has always been a matter of complete indifference to me. I would have helped you just the same, I am a citizen of the world, you're a human being. My sister.'

(Is it the beer, something's out of joint. That's not what he is supposed to be telling me, better he should hate me because I belong to the race of the oppressors, should want to kill me, to fuck me to death. To free himself from me, violently. Instead, he's rubbing my nose in his brotherly love!)

'One must be virtuous. Those women who flaunt themselves, who take drugs, drink alcohol, go to bed with anyone, boy, haven't I known plenty. Bed and bed again, and then more bed. At thirty they look like death, you'd think they were fifty. How old are you?'

Isn't he going a bit strong? But she, drunk, beatific, stares at those eyelashes which curve, nearly at a right angle, a living solution to the problem of the squaring of the circle. The shell-like white of the cornea, the dark water of the irises. Your eyes since I lost their incandescence flat calm engulfs my jibs the shiver of *vae soli* gurgles beneath my ribs.

'Twenty-nine.'

'And see, you look so fresh. That's because you've led such a virtuous life. Take off your coat.'

As if hypnotized, she complies.

'You're well made, you're still young. But if . . .'

If.

Had we but world enough and time this coyness lady were no

crime. Something's wrong something's upside down. She sips her beer, clinging to the coolness of the glass. Waiting till she can't take any more, then she'll get up and go.

But just when, anger growling, she stretches her hand towards her crutches, he stretches out a tender daring hand. Lifts her fringe. Claiming a lover's prerogative over her. The caress winds through her every nerve. Lances her breasts. And she stays in her seat.

'You're pretty you know let me tell you a story.'

Drunkenness, fatigue, bewilderment, she finds it difficult to follow his American voice. Steps into a fog, hands stretched out towards the possible, eyes dilated with not-seeing. Then a dark gallery she does not yet know it is immense, where the horizon is obstructed sometimes on the right sometimes on the left by screens. You have to walk around the screens. Each time you come across yet another one. Ebony they are, inlaid with ivory birds stuck in mid-flight. Beyond the walls of the gallery you can sense the tall shudder of trees, leaves rubbing together, kneaded by the wind, stoned by the rain. They're dripping to the ground already a lake, a heavy crystal shower dripping from them, and in the inside dryness screen after screen is being pierced. Or has it to do with this young German girl, blond, virgin, brought up by her grandmother in such innocence she did not even know she had a sex. And in some dark flat, between two flights, the pilot brother, the evening of a chaste wedding, reveals to her, through gentle probings of her hand held in his, that she has a maidenhead, to pluck it slowly.

'You understand now, don't you? Why I love you like a sister? You are my sister in God.'

For her there has never been will never be going beyond the screens. Ivory birds flying away into an ebony sky. And her warm dryness will never be united, all walls burst open, to the streaming outside coolness. Her eyes ache from imagining her breasts laid against the slim chest; and the bitterness of the beer, suddenly, is intolerable, there's this pressure inside her. She says 'I must go to the toilet.' She'll make her escape from there.

She combs her fringe nostrils filled with a frank yes frank smell of urine and black soap; hands still wet slipping on the handles of the crutches, hobbles towards the back stairs.

'You've got the wrong exit.'

There he is, leaning against the telephone, waiting for her.

'I thought perhaps you were feeling sick, so I came to find you.'

Implacable brotherly love. I give up. She wants to laugh. He has her by the elbow again, he helps her up the steps, talks, talks in the street, holds her again, with loving care, down the underground stairs.

The train is nearly empty: sad revellers, lone women. She, all black long in-between the lights of deserted stations, feels nothing but a weary bewilderment; fog stands between her and this man she's so strained her eyes to see.

And then, in Châtelet station, in the draught of an intolerable bend, nobody about, walls tiled with white like a Turkish bath, he says, she thinks she hears him say, 'and if I had wanted to would you also?'

What's she got to lose?

'Maybe.'

'I dislike short affairs. Are you really going away tomorrow?'

'I have to.'

'Can't you put if off for a few days? We could meet again, tomorrow night for instance.'

'I have to go.'

'That's just too bad then.'

A few more steps, on three legs and two crutches, and he stops her again.

'Kiss me.'

He offers his cheek to her, and she plants a big angry kiss on it. The cheek is smooth, and she smells, as she brushes it, his smell of warm fog.

'I haven't kissed you on the mouth, don't you see, because it would have changed everything. You understand, don't you, why I can't give you my mouth? I am your brother.'

That's the stabbing with a knife of our Dutchman.

Once more, he helps her into the train, keeping the doors open with his foot until he's made sure she's all, legs and crutches, in: sits next to her. She now feels bizarrely sisterly. We understand each other, we two, I know what game you're playing and you smelt mine out from the first. I would have had a better deal out of my pervert. Perhaps. The train rolls on. She stares at the slim thighs inside the corduroy, not for me, these thighs, for some German virgin, or some blond nymph from the Old South.

Cité, and as Saint-Michel approaches, the rolling eases up. To a screeching of brakes.

'Are you sure you'll be all right all the way to Porte d'Orléans? Don't you want me to go on with you to the end?'

'You've gone far enough.'

'Give me another kiss.'

She delivers the noisiest kiss she can manage. At least make the ladies in the train turn and stare. Squeezes her shoulder, he's out, raises a hand, turns his back on her, hand which has been holding her elbow now back deep inside the vertical pocket of the leather jacket. Separate. From her, from everything. Almost frail after all now seen from a distance. Free. A strange black man in the crowd scaling speeding up the stairs. Outside soon.

And the fog thins out, and the rolling takes her over again. Don't I get had. Born for it. In the window, a mirror in the tunnel, her eyes shine as if they were black.

A slav gentleman, slavly, frankly, maturely lubricious is sitting opposite her. She smiles at him. He finds her broken leg immensely interesting. As he talks about it, he caresses the plaster. His hands look like warm hands, his glance, genuinely curious, pierces through the fog. He's a doctor, he's a Bulgarian . . .

The train rolls on towards Porte d'Orléans.

•

KATHY ACKER

New York City in 1979

(1981)

A native New Yorker, Kathy Acker was associated with the Fluxus group of artists and film-makers in the 1960s and with the early punk rock scene in the 1970s, when she first began to attract attention in the underground presses. It was a few years, however, before she broke through to wider audiences with such controversial books as Blood and Guts in High School *(1978),* Great Expectations *(1982) and* Don Quixote *(1978): 'Plagiarism,' she remarked, 'became a strategy of originality.'*

Her writing, which includes plays as well as fiction, has been described as post-punk feminism, though her wild and wonderful stuff defies easy classification.

Some people say New York City is evil and they wouldn't live there for all the money in the world.

These are the same people who elected Johnson, Nixon, Carter President and Koch Mayor of New York.

The Whores in Jail at Night

— Well, my man's gonna get me out of here as soon as he can.

— When's that gonna be, honey?

— So what? Your man pays so he can put you back on the street as soon as possible.

— Well, what if he want me back on the street? That's where I belong. I make him good money, don't I? He knows that I'm a good girl.

— Your man ain't anything! Johnny says that if I don't work my ass off for him, he's not going to let me back in the house.

— I have to earn two hundred before I can go back.

— Two hundred? That ain't shit! You can earn two hundred in less than a night. I have to earn four hundred or I might just as well forget sleeping, and there's no running away from Him. My baby is the toughest there is.

— Well, shit girl, if I don't come back with eight hundred I get my ass whupped off.

— That's cause you're junk.

— I ain't no stiff! All of you are junkies. I know what you do!

— What's the matter, honey?

— You've been sitting on that thing for an hour.

— The pains are getting bad. OOgh. I've been bleeding two days now.

— OOgh OOgh OOgh.

— She's gonna bang her head off. She needs a shot.

— Tie a sweater around her head. She's gonna break her head open.

— You should see a doctor, honey.

— The doctor told me I'm having an abortion.

— Matron, Goddamnit. Get your ass over here matron!

— I haven't been bleeding this bad. Maybe this is the real abortion.

— Matron! This little girl is having an abortion! You do something. Where the hell is that asshole woman? [The matron throws an open piece of Kotex to the girl.] The service here is getting worse and worse!

— You're not in a hotel, honey.

— It used to be better than this. There's not even any goddamn food. This place is definitely going downhill.

— Oh, shutup. I'm trying to sleep. I need my sleep, unlike you girls, cause I'm going back to work tomorrow.

— Now what the hell do you need sleep for? This is a party. You sleep on your job.

— I sure know this is the only time I get any rest. Tomorrow it's back on the street again.

— If we're lucky.

LESBIANS are women who prefer their own ways to male ways.

LESBIANS prefer the convoluting halls of sensuality to direct goal-pursuing mores.

LESBIANS have made a small world deep within and separated from the world. What has usually been called the world is the male world.

Convoluting halls of sensuality lead to depend on illusions. Lies and silence are realer than truth.

Either you're in love with someone or you're not. The one thing about being in love with someone is you know you're in love: you're either flying or you're about to kill yourself.

I don't know anyone I'm in love with or I don't know if I'm in love. I have all these memories. I remember that as soon as I've gotten fucked, like a dog I no longer care about the man who just fucked me who I was madly in love with.

So why should I spend a hundred dollars to fly to Toronto to get laid by someone I don't know if I love I don't know if I can love I'm an abortion? I mean a hundred dollars and once I get laid I'll be in agony: I won't be doing exactly what I want. I can't live normally i.e. with love so: there is no more life.

The world is grey afterbirth. Fake. All of New York City is fake is going to go all my friends are going crazy all my friends know they're going crazy disaster is the only thing that's happening.

Suddenly these outbursts in the fake, cause they're so open, spawn a new growth. I'm waiting to see this growth.

I want more and more horrible disaster in New York cause I desperately want to see that new thing that is going to happen this year.

JANEY is a woman who has sexually hurt and been sexually hurt so much she's now frigid.

She doesn't want to see her husband any more. There's nothing between them.

Her husband agrees with her that there's nothing more between them.

But there's no such thing as nothingness. Not here. Only death whatever that is is nothing. All the ways people are talking to her now mean nothing. She doesn't want to speak words that are meaningless.

Janey doesn't want to see her husband again.

The quality of life in this city stinks. Is almost nothing. Most people now are deaf-mutes only inside they're screaming. BLOOD. A lot of blood inside is going to fall. MORE and MORE because inside is outside.

New York City will become alive again when the people begin to speak to each other again not information but real emotion. A grave is spreading its legs and BEGGING FOR LOVE.

Robert, Janey's husband, is almost a zombie.

He walks talks plays his saxophone pays for groceries almost like every other human. There's no past. The last six years didn't exist. Janey hates him. He made her a hole. He blasted into her. He has no feeling. The light blue eyes he gave her; the gentle hands; the adoration: AREN'T. NO CRIME. NO BLOOD. THE NEW CITY. Like in Fritz Lang's METROPOLIS.

This year suffering has so blasted all feelings out of her she's become a person. Janey believes it's necessary to blast open her mind constantly and destroy EVERY PARTICLE OF MEMORY THAT SHE LIKES.

A sleeveless black T-shirt binds Janey's breasts. Pleated black fake-leather pants hide her cocklessness. A thin leopard tie winds around her neck. One gold-plated watch, the only remembrance of the dead mother, binds one wrist. A thin black leather band binds the other. The head is almost shaved. Two round prescription mirrors mask the eyes.

Johnny is a man who don't want to be living so he doesn't appear to be a man. All his life everyone wanted him to be something. His Jewish mother wanted him to be famous so he wouldn't live the life she was living. The two main girlfriends he has had wanted him to support them in the manner to which they certainly weren't accustomed even though he couldn't put his flabby hands on a penny. His father wanted him to shut up.

All Johnny wants to do is make music. He wants to keep everyone and everything who takes him away from his music off him. Since he can't afford human contact, he can't afford desire. Therefore he hangs around with rich zombies who never have anything to do with feelings. This is a typical New York artist attitude.

New York City is a pit-hole: since the United States government, having decided that New York City is no longer part of the United States of America, is dumping all the laws the rich people want such as anti-rent-control laws and all the people they don't want (artists, poor minorities, and the media in general) on the city and refusing the city Federal funds; the American bourgeoisie has left. Only the poor: artists, Puerto Ricans who can't afford to move . . . and rich Europeans who fleeing the terrorists don't give a shit about New York . . . inhabit this city.

Meanwhile the temperature is getting hotter and hotter so no one can think clearly. No one perceives. No one cares. Insane madness come out like life is a terrific party.

In Front of the Mudd Club, 77 White Street

Two rich couples drop out of a limousine. The women are wearing outfits the poor people who were in ten years ago wore ten years ago. The men are just neutral. All the poor people who're making this club fashionable so the rich want to hang out here, even though the poor still never make a buck off the rich pleasure, are sitting on cars, watching the rich people walk up to the club.

Some creeps around the club's entrance. An open-shirted skinny guy who says he's just an artist is choosing who he'll let into the club. Since it's 3.30 a.m. there aren't many creeps. The artist won't let the rich hippies into the club.

– Look at that car.

– Jesus. It's those rich hippies' car.

– Let's take it.

– That's the chauffeur over there.

– Let's kidnap him.

– Let's knock him over the head with a bottle.

– I don't want no terrorism. I wanna go for a ride.

– That's right. We've got nothing to do with terrorism. We'll just explain we want to borrow the car for an hour.

– Maybe he'll lend us the car if we explain we're terrorists-in-training. We want to use that car to try out terrorist tricks.

After forty-five minutes the rich people climb back into their limousine and their chauffeur drives them away.

A girl who has gobs of brown hair like the foam on a cappuccino in Little Italy, black patent leather S&M heels, two unfashionable tits stuffed into a pale green corset, and extremely fashionable black fake leather tights heaves her large self off a car top. She's holding an empty bottle.

Diego senses there's going to be trouble. He gets off his car top. Is walking slowly towards the girl.

The bottle keeps waving. Finally the girl finds some courage heaves the bottle at the skinny entrance artist.

The girl and the artist battle it out up the street. Some of the people who are sitting on cars separate them. We see the girl throw herself back on a car top. Her tits are bouncing so hard she must want our attention and she's getting insecure, maybe violent, cause she isn't getting enough. Better give us a better show. She sticks her middle finger into the air as far as she can. She writhes around on the top of the car. Her movements are so spasmatic she must be nuts.

A yellow taxi-cab is slowly making its way to the club. On one side of this taxi-cab's the club entrance. The other side is the girl writ(h)ing away on the black car. Three girls who are pretending to be transvestites are lifting themselves out of the cab elegantly around the big girl's body. The first body is encased into a translucent white girdle. A series of diagonal panels leads directly to her cunt. The other two dresses are tight and white. They are wriggling their way toward the club. The big girl, whom the taxi-driver refused to let in his cab, wriggling because she's been rejected but not wriggling as much, is bumping into them. They're tottering away from her because she has syphilis.

Now the big girl is unsuccessfully trying to climb through a private white car's window now she's running hips hooking even faster into an alleyway taxi whose driver is locking his doors and windows against her. She's offering him a blow-job. Now an ugly boy with a huge safety pin stuck through his upper lip, walking up and down the street, is shooting at us with his watergun.

The dyke sitting next to me is saying earlier in the evening she pulled at this safety pin.

It's four o'clock a.m. It's still too hot. Wet heat's squeezing this city. The air's mist. The liquid's that seeping out of human flesh pores is gonna harden into a smooth shiny shell so we're going to become reptiles.

No one wants to move anymore. No one wants to be in a body. Physical possessions can go to hell even in this night.

Johnny like all other New York inhabitants doesn't want anything to do with sex. He hates sex because the air's hot, because feelings are dull, and because humans are repulsive.

Like all the other New Yorkers he's telling females he's strictly gay and males all faggots ought to burn in hell and they are. He's doing this because when he was sixteen years old his parents who wanted him to die stuck him in the Merchant Marines and all the marines cause this is what they do raped his ass off with many doses of coke.

Baudelaire doesn't go directly toward self-satisfaction cause of the following mechanism: X wants Y and, for whatever reasons, thinks it shouldn't want Y. X thinks it is BAD because it wants Y. What X wants is Y and to be GOOD.

Baudelaire does the following to solve this dilemma: he understands that some agency (his parents, society, his mistress, etc.) is saying that wanting Y is BAD. This agency is authority is right. The authority will punish him because he's BAD. The authority will punish him as much as possible, punish me punish me, more than is necessary till it has to be obvious to everyone that the punishment is unjust. Punishers are unjust. All authority right now stinks to high hell. Therefore there is no GOOD and BAD. X cannot be BAD.

It's necessary to go to as many extremes as possible.

*

As soon as Johnny sees Janey he wants to have sex with her. Johnny takes out his cock and rubs it. He walks over to Janey, puts his arms around her shoulders so he's pinning her against a concrete wall.

Johnny says, 'You're always talking about sex. Are you going to spread your legs for me like you spread your legs all the time for any guy you don't know?'

Janey replies, 'I'm not fucking any more cause sex is a prison. It's become a support of this post-capitalist system like art. Business-men who want to make money have to turn up a product that people'll buy and want to keep buying. Since American consumers now own every object there is plus they don't have any money anyway cause they're being squeezed between inflation and depres-sion, just like fucking, these businessmen have to discover products that obvious necessity sells. Sex is such a product. Just get rid of the puritanism sweetheart your parents spoonfed you in between materialism which the sexual revolution did thanks to free love and hippies sex is a terrific hook. Sexual desire is a naturally fluctuating phenomena. The sex product presents a naturally expanding market. Now capitalists are doing everything they can to bring world sexual desire to an unbearable edge.

'I don't want to be hurt again. Getting hurt or rejected is more dangerous than I know because now everytime I get sexually rejected I get dangerously physically sick. I don't want to hurt again. Every time I hurt I feel so disgusted with myself – that by following some stupid body desire I didn't HAVE to follow, I killed the tender nerves of someone else. I retreat into myself. I again become frigid.

'I never have fun.'

Johnny says, 'You want to be as desperate as possible but you don't have to be desperate. You're going to be a success. Everybody knows you're going to be a success. Wouldn't you like to give up this artistic life which you know isn't rewarding cause artists now have to turn their work/selves into marketable objects/fluctuating images/fashion have to competitively knife each other in the back because we're not people, can't treat each other like people, no feelings, loneliness comes from the world of rationality, robots, everything one as objects defined separate from each other? The whole impetus for art in the first place is gone bye-bye? You know you want to get away from this media world.'

Janey replies, 'I don't know what I want now. I know the New York City world is more complex and desirable even though everything you're saying's true. I don't know what my heart is cause I'm corrupted.'

'Become pure again. Love. You have to will. You can do what you will. Then love'll enter your heart.'

'I'm not capable of loving anyone. I'm a freak. Love's an obsession that only weird people have. I'm going to be a robot for the rest of my life. This is confusing to be a human being, but robotism is what's present.'

'It's unnatural to be sexless. You eat alone and that's freaky.'

'I am lonely out of my mind. I am miserable out of my mind. Open open what are you touching me. Touching me. Now I'm going into the state where desire comes out like a monster. Sex I love you. I'll do anything to touch you. I've got to fuck. Don't you understand don't you have needs as much as I have needs DON'T YOU HAVE TO GET LAID?'

– Janey, close that door. What's the matter with you? Why aren't you doing what I tell you?

– I'll do whatever you tell me, nana.

– That's right. Now go into that drawer and get that cheque-book for me. The Chase Manhattan one, not the other one. Give me both of them. I'll show you which one.

– I can find it, nana. No, it's not this one.

– Give me both of them. I'll do it.

– Here you are, nana. This is the one you want, isn't it?

– Now sit yourself down and write yourself out a cheque for ten thousand dollars. It doesn't matter which cheque you write it on.

– Ten thousand dollars! Are you sure about this, nana?

– Do what I tell you. Write yourself out a cheque for ten thousand dollars.

– Uh O.K. What's the date?

– It doesn't matter. Put any date you want. Now hand me my glasses. They're over there.

– I'm just going to clean them. They're dirty.

– You can clean them for me later. Give them to me.

– Are . . . you sure you want to do this?

– Now I'm going to tell you something, Janey. Invest this. Buy

yourself 100 shares of AT&T. You can fritter it away if you want.
Good riddance to you. If your mother had invested the 800 shares
of IBM I gave her, she would have had a steady income and
wouldn't have had to commit suicide. Well, she needed the money.
If you invest in AT&T, you'll always have an income.

– I don't know what to say. I've never seen so much money
before. I've never seen so much money before.

– You do what I tell you to. Buy AT&T.

– I'll put the money in a bank, nana, and as soon as it clears I'll
buy AT&T.

At ten o'clock the next morning Nana is still asleep. A rich
salesman who was spending his winter in New York had installed
her in a huge apartment on Park Avenue for six months. The
apartment's rooms are tremendous, too big for her tiny body, and
are still partly unfurnished. Thick silk daybed spreads ivory-handled
white feather fans hanging above contrast the black-and-red 'natural-
istic' clown portraits in the 'study' that give an air of culture rather
than of call-girl. A call-girl or mistress, as soon as her first man is
gone, is no longer innocent. No one to help her, constantly
harassed by rent and food bills, in need of elegant clothing and
cosmetics to keep surviving, she has to use her sex to get money.

Nana's sleeping on her stomach, her bare arms hugging instead
of a man a pillow into which she's buried a face soft with sleep.
The bedroom and the small adjoining dressing-room are the only
two properly furnished rooms. A ray of light filtered through the
grey richly laced curtain focuses a rosewood bedstead covered by
carved Chinese figures, the bedstead covered by white linen sheets;
covered by a pale blue silk quilt; covered by a pale white silk quilt;
Chinese pictures composed of five to seven layers of carved ivory,
almost sculptures rather than pictures, surround these gleaming
layers.

She feels around and, finding no one, calls her maid.

'Paul left ten minutes ago,' the girl says as she walks into the
room. 'He didn't want to wake you. I asked him if he wanted
coffee but he said he was in a rush. He'll see you his usual time
tomorrow.'

'Tomorrow tomorrow,' the prostitute can never get anything
straight, 'can he come tomorrow?'

'Wednesday's Paul's day. Today you see the furrier.'

'I remember,' she says, sitting up, 'the old furrier told me he's coming Wednesday and I can't go against him. Paul'll have to come another day.'

'You didn't tell me. If you don't tell me what's going on, I'm going to get things confused and your Johns'll be running into each other!'

Nana stretches her fatty arms over her head and yawns. Two bunches of short brown hairs are sticking out of her armpits. 'I'll call Paul and tell him to come back tonight. No. I won't sleep with anyone tonight. Can I afford it? I'll tell Paul to come on Tuesday's after this and I'll have tonight to myself!' Her nightgown slips down her nipples surrounded by one long brown hair and the rest of her hair, loose and tousled, flows over her still-wet sheets.

Bet – I think feminism is the only thing that matters.

Janey (yawning) – I'm so tired all I can do is sleep all day (only she doesn't fall asleep cause she's suddenly attracted to Michael who's like every other guy she's attracted to married to a friend of hers).

Bet – First of all feminism is only possible in a socialist state.

Janey – But Russia stinks as much as the United States these days. What has this got to do with your film?

Bet – Cause feminism depends on four factors: First of all, women have to have economic independence. If they don't have that they don't have anything. Second, free day-care centres. Abortions (counting on her fingers). Fourth, decent housing.

Janey – I mean those are just material considerations. You're accepting the materialism this society teaches. I mean look I've had lots of abortions I can fuck anyone I want – well, I could – I'm still in prison. I'm not talking about myself.

Bet – Are you against abortions?

Janey – How could I be against abortions? I've had fucking five of them. I can't be against abortions. I just think all that stuff is back in the 1920s. It doesn't apply to this world. This world is different than all that socialism: those multinational corporations control everything.

Louie – You just don't know how things are cause the feminist movement here is nothing compared to the feminist movements in

Italy, England, and Australia. That's where women really stick together.

Janey – That's not true! Feminism here, sure it's not the old feminism the groups Gloria Steinem and Ti-Grace, but they were *so* straight. It's much better now: it's just underground it's not so public.

Louie – The only women in Abercrombie's and Fitch's films are those traditionally male-defined types.

The women are always whores or bitches. They have no power.

Janey – Women are whores now. I think women every time they fuck no matter who they fuck should get paid. When they fuck their boyfriends their husbands. That's the way things are only the women don't get paid.

Louie – Look at Carter's films. There are no women's roles. The only two women in the film who aren't bit players are France who's a bitch and England who's a whore.

Janey – But that's how things were in Rome of that time.

Bet – But, Jane, we're saying things have to be different. Our friends can't keep upholding the sexist state of women in their work.

Janey – You know about Abercrombie and Fitch. I don't even bother saying anything to them. But Carter's film: you've got to look at why an artist does what he does. Otherwise you're not being fair. In ROME Carter's saying the decadent Roman society was like this one.

Louie – The one that a certain small group of artists in New York lives in.

Janey – Yeah.

Louie – He's saying the men we know treat women only as whores and bitches.

Janey – So what are you complaining about?

Bet – Before you were saying you have no one to talk to about your work. That's what I'm saying. We've got to tell Abercrombie and Fitch what they're doing. We've got to start portraying women as strong showing women as the power of this society.

Janey – But we're not.

Bet – But how else are we going to be? In Italy there was this women's art festival. A friend of ours who does performance dressed as a woman and did a performance. Then he revealed he was a man. The women in the festival beat him up and called the police.

Michael – The police?

Janey – Was he good?

Bet – He was the best performer there.

Louie – I think calling the police is weird. They should have just beaten him up.

Janey – I don't like the police.

I Want All the Above to be the Sun

Intense Sexual Desire is the Greatest Thing in the World

Janey dreams of cocks. Janey sees cocks instead of objects. Janey has to fuck.

This is the way Sex drives Janey crazy: Before Janey fucks, she keeps her wants in cells. As soon as Janey's fucking she wants to be adored as much as possible at the same time as, its other extreme, ignored as much as possible. More than this: Janey can no longer perceive herself wanting. Janey is Want.

It's worse than this: If Janey gets sexually rejected her body becomes sick. If she doesn't get who she wants she naturally revolts.

This is the nature of reality. No rationality possible. Only this is true. The world in which there is no feeling, the robot world, doesn't exist. This world is a very dangerous place to live in.

Old women just cause they're old and no man'll fuck them don't stop wanting sex.

The old actress isn't good any more. But she keeps on acting even though she knows all the audiences mock her hideousness and lack of context cause she adores acting. Her legs are grotesque: FLABBY. Above, hidden within the folds of skin, there's an ugly cunt. Two long flaps of white thin speckled by black hairs like a pig's cock flesh hang down to the knees. There's no feeling in them. Between these two flaps of skin the meat is red folds and drips a white slime that poisons whatever it touches. Just one drop burns a hole into anything. An odour of garbage infested by maggots floats out of this cunt. One wants to vomit. The meat is so

red it looks like someone hacked a body to bits with a cleaver or
like the bright red lines under the purple lines on the translucent
skin of a woman's body found dead three days ago. This red leads
to a hole, a hole of redness, round and round, black nausea. The
old actress is black nausea because she reminds us of death. Yet she
keeps plying her trade and that makes her trade weird. Glory be to
those humans who are absolutely NOTHING for the opinions of
other humans: they are the true owners of illusions, transformations,
and themselves.

Old people are supposed to be smarter than young people.

Old people in this country the United States of America are treated
like total shit. Since most people spend their lives mentally dwelling
on the material, they have no mental freedom, when they grow old
and their skin rots and their bodies turn to putrefying sand and
they can't do physical exercise and they can't indulge in bodily
pleasure and they're all ugly anyway; suddenly they got nothing.
Having nothing, you think they could at least be shut up in opiated
dens so maybe they have a chance to develop dreams or at least
they could warn their kids to do something else besides being
materialistic. But the way this country's set up, there's not even
opiated homes to hide this feelinglessness: old people have to go
either to children's or most often into rest-homes where they're
shunted into wheelchairs and made as fast as possible into zombies
cause it's easier to handle a zombie, if you have to handle anything,
than a human. So an old person has a big empty hollow space with
nothing in it, just ugh, and that's life: nothing else is going to
happen, there's just ugh stop.

Anything that Destroys Limits

Afterwards Janey and Johnny went to an all-night movie. All
during the first movie Janey's sort of leaning against Johnny cause
she's unsure he's attracted to her and she doesn't want to embarrass
him (her) in case he ain't. She kinda scrunches against him. One
point Johnny is pressing his knee against her knee but she still ain't
sure.

Some Like It Hot ends. All the rest of the painters are gonna leave
the movie house cause they've seen *The Misfits*. Separately Janey

and Johnny say they're going to stay. The painters are walking out. The movie theatre is black.

Janey still doesn't know what Johnny's feelings are.

A third way through the second movie Johnny's hand grabs her knee. Her whole body becomes crazy. She puts her right hand into his hand but he doesn't want the hand.

Johnny's hand, rubbing her tan leg, is inching closer to her cunt. The hand is moving roughly, grabbing handfuls of flesh, the flesh and blood crawling. He's not responding to anything she's doing.

Finally she's tentatively touching his leg. His hand is pouncing on her right hand setting it an inch below his cock. Her body's becoming even crazier and she's more content.

His other hand is inching slower towards her open slimy hole. Cause the theatre is small, not very dark, and the seats aren't too steep, everyone sitting around them is watching exactly what they're doing. Her black dress is shoved up around her young thighs. His hand is almost curving around her dark-pantied cunt. Her and his legs are intertwined. Despite fear she's sure to be arrested just like in a porn book because fear she's wanting him to stick his cock up her right now.

His hand is roughly travelling around her cunt, never touching nothing, smaller and smaller circles.

Morning. The movie house lights go on. Johnny looks at Janey like she's a business acquaintance. From now on everything Janey does is for the purpose of getting Johnny's dick into her.

Johnny, 'Let's get out of here.'

New York City at six in the morning is beautiful. Empty streets except for a few bums. No garbage. A slight shudder of air down the long long streets. Pale grey prevails. Janey's going to kill Johnny if he doesn't give her his cock instantaneously. She's thinking ways to get him to give her his cock. Her body becomes even crazier. Her body takes over. Turn on him. Throw arms around his neck. Back him against car. Shove clothed cunt against clothed cock. Lick ear because that's what there is.

Lick your ear.

Lick your ear.

Well?

I don't know.

What don't you know? You don't know if you want to?

Turn on him. Throw arms around his neck. Back him against
car. Shove clothed cunt against clothed cock. Lick ear because
that's what there is.

Obviously I want to.

I don't care what you do. You can come home with me; you can
take a rain check; you cannot take a rain check.

I have to see my lawyer tomorrow. Then I have lunch with Ray.

Turn on him. Throw arms around his neck. Back him against
car. Shove clothed cunt against clothed cock. Lick ear because
that's what there is.

You're not helping me much.

You're not helping me much.

Through this morning they walk to her apartment. Johnny and
Janey don't touch. Johnny and Janey don't talk to each other.

Johnny is saying that Janey's going to invite him up for a few
minutes.

Janey is pouring Johnny a glass of Scotch. Janey is sitting in her
bedroom on her bed. Johnny is untying the string holding up
her black sheath. Johnny's saliva-wettened fingers are pinching her
nipple. Johnny is lifting her body over his prostrate body. Johnny's
making her cunt rub very roughly through the clothes against his
huge cock. Johnny's taking her off him and lifting her dress over
her body. Janey's saying, 'Your cock is huge.' Janey's placing her
lips around Johnny's huge cock. Janey's easing her black underpants
over her feet.

Johnny's moaning like he's about to come. Janey's lips are
letting go his cock. Johnny's lifting Janey's body over his body so
the top of his cock is just touching her lips. His hands on her
thighs are pulling her down fast and hard. His cock is so huge it is
entering her cunt painfully. His body is immediately moving quickly
violently shudders. The cock is entering the bottom of Janey's
cunt. Janey is coming. Johnny's hands are not holding Janey's
thighs firmly enough and Johnny's moving too quickly to keep
Janey coming. Johnny is building up to coming.

That's all right yes I that's all right. I'm coming again smooth of
you oh smooth, goes on and on, am I coming am I not coming.

Janey's rolling off of Johnny. Johnny's pulling the black pants
he's still wearing over his thighs because he has to go home.
Janey's telling him she has to sleep alone even though she isn't

knowing what she's feeling. At the door to Janey's apartment Johnny's telling Janey he's going to call her. Johnny walks out the door and doesn't see Janey again.

•

YUAN CH'IUNG CH'IUNG
A Lover's Ear
(1985)

Born in Taiwan in 1950, Yuan Ch'iung Ch'iung has written stories, essays and (under a pseudonym) poetry, as well as working busily as a scriptwriter for Taiwan's daytime TV soaps.

Short-short stories have a long tradition in Taiwanese literature, but Yuan's are unusual in that they scorn the customary twist-in-the-tail structure and neat ending; hers tend to evoke moods and to leave questions unanswered. As her translator Howard Goldblatt notes, 'Some of her work is slightly bizarre, some is surprisingly (and gently) erotic; "A Lover's Ear" has traces of both qualities.'

He noticed that she carried an earpick in her purse. She told him that her ears itched from time to time, and she carried it with her so she could clean her ears whenever she felt like it.

He asked her if she would mind cleaning his ears for him. They also itched from time to time.

The two of them had strong feelings for one another by this time, and they had already done a lot of things together.

In fact, she had used her earpick only on herself, never to clean anyone else's ears. She had always felt that cleaning someone else's ears was the height of intimacy – except, of course, when it was done professionally. Her own mother had been the only other person ever to clean her ears. It seemed to her that if a relationship was lacking either in passion or in trust, there was little chance that one person would clean the other's ears.

She giggled nervously. 'Now?' she asked.

They had agreed to meet somewhere else this time, at some open, well-lighted place where there were lots of people. A public place. She had insisted on it. She had told him she didn't want to go to his place or to her place. There was so much passion in their relationship at that point that whenever they were alone they fell immediately into each other's arms. That left them no time to do anything else.

He smiled in return. Taking her hand in his and holding it tightly, he looked her straight in the eye and said softly and a little conspiratorially, 'Yes, now.' The very same tone of voice he always used when he wanted to do *it*. He would say, 'I want to put it in.'

She could tell she was blushing. Two women at the next table were just then talking about a man. No more than three paces separated the two tables, so that every word the two women said came through as clear as a bell.

He was sitting opposite her, but fortunately the table was small. She told him to lay his head down on the table, the right side up. His large head took up nearly half the tabletop. Since it was right there in front of her, she could work on his ear with ease. She was able to look straight down into his ear canal. He had fleshy ears and a wide opening to his ear canal. It was strange how you could know absolutely everything about someone you were in love with, how you could see the most private parts of his body, yet surprisingly would never really notice his ears. Since the lighting was on the dim side, she couldn't see all that clearly as she cleaned his ear. She asked if she was hurting him. 'No,' he said.

When she had finished with the right ear, he turned his head to the other side. Neither of them spoke while she was cleaning his ear, so they could hear every word spoken at the next table. One of the women was saying to the other, 'What in the world could have happened? With all that love, I just don't understand it.' They were discussing a relationship that had gone sour for no apparent reason. She was concentrating so hard on cleaning his left ear that her eyes began to blur; just then her hand slipped. 'Ouch!' he complained tenderly, as though the pain itself were an expression of love. 'Oh-oh,' she hastened to apologize. 'I'm sorry.' Drops of blood appeared on the inside wall of his ear. She didn't have the nerve to tell him. 'I'm not going to do it any more,' was all she said.

He sat up and felt around in his ear with his pinky. His eyes narrowed as he savoured the feeling. He then gave her the oddest look as he said: 'That was sort of like putting it in, wasn't it?'

They broke up not long after that.

Their break-up was accompanied by a very unpleasant scene. It took her a long, long time to get over her feelings of loathing for him and pity for herself. Her only reaction to the news that he had gotten married was indifference – not a trace of emotion. He had become totally irrelevant to her life.

From now on, she reflected, his wife can clean his ears for him.

Inexplicably, this thought saddened her – she suddenly felt very, very sad.

Translated by Howard Goldblatt

•

AMY YAMADA

Kneel Down and Lick My Feet

(1988)

Amy Yamada has a reputation as Japan's most liberated woman writer. Born in 1959, she began writing in earnest in the 1980s, when she burst on to the scene with her novel Bedtime Eyes *(1985), which told frankly and unromantically of a relationship between a Japanese woman and a black American soldier – an approach quite contrary to the traditional Japanese vagueness about such matters.*

Bedtime Eyes *became a major feature film, and more short novels followed in 1987:* Jesse's Spine, Fingerplay, Soul Music Lovers Only *and more.* Ponchan is Here *(1990) is a collection of short stories, and Yamada is also in demand by both fiction and music magazines.*

The following story was developed into a novel bearing the same title, which was published in Japan in 1988.

It's not as if she's some priss who doesn't know a thing about men, but the first time Chika saw me spit in a guy's mouth, she had to run to the toilet. I mean, really. She's the one who came to me begging, Shinobu, Sis, I need to make some money. Help me find a job. What was I supposed to do? I was the same way at first. When I got started in the business, seeing men humiliated like this made me want to puke. But after a few years it's like any job. Your own craft is the only thing you can believe in. If it makes guys salivate and snuggle up, or if it makes them shit before my eyes, it's all the same to me. Men look up to me from all fours and I pity them. I grind my high heels into their pitiful little cocks and watch their faces twist while I drag on a cigarette. And then I say: *Kneel down and lick my feet.*

I hadn't heard from Chika in a while when one afternoon she called to ask if I knew of any jobs. And I said to myself, Just like I thought, things are going sour with her old man. So I asked, but she said, No, things're going great. She sounded cheerful enough. She said his birthday was coming up and she wanted to give him a present, so she needed to make some money. Which made me think, This girl is crazy.

Years ago, she was happy with next to nothing. She'd turn a few tricks and had a nice living. She wasn't lazy either. Worked every day, but she spent all her money on books, records, clothes, and all she'd eat was a little nibble of French bread. I'd scold her and tell her she ought to put a little more in her stomach, and she'd turn to me with a straight face and say, Well, Sis, why don't you introduce me to some nice rich old man? I never dreamed she'd be asking me to find her work so she could buy a present for some guy. Nor could I believe how fast she left her favourite glitzy Akasaka and Roppongi nightspots behind. Left her dull black guy, too, and his dumb kid, who she never let out of her sight for a second, just to move to this dead-end base town.

Still, Chika and I had been through a lot of good and bad times together. So, despite my doubts that this hypersensitive girl would make the necessary adjustments, I decided to bring her into this S&M club. With apologies in my heart to her old man. Actually, I've done worse myself. But this line of work is, surprisingly, quite safe, and you don't have to sleep with anybody you don't like. At first it's weird, but once you get used to it, it's like manual labour. You get rid of your frustrations, and you make some money. And it's not a bad profession, either. No other line of work lets you see so many men revert to their natural state. Plus it's nice to have men wait on you for a change. Ginza bar hostesses, by far the bigger fools, put up with more crap for much less money.

The next day Chika came to the club, and the owner – Pops we call him – liked her from the start. She'll be very popular, he said. What an insult! After the years I'd spent polishing her to a fine gleam, when the two of us go to town we get *anything* we want from any man we want!

Chika was Chika, all big eyes and silence at first. She's the lively, joking-around type, but as she listened to what we do here, I could see her sliding into the dumps. As it turned out, that was only because she heard that the first three or four days would be a trial period she wouldn't get paid for. It's the way it has to be. The customers' lives are at stake here. Pops let me teach Chika the ropes. She didn't know the letter S about S&M. She'd modelled for S&M magazines plenty of times, but modelling means you don't have to do anything but get tied up and have your picture taken. Neither the 'doers' nor the 'done to' have any idea what's going on. We know a well-known S&M writer who can't even handle a rope.

There's S&M clubs, and then there's S&M clubs, if you know what I mean. And that's where most amateurs make their first mistake. Some clubs are run by gangsters. The charges are outrageous, and the clubs tend to be filthy. They don't even disinfect the enema equipment before they shove it up the next customer's butt. Talk about breeding grounds for AIDS. In some places, the girls actually have *sex* with the customers. Guys'll call up for the first time and ask, Afterward is she gonna let me do it? As if it were *natural*! The girl who answers the phone is used to this. She tells them politely that queens don't consort with slaves. The fact is, guys who are really after a woman's body can't be called true lovers of S&M. They should just splash cold water on their faces and come back later. Guys who truly love S&M are sincere.

This place is called the Queen's Palace. It's a club for guys who want to get picked on. We don't get many misguided souls who want to tie up women or anything silly like that. So I feel safe. Even someone like me who doesn't really get off on S&M can have a good time. Show me another place where women have slaves in this day and age! Show me another job where you can abuse men and have them thank you for it.

What's more, this place is clean, almost disturbingly clean. All equipment is disinfected after use. The men wear condoms start to finish, the rooms are made spanking clean after each round of play, and, of course, we disinfect our hands with ethanol. So there's nothing to worry about. Still, Chika was frightened of the whole thing – until I got her to put on some black underwear. It's

amazing how a black leather brassière and panties, black seamed
stockings, and a black garter belt can make even a total amateur
like her look like a real queen. I, on the other hand, wear a French
lace camisole and needle-spike heels. Chika likes to play the bad
girl. She makes a point of shocking detectives with her black silk
lingerie when she's called down to the police department. She
actually gets off exposing herself in front of people like that. Try
not to look too sweet, I tell Chika, as I open the door to the room
where a client is showering.

Let me see – what was it Mr Yamamoto liked? Oh, I remember,
he's the old coot who always takes the full course, *hard*. This might
be a little tough for Chika to watch right when she's starting off,
but what the hell. Sooner or later she's going to have to do at least
this much herself. The sound of the water stops. Mr Yamamoto is
coming out of the shower. In an instant, I have put on the face of
the Queen.

I sit on the red velvet throne with my legs crossed. Stark naked,
the man approaches. He sits at my feet. He sure does look like a
slave. In real life, the guy is president of a big company and spends
his time bullying his employees. Chika sits in the chair beside me
and watches us play-by-play.

'Queen Shinobu, it is an honour to be your humble plaything
today.'

'You are a despicable little slave.'

'Absolutely, your Highness.'

At this point, if the answer is unsuitable, I kick the slave away
and shriek, What kind of an answer is that! But Yamamoto knows
his part. There's nothing wrong with his answer.

'Well, then, slave, put this on that filthy thing between your
legs,' I say, throwing a rubber in his face. This is a problem for
guys who are too tense or whose sorry little pricks are too small.
They can't keep it on. When that happens I clamp it on with a
clothes-pin.

By now I've seen hundreds of pricks, and they're basically all the
same. But the way men are so attached to that one little part of
their bodies, the way they're thrilled or pained by whether it's big
or small, well, I think it's cute. The only thing a woman cares
about is whether the prick is attached to the man she loves or
whether it's attached to some other man. Or maybe it's only me.

No, Chika says the same thing. What makes one man's dick special is a woman's thoughts, right? I don't care how many pricks I have to look at in my line of work. They just look like a bunch of wriggly vegetables out of some cartoon. Maybe there are vegetables that really look like that – maybe only in fairy tales.

I make a habit of having the slaves massage my legs as I think about what to put on the day's menu. That's part of the game, too. Most men like women's legs, but masochists are crazy about them. Getting to rub a fishnet-stockinged leg gets their mouths watering. And if they start to slobber on your leg and you give them a little kick in the cheek, the job's almost done. The guy's thing, lifeless as a sea slug until then, is standing straight up in a second. Some guys go wild for black high heels and will lick them all over, even the soles. We call this 'purification' – but it means that *good* shoes would be a waste. One time I was out shopping with the mama of the club. We were passing by a shoe store, and I said, Look, Mama, let's find a nice pair of shoes. How about these? Don't you think they're great? She just looked at the price tag and said, Oh, Shinobu, they're too expensive. You're just going to let people lick them. Very matter-of-factly, out loud. The shop employees turned and stared at us in shock. The air in the store went cold. Mama and I put on these weak little smiles and walked out of the place.

When I first got into this business, I was just like Chika. I didn't know what to think, but you get used to it. When you get right down to it, there are an awful lot of sadists and masochists in the world. People call this a perversion, but you have to wonder, if there are this many so-called perverts in the world, what is normal? These people know a hell of a lot more about human joy than all those teenagers fucking around without a whisper of love. If it were just a matter of sex, animals can do it. But only people can indulge themselves with a *taste* for carnal pleasure. For some people this is a search for love, but for others it's a thirst for S&M, or romance. S&M is an underground pleasure, but don't you think that's the way sex should be? Everybody has some secret sexual kick. Compared to the rubes who get their kicks from ogling smelly farm girls in trash magazines, the men who pursue their deepest pleasures in the world of shadows are far superior beings. Men who like their women young and virginal don't understand a bloody thing, but what can you do about it?

When I first told Chika about S&M, she thought it sounded great because all she could think of was high-minded stuff like *Histoire d'O* and Sacher-Masoch. But when it's a job, you have to cut through that sentimental crap. Make a mistake and you end up with shit on your hands. With a little practice, though, it's no problem. It's easy to learn how many condoms to put on the vibrator you stick up a guy's ass and how to use the tissue paper to clean up afterwards so you don't even have to touch him. It becomes second nature. What's hard is when you have to tie a guy up. There's lots of variations and you have to learn how to avoid those places where, if a rope digs in, you're in trouble. The basic form is called the tortoise-shell truss, but there is no end to the number of advanced techniques. There are pros who specialize in nothing but ropes. By the time you've learned the ropes, your hands are covered with blisters, but you have learned a skill. Me, I can always go to work for a packing company.

So, after having the poor jerk do my merciless bidding for a while, I decide to tie him up and hang him upside-down from the ceiling, his head resting on the floor. Now the fun begins. I sit on his head and abuse his nether parts. Chika says that looks like something she could do, so I let her. Naturally there's a right way and a wrong way to sit. Properly, you should mount the guy's face – astride his forehead so he can breathe easily. It also keeps the guy from getting the wrong idea and trying to stick his tongue up you. There are some slaves who want to be the Queen's chair so badly they cry. On them, I sit a little harder, give them the extra enchantment of having trouble breathing.

Chika gives out a little squeal of joy as she sits on the guy's face. I scold her, saying, Stop that, you're the Queen, you must be more strict with him. Okay, she says and sticks out her tongue at me. The fool! If she acts too cheerful, she'll put the customer in a bad mood. Take it easy, Chika. A woman is always a Queen. I wrench open the man's mouth and begin to spit in it. A dead hush falls over everything.

'I want to be the Queen's chamberpot.'

He says that with such an ecstatic expression that that's when Chika has to run to the toilet. C'mon, I think, we're just getting started. This guy does say the cutest things, though. As a reward, I'm going to punish him but good. You have to leave yourself room to smile. We're no amateurs here. When a slave says things like that to me, it gets me hotter and puts an extra snap into my whip hand. This guy here is at his peak and will allow himself to do anything. I'm only too happy to oblige. I know all I need to know about that *other* world which doesn't begin to measure a man's *real* character. How bored men and women can get in that existence.

When Chika creeps back into the room, an embarrassed look on her face, the slave is still tied up and upside-down and I'm whipping his back. Look! I say, Queen Chika has returned to look upon your vile body. Got to keep the situation in hand. She apologizes to me, and quietly stands close to see how I use the whip. I've got to teach her how to make a loud noise without leaving a mark. It takes a sharp snap of the wrist. Most girls get a sprain when they start. And most beginners can't control where the whip lands. That can be a problem. Around the ribs, it's easy to leave marks that won't go away. But most people have to go back to their ordinary lives when they walk out of here, so our job is to keep things like that from happening.

Language is one of the most critical things in this kind of play. You need to speak in a dignified manner, but you must also be polite and show respect. Not least of all to yourself. We queens are terribly important personages after all. It behoves us to use words that elevate all our actions. Think about this in an unromantic context, and you can't keep from laughing, saying stuff like Beseech the queen that you might grovel before her honourable legs and receive the venerated punishment. You could chew off your own tongue on those phrases. Slaves who exalt the queen's every action call my piss holy water.

Aside from language, there's one other rule to this game. That is, after abusing the client you have to be nice to him. Anybody who gets hurt all the time is bound to get upset. You have to create a sense that you're punishing the client because you love him. The very whip of love. This is a world of whips and treats. That trade-off is the ultimate taste of the sweetness of life. Technique takes a secondary role. That's why lots of clients say they are completely satisfied with purely verbal play.

But isn't everything like that, really? Love that's only fun makes you soft. A little essence of suffering is what lights the fires of love.

Chika is one other woman who understands this very well, so I
think she'll get good at this. But it's so true, no?

You know what I really hate? Men and women who think
they're having an adult relationship because they can behave coolly
to one another. That's the sort of thing kids do when they want to
feel grown up. Real adults know what it means to suffer; they've
savoured difficulty. People who casually sleep together and casually
break up don't know anything about love. A real adult, no matter
how much he or she wants to sleep with someone, endures not
sleeping with them and learns to deal with pain. Sure, sleeping
around is just another form of play. And from the most trivial play,
a serious love can be born, as both Chika and I have experienced.
So it's hard to say. Way back when Chika and I used to play the
field, we were something else. We were wanton. We ran our risks
and we had our regrets. But one thing Chika managed that I never
could – she could always find a good point in a guy and tell me
about it. She'd say that some day these experiences would count in
our favour, though how she couldn't say.

I tie the guy up good, cross-legged, and shove the rubber dick
up his ass. I loosen the ropes to free up his hands and let him
masturbate in front of me. We finish right on time. Of course he
has to dispose of the condom himself. The sight of a man masturbating with a condom on is pitiful. I talk him through the whole
thing. It's a form of hypnosis. At times like these, I think men are
quite delicate. If I say the wrong thing at the wrong moment, it's
all over for them. If there were a man who could talk to a woman
in bed the way I talk, women would come just listening to him. But
there aren't many men like that, men who can say enough of the
right things in bed. Relatively speaking, foreigners are better at it.
Men who can speak in a way that is both obscene and refined,
crude and sincere. Most Japanese men don't have it in them. If you
find one who can talk, it's usually just a string of words you can't
say on television. Not like that Frenchman, whatzisname, Chika,
what was the guy's name? The guy who was Jane Birkin's . . .
Yeah, Serge Gainsbourg. No guy like him. Nobody even comes
close. It might make things a little awkward, but that's okay. Love
can hide a multitude of sins. But no matter how much in love you
are, a guy who keeps at it without a word is a big turn-off. One
part inspiration and nine parts perspiration. It pisses me off to

think of all the guys with no talent for sex getting their way in this world. Their women are just as bad, pretending they feel something. Men might not know it, but there are lots of women out there who pretend to come. It's a simple performance. And men are easily fooled. My women friends are all good women who like men, but there are plenty of them who have never come once sleeping with a man. They have no trouble masturbating to a climax though. It's a shame. They're too easy on their men and that's not right. They should teach them the truth about women's bodies.

'Shinobu, is that girl who was just here a new queen?'

Mr Yamamoto has changed his clothes, and he's got his company president face back on. I no longer speak arrogantly, am back to my normal voice.

'That's right. She still has a long way to go, but some day you'll be asking for her.'

'Well, you'll have to train her well before that day comes.'

'What are you saying? All our girls are top drawer.'

After the session, it's fun to talk with a client you've gotten to know well. With first-time clients, it's important to be friendly and show them you're not really the frightening bitch they think you are. There are all kinds of clients. I remember one guy who was an orchestra violinist. After his session, he gave a little concert for all the queens who weren't busy. Right there in the room, with pulleys and chains hanging from the walls, he played this *humoresque*. It was so beautiful, the bow moving back and forth in front of the cage. When Chika heard that story she got this faraway look on her face and sighed, Oooh, just like a Kuniyoshi Kaneko painting! Like I'm supposed to know who this artist is . . .

Another time, as a client was showering after his session, I took a look at the book he left on the table, and it was in some difficult-looking foreign language. As I was leafing through it, the young guy stuck his head out of the shower, and this totally changed bright-boy expression came over him. Your majesty, he asked, do you like García Márquez? Again I ask you, Me? I never heard the name. But when Chika heard the story she said, Outasight! If only I could have customers like that. I think she meant it.

Plenty of these people seem to have highly developed personal aesthetics.

One customer always brings me a new set of lingerie; another always brings me love letters. But no matter how well I get to know them, very few of my clients ever ask me to meet them away from the shop. Everybody who comes here wants to be entering another world. That goes for me and the other queens, too. Some of us go home to husbands and children who don't know anything about this. Some are strait-laced office workers. Some are just pulling the wool over their parents' eyes. I have a man of my own, and for that matter so does Chika. When I'm with my man, I don't talk big the way I do at work. In his arms, I'm as cuddly as a kitten. People really do have an A-side and a B-side. They're complicated.

Men come here and bare their true selves. And then *we* go home and bare our true selves in our own man's arms. Or maybe those aren't our true selves. We all want the man we love to feel good, so sometimes we flirt in a way that's totally out of character. So maybe our true selves aren't really anywhere but inside us. All people are actors to some extent, except when they're completely alone. That's why, in my heart, I don't believe anything about anybody. But that doesn't mean that I hate them. It's just obvious. No matter how much you trust somebody, that person's acting, at least a little. So all you guys who trust your wives while you go out and blow the company's entertainment budget on some Ginza bimbo better get smart. Before you know it, your ass is going to be in never-never land.

'Well? You think you're up to it?'

Chika answers with an ambiguous smile.

'I don't know. It takes skill to get a big man all tied up and hanging like that. But when it comes right down to it, there's not many things I can do, so I guess I have to try. I've tried all kinds of things. I know there're limits to what I can do. And I know all about what I can't do, the things that disturb me in my heart, disrupt my own time. Being a hostess is okay, but I'm sick of putting up with the abuse when I meet some customer outside the bar. I've had my fill of sleeping with strange men. So in that sense, this line of work seems made for me. One at a time, each time a complete little act. I have a short attention span. Really, I'd be good at office work somewhere, get done by five, but with a pink-collar job like that I could never afford all the things I want.'

That was Chika's grumbling analysis. Work that would disturb her in her heart. Come to think of it, when she worked in the bar, she would always run straight home at quitting time and the mama scolded her for that. She has this surprisingly well-defined no-trespassing zone. In night-life trades, usually, hearts and bodies flow together and eventually your personal life gets dragged into it. But she clearly rejected that. It was all a joke to her. When she screwed some rich old man to make a little pocket change, she never acted the sweet young lady, because this was only a tempo-rary withdrawal he'd made from her love bank. She never met him halfway, never played up to him, never gave of herself. When his two hours were up, it was, well, *sayonara*. Just like an American call girl. Not at all like a Japanese hotel whore. And she was the one who decided she would make her money that way. Totally shame-less, full of pride. In not playing up to her tricks, by keeping her love for her man, though, she's just like me.

I might raise a frown or two when I say this, but I think that selling your body and working for a company are pretty much the same thing. Just ways to make money. People who need a lot of money have to pick the job that'll get it for them. Chika and I have been that way for a long time. There were always lots of things we wanted. Not that we ever worked in massage parlours or anything, but we've both made money by sleeping with men. Of course, we had our standards. We wouldn't do it with someone who was repulsive. Though it's true that some repulsive people might be considered handsome in ordinary society.

I don't remember ever feeling it was a sin to make money with my body. I only felt it was a sin when I sold, not my body, but my dignity, when business was off and I had to pretend to like some man I didn't like. That can make you puke, really. Well, that was when I was a bar hostess. There seem to be plenty of women who do the opposite, but I don't presume to say anything about them. And that's why I don't like it when people like that say things about women who live like us. Different people have different values.

It seems I didn't have to worry so much. Within a week, Chika was like an old hand. She was quick. She learned the ropes. She even learned to tie a man up and hang him from the ceiling. More than anything, she seemed to like the fact that she didn't have to hang out with the customers afterwards, that each session was a discrete little drama. And she seemed to be indulging her own ingenuity as well. She used music and candlelight, seemed to enjoy her own performances. Gee, Sis, she'd say, this work seems to suit me. Men really have a whole lot of sicknesses deep inside. And I'd think of all the men I tossed aside over the years and bite my lip.

Chika is so young, and yet the things she says, her eyes filling with tears, show she understands so much. There are plenty of men, she'd say, who I'm sorry I treated the way I did. I would never have done it if I knew what I know today. Such murmurs of the heart seemed to be her forte. In a way, she couldn't stand anything that would cause her to hate. She honestly seemed to understand the things I had been telling her.

One day, though, when Chika had become as good as any of the other queens, with a long list of clients of her own, she came rushing up to me, white as a sheet, pleading, 'You've got to help – I can't handle this guy by myself.'

'What are you saying? Nothing should shock you any more,' the club mama and I said as we entered her room.

There we found a young man with a timid smile on his face.

'What an imp! What lowly punishment have you begged the queen for?' I spoke in my regal voice.

'I'm sorry, I'm sorry,' he apologized, on the verge of tears.

'What's this?' asked the other queens, who'd all assembled in the room.

'Well, actually, I wanted her to stick me with needles,' he answered.

'What? Chika, I've taught you how to do that! What's your trouble?'

'He . . . he doesn't want the regular needles,' she said, opening a box he'd brought with him. In it were hundreds of heavy sewing needles.

'Sir, we don't use needles like this here. We use sterile, disposable hospital needles,' said the club mama.

It's fairly common for us to use hospital needles, sticking them in a customer's nipples or through a layer of skin in his scrotum. If you do it with a good strong jab, there's not that much pain or blood. New queens may be a little squeamish, but it's no big deal.

'But that's not what I . . .' he began to explain, but he had trouble speaking. 'I want her . . . to stick all of these . . . sewing needles into my . . . penis.'

The queens shrieked in alarm.

'And after that I want her to stick that . . . writing brush all the way up the . . . hole in my penis.'

The queens shrieked again. Mama was the only one who kept her cool.

'You get an erection that way?' she asked.

'Yes,' he said, shamefully.

'You'll bleed a lot. The blood all collects there,' Mama continued. 'Have you ever done this before?'

'Yes,' he said. 'So don't be shocked. Rather than do it myself, I came here because I thought it would be better to have a beautiful woman do it.'

'I wouldn't do it,' the queens said and ran off. In the end, only Mama, who has seen all the bitter and the sweet in this world, and I, who have twice the courage of your average person, were left. Chika, despite her weakened state, sat in the corner of the room and watched as we went to work.

We put the first-timer in a chair, dimmed the lights, and faced him. I sterilized the sewing needles with ethanol and handed them one by one to Mama, who jabbed them into his penis. I wondered if the guy would be all right. The needles he brought were old. Some were rusty.

As Mama stuck him with needle after needle, his prick became engorged. It got harder and harder to put the needles in. If she stopped mid-thrust, his face twisted in pain. Mama scolded him after each needle. In time, he got a full-blown erection, and the protruding ends of the needles disappeared completely into his prick. I thought to myself, I don't want to be around when they come out, because he's going to bleed *all over the place*.

The more his crotch began to look like a pincushion, the more ecstatic the young man's expression became.

Mama began to speak in a loving voice, in that dim room oozing with insanity. It was enough to make me shiver, in spite of myself. Times like this, I really admire Mama. She's a real pro.

'How's that? This is what you wanted. It hurts, doesn't it? Tell me it hurts. Then I'll forgive you.'

'It doesn't hurt. It doesn't hurt at all.'

'You really don't know how to listen, do you? If you want to be such a bad boy, we'll have to do this all over again.'

'Forgive me. It's all my fault. I won't do it again. I beg of you.'

'Too late now. You should have caught on sooner. I can no longer forgive you. Hand me another needle.'

Their conversation went on for a long time, the drama building to a pitch. I glanced at Chika, who was staring speechless at this punishment. There were only a few needles left. Mama also noticed this and seemed to be trying to bring the guy to a climax. I passed the last needle to Mama.

'Look, your prick is full of needles. Shall we cut it off and put it in the sewing box? This is the last needle. When this one is in, your punishment will be finished. You will be mine, utterly.'

Mama paused and jabbed in the last needle.

In a burst the man ejaculated. He screamed out: '*Mother! . . . Mother! . . . Oh, Mother!*'

I looked at Mama, and she, without a word, was looking at me. Bliss had infused the young man's expression. My chest was filled with emptiness and pain.

'Shinobu, turn on the light!'

I got ahold of myself and turned on the light. The man appeared to be waking from a dream.

'Now we're going to take the needles out. This may hurt,' Mama reassured him, 'but you're going to be fine.'

'I'm used to it,' he said.

I brought a towel over and spread it at his feet. Mama waited to get started. The man began talking quietly.

'I was an illegitimate child, and people teased me about it when I was little. My mother – I mean the mother who took me into her house – was the only one who was kind to me. But there were times, I guess, when she couldn't take it any longer. She would call me to the room where she was sewing kimonos, and she would do things to me like we just did. It became a kind of habit. A strange habit. She's dead now. But I can't ever forget her.'

With each needle Mama pulled out, the man interrupted his speech. Still, he talked to the end. Around him was a sea of blood. He looked pale, but satisfied.

I commandeered the towel and said, 'What will it be, then? Do you still want the brush today?'

'You mean we can do more?' he asked. 'No, that's OK. I'm quite happy for today. Usually when I go to S&M clubs, the women are afraid of me and won't do what I want. No, I'm very happy. Mama, you were truly just like my mother.'

Mama smiled and said, 'Well, come back again any time,' then left the room. The man bowed deeply.

I thought Mama was fabulous. In this world, being young and cute doesn't mean a thing. I still have a lot to learn.

For all the blood the guy had lost, the bleeding stopped unbelievably quickly. He went into the shower. I was thinking, maybe I'll start to clean up, when I looked around and saw that Chika had fainted. What a sad sight! I left her there and switched on the vacuum cleaner. The sound roused her.

'What a mess,' I started swearing.

Chika's eyes gleamed. That sad, frightened look had vanished completely.

'Sis, life is amazing, isn't it?' she said, nodding to herself.

'What do you mean – fainting at the sight of blood and babbling about life?' I said and made her help me clean up.

The man came out of the shower, looked at us, and said flat out, 'Oh, Chika, you still here?'

She pouted and looked away.

Translated by Terry Gallagher

•

ISABEL ALLENDE
Our Secret
(1989)

Born in Peru and brought up in Chile, Isabel Allende worked as a journalist for many years before starting to write fiction in 1981. Her first novel, The World of the Spirits, *won worldwide acclaim, and it was followed two years later by the equally successful* Of Love and Shadows. *The stories in* Eva Luna *and* The Stories of Eva Luna *are set in the dazzling landscapes of South America, mingling themes of politics and poverty, passion, pain and tragedy. 'Our Secret' is from the latter book.*

She let herself be caressed, drops of sweat in the small of her back, her body exuding the scent of burnt sugar, silent, as if she divined that a single sound could nudge its way into memory and destroy everything, reducing to dust this instant in which he was a person like any other, a casual lover she had met that morning, another man without a past attracted to her wheat-coloured hair, her freckled skin, the jangle of her gypsy bracelets, just a man who had spoken to her in the street and begun to walk with her, aimlessly, commenting on the weather and the traffic, watching the crowd, with the slightly forced confidence of her countrymen in this foreign land, a man without sorrow or anger, without guilt, pure as ice, who merely wanted to spend the day with her, wandering through bookstores and parks, drinking coffee, celebrating the chance of having met, talking of old nostalgias, of how life had been when both were growing up in the same city, in the same barrio, when they were fourteen, you remember, winters of shoes soggy from frost, and paraffin stoves, summers of peach trees, there in the now-forbidden country. Perhaps she was feeling a little lonely, or this seemed an opportunity to make love without complications, but, for whatever reason, at the end of the day, when they had run out of pretexts to walk any longer, she had taken his hand and led him to her house. She shared with other exiles a sordid apartment in a yellow building at the end of an alley filled with garbage cans. Her room was tiny: a mattress on the floor covered with a striped blanket, bookshelves improvised from boards stacked on two rows of bricks, books, posters, clothing on a chair, a suitcase in the corner. She had removed her clothes without preamble, with the attitude of a little girl eager to please. He tried to make love to her. He stroked her body patiently, slipping over her hills and valleys, discovering her secret routes, kneading her, soft clay upon the sheets, until she yielded, and opened to him. Then he retreated, mute, reserved. She gathered herself, and sought him, her head on his belly, her face hidden, as if constrained by modesty, as she fondled him, licked him, spurred him. He tried to lose himself; he closed his eyes and for a while let her do as she was doing, until he was defeated by sadness, or shame, and pushed her away. They lighted another cigarette. There was no complicity now; the urgent anticipation that had united them during the day was lost, and all that was left were two vulnerable people lying on a mattress, without memory, floating in the terrible vacuum of unspoken

words. When they had met that morning they had had no extraordinary expectations, they had no particular plan, only companion-
ship, and a little pleasure, that was all, but at the hour of their
coming together, they had been engulfed by melancholy. We're
tired, she smiled, seeking excuses for the desolation that had settled
over them. In a last attempt to buy time, he took her face in his
hands and kissed her eyelids. They lay down side by side, holding
hands, and talked about their lives in this country where they had
met by chance, a green and generous land in which, nevertheless,
they would for ever be foreigners. He thought of putting on his
clothes and saying goodbye, before the tarantula of his nightmares
poisoned the air, but she looked so young and defenceless, and he
wanted to be her friend. Her friend, he thought, not her lover; her
friend, to share quiet moments, without demands or commitments;
her friend, someone to be with, to help ward off fear. He did not
leave, or let go her hand. A warm, tender feeling, an enormous
compassion for himself and for her, made his eyes sting. The
curtain puffed out like a sail, and she got up to close the window,
thinking that darkness would help them recapture their desire to be
together, to make love. But darkness was not good; he needed the
rectangle of light from the street, because without it he felt trapped
again in the abyss of the timeless ninety centimetres of his cell,
fermenting in his own excrement, delirious. Leave the curtain open,
I want to look at you, he lied, because he did not dare confide his
night terrors to her, the racking thirst, the bandage pressing upon
his head like a crown of nails, the visions of caverns, the assault of
so many ghosts. He could not talk to her about that, because one
thing leads to another, and he would end up saying things that had
never been spoken. She returned to the mattress, stroked him
absently, ran her fingers over the small lines, exploring them. Don't
worry, it's nothing contagious, they're just scars, he laughed,
almost with a sob. The girl perceived his anguish and stopped, the
gesture suspended, alert. At that moment he should have told her
that this was not the beginning of a new love, not even of a passing
affair; it was merely an instant of truce, a brief moment of innocence,
and soon, when she fell asleep, he would go; he should have told
her that there was no future for them, no secret gestures, that they
would not stroll hand in hand through the streets again, nor share
lovers' games, but he could not speak, his voice was buried

somewhere in his gut, like a claw. He knew he was sinking. He tried to cling to the reality that was slipping away from him, to anchor his mind on anything, on the jumble of clothing on the chair, on the books piled on the floor, on the poster of Chile on the wall, on the coolness of this Caribbean night, on the distant street noises; he tried to concentrate on this body that had been offered him, think only of the girl's luxuriant hair, the caramel scent of her skin. He begged her voicelessly to help him save those seconds, while she observed him from the far edge of the bed, sitting cross-legged like a fakir, her pale breasts and the eye of her navel also observing him, registering his trembling, the chattering of his teeth, his moan. He thought he could hear the silence growing within him; he knew that he was coming apart, as he had so often before, and he gave up the struggle, releasing his last hold on the present, letting himself plunge down the endless precipice. He felt the crusted straps on his ankles and wrists, the brutal charge, the torn tendons, the insulting voices demanding names, the unforgettable screams of Ana, tortured beside him, and of the others, hanging by their arms in the courtyard.

What's the matter? For God's sake, what wrong, Ana's voice was asking from far away. No, Ana was still bogged in the quicksands to the south. He thought he could make out a naked girl, shaking him and calling his name, but he could not get free of the shadows with their snaking whips and rippling flags. Hunched over, he tried to control the nausea. He began to weep for Ana and for all the others. What is it, what's the matter? Again the girl, calling him from somewhere. Nothing! Hold me! he begged, and she moved towards him timidly, and took him in her arms, lulled him like a baby, kissed his forehead, said, go ahead, cry, cry all you want; she laid him flat on his back on the mattress and then, crucified, stretched out upon him.

For a thousand years they lay like that, together, until slowly the hallucinations faded and he returned to the room to find himself alive in spite of everything, breathing, pulsing, the girl's weight on his body, her head resting on his chest, her arms and legs atop his: two frightened orphans. And at that moment, as if she knew everything, she said to him, fear is stronger than desire, than love or hatred or guilt or rage, stronger than loyalty. Fear is all-consuming . . . and he felt her tears rolling down his neck. Everything stopped: she had touched his most deeply hidden wound. He had a presentiment that she was not just a girl willing to make love for the sake of pity, but that she knew the thing that crouched beyond the silence, beyond absolute solitude, beyond the sealed box where he had hidden from the Colonel and his own treachery, beyond the memory of Ana Díaz and the other betrayed *compañeros* being led in one by one with their eyes blindfolded. How could she know all that?

She sat up. As she groped for the switch, her slender arm was silhouetted against the pale haze of the window. She turned on the light and, one by one, removed her metal bracelets, dropping them noiselessly on the mattress. Her hair was half-covering her face when she held out her hands to him. White scars circled her wrists, too. For a timeless instant he stared at them, unmoving, until he understood everything, love, and saw her strapped to the electric grid, and then they could embrace, and weep, hungry for pacts and confidences, for forbidden words, for promises of tomorrow, shared, finally, the most hidden secret.

Translated by Margaret Sayers Peden

•

ELIZABETH COOK
Billets Doux
(1989)

A part-time teacher in London prisons, Elizabeth Cook has written a study of the poetry of the Renaissance, Seeing Through Words *(1986), has translated Seneca's play* Thyestes, *and has edited a new edition of the works of John Keats. 'Billets Doux' is an amusing story about adultery.*

I was thirty last January and am old enough to enjoy the fact that my lover thinks of me as a younger woman. My lover is fifty but looks much younger, perhaps because he is slightly fat – not paunchy, but sleek – and this keeps his skin from getting that crêpey look that some skin gets. I, on the other hand, am rather thin. I used to think that I looked better with clothes on than off –

I can wear almost anything – but my lover doesn't agree. I am not particularly beautiful but I have got the most astonishing red hair. It is very long and full and it springs out of my head like fiery thoughts.

My lover's wife is thirty-eight but she doesn't look it. She is really beautiful. She looks like a Swede but she isn't one. She is statuesque and, without being at all fat, everything about her goes in curves. She is like cream and her hair is ice-blond. She is a famous cookery writer and I am always seeing her on television, tasting things or talking about the food she's eaten abroad. Needless to say she's a wonderful cook. Apart from seeing her on television I don't really know her, but she does come into the library where I work sometimes. The books she gets out are usually for some kind of research she's doing on food in the past. My lover says he's always having to eat things she's trying out from fourteenth-century recipes. But he wouldn't look so plush and well if they were bad.

I cook very badly indeed. My father used to say that no one would ever marry me for my cooking. And he was right I'm glad to say. But my lover likes dressing me up and taking me out for meals. With his wife cooking at home all the time it's his only chance to eat out. And he likes spending money on me. He's always giving me underclothes. He says he likes it when he's sitting opposite me in a restaurant and he knows what I've got on underneath: probably silk camiknickers and some kind of lacey suspender belt. Men are very traditional when it comes to underwear.

A few months ago my lover took me to a new Indonesian restaurant about thirty miles from here (we never go out in this town because we don't want anyone to see us). The food was very good – all sorts of little bits, very beautifully presented and not overcooked and not at all filling. This was important because we were going back to my house to make love and nothing spoils love-making more than being stuffed.

We had been looking forward to this night because his wife would be on an aeroplane to Singapore and there was no way she could phone him to make sure he was at home like he'd said. So he was going to spend the whole night with me and, even though we wouldn't sleep as much as an ordinary couple would, we would have breakfast together (that means instant coffee) before we both went out to work.

We were as careful about not drinking too much as about the eating. But when we got home I asked my lover to bath me and then he produced a bottle of champagne which was just right. He soaped me all over very carefully in a kind of neutral way – not lingering anywhere except to massage my nipples where they poked out through the cream of the lather. And then when I stepped out he dried me in a big towel as if he were my mother.

He had wanted to get in the bath too but he was always so clean I didn't want him to get any cleaner. I wanted there to be something to taste when I started on him. After he had rubbed me dry he found some oil I had in the bathroom and I lay on my tummy on a towel on the bed while he went over me with his hands, very slowly and deliberately, kneading the oil in. He started off at my shoulders and then moved inwards to my spine and then down over my hips and buttocks and then instead of sliding his hand in, he moved on down my legs one at a time, until he had massaged even the soles of my feet.

By that time I was ready to eat him in one gulp but he still had all his clothes on and he looked very calm and reflective. So then it was my turn to work on him. I made out like I wasn't in a hurry either. I behaved more like a valet than a lover as I took his clothes off and hung them neatly over the back of my chair. I didn't even pause when I unzipped his fly. I just let him step out of his trousers and then I folded them too. And then I pulled his socks over his heels and pushed them into the toes of his shoes and put the shoes together in a pair.

And then I held out my hand to invite him over to the bed. He lay down and I began the feast down at the nape of his left heel. And then I made my way round to the inside of his shin and went up, just dabbing at him with my tongue at first and then as I got up higher licking more wetly so as I got to the inside of his thigh I could really feel the hairs of his leg dragging against the grain of my tongue. But I didn't move on beyond the crease at the top of his thigh; I moved straight down to the toes on his right foot and moved slowly up that leg. Careful as a cat I was. I didn't want to miss one scrap of cream.

It wasn't till I'd nearly reached the top of his right thigh that I found her message to me. But I couldn't have missed it because it stood out like a rose in full bloom. It really was a beautiful print she had made. I would not have expected less from such expert teeth. And it was very well placed – like a stylish tattoo – about an inch below where his balls would graze his thigh when he was standing.

I paused for a moment in my work, my tongue inert a few centimetres off from the rose. My lover groaned a little – it was not so much from pleasure as a nudge to go on. So I did; moving inwards this time, licking the wiry hair on his balls and feeling the weight of his balls as they lolled against my tongue, and then moving up in the crease between balls and thigh wondering whether to start in at the root of his cock. But all the time I was thinking about her message and what I should do about it. Should I ignore it? I certainly wouldn't ignore him, if that was what she'd been thinking. Or should I respond in kind? My tongue was still toying with the crown of hair at the base of his cock when I made up my mind. I moved up a few inches to where his belly began, soft and hairless. I found a spot I liked and nuzzled my nose in it first; and then I took it between my lips and held on like a clam and sucked. But then I thought NO. He'll see that. I stopped at once. It wasn't much of a mark I'd made so far. If I rubbed his belly a bit the blood would flow away. I gave the spot a perfunctory kiss and moved down.

Not to her side (she'd taken right). My mouth moving like a metal detector over him I made for a place that felt right. It was almost in the crease where it begins to be sweaty and to smell like Brie, and this time I used my teeth. I could feel his balls tighten with excitement and this excitement communicated itself to me pretty fast. I only glimpsed the rose I'd made as I took my mouth away. But I was pleased to see that it was brighter than hers.

And to be honest I didn't give it another thought. Not until about three weeks later when, without wishing to be repetitive, I found myself lingering on the same area of my lover's anatomy. And she'd done it again. Not once, but many many times. Some had bloomed and faded, born to blush unseen. But three new ones stood out proud and bright. Mine had of course disappeared by then; but I felt sure she must have seen it. Why else would she have been so assiduous in replacing each paling print with one that was fresh and new and couldn't be missed? She had to be answered.

Quality rather than quantity I thought – and was sure that she'd agree since her quantity had only been a matter of securing visibility. I decided to match the best of her new ones. A little lower than my last, but still high up on the inside of his left thigh. My print was exactly opposite hers: like a lipstick kiss where his thighs would touch each other. He'd moaned, and pressed down on my head as I was doing it. He was having a good time these days.

We managed to see quite a lot of each other at that time. She was working on a new series and making a lot of short trips to Italy and Spain. (She has a great deal of energy – she can get off an aeroplane and just carry on.) And my lover's a bit of a baby – he doesn't care for being on his own. And I think he probably assumes that she goes off with all kinds of men when she's away. But I know better. She has told me of her constancy and I have told her of mine. Yes. She and I continued to speak to each other. We became increasingly exact and resourceful in our markings. Quite witty really: as I prized his buttocks apart to place a mark she'd have to hunt for, I saw she'd got there first. My reply simply meant '*touché*'. But sometimes I was the leader. In an attempt to break with the genital fixation we'd got into, I sucked out a beautiful cupid's bow on the sole of his (right) foot. And sure enough – five days later – it was kiss for kiss: a mark to match on his left sole. We'd swapped grounds. It was free for all.

My lover's inner thighs were by now speckled with bites. He reminded me of an old chair the painters had found to stand on when they were decorating the library. Cigarettes had been stubbed out all over it making weals in the paint, and the men went on squashing their fags out on it till it was stippled like a steel band's drum. I began to pity his poor thighs and let them be.

Besides, there are other things to do than bite. Licking and touching for instance. I think people make too much fuss over genitals. They limit their possibilities by assuming that cocks are the only things that can go anywhere and that cunts are the only places to go. But the way I look at it each pore of anybody's skin can be a cock or a cunt depending on its mood. Haven't you felt your skin when it's up and searching, pressing out and straining to get into every dent and cranny your lover's skin might offer? But then at other times each pore softens and opens into an eyelet longing to be filled. Skin's like Velcro: hooks and loops, whichever one at will, and it can play the game of man and woman, fucker and fucked, in a much more nimble way than genitals can. That was one of the things I'd liked about my lover. He knew about skin. Touching for him was not a cursory business to be undergone because women liked it – get them horny so the real show could start. With us any part could become our sexual centre and it could be hooked or looped or slippery as silk.

But that began to change after the biting correspondence began. As my tongue tip played with the hairs above his belly, feeling the energy that hovered to meet me, his palm would push down on my scalp and force me under to nose in on his cock and balls. And he'd go on pressing me, forcing my face closer and closer in till I'd submit and make yet another mark with my lips and teeth. And then he'd groan and I could imagine his cock arching out into a stretch and then ready to go into me. I expect it was the same for his wife.

After a while the bites I gave were sulky and obliging and not for her in any way. I just wanted him to stop holding my head down and I'd bite to get it over with though I could hardly bear to do it with the skin down there so bruised and tender. But he loved it. He wanted nothing else but to be gnawed at in his bruised parts and then to ram in his cock and fuck.

Other things changed about him too. There was something driven and distracted about him which left me feeling there was not much point in saying anything at all. In the past we'd had crazy, fantasy conversations: we'd choose characters for an evening and then see how far we could go with them, using them on the other people we met and keeping straight faces. But I stopped when he began to smile like he was humouring me. Whatever we did – for we went on going for drives and walks as well as out for meals – I began to get the feeling that he was mentally drumming his fingers until the time we could get home and into bed. It's hard to explain why it was so unpleasant: it wasn't like the old, shared excitement when we took pleasure in everything we did together and, even though we were longing to touch each other more, there was a fineness in the waiting. No; it was different. Worse. I'd begun to feel like an adjunct. Something to be endured and put up with because what he wanted – which was not me – couldn't be had without me.

Which explains why I haven't seen him for a month. He's been persistent – even urgent – in his attempts to see me but he hasn't found the right tone of voice yet. One touch of the old lightness and I'd be back like a shot. I miss that, but he seems to have lost it.

But I've seen more of her recently. She's been using the library quite a lot and I've had to help her over some inter-library loans. She's looking a bit drawn. Perhaps the pace of her life is catching up with her, but I don't like to see it. And her creamy skin isn't glowing in quite the old way. She was talking to me the other day when it was time for my tea break. So I said why didn't she join me. We went to the old-fashioned tea rooms down the road and sat among the old ladies with their hats. I was so pleased to have her with me that I ordered a plate of mixed cakes. It upset me to see her wasting away and I wanted to watch her tuck in.

•

IVA PEKÁRKOVÁ
Truck Stop
(1989)

Iva Pekárková is one of New York City's few female cab-drivers. Born in Prague in 1963, she studied biology before leaving Czechoslovakia in 1985. After a year in an American refugee camp, she found her way to the United States.

Harking back to her experiences in socialist Czechoslovakia, Truck Stop Rainbows *(1989) was her first novel, from which the following episode is taken. A second novel,* The World is Round, *is in progress between cab rides.*

I lay on the front seat of the Liazka, letting the motor rock me to sleep, listening to the rain and dreaming. We were now descending the serpentine road that cut down the mountainside in waves toward Moravská Třebová. White beech trunks flashed by in the windows. I sat up again, just so I could savour them. The yellowish lights of the rig licked the tall, slender, silvery-grey trees, rigid and gloomy as dancers frozen in mid-step. At that moment I couldn't stop looking at them (in fact, I had never been able to). It was strange: every time, absolutely every time I rode through here, I recalled a certain moment from my childhood. The little East

German Trabant diligently negotiates the hairpin turns, the rain; Father drives, skilfully and with exaggerated caution; drops of water collide on the windows, the air smells moist, and two little girls in the back seat trace the raindrops with their fingers. The streaming drops web the view, and the girls gaze out at the world with eyes full of wonder. The younger one occasionally touches her mother's back, warm and fragrant. She needs to reassure herself, confirm by touch that Mother is here, that she will turn to her, that she will reach back her gigantic hand so both children can grasp her fingers, like shipwrecked sailors reaching for floating beams. And the girls hold on, gripping the hand, as if they already feel the need to fight against the unfair, vertical force of time that separates age from age, mother from child. The children protest the force they will come to feel, even though it hasn't yet touched them. The family is returning from an outing; and along the road, bathed in a light summer shower, stand the bleached, tremendously tall trunks of the beeches, radiating light into the countryside.

That memory returned to me again and again, every time I descended that hillside with those silver beeches on the way down toward Třebová from the highway rest stop. For a long time I'd searched for this whitest of all beech stands; for years it seemed that it must have been just an image from a dream I had no right to consider a part of reality. Then later, when I actually discovered that piece of countryside after all, it was as if someone had laid a bouquet of rainbows at my feet.

How often I recalled it! I looked forward to it. Sometimes the countryside, a single stretch of land or section of road, will take root in your consciousness more deeply than things you encounter every day.

Those white, straight, unchanging beeches served to remind me that I, too, had once had a childhood.

As a matter of fact, it's strange how quickly and ungratefully a person can forget. Year after year, the faces of people close to me dissolved in my memory, and I purposely wouldn't look at their photographs because I knew how quickly such snapshots could take hold. They become etched in the mind and bury living images – dissolve them into nothingness. And I couldn't allow them to.

Only those trees . . . the whitest beeches in the entire republic . . . could trigger the flow of memories in me. I knew a couple of stretches of earth with this power. Sweet hidden springs of memories. Not melancholy memories, by any means.

So I could actually even be happy.

I could ride along through the rain in a strange yet familiar truck and recall sweetly how I, too, had once been young.

The wipers tenderly washed away the salty tears from my heart. The rain diluted the bitterness of my thoughts – and I could feel as safe and protected as in my mother's arms, which no longer existed. I was able to curl up blissfully in the sound of the motor and become someone else again for the instant.

I lay my head down again and thought about the magic of the Night Road.

I felt the Magic of Night between my knees: how it slowly rose up the insides of my thighs to warm my lap.

I thought about the Magic of Night and my heart began secretly to pound.

The Magic of Night surged inside my bra, making my nipples rise, like the caress of someone's tender, eager hand.

It was interesting how closely connected memories of childhood were with adult appetites; I pictured (behind closed eyelids) the driver's smile and his eyes . . . The colour of someone's eyes never meant anything to me, but his gaze always stuck in my mind – I could always recognize a person by his look.

The driver had a translucent blue gaze. Perhaps a little common, but understanding and serene. The kind I liked.

My hair, with its familiar silky texture, lay in readiness over the gearshift. Soft and supple hair, telegraph wires, antennae, electrical connections transmitting the Magic of Night from me to the driver's hands.

No, I didn't pick men up on the road, and I didn't try to get picked up. I didn't collect men and experiences in a deliberate way. Insinuation was against my nature – and so far nothing much could have been inferred from my eyes or body language. I always left the decision to my precious Serendipity until the very last instant. But for a long time my electric hair had served as a wordless agreement between me and anyone who understood.

We were now passing through Třebová, and we had to downshift on the cobblestones of the town square. I breathed the damp fragrance of rain deep into my lungs, and I already felt the driver's strong (and familiar) hand absorbing the electricity from those golden strands. I was drowsy, aroused, snug.

Because when that hand again made its way down to the gearshift (where it no longer had any legitimate business) and waded through my gilded thicket all the way to my forehead, it was clear that our truck would be stopping at the familiar shadowy rest stop just outside of Olomouc tonight.

It was nice.

Yes, that's the right word: nice.

Not unforgettable, but it had a charm of its own; after all, I'd learned long ago to reject the most ordinary experiences in advance. This embrace didn't remind me of anything that had gone before; it didn't fill me with those deep, intrusive memories, as so often happened in less skilful arms. On the contrary, everything from the past was washed away, took its normal place in my mind – and the love-making alone won its rightful place.

Even the rest stop (which I knew well from other nights and which he must have known just as well) belonged to us alone that night, including the lights of passing cars, including the sound of the rain, including the rocking motion imparted to us by each passing truck. The cab belonged to us alone, secluded, secure.

We said nothing.

We both belonged to the distance, to restlessness, road dust, and unexpected adventures – this was so implicitly obvious that we didn't need to speak about it.

The driver was one of those who understand.

We were both molecules of a great, almost completely stifled, age-old longing. A longing more powerful than love or lust, a voracious longing for the freedom, horizon, and azure of those mountains near the border. I'd learned which people carried this longing within them. He had it. And so, since we were parts of the same whole, it was pleasurable to connect for an instant, but that wasn't the most important thing.

It was important to keep driving, to go farther, to continue living, to take off somewhere into the womb of never-ending highways, roads, and footpaths that converged at the vanishing point of the infinite.

At that moment I had the infinite within me.

I felt that living, magnificent, absurd, and useful physical append-age; I savoured its penetration and felt the savage heartbeat pulsing within it. I savoured my body and gave it up to be savoured; I pressed myself into those wonderful arms, familiar and strange, like a cradle.

Sure, I knew perfectly well that each of us had learned every one of those supple, intoxicating motions in which we were joined from someone else, but that made no difference to us at the time. It was controlled love-making, certainly not one of a kind, but still, for that moment, unique.

Nestled in those firm, tender arms, caressing and desiring me, I thought simply of nothing.

And this, precisely this, was the unrepeatability I was always searching for, that fundamental, perfect, pure ecstasy of soul and body.

I didn't succumb to the wedding madness that had afflicted my entire class.

In our third year, at a time when, as I've already said, personalities were taking shape, the overwhelming majority of my once fickle classmates began pursuing serious relationships.

My former colleagues from high school had become worthy mothers long ago: they'd all fallen into it together, before they'd even turned twenty, and – convinced that it was necessary to atone for their sins – they couldn't pluck up the courage to present themselves before the abortion committee. They got married as a sort of afterthought, at times to men they didn't know all that well, because pregnancy loomed a lot larger than any vision of conjugal life. Sometimes they regretted being tethered so soon to diapers and the kitchen range, but they never forgave anyone who failed to procreate. They elevated parenthood to some kind of hereditary duty, the fate of the normal individual, who was forced to bear it with head bowed in grey acquiescence.

My clever university compatriots, however, took a more premedi-tated approach to marriage, duly weighing all the pros and cons; they judiciously chose the least unsuitable groom and then – as I interpreted it – they persuaded themselves they had real feelings for him.

The whole class was gripped by panic: hurry, girls, get him! Get hitched before the state boards or you're a rotten egg!

I didn't succumb to the universal hunting spirit, even though I have to admit that there really was a grain of truth to the graduation theory.

The 'few good men' – just like in a provincial village! – were picked over one by one, so that in the eyes of the average woman the only men past the age of twenty-five who remained unmarried were worthless paupers, inveterate Casanovas, mother's boys, and one or two who had managed to get divorced and who, of course, were already paying alimony for two or three kids.

In the big picture, our little world really was a village, a hamlet of two hundred people and without much of a selection, where the easiest (and safest) thing to do was to find yourself a partner from the next cottage over and apply the screws until that happy wedding day.

No one wanted to remain single, and people were looking for security; they didn't want to take any chances. A sparrow in your palm is better than a pigeon on the roof.

So in our third year even extremely pretty and desirable girls were starting to get jumpy and to search, evaluating boys as husbands and as progressives, sending out wedding announcements or quietly envying their luckier friends who had already taken the plunge and were out of the woods of insecurity.

The objects of envy became men and husbands, instead of strong emotions, fulfilment, or good relationships. It was important to enjoy yourself enough in your youth and still manage to snare Mr Right before the transition from young beauty to old maid. In our third year all these potential old maids were saddling up in droves for the hunting season.

Believe me, I didn't share in this universal marital frenzy. It goes without saying that the dismal spectre of an ageing world picked clean of men, who in and of themselves are quite worthwhile, did sometimes pass before my eyes, but somehow I never really recognized it. If there existed a person I'd want to stay with until the end of time, I'd find him eventually. I could wait. And if no such person existed in the whole wide world (which seemed more likely to me), then I could easily live out my life and die single. I was sure of that.

I wasn't looking for any security.

In a world fenced in by barbed wire — a world of filth, sickness, and radioactivity, a world as tired and worn as a pair of jeans that haven't been washed for five years — the concept of security was absurdly subjective.

The security seekers were desperate escapists; they sought shelter from the hurricane under their bedsheets; at the sight of blood they closed their eyes and plunged their ostrich heads into the sands of their private wastelands. In the shadow of the mushroom cloud they scratched out little trenches in their gardens and brought their one-and-onlies home hand in hand, to have someone to lean on.

I wasn't looking for the security of anyone's embrace: to my taste, that was too high a price to pay in jealousy and captivity. I didn't need any of that. For me the most beautiful security was serendipity.

The serendipity that ruled everywhere.

The serendipity of the rainbow.

The magnificent, alluring, dangerous, and dependable Serendipity of the road.

Serendipity, whose only law was that she brought you the most iridescent adventures precisely when you expected them least and wanted them most.

The serendipity of the instant, who could give you anything, as long as you knew how to obey her.

And in this I saw the possibility of being truly happy.

While my peers sought shelter and pseudo-security, I was learning to live for the moment. That immediate instant that passes away but always leaves its imprint on the consciousness. That instant, profound but not heavy, without obligation. Magical in its lack of context.

You might object that too great a number of momentary memories causes life to splinter. To swerve off course. To lose its unity and direction. But that's exactly what we wanted. In the face of that prefabricated blueprint that sought to entrap us like little screws in a machine in a factory dedicated to the destruction of the world and the eradication of rainbows, Patrik and I armed ourselves with our philosophy of instants. Yes, from our childhood we had hunted those multicoloured, uncontrolled, unexpected instants, sweet and bitter alike, and the more of these instants we caught, the more we wanted to catch and the better we got at it.

*

I lay in the truck on the cot (which was both strange and familiar) and experienced the instant.

The tiny cabin light shone above our heads (because sometimes you've got to give all the senses a chance, not just touch), and I wondered whether the shadows on the curtain that concealed us had revealed any of our intimacy: the hilly landscape of my heaving breasts as I lay on my back; his torso and his trembling head as he supported himself over me on one elbow, stroking my stomach with somewhat proprietary tenderness.

I sprawled out, domesticated, on the single cot, formed my lips into a half smile – and engaged all my senses, one after the other, so that the image of the day would sink in as deeply as possible.

I'd already checked out the situation, the dazzlingly white light illuminating the fluid on my raised hand, the shadows darkening into the background beyond my legs, and the almost unreal shifting colours of twilight.

And the face, with its pleasant (and now partly closed) eyes and overly large nose, whose elongated black shadow created a disturbing and harsh effect, artificially comical, like a circus clown. I touched the veins on his temple with my index finger, the moist dew of sweat caressed my fingertip, and beneath it I could feel the flow of blood. Touch. I closed my eyes, and with only red and yellow circles from the light penetrating my eyelids, I explored the skin of that strange familiar body with my free hand, and with my buttocks I registered the slightly sticky impression of the synthetic-fabric sleeping bag underneath me. It was hot, steaming hot. I cooled my shoulder on the iron wall behind me, gratefully remembering the people who made the Liazka, who couldn't upholster it, even with cheap vinyl. In a Volvo or Mercedes you had to open a window, but the Liazka was permeable to the night coolness. I could taste the difference in temperature between the sweaty supple body next to me and that sheet-metal panel. I inhaled.

The ever-present smell of dust. The overpowering, almost suffocating, deliciously animal concentration that requires at least two (but there were more!) physical scents. The smell of the worn blanket, and the distant smell of night, passed on to us through the window, opened a crack to the universe.

The smell of oil. Not unpleasant.

Whiffs of old, familiar smells, smells of the road, smells that cropped up in every cab of every truck on that Northern Road of ours. Common odours and odours all their own. Forgotten, but recalled upon in every subsequent encounter.

(I've never collected souvenirs. Gifts, rings, earrings. But if I could, I'd save whiffs of beautiful nights in a little pouch on my chest, the way Indians keep the scents of the prairie.)

All the while, large and small raindrops had been drumming on the resonant metal roof. It was possible to hear each of the largest, less frequent drops as it burst on the metal, scattering a rosette of smaller drops. The roof answered the watery assault onomatopoetically, and the resulting performance was musical and balmy.

I listened to the car engines which appeared on the auditory horizon, changed pitch like an approaching bumble-bee or helicopter, then whizzed by, rocking us gently before buzzing off into the distance.

The driver whispered compliments in his warm Central Slovak, and I smiled gently, like a beautiful woman who has just been well laid. And in fact, I had been well laid, and I wanted to let him know, but I wasn't sure yet what method I would choose.

I had saved the sense of taste for last, and I licked his chapped lips, the lips of a man, lips that had proved they could be attentive and tender to me. I caressed his cheek with my cheek; it was rough, and he sheepishly ran his hand through the stubble, making it rustle. I tasted the sweat on his throat and shoulder, and that completed my experience of the instant.

But on my left hand his seasoned, gorgeous sperm lay cooling and drying.

I spread it over my palm and played with it.

'You've got the most beautiful sperm I've ever seen in my life,' I said. 'Fragrant, smooth, pearly, and sparkling. Gorgeous sperm, a man's sperm.'

He didn't believe me.

Of course, in a certain sense he was right not to believe me, since I had a reserve of such absolute confidences for everyone I met; I expected my nocturnal friends to divide every compliment by the coefficient of transience, the way I always did.

But he really was listening to me, letting it all pass through his head, and I (as I rambled on) realized that I was raising for him the coloured arc of a new rainbow.

'You've got gorgeous sperm,' I whispered, and in the light of the little lamp I revealed to him the magic of its translucent, milky sheen. I showed him those millions of invisible, vivacious little creatures. 'Sperm is a source of both hope and fear. Some administer sperm as a life-giving elixir, because it contains life and is infected with life; some throw it away, rid themselves of it, wipe it off on a rag, despise it. Sperm is the bearer of life and death. Sperm is conception or contamination. Sperm is the union of animal juices; sperm is the seal of an eternal bond or complete nonsense. It's up to you how you look at it: sperm is everything. I love it . . .'

I didn't finish. Actually, I was interrupted. Because he took off on a journey down my body. And while he caressed and licked all those gorgeous, erogenous nooks he hadn't yet explored, I could concentrate only on his eager, grasping lips.

I watched.

He held my hips in his arms and it was wonderful to see those tanned and muscular veined hands on my skin. I watched. He was in no hurry.

I was in no hurry either; I felt safe in his warm, calloused hands.

And then, when he took me again, perhaps more tenderly than the first time, I knew that I had succeeded after all in awakening in him the rainbow that would unite us throughout the rainy night, until daybreak.

He held me in his arms like a little girl, like a doll, sheltering me from the world and its tragedies, and I felt like crying.

I came again and then again, until I was weak as a baby, and he smiled down at me and kept me safe.

Then, when the pleasure was too much, he suddenly rose up over me, and with his penis in both hands he delivered an arc of semen on to my body. It was a gift.

'There you are,' he said softly and tenderly. I cried out.

And although there was a void in me after him, I kept crying out while he intently, carefully, spread that frothy, mysterious substance over my stomach, my breasts, my face. I could feel my skin growing taut and beautiful, and again I sensed those indescribable hot waves and shudderings that freed me from the pain of the world.

Always for an instant.

Translated by David Powelstock

EVELYN LAU
Fetish Night
(1993)

Born in Vancouver in 1971, Evelyn Lau wanted to be a writer from an early age. At twelve she was writing for magazines and winning prizes for her poetry, but her Chinese immigrant parents wanted her to train as a doctor and forbade her to continue. After a furious row she left home to try and survive on her own. She was then fourteen.

She was raped, had psychiatric treatment, became a prostitute and a drug addict – and continued to write. She told her story in Runaway: Diary of a Street Kid *(1989), which became a bestseller in Canada, and in 1992 she became the youngest poet ever to be nominated for Canada's Governor General's Award.*

'Fetish Night' comes from her first collection of short stories, Fresh Girls *(1993), and is drawn from her first-hand knowledge of life on the streets.*

The club is black-painted, underground. Sabina hears the rattle of the chains before she reaches the end of the narrow corridor. The clunk of boot heels on the floor, the creak of tight leather pants. Justine walks slightly ahead, her body sharp and as purposeful as an arrow. When Justine's jacket swings open, Sabina sees her friend's familiar breasts exposed, the squarish nipples sticking out like antennae from her chest.

The bartender is naked, but his piercings give him the appearance of being dressed, thin crescents of gold and silver jutting from different points in his body. Justine orders soda, Sabina a vodka on ice. Together they make a quick tour of the club, squeezing between knots of people wearing smooth black leather or bare skin, many glittering with studs and rings. Several men have hoods fitted over their heads, resting like mantles on their shoulders. An oriental woman stands against the wall, a latex sheath outlining her curves, plucking with a red fingernail at the juncture where stocking and garter belt meet. A blonde wearing a cocktail dress and a loop of gold and diamonds around her neck is being strapped stomach-down to a table, ropes and cuffs materializing to curl around her waist, wrists, ankles. A slave hangs his head by the doorway, a spattering of tiny bulbs blinking around his crotch, his girlfriend pressing the button in a small box tucked into the rear of his underwear.

Over by the piano, Sabina notices a man watching her steadily, with his hands clasped in front of him. He lowers his eyes when she returns the gaze but does not move otherwise, as though chained to the spot. She decides to ignore him for now, moving to the lounge area where there are paintings on the wall she can't quite make out in the dark, but they seem to be landscapes: men in bulky sweaters walking dogs near cliffs, waves crashing against rocks and spraying the sky. She chooses a plush, high-backed chair, and Justine clambers on to the arm, resting one foot on the seat and dangling the other leg. Stroking Sabina's hair with one hand, she points out the key players with her cigarette in the other – the internationally known male dom, the female pain freak who was runner-up in several tattoo contests, the transsexual centrefold model. In the dark the model's eyes are a wet washed-out blue, wide and heavily lashed above the cheekbones where the skin is stretched tight enough to break.

Sabina sets her drink on a wooden table beside her. The glass is sweating from the melting ice and the heat of the bodies in the room. The club is full, each person taking up extra space with the accoutrements they wear, the collars protruding with nails and screws, the paddles and whips hanging from belts looped around their hips. Across from her, two girls barely out of their teens are huddled together on a corner of a couch. One is wearing a headband which tugs all her hair off her forehead, making her appear even younger and more vulnerable. They say nothing to each other, but watch with the nervous, insatiable gaze of voyeurs. No one in the club approaches them.

The whipping has been going on for some time. A man is stretched out unrestrained on a table, gripping a piece of leather between his hands. He is naked except for underwear and a leather collar and bracelet. Another man, wearing a fluffy shoulder-length wig and lipstick, his body tightly laced in garter belt and a merry widow, is circling him expertly, flicking at his legs and the slope of his back with whips of various sizes. After half an hour of warm-up he is dancing around his lover, his arm rising and falling with tireless strength, blows hailing upon the man's body. As the flogging crescendoes, Justine scrambles closer to Sabina until she is almost sitting on her lap, the soda forgotten in her hand. Sabina curls her arm under her friend's jacket and presses her breast comfortingly. The man on the table has already taken more pain than anyone she has seen, but it is a while yet before he begins to bite on the leather strap in his hands, like a woman giving birth. Shouts escape his lips, and he turns his face towards Sabina. His eyes are black and tortured and he is staring straight at her. It seems for a moment as if he is trying to draw strength from her face, which she keeps impassive. His eyes hold hers as his lover whips him with all the strength in his arm in the now utterly silent club, his eyes tell her not to blink or breathe, not to disturb the spell. Only when he ducks his head down again to clamp his teeth on the strap does Sabina's heart start beating again, hurtfully, as if she is being pounded repeatedly from inside her chest. The whipping must stop but it doesn't stop, the people standing around in their elaborate costumes no longer seem threatening, their chains hang limply by their chaps, one or two women are stepping forward to tell the man he is whipping the same spot repeatedly, he mustn't do that, he's hurting him too badly, and still the whip descends on breaking flesh and the walls and the ceiling are ringing with its sound. The man on the table is finally crying, his whole body rising and falling with his sobs as if his body was a white and pink wave of raw flesh.

Long after any tolerable ending, the beating stops. His wigged lover, breathing hard, tugs the strap tenderly out from between his fingers and helps him off the table. The man staggers and almost falls, and the two make their way supporting each other through the crowd. People clear a wide path for them, and the silence takes a long time to form again into conversation. People cough and clear their throats, testing their voices as if using them for the first time. In a corner, before they disappear through a doorway, the man in the wig kisses his bleeding lover, and Sabina hears for a moment their soft, commiserating laughter.

The man who has been watching Sabina all evening is suddenly,

magically, on his hands and knees in front of her. She looks at
Justine and shrugs; her friend grins and moves into another chair,
tucking her knees up to her naked chest, drawing on her cigarette.
The man kisses the floor around Sabina's feet, and when she
crosses her legs he cautiously moves towards her dangling shoe.
His face reminds her of a storm cloud — soft brown curls, bushy
eyebrows, large turbulent eyes, and a bow mouth in a round face.
Reaching between his legs her hand collides with the pendulum of
his penis, cloaked in rich, supple leather. Without being asked, he
draws a whip from the belt around his waist the way a soldier
might unsheathe a sword, surrendering it to her, and she begins to
step around him in the first stages of the tormentor's dance, the
music familiar and dependable, the whack of leather against skin,
the small unchecked cries of pain.

. . .

Sabina's slave is circling the club now, as he has been ordered to
do, his ass raised high and his forehead bent to the ground. He is
alternately barking and howling. People make room for him, glancing at Sabina curiously, smiling now that the tension from the
man's whipping on the table has been replaced by a more playful
mood. A girl with cropped hair and rings piercing the skin of her
temples, nose and neck asks to borrow the slave for a ride, and
when Sabina assents she climbs nimbly on to his back and digs the
heels of her ankle boots into his side, yipping, her small neat body
arched in pleasure. Occasionally she reaches behind her to strike his
rump with a leather strap. When the slave returns, head bent, to
Sabina's side, the girl dismounts him and thanks her, returning him
with a bow and a flourish of her hand.

Fetish Night is almost over. Lights blink on in different parts of
the club, exposing white faces and garish make-up on the women
and some of the men. Sabina heads for the bathroom, which is a
modern, unfriendly cavern of mirrors and polished cement. She and
Justine leave through lit passageways, brushing against the other
club-goers who appear startled in their states of transition, many
carrying changes of clothing draped in rustling bags over their
arms.

. . .

Outside, taxis line the block. People emerge from the change room at the rear of the club, unrecognizable in shirts and slacks, jeans, pantihose and trench coats. The sky is lit by street lamps and a light, cold rain has begun to fall, sticking in the air like snow. Justine waves at a taxi, digging her other hand into her tight leather pants for warmth. Someone touches Sabina hesitantly on the arm and she turns to find her slave with his eyes lowered, handing her a folded piece of paper. She opens it to find his phone number, but when she turns to say goodbye he has already disappeared, down the block or into a cab, or back into the shadows between the broken, shuttered buildings in the neighbourhood. As she slides into the waiting cab, Justine points out the man who had been whipped on the table. Sabina would not have known it was him, otherwise. He is fully dressed and walking with an easy, swinging gait down the street, his denim-clad, de-wigged lover beside him. As they round the corner she notices they are almost the same height, their shoulders bumping gently as they disappear from sight.

•

SVETLANA BOYM
Romances of the Era of Stagnation
(1993)

Svetlana Boym lectures in the Comparative Literature Department at Harvard University, Massachusetts. An expatriate Russian, she won an award for new writing by Russian women with her story 'Romances of the Era of Stagnation', which was published in the anthology Chego Khochet Zhenshchina *(1993).*

She has also written Death in Quotation Marks: Cultural Myths of the Modern Poet *(1991) and* Common Places: Mythologies of Everyday Life in Russia *(1994), as well as film scripts, essays and fiction. She is Film Editor of* The Slavic Review.

'You are frigid,' he told her as they passed by the Gorky monument on Kirov Avenue. She was sorry that he no longer touched her shoulder under the thick wool coat but walked aloof, chewing pink

Finnish gum. Frigid – *frigidna*. *Frigida, fetida, femida* – she must
have been a Roman goddess, with small classical breasts and pupil-
less eyes of cool marble. It might have been her on that photo in
the history textbook, standing side by side with handsome Apollo
who had lost his masculine arms. Right before the barbarian
invasion . . . or was it right after? She caught her embarrassed
reflection in the window of the Porcelain Shop. It felt uncomfort-
ably damp and raw. She wanted so much to replay the whole scene,
to put his hand back under her wool coat, to experience the
meaningful weight of his warm finger, to press her cheek against
his frosted moustache in that split second right before they got
to the faded neon P of the Porcelain Shop. But it was too late
now; he would not give her another chance, another touch. They
were already crossing the tram routes and parting by the fence of
the park with the poster for Leningrad Dixieland. Season: 1975.

'Excuse me, miss, are you the last?'
   'Yes.'
   'Well, miss . . . not any more. Now, I am after you. So what are
we queuing for? What's on offer? Grilled chickens or "Addresses
and Inquiries"?'
   'Addresses and Inquiries, I hope.'
   'Good . . . good . . . let's hope together. That's the only thing we
can do these days – hope. Right? I see you are not from around
here . . .'
   'No. I am from here . . .'
   'Oh yeah? You sure don't look like it . . . Forgive my curiosity,
miss, if you are from around here, why are you queuing for the
Information Kiosk?
   'Just looking for my schoolfriends . . .'
   'Oh, OK. One has to do that from time to time . . . I thought
you were some kind of foreigner or something . . .'

Anya realized that she had forgotten how to make small talk in
Russian. She had lost that little invisible something that makes you
an insider, a tone of voice, a gesture of habitual indifference, half-
words half said and fully understood. Anya had emigrated from the
Soviet Union fifteen years ago: she was told then that it was once
and for ever, that there would be no way back for her: it was like

life and death. Now she was able to visit Leningrad again. The city had changed its name, and so had she. She came back as an American tourist and stayed in the overpriced hotel where you could drink chilled orange juice at the bar, that item of bourgeois charm. Like other idle Westerners she began to collect communist antiques, little Octobrist stars representing the baby Lenin with gilded curls, red banners with embroidered golden inscriptions 'To the Best Pig Farmer for the Achievement in Labour' or 'To the Brigade of High Level of Culture'. Occasionally she wanted to pass for a native, and betrayed herself in passing.

Anya was born on the Tenth Soviet Street in Leningrad and now she lived on the Ninth West Street, New York. Could she make small talk in New-Yorkese? Yes, of course. During these years she had learned how to be a foreigner-insider, a foreigner-New-Yorker, together with other resident and non-resident aliens, stateless legal and illegal city dwellers. She was among the lucky green-card-carrying New Yorkers and could demonstrate her picture with a properly exposed right ear and a fingerprint. New York felt like home. It struck her now that she was much more comfortable in a place *like* home than at home. She was a regular at *Lox Around the Clock*, and could spell her name in two seconds over the phone. 'R-o-s-e-n-b-l-u-m A-n-y-a. No, it's not Annie, it's n-y, like in "New-York". – Thank you. – You too.'

Of course, she had an accent, but it was 'so very charming', a delicious little extra, like the dressing on a salad that comes free of charge with an order of Manhattan chowder – 'What dressing would you like on your salad, dear?' the waiter would ask her. 'Italian, French, Russian or blue cheese?' 'Russian, please,' she would say, 'and lots of fresh pepper.'

She worked freelance doing voice-overs for commercials whenever they needed accents. The last one she did was 'La Larta, European youglette, passion fat-free – I can't believe it's not yogurt.' Female voice: 'Remember the first taste of Larta. Was it in Lisboa? Sofia? Odessa? (A mountain landscape, the peaks of Caucasus and the sparkling sea – a woman with the sensual lips of Isabella Rosellini, her face shining with Lancôme.) Remember La Larta – natural and fresh like first love.'

'Oh,' said the director, 'you have to pronounce each sound distinctly – *L* is soft and French; the back of your tongue touches the palatal – let me show you. Look here, softly but firmly, and then breathe out on the a. Open your lips, yes yes, as if for a kiss . . . Then tease me, go ahead tease me with your rrr – roll it deep in your throat – yes – rr stands for mystique; and then you come out again, playful and light, letting your tongue tickle your teeth. *Ta-ta-ta – LLarrta-ta-ta – ta-ta –* the viewer wants to taste it now. Yes, yes, yea. Larta passion fat-free.'

And then Anya did several AT&T commercials speaking over the falling Berlin Wall. But this happened a few years ago, when it was still news. In any case, these were only temporary jobs. Eastern European accents went in and out of fashion. Anya was an understudy for the new line of soft drinks: 'A revolution is brewing in the Orient. A revolution in Cola,' but the role was given to a Romanian. She must have had better connections.

'Are you queuing for inquiries?'

'Yes . . .'

'And where is a queue for addresses?'

'It's here too.'

'Well, I actually need a phone number . . . Of course, it would be great to get a home address too, but I know they're not listed . . . It's dangerous now . . . I don't blame them. What you really need nowadays is an iron door . . . Don't look at me like that . . . You think I'm joking . . . I know you're young, miss, you might think – an iron door, well, that's a bit much . . . but let me tell you I know a really honest guy, used to be an engineer in the good old days . . . he makes excellent iron doors. Real quality iron. You can call him, tell him I gave you his number . . .'

'Thanks. I'll think about it . . .'

'Well, don't think too long or it will be too late . . . No, of course, spit when you say it. Touch wood. We don't wish anything bad to happen . . . Maybe there will be law and order in this land one day . . . or at least order . . .'

'Hm . . .'

'Come to think of it, maybe they don't list the phone numbers either. Have you got a pen, miss? Oh this is great "Ee Lo-ve Nyuu York . . ." Did you get it in Gostiny Dvor or in the House of Friendship?'

*

Anya began to fill out her inquiry cards to avoid further discussion of iron doors. She wanted to find her first teenage loves, Sasha and Misha, with whom she had had her first failed perfect moments. Both relationships had been interrupted. With Sasha, they had split up after this declaration of frigidity and a clumsy wet kiss; with Misha, they had to separate after sealing a secret erotic pact of Napoleonic proportions. She would have liked to update their love stories, to recover a few missing links, to fill in the blanks. They were complete antipodes, Sasha and Misha. Sasha was blond, Misha dark; Sasha was her official story, Misha secretly telephonic; Sasha was beautiful, Misha intellectual. Sasha knew too many girls and Misha had read too much Nietzsche at a young age. It was almost twenty years ago and the song of the moment was called 'First Love'. 'Oh, the first love, it comes and goes with the tide,' sang the Yugoslavian pop star, the beautiful Radmila Karaklaic, blowing kisses out to the sea somewhere near the recently bombed town of Dubrovnik . . .

In his white coat with blood-red lining, Sasha was beautiful; he had a long black scarf and the aura of a black-market expert. He sang the popular song by Salvatore Adamo about the falling snow: 'The snow was falling and you wouldn't come this evening; the snow was falling and everything was white with despair . . .' '*Tombait la neige . . . tu ne viendrais pas ce soir . . .*' His masculine voice caressed her with the foreign warmth. French snow was falling over and over again, slowly and softly, slowly and softly . . . How was it possible that she wouldn't come that evening? Oh, she would, she must come . . . and she just couldn't resist. She recalled the shape of his lips, soft, full and cracked, but didn't remember at all what they were talking about. Oh yes, she was a bit taken aback when she found out that he had never read Pasternak. On the other hand, he was a real man and sang beautiful songs. He put his hand under her sweater. He touched her. He tried to unfasten her bra, those silly little hooks on the back, but they just wouldn't yield to him . . . 'Oh, it doesn't matter. Let me help . . .' But he knew that a man must be a man, there are things that a man must do alone . . . At that moment a noise in the corridor interrupted them. It was Sasha's father, a former sea captain, coming home after work. The problem was that they did not have anywhere to go: there were no drive-ins, no cars, no back seats available for them; no contraception

and only the cheapest Bulgarian wine. Like all Leningrad teenagers
they went to walk on the roofs of the Peter and Paul Fortress. That
was a minor transgression. They walked right under the sign 'No
dogs allowed. Walking on the roofs is strictly prohibited . . .' They
would get all icy and slippery and one could easily slip, distracted
by the gorgeous panorama of the Neva embankment. But it was
quite spectacular, the imperial palace dissolving in the mist, dark
grey ripples on the river, a poem or two . . . Wait, do you
remember how it goes . . .? 'Life is a lie, but with a charming
sorrow . . .' Yes, she would say, yes . . .

But that day they parted before the entrance to the park. On the
way she worried that her nose was becoming frozen red and that
she didn't look good any more. She was too embarrassed to look at
him and could only catch glimpses of his blond curls, his scarf and
the dark birthmark on his cheek. Then there were some clumsy
gestures and an unexpected wetness on her lips. Did I kiss him or
not? She tried to concentrate because this was supposed to be her
perfect moment.

'You are frigid,' he said very seriously.

Frigid . . . frigid . . . a blushing goddess. So, that's what it was
called? This clumsiness, arousal, alienation, excitement, tongue-tied-
ness, humidity, humility, humiliation.

'Are you waiting for apricot juice?'

'No . . .'

'You mean the apricot juice is gone? I don't believe it . . . this is
really incredible . . . All they got is the Scottish Whisky.'

'Miss, where are you from?'

This time Anya did not protest. She began to fill in Misha's card
– all in red ink. Misha did not know French songs and did not care
much about Salvatore Adamo. They spoke only about Nietzsche,
orgasms and will to power. 'Orgasms: they must be simultaneous
or nothing at all. They are beyond good and evil . . . For protection
women could simply put a little piece of lemon inside them. It's the
most natural method, practised by poets during the Silver Age . . .'
If her relationship with Sasha was a conventional romance with
indispensable walks on the roofs of the fortress, her relationship
with Misha was an example of teenage nonconformism. They dated
mostly on the phone and saw each other only about three times

during their two-year ongoing erotic conversation. She could still hear his familiar voice, which had already lost its high boyish pitch and acquired a deep guttural masculinity, resounding in her right ear.

When she thought about Misha, she saw herself sitting in a clumsy pose on an uncomfortable chair near the 'communal' telephone, counting the black squares on the tiled floor. The telephone was placed in the corridor and shared by all the neighbours of the apartment. While talking to Misha she had to lower her voice, because her neighbour Valya, the voracious gossiper, was conspicuously going back and forth between her room and the kitchen, slowing her steps near the phone. The rest of the time she was probably standing behind the doors of her room, busy filling in the gaps in Anya and Misha's fragmented dialogue. With Misha she was very intimate but their intimacy was safe, and the distance protected them from self-censorship. They knew that they were partaking in a larger system of official public communication. The invisible presence of the others, the flutter of slippers in the corridor, pleasantly tickled their nerves.

Anya met Misha on the Devil's Wheel – a special whirligig in the Kirov Park of Culture and Leisure. Misha fell victim to the calumny of Anya's girlfriend, Ira, who observed his immediate affection for Anya. 'He's handsome,' Ira said, 'but he has smooth rosy cheeks like a girl . . . you know what I mean . . .'

'He has smooth rosy cheeks like a girl . . .' – this strange sentence haunted Anya for the whole day, that beautiful spring day when they were riding on the whirligig trying to touch each other in the air in a moment of ephemeral intimacy, and then push each other away, swinging on the chains. The song goes like this:

> Just remember long ago in the spring,
> We were riding in the park on Devil's Wheel.
> Devil's Wheel, Devil's Wheel
> and your face is flying near me.
>
> But I am swinging on the chains,
> I am flying – OH!

'Akhkh . . .'
    'Oh?'

'Akh – "I am swinging on the chains. I am flying". Akh, Akh.'

'I thought you were humming the old song "Devil's Wheel". Haven't heard it on the radio for ages . . . It must be ten years old . . .'

'Yeah . . . I don't know why it stuck with me.'

'It's a nice song. I remember our great talent Muslim Magomaev used to sing it on the TV on New Year's Eve. It was when I was still married to my ex-wife and our son was in the army . . . She would be making her New Year potato salad in the kitchen with my mother-in-law and I would watch TV, that show called "Little Blue Light". And then there would be a clock and the voice of comrade Brezhnev – first it was comrade Brezhnev himself, then his voice, and in the last years the voice of an anchorman reading Brezhnev's speech – poor guy had a tic – but the speech always sounded so warm and familiar and it went so well with a little glass of vodka and herring: "Dear Soviet citizens . . . The coming year promises us further achievements on our victorious road to Communism . . . I wish you good health, happiness in your personal life and success in your labour." And then Muslim Magomaev would sing "Devil's Wheel": "Just remember long ago in the spring, we were riding in the park on Devil's Wheel. Devil's Wheel, Devil's Wheel . . ." I know these days you're not supposed to remember things like that . . . Now it's called "the era of stagnation . . ."'

'But it was such a good song . . .'

Anya was afraid to lose Misha's face for ever at the next turn of the whirligig. 'Devil's Wheel, Devil's Wheel, and your face is flying near me.' The words of this popular song shaped their romance. But in this whirlpool of excitement, in the swings of the Devil's Wheel, in the cool air of a Russian spring, his cheeks were getting rosier and rosier. The obscene girlish words froze on the tip of her tongue. He blushed like a girl. They were doomed . . .

They would have been a strange couple anyway – his girlish rosy cheeks and deep masculine voice, and her boyish clumsiness and long red nails painted with an imported Polish nail-polish. They didn't know what to do with their excessively erotic and intellectual selves. After the encounter on the Devil's Wheel there were months of phone calls. They carefully planned their next meeting and always postponed it. Finally they decided, now or never, they would conduct a secret ritual, the deepest penetration into the mysteries of the soul.

She left her house and walked away from the city centre. She passed the larger-than-life portrait of Lenin made of red fishnet in the 1960s. Behind the monument to the Russian inventor of radio there was urban no man's land, the old botanical gardens with ruined greeneries, endless fences made of wood and iron. This was the border zone – exactly what Misha looked for to perform their secret ritual. 'This could be done once in a lifetime,' he said seriously. 'Napoleon did it to Josephine.'

She had to stand against the iron fence with her hands behind her back and open her eyes very wide. Then he touched her eye with his tongue. He touched it deeply, trying to penetrate into the darkness of the pupil. For a second he lingered, and then licked the white around her eyelids as if drawing the contours of her vision from inside her. Her gaze acquired some kind of primordial warmth and humidity. They paused for a moment. Her eyes were over-flowing with desire.

They never condescended to kissing, holding each other, or saying a romantic 'I love you' on the roof of the fortress. They despised these conventional teenage games. They committed a single Napoleonic transgression, a dazzling eye contact, a mysterious pact of intimacy signed with neither ink nor blood.

'Miss, you'll have to rewrite this . . . We do not accept red ink. And try to be neat . . .'

'Forgive me. I have terrible handwriting . . .'

'That's your problem. And hurry please, we close in an hour . . .'

'But we've been waiting an hour and a half.'

'Well, yesterday, people stood for three hours under drizzling rain. Be grateful that you're queuing for information, not for bread . . .'

'Oh, by the way, speaking of bread, you should have seen what they sell in the cooperative bakery around the corner. Their heart-shaped sweet breads are now five hundred roubles apiece . . . I mean this is ridiculous . . . They used to be twenty kopecks – maximum.'

'What are you talking about? We didn't even have heart-shaped breads before . . . If it were up to you and people like you, we would still live in the era of stagnation or, even worse, in the time of the great purges . . . You just can't take any change . . .'

'Hey, comrades, ladies and gentlemen, whatever . . . Stop yelling in line. These working conditions are impossible! I can't give out any information with all of this shouting!'

And in New York there are a hundred kinds of breads – Anya suddenly felt ashamed of it – bread with and without calories, with and without fat, bread which is not really bread at all, but only looks like it. This bread will never get stale; it is non-perishable, eternally fresh and barely edible. So sometimes you have to rush to an expensive store miles away to fetch foreign bread that lasts only for a day, that is fattening and crusty and doesn't fit in the toaster. So she did not express her views on the heart-shaped cakes. She tried hard to remain neutral and friendly with all the strangers in the line and concentrated on filling out her inquiry cards. But those two repulsively intimate episodes were her main clues for Sasha and Misha. The rest was the hearsay of well-meaning common friends, rumours, and most of them fifteen years old.

Sasha, rumour had it, was married and drinking. Or rather, at the beginning he did everything right – he flirted with the black market in his early youth, but then cut off all his blond curls and ties with foreigners and entered the Military Naval Academy. He married his high-school sweetheart, whom he had begun to date in the resort town of Z just about the time of their romance, and who had heroically waited for him through all those years. Of course, they had a very proper wedding in the Palace of Weddings on the Neva embankment and they placed the crown of flowers in the Revolutionary Cemetery and took lots of pictures with her white lacy veil and his black tuxedo. Sasha wanted to be a noble army officer, like his father, a youngish-looking, well-built man, who often played tennis at the courts of the town of Z. He was made of the 'right stuff'. But then something unforeseen occurred. Some time in the early 1980s he started to develop strange symptoms, losing hair and getting a dark rash on his arms . . . Nobody was sure what it was . . . During his service somewhere in the Arctic Circle, Sasha might have received an excessive dose of radiation. But those were the things that one didn't talk about, you know what I mean . . . He quit the service, left the city and underwent special medical treatment somewhere far away. He came back completely cured. Anya's distant cousin, Sasha's occasional tennis partner, said that he was in Leningrad, but that he had moved from his old apartment and no longer spent summers in the town of Z. Another common friend had spotted him in the subway passage, but Sasha didn't say hello. But the crowd was moving fast, the light was dim, and, who knows, it might have been someone else altogether . . .

As for Misha, he was considered lucky . . . Like Sasha, he did not keep in touch with the old friends, but then again, those old friends did not keep in touch with each other, just gathered occasionally, once in a long while for someone's birthday or a farewell party. Misha started as unconventionally as one would expect of him. In the late 1970s he managed to get into the philosophy department, which was an almost impossible thing to do without connections. So he had to settle for the evening division, in which case he had to serve time in the Soviet army. What might have seemed like a tragedy turned out to have a peculiar 'happy ending'. Misha spent two years in the Far East, in the most dangerous area near the Chinese border. He told her during one of their last long conversations after he returned from the army that in his detachment he was the only person with a high-school education. So he could satisfy his will to power. The soldiers polished his boots, squatted in front of him and methodically brushed away every tiny bit of dust. He liked it. He said that of all things in the world, he loved power the most. Anya thought that he must have still been into Nietzsche. By the age of twenty-one he was chosen to enter the Communist Party on a special basis, two years before the official age of eligibility, which was twenty-three. During the 1980 Russian Olympic Games – the last epic event of the Brezhnev era – Misha was elected to the Leningrad Olympics Committee. He called her then, appearing very friendly, and promised to get her some Ceylon tea which had long vanished from the stores and could only be acquired by the privileged few.

She couldn't forgive him for this tea for a long time. Perhaps it was not the tea itself but a certain tone of voice . . . That year she became something like an internal refugee and had to leave the university, 'expelled voluntarily'. She applied for emigration and soon after that friends stopped visiting her. Occasionally they called

from the public phones and spoke in strange voices, and then when
something squeaked in the receiver, quickly bid their farewells:
'Forgive me, I am out of change. I'll call you later.' Anya was
running endless errands, as a therapy against fear, collecting the
'inquiry cards and papers' – *spravki* – to and from various depart-
ments of Internal Affairs . . . And yes, good tea was really hard to
get in those days, especially the sweet and aromatically prestigious
Ceylon tea. She often imagined meeting Misha somewhere in the
noisy subway, in the midst of a crowd. He would proudly wear his
great tan and fashionable brand new T-shirt with the winking
Olympic bear, made in Finland. 'I've been transferred to Moscow,
you know,' he shouted at her. 'I've been very busy lately.' 'Me too,'
Anya shouted in response. 'I am emigrating, you know.' She knew
she was compromising him at that moment, that she was saying
something that one did not talk about, something that one could
only whisper in private and never on the phone. A few strangers
conspicuously turned around to look at them as if photographing
Misha's face and hers with their suspicious eyes. And then Misha
blushed, in his unique girlish fashion, his cheeks turned embarrass-
ingly rosy as in those teenage years, and he vanished in the crowd.

But all of this took place many years ago, and Anya no longer
had any problems with tea. Those fragments of intimacy with
Misha and Sasha, tactile embarrassments and unfulfilled desires,
were the few things that remained vivid in her mind from the 'era
of stagnation'. Those incomplete narratives and failed perfect moments were like fragile wooden logs, unreliable safeguards on the
swamp of her Leningradian memory that otherwise consisted of
inarticulate fluttering and stutters, smells and blurs.

Anya had already performed some of the obligatory homecoming
rituals, but they were too literal and therefore disappointing. She
walked by the ageing but still cheerful Gorky on the renamed
Kirov Avenue, approaching the windows of the Porcelain Store,
which now sold all possible commercial goods from chicken grills
to Scottish Whisky and Wrangler jeans. Across the street from the
square with the monument to the Russian inventor of radio (whose
invention, among many other things, is now called into question)
she searched in vain for the red shadow of Lenin made of fishnet.
The house where she used to live was being repaired and on the
broken glass door of the gala entrance she found a poster advertising

a popular Mexican soap opera, 'And the Rich Also Cry'. Otherwise the facade looked exactly as in the old days, but it appeared more like an impostor for her old house, or a stage set that clumsily imitated the original. Anya climbed up to their communal apartment through piles of trash. The place looked uncanny. The old communal partitions, including the secret retreats of the neighbour aunt Valya who bore witness to her teenage romances, were taken apart and the whole narrative of communal interaction was destroyed. On the floor she found broken telephone wires, worn-out slippers and pieces of a French record. She looked through the window: black bottomless balconies were still precariously attached to the building and a few rootless plants continued to inhabit them. A melancholy lonely drunk urinated near the skeleton of the old staircase.

'Comrades, Ladies and Gentlemen. Remember who is the last in line and no more lining up after that. Can I trust you?'

'But of course . . . We are all family here, miss. We know who stood in line and who didn't.'

'Hurry up, comrades. Prepare your inquiry cards neatly. Be sure to include name and patronymic, place of birth, nationality, permanent address . . . We are short of time here . . .'

Indeed we are short of time, thought Anya. We are all only a phone call away from each other. Misha, Sasha, let's all get together. Let bygones be bygones – God, we used to learn so many proverbs in our English classes and then never had occasion to use them . . . Let's chat, remember the golden seventies, have a drink or two. What do you think? There are so many blank spots in our life stories, and we don't have to fill them all, it's OK. We'll just have fun. Let's meet in some beautiful spot with a view, definitely with a view. We don't need broad panoramas, no. And I don't think the Temple of our Saviour in Blood is such a good place. (I heard they took the scaffolding down and you can actually see it now; it's restored after so many years . . .) Let's meet on a little bridge with golden-winged lions. 'Let's tell each other compliments, in love's special moments' – I didn't make up this song; it really existed.

Take it easy, Sasha . . . I know what had happened. I've heard . . . I don't have much to say about it, only that it could have been worse . . . Listen, you looked really gorgeous in that white coat with red lining and I was completely and totally seduced by that silly song . . . I must have had a real crush on you. I even forgave you for not reading Pasternak. It's just that we took ourselves so seriously in those days, you and me . . . But tell me, where did you get that cruel Latin word 'frigid'? In America, you know, women are rarely frigid, but the weather frequently is . . .

Hey, Misha. I've really forgotten about that Ceylon tea of yours . . . it doesn't matter any more, I've brought you some Earl Grey . . . Remember our telephonic orgasms in the communal corridor? God, I wish someone had taped those . . . Should we try to continue in a more sedate grown-up fashion and shock the long-distance operator? I think I know something about you from the time your army boots were still unpolished. The taste of your tongue in my eyes . . . Where are you now? Way up or low down? As usual, beyond good and evil? I am joking, of course; you might have forgotten your high school Nietzsche . . .

Me, I'm fine really. I love New York, as they say. Like New Yorkers, love it and hate it. It feels like home and I feel a bit homesick now, for that little studio of mine on the Ninth West Street, bright but rather messy, without pretence of cosiness. Sometimes I go travelling to the end of the world, or at least to the southernmost point in the United States. Last time I nearly slipped on the wet rocks. You see, you need that, to get a perspective, to estrange yourself. It's dangerous to get attached to one place, don't you think?

And yes of course I must be having great sex. For that's what we do 'in the West' and it couldn't be otherwise. It's actually almost true and not a big deal. I have a Canadian boyfriend, we are working out a lot. Sometimes he says that he hasn't found himself yet. (Found whom, you would ask . . .) I know it might sound funny here, some people try to lose themselves and others to find . . . Well . . . let's have a cup of coffee . . .

Where shall we sit? You are local, you must know places. Yesterday we tried to have a drink with my old girlfriend and we couldn't find a place to sit. It was raining. So we ended up going to the movie theatre, The Barricade, on Nevsky. They have a nice coffee shop. We even bought the ticket to the movies, just in case. They were showing *Crocodile Dundee*. The cleaning woman tried to get us to go to see the movie theatre. 'Hey, kids. Oh it's such a funny movie,' she said. 'You just can't stop laughing. Our movies are never funny like that.'

'No,' I said, 'we paid for the ticket but really we just want to sit in the coffee shop since it's open till the next show.'

'But – it can't be done,' she said, 'the coffee shop is for movie-goers only and what kind of movie-goers are you?'

'I have already seen *Crocodile Dundee*,' I protested.

'It's impossible ... Don't try to fool me. This is the first night ...'

'I saw it in the drive-in in New London,' I insisted ...

'Look, miss, leave the coffee shop this very minute. I tell you that in Russian, loud and clear. Coffee is for movie-goers only.'

Maybe we'll see a movie, Misha, something very slow, with long, long takes. Wait, Misha, don't rush ... I am sure we'll find a place near by ... I would have invited you for a bagel, but it's far away ... We could talk about Napoleon. He is sort of out of fashion now ... I bet the waitress would take us for ageing foreign students ...

'The information kiosk closes in fifteen minutes.'

'Wait, dear miss, you've promised us so much ... we've waited for so long ...'

'This is public abuse. I demand the "Book of Complaints and Suggestions" ...'

'I am sorry, comrade, we don't have it at this branch of the Information Kiosks. You would have to go to the Central Information Bureau on Nevsky Avenue. But they close at two today, so you are too late. And tomorrow they have a day off.'

'That's the whole problem ... Whatever the reason, Russian people love to complain ... I would have prohibited those "Books of Complaints and Suggestions" ... What we need is "The Book of Constructive Proposals".'

'And who are you, mister? Are you a people's deputy, or what?'

'No, I am not.'

'Well, we are very glad that you are not the people's deputy. People have a right to information. If they can't get the information they can complain ... We've been silenced for too long ...'

'So what? Before we didn't have any information, now it's all over the place ... But who needs it when we can't afford toothpaste! We don't have toothpaste, but we've got glasnost to freshen our breath . . . Information . . . If you want my opinion, there is too much information these days, too much talk and no change . . .'

'Excuse me,' said Anya very politely. 'It is written here clearly: "The Information Kiosk is open from 11 a.m. to 5 p.m., Monday–Thursday." Today is Thursday and it is quarter to four now, therefore the kiosk should be open for another hour and fifteen minutes.'

'Hey, lady . . . and who do you think I am? Do you think I can't read or something? You try working here for a fucking hundred roubles per hour. I would be making twice as much in the cooperative bakery . . . But I stay here all the same. I feel sorry for folks like you, filling out those fucking inquiry cards in the cold . . . Someone has to give people information they need . . .'

'Excuse me, miss . . . Where are you from?'

Translated by the author

•

L. A. HALL
Harmonizing Polarities
(1995)

A secret writer of fantasy and science fiction from an early age, L. A. Hall is now publishing some of her stories and she has recently completed her first novel. She has also written extensively on sexuality in history in such books as Hidden Anxieties: Male Sexuality 1900–1950 *(1991) and* The Facts of Life: the Creation of Sexual Knowledge in Britain 1650–1950 *(1995), and reviews for* The Times Literary Supplement *and other journals. 'Harmonizing Polarities' blends fantasy and the erotic in a highly original way.*

The white cat stirred, pink mouth opening in a mew. Alkestis jerked awake. It was perhaps too snug, here beside her fire, surrounded by cats. Had Kammeren not told her time and again that sloth and lethargy were not the same as the passivity requisite for the maintenance of the Balance? The ginger cat whined at her, coming to rub at her feet. 'No, it's not time for feeding yet.'

And then she heard it too: the distant thud of knocking on the door. 'So who can it be? Some new ploy of Megarik's, do you think?' She had offended the aristocratic wizard-minor years ago by refusing to take him on as her apprentice.

She stepped out of the cosy room and into the corridor.

She knew that she herself risked the Balance through her delay in taking an apprentice, becoming open to having one forced upon her – Megarik or some tool of his – to learn from her and then use the power as it had never been meant to be used. The time was ripe. Delay too long and Perastis would pass Beyond, and their chain would be past and present without a future.

She opened the door.

Woefully unsubtle, she thought. Do they want me to empty out the cup simply for a pretty face? They should know better than that. Though, perhaps, if he had not been shivering like a half-drowned kitten in the wind that always whipped around that corner, if he'd been warm and dry and clean, there might have been a moment or two of temptation to fight. It was so long since she'd lain replete in Kammeren's arms and heard him say 'Well, my dear, that was the last time.' – 'But why didn't you tell me?' – 'Did you want the last time to be inauspiciously marred by your knowledge that that was what it was?'

'Yes?' she said to the trembling auburn-haired boy.

'Lady Alkestis ai Kammeren ai Perastis, I have come to ask to be your apprentice.'

Oh yes. She beckoned him in. If it were some ploy of Megarik's, she'd find out what she could. What sort of hold could Megarik have on what she could see, now, in the light, under the plastered hair, the soaking cheap coarse garments of a seafarer – as she had seen the inherent beauty of cats which had arrived similarly disadvantaged on her doorstep, half-starved, patches of fur clawed out, soaked, scared – was a lovely thing?

The tortoiseshell matron slunk out from under the staircase, heavy with impending young. She wound herself round the dank ankles of the newcomer, purring, and rolled over on her back, hoping to be tickled. The boy stooped to do so, and then jerked up again. 'Lady Alkestis, I'm sorry.' She waved him along the corridor. A point in his favour, but no more than that.

Wanting to strip those shabby wet things from this new arrival and rub him down with warm towels until he purred did not make him any less dangerous – rather more. Had Megarik – no. A pure chance of the inclement day that his tool had arrived in such a condition.

She ushered the boy into the parlour; the fluffy white and the ginger cats came up to nose at him, and then, from somewhere, the shining pure black dropped beside him. Megarik, she recalled, had cowered back a little, muttering 'Nice kitties' between clenched teeth. This one knelt and spoke to them in little words of love, finding out where they liked to be stroked or scratched.

'Oh. Lady Alkestis.' He scrambled to his feet, blushing becomingly. 'I'm sorry.' Colour returned to the pale cheeks.

'So, what do you want with me, Master –?'

'Rieth.' he said. 'Just Rieth.' He twisted his finely shaped hands together. 'It'll likely sound foolish to you,' he said, 'but I've been told I have the wizard-gift.' Alkestis was intrigued in spite of herself. What harm in testing him? Even if it were some ploy by Megarik. And there was something about this boy . . .

Auburn hair and high cheekbones and the look of a body that would be good to hold, she chided herself.

'Completely untrained?' She raised her eyebrows. 'And yet you come to a wizard-major to be apprenticed?'

Colour burnt across Rieth's cheekbones, as he muttered something incoherent. He pulled himself upright and said, more clearly, 'I'm sorry to have wasted your time, Lady Alkestis. May I go now?'

'Stay!' Halfway to the door, he felt himself being turned around to face her once more. The eyes were wide open and wide awake. 'Your sheer temerity merits some reward.' She stood up and crossed to where he was standing frozen. Placing her hands on his shoulders, she bent her forehead to touch his.

Dazzling darkness exploded in his skull.

After an uncountable measure of time, it stopped. She let him go, and he staggered. Wanting to cringe at her feet, at the power revealed by this plump middle-aged spinster surrounded by pussy-cats. He whimpered, frightened.

'Yes,' she said. 'You do indeed have the gift.'

'I do?' His head hurt.

'Very much so. I will take you as my apprentice: subject to certain further tests. But that can wait until you've got out of those wet clothes and had a bath.'

'A b-b-bath?'

'You do know what a bath is?' she said with kindly impatience. 'Take those dreadful clothes off.'

'Here?' But he complied, too scared of her to think of protesting. She looked at the soggy pile on the floor with disdain. It vanished. A robe appeared. He looked at her and at it, trying to conceal himself with his arms, not at all successfully.

'Put that on. I'll show you to the bathroom.'

The ginger and black cats followed them up the stairs and along the landing, and dashed in as she opened a door. The room was full of warm steam, and smelt delicious. Peering through the clouds of moisture, he perceived a deep sunken pool full of what had to be very hot water. Racks at one side held soap, pots of lotion, brushes, towels, combs, razors, all that one could need.

'Get yourself clean; then come through that door.' She gestured towards a door in the far wall. 'But really clean!' She left him, to his great relief. He had feared that she would watch him bathe, if not get in and scrub him herself to make sure.

He slithered out of the robe and into the water, watched with avid interest by the two cats. Oh. It was so good, the hot water around him, the scented oils and lotions, as he scrubbed and soaked and massaged the fine soap, so different from anything encountered on ship board, into his hair. Reluctantly he climbed out and wrapped himself in one of the thick towels. The only thing that stopped him from purring with contentment was Alkestis's remark about further tests. He rubbed his wet hair with a towel, ran a comb through it wincing as the teeth snagged on tangles. Felt the squeak of cleanness: how long since that had been the case? He ran a hand over his chin. It would do. Wrought up as he was, his hand might slip while shaving, leaving unsightly gashes.

Sighing, he slipped the robe back on, fearing to keep Alkestis waiting, and went to the door she had indicated. It opened softly at his touch, revealing a dimly lit chamber. The cats thrust past his legs and leapt from the soft carpet on to the bed. A plump hand caressed them.

'Ah. Rieth.' He blinked. Alkestis's bedchamber. But . . . surely

. . . she could not . . . a wizard-major wouldn't . . . or was it merely a trick, the talk of apprenticeship? . . . or some kind of trial. 'Get in.' She patted the space beside her. Her eyes were not sleepy at all. He shivered. 'You have to make love to me.'

'I . . . have to . . . what?'

She sighed. 'It is a necessary part of the relationship between wizard-major and apprentice. It was so between Kammeren and me, between Kammeren and Perastis, and so on back through the generations. It's essential, part of the balancing of polarities.'

'Oh.' Knowing that he could not conceal, in the loose robe without a sash, that he was not at all aroused, he had no idea what to do. 'Um.'

'It doesn't require that you do anything different from the usual. Not at this early stage, anyway.'

But I can't do anything, he thought desperately. What will she do? It seemed to him that in the half-light her eyes glinted at him like the cats'.

Alkestis gave one small testy sigh and twitched the cover away. Underneath she was naked. Rieth gasped. Lush creamy curves that he had never suspected under that plain severe dress. Rich brown hair tumbling loose about her shoulders. She was magnificent. Rieth fell to his knees. 'Lady Alkestis, it will be a pleasure.'

'It had certainly better be.' She put out a hand. 'Come here.' He did not know about the harmonizing of polarities, had only the vaguest idea of what they might be: but he did know how to give and receive pleasure. He took the ripeness of her into his arms, letting his lips fall to hers.

She had forgotten, probably just as well, what she had been missing while the cup filled. Oh, the odd twinge, here and there, but her naturally lethargic nature had served to keep her chaste. As the severely dressed cat-loving spinster, one had remarkably few offers to turn down. To go looking would have been too much trouble. But she had been quite right that Rieth's body would be good to hold. She had not even thought of how good his arms would feel around her. She had certainly never anticipated that he would already have remarkable erotic skills: that at least was one part of his training which she would not have to start right from basics. It had taken a long time for her to reach that pitch of competence, not that getting there hadn't provided her and Kammeren with a great deal of virtuous enjoyment.

She slid her lips along the elegant line of his collar-bone. So beautiful: an unexpected bonus. That amazing raw wizard-gift. Untrained yes, but at least not badly trained, nothing to unlearn there, she would not have to spend precious time getting him out of pernicious habits. And now Megarik could not force himself or an apprentice of his choosing upon her. Above all, the Balance steadied a little. Already she could tell, even without going out on to the Planes.

'Mm. Lady Alkestis, do you like this?' She mirrored his action back, a game he soon learned, he might never have heard the word 'polarities' before but he had an instinctive feel for harmonizing them.

There was one easy way to get out on to the Planes, she thought. She'd never have thought of trying it with a raw apprentice, but she'd never anticipated an apprentice with Rieth's skills. Carefully she began to synchronize their breathing: he picked it up at once, so attuned was he to each movement of her body. Right; right; completely attuned. Change the rhythm – yes – yes – now!

And they were floating out. She could feel Kammeren's warm contentment that at last she had steadied the teetering Balance. More distantly she was aware of Perastis, a brief image of the old woman gathering herbs on the hills below her cave. Automatically she checked the Balance. Yes. Better.

But she could feel Rieth becoming bewildered and disorientated, losing attunement, and plunged back into the reality of her bed, Rieth in her arms trembling and shaking.

'Lady Alkestis, what happened? Never before – it's never been like that.'

'What,' she asked carefully, 'did it seem like to you?'

'Dark – and then flashing colours in the darkness – and voices whispering but I couldn't make out what they said. And – and a feeling like an enormous clock ticking or a heart beating.' One needed to learn how to see the Planes. One with so little training might well experience an inchoate whirling. 'Lady Alkestis – what did that?'

She stroked the side of his face, partly to soothe him and partly because the act gave her pleasure, rough and smooth contrasting beneath her fingers. 'I took you out on to the Planes,' she said. 'It is something that we with the wizard-gift can do. There are other ways, but this is one of the quicker and more pleasant.'

'The Planes?' he asked.

'It's hard to explain,' she said. 'They touch our world, but they are not our world, one can move from one to another, time is different there – that one heartbeat before climax can be a long time there.'

He slumped down beside her, pulling away a little. The cats, picking their moment with exquisite timing, jumped into the bed. Alkestis ran a finger down the spine turned towards her. 'Did I surprise you then, beautiful Rieth?'

He turned over, looking sulky. 'I was scared,' he muttered. 'You might have told me.'

'If I'd told you we wouldn't have been able to do it; my only chance was leading you into it like that.'

'While you – and I – we were ...' He looked profoundly shocked. She wanted to hug him, so sweet, and ran a finger over his lips.

'Yes. While we were joined in intense pleasure, one breath from culmination.'

'And those – people? – I felt out there – they're not dead, are they?'

'No.' Oh dear, what did they learn in the Islands? 'Kammeren and Perastis both still live, it is not the place of the dead.' She cupped the sullen face in her hands and kissed him. She had stormed and raged at Kammeren, then spent days of frozen silence. The early days of apprenticeship could be awful, and this particular obligation had come as more of a shock to her than it did to Rieth: she had powerfully resented sharing Kammeren's bed, assuming it the price paid to learn and not part of the learning itself. It had taken Perastis, her first time out on the Planes, to scold a little sense into her. To point out that it was she herself she was hurting by lying like a stone next to Kammeren.

'Sweet,' said Alkestis, 'you need some breakfast.' She thought: what would they like? A tray appeared with hot flaky rolls, butter, preserves, fresh fruit, and hot chocolate. 'Will this do for you?'

Rieth leant over, took a roll and buttered it liberally. He broke off a piece and popped it into Alkestis's mouth. 'I don't think I've ever breakfasted so well in my life.' She leant back against plump pillows and reached for the mug of foamy chocolate. He looked a little shocked: people always seemed to expect that the wizards-major either lived in austere celibacy, or else devoted their lives to orgiastic rituals. There was a time for everything under the Balance, though two lovers in a lifetime, at widely separated periods, could hardly be described as orgiastic, however much fun you had harmonizing the polarities together.

They pushed the tray aside, not finished enough for her to dematerialize it but enough so that it got in the way of the exchange of languid caresses. She fed Rieth grapes from her own lips, remembering doing the same to Kammeren. Had Perastis done so with him, too?

A cat mewed gently. Something was wrong.

Megarik. Pounding on the door as if he were a warden raiding an illegal still. She swung out of bed, materializing clothes on to her body, making sure her hair was neat and tidy and smooth against her head. She beckoned to Rieth, who looked down a little astonished to find himself clothed. 'Come.'

Leaving Rieth in the parlour surrounded by cats, she went to admit Megarik, who was stamping and fretting on the doorstep. 'How much longer will you shilly-shally, Alkestis?'

'The Balance holds,' she drawled. Megarik's affectation was to make himself look taller and more aquiline than nature intended, with more hair on his head. She forbade herself the petty move of stripping him of illusions. Opening the door, she ushered him into the parlour. 'And is secured by my taking an apprentice.'

'That dockside catamite?'

'Oh, you've met already?' she purred.

'Anyone who didn't seclude themselves from the world the way you do could recognize the type. But my dear Alkestis' – a couple of the cats hissed softly and Megarik twitched – 'you don't expect me to believe that this – night's companion – is truly your apprentice. A jest.' He gave her a mirthless smile.

'No jest. My apprentice. Rieth ai Alkestis ai Kammeren.'

'So you persist in this foolish charade to thwart me?'

'In order to maintain the Balance, Megarik.'

'Balance! What consideration of this Balance of yours would finally move you to unleash your powers?'

'Not my Balance, Megarik. If you don't know that, no wonder you're a mere wizard-minor.' She looked at him directly. He quailed. 'You may go.' She turned to look at Rieth: he looked frightened. But, underneath, a core of determination. He would do.

The warm room was stifling. Initially Rieth had relished the warmth, the baths, the soft bed. He'd never lived anywhere so unobtrusively elegant and luxurious. But now he felt suffocated, yearning for the wind blowing in his hair. He wanted to go down to the dockside and smell the sea air.

Alkestis had never told him he might not leave the house. Surely he could go for a walk – and if she were perturbed for a few moments, so much the better. The cats were allowed more liberty than he, sliding out of their flap-door at night to wail on the tiles, coming in during the day with bloody prey in their mouths. He would go out.

As he crossed the harbour front he tossed his head at the occasional low whistle. Oh, this was the place he belonged, he thought, a harbour tavern was always home.

He slid in and found a table, then realized that he had no money. It did not distress him: soon someone would offer to buy him a drink, he could be sure. A grizzled captain yarning with the bartender looked around with interest. He seemed about to step over, but then two new arrivals entered.

'Uptown folks,' someone growled, but very softly. A man and a woman, whose plainness of dress did not disguise the sumptuous-ness of the expensive fabrics. Rieth had met similar kinds before, seeking excitement. Harmless enough, on the whole, wanting the thrill of danger without the reality.

They stood in the doorway, looking around, and then approached Rieth's table. 'Permit us to buy you a drink.'

'Thank you, your honours. I'll have the rum.' You could be reasonably sure of the rum in a place like this, and the day was cool enough for him to prefer it. The couple sat down beside him: three thick glasses and a whole bottle appeared on the table. The man grinned and poured out.

'Here's to you, you beauty.'

As the level in the bottle fell steadily, the woman matching them glass for glass, Rieth found his own head was growing a little muzzy. On both sides a knee pressed intently against his own. The woman took his hand, tickled the palm. She looked across him to her companion. 'Enough to go round,' she murmured.

The man nodded. 'I'll fix it up,' he said, and moved over to the bar, where he engaged the bartender in low-toned conversation.

The woman walked her fingers up Rieth's arm, playfully. Her knee still nudged his. He recognized the game, and was prepared to play along. A hand under his elbow lifted him to his feet: he staggered a little as he was drawn through a curtained doorway and up a twisting staircase.

'He's not too drunk, is he?' asked the man. The woman laughed. Rieth turned his head to protest that he was not drunk at all – his head was harder than that – and nearly stumbled on the stair. At the top of the staircase a door stood open: his companions steered him into the room, giggling, and closed the door carefully, shooting the bolt. Fingers fumbled at his clothes, and before he knew where he was he was lying between the two of them, all of them naked.

The woman giggled, her hands becoming shameless. Other, larger, harder hands touched him: Rieth stretched like a cat being stroked, too drowsy to be active but relishing the attentions. The rum must have been far more potent than he had thought. Through the fog he heard them murmuring things like 'So easy . . . the price of a couple of glasses of rum . . . the little wanton' as they arranged him for their mutual gratification with an expertise that betrayed that this was far from the first time they had played this game. Rieth moaned softly, too far gone to identify which touched him.

'Now!'

Dazzling darkness exploded in his skull.

Perhaps she had been pushing Rieth too hard, making up for her own dilatoriness. She might have predicted an escape to his old haunts, and even the further consequences: Rieth was like a cat that would go to any warm lap, she knew. But like a cat would return to home where he was fed. She hoped. But there was something more seriously wrong than a rebellious moment. Something murky and wrong, something that unsettled the Balance, something connected with Megarik: those two were no simple pleasure-seekers.

She stroked soft fluffy white fur, felt the purr resonate through her own hand. Megarik would surely not delay in coming to crow over her.

But Megarik did not come. He was learning the uses of suspense, was he? Well, thought Alkestis as she lay in bed surrounded by cats grateful for the return from exile, it will not do that little hussy any harm to have a cold worried night, perhaps it will teach him a lesson. Why should I make the effort to seek for him: I can find it out readily from Megarik in the morning.

But it was nearly noon by the time Megarik arrived.

'You had better find yourself a new apprentice.' She raised her eyebrows, decided not to make any comment, and lowered them once more. 'Your poppet has levanted.' But under the appearance of hand-rubbing glee, Megarik was very very worried about something. 'He's left – sailing captain's pet, I expect.'

'No one could leave by sea with the present prevailing wind, Megarik. Tell me the truth.'

'Alkestis, I have told you the truth. He's gone.'

'Gone where?' Her eyes blazed at him: the white cat hissed and spat, fur on end. 'Your tampering must have sent Rieth out into the Planes, probably by sheer accident.'

Megarik hung his head. 'I was just moving him to a place of safety . . .'

'The Planes are not a horse and carriage for easy transport, are they? Perhaps this will restrain you from tampering in future.'

'You wizards-major! You sit here in your fine houses on the bounty of Noyarth prating of the Balance and doing nothing.' He was sincere: not just hatred-driven.

'So I must get him back.'

'Alkestis, I forbid you. Leave him be. Take a more fitting apprentice, not that scum of the dockside, that whore.'

'Megarik, Balance-holder chains are not formed on the basis of social acceptability. The Balance chooses. It has nothing to do with birth or good breeding – it was mere chance that Kammeren was a gentleman. I shall bring Rieth back.'

Megarik banged out of the door without farewell. She shook her head.

Sadly slack in practising the disciplines, she did not look forward to a prolonged search on the Planes. She had substituted lethargy and laziness for alert passivity and sensitive responsiveness to the state of the Balance. As bad in its way as Megarik's insistence on visible activity. Her cool, slothful, inherently solitary nature had been as much a hindrance to becoming a wizard-major as Rieth's promiscuity might prove. (How would he ever manage the long years of letting the cup fill?)

But it was her sloth, his indolent obligingness, that were nearer the heart of the matter than Megarik's restless bustling.

Waves battered at Rieth. Cold, cold, cold, these northern waters. Had they thrown him in then, to drown? He had been exceedingly foolish, he realized, as memory of what had brought him to this pass returned. Megarik must have taken the shortest way to remove the source of his disapproval.

The sound of breakers crashing on to rocks: a thin line of darkness solid in the dimness. Wearily he made himself kick more strongly in that direction, until, gasping, he dragged himself up the beach, forcing himself above the tideline, over rough pebbles, to where dunes gave some kind of shelter. He curled up under one of them and fell asleep.

He waked, blinked and stretched and stood up. The storm had died down, the sea no longer surged furiously, the sun was out and the sky looked as though it only needed a little time for the faint cloudy haze to disperse.

He climbed over the dunes and further inland. There was not very far to go: the island was small, with no fresh water supply that he could see. He swallowed, and then realized that he was not thirsty, as he would have expected. Or hungry. He sat down on the beach and looked out to the sea stretching completely blank on every side. No ships, no other land. Just that vast expanse of water and this tiny island. He shivered and looked down at himself. The ragged clothes of a seaman battered in the waves. Not the clothes he had been wearing when he had set out on his jaunt to the dockside. But then, he had been relieved of those.

Alkestis had picked him off the street like a stray kitten. Her own feelings did not come into it: the cats came and went, she did not fret, left them free to do so. If one of them had been taken by Megarik to use as a lever, she would have been angry, but not at the cat. But he, unlike a straying cat scooped up and stuffed into a sack, had brought about his own entrapment. Laid her open to Megarik's manipulations, and endangered the Balance she was so anxious to preserve. She would be angry for that. Rieth buried his head in his hands. Rather stay here for ever than face her. His bravado in defying her had evaporated, leaving him queasy and scared.

Alkestis found herself halfway up a cliff with the sea beating at its foot. No way but down: and what then? She shaded her eyes from the sun glaring down, and looked out into the distance. A vast empty expanse of ocean.

She had no illusions that Rieth felt anything that would lead his pseudo-reality to welcome her. However often he succumbed to her in bed, groaning soft endearments, what he primarily felt was resentment. As one did, early in apprenticeship. As she had felt for Kammeren. As Kammeren had felt for Perastis. And so back along the generations.

If Rieth did not want to be found . . . Time did matter. Though it ran so differently in the Planes, it existed there none the less. And on the Planes one did not eat or drink, had no desire to, did not know the lack. And after long enough one died of starvation.

Almost on the horizon, a small dot of island.

Rieth was there. Couldn't he feel what it was doing to the Balance? Very likely not.

So how did she reach him? To try and change such a powerful pseudo-reality would not be easy. Simpler to try small alterations rather than radical measures. It was too far to extend a bridge to the island. It would have to be a boat. Alkestis grimaced. She was not an Islander like Rieth to be as at home on the water as on land. She would just have to manage.

Skidding and sliding down the cliff, she found, as she expected, a small rowing-boat at the bottom. Pushed it out beyond the surf, climbed in and shipped the oars. She looked over her shoulder to set her course, and bent to rowing.

Her back ached. Her hands hurt. The glare of the sun on the water hurt her eyes. It seemed that she had been rowing for hours, and the island got no nearer. Her shoulders creaked and protested at every stroke she pulled.

But she must have been getting closer: there were small white caps to the waves, and the boat began to pitch and toss unpleasantly. It was apparent that Rieth did not want her company. Alkestis tightened raw-feeling hands around the oars, and put her aching back into each pull. Lightning sizzled past her into the sea. Thunder crackled overhead.

She felt the Balance swaying like a child's top when the momentum begins running down.

A wilder wave than before snatched one oar from her hand. She lurched round to the stern with the single oar left, trying to scull. In such a sea it was of no avail: the little boat pitched helplessly at the waves' mercy, and finally turned turtle.

Alkestis, unable to swim, paddled frantically with hands and feet. Could she, in the short time left, summon up the powers at her command, with one last effort of will try to undo this mess?

Hands grabbed at her, and she struggled. Oh, too much, to try and make sure she drowned. A hand smashed into her chin, and she knew no more.

I couldn't just let her drown, he thought. I didn't know she couldn't swim. He huddled in among shrubbery which he didn't think had previously covered the island, which seemed bigger, too. I should have taken the boat and gone.

Gone where? If Alkestis had got this far in pursuit of him, in that cockleshell of a vessel, he had no great hopes of permanently evading her. But if he hid maybe she'd think he'd escaped somehow and leave the island. Now he had the storm and her near-drowning to add to his crimes, he really didn't want to encounter her. He curled up and whimpered.

– Well, little kitten? – Even though she was standing before him (he could see the hem of her skirt and the toes of her boots but didn't dare to lift his gaze any higher) the voice spoke inside his head. – That's the way it is, on the Planes. –

– I didn't know you couldn't swim! – His mind could not even begin to encompass the ways in which Alkestis might punish him. He wanted to be brave, to defy her, but could not lift his eyes to hers.

– Punish you? – There was an offended feeling to the question. – You're my apprentice, part of my chain, and I've come all this way to find you. Why should I punish you? –

His head jerked back and he stared up at her. His loving ambitious mother had severely chastised him on each return from the dockside excursions she thought so fatal to his prospects.

– You're not my child. You're my apprentice, part of the chain. I simply came to fetch you back: which may feel like punishment, I suppose. – She knelt down beside him. – I'm sorry it has to be this way. Perhaps I took the wrong decision when I took you for my apprentice, perhaps my motives were not sufficiently clarified, I was too worried by Megarik's harassment. Unfortunately it's hard if not impossible to undo. –

– I'm not the right apprentice for you. –

– Perhaps I am the wrong wizard-major. –

Rieth looked at her slumping shoulders, her bowed head. Was she offering to release him? It felt not like liberation but like being cast into exile. He stretched out a hand to cup her chin, lifted her face to look at him. Was about to communicate in this new strange way, and then, instead, leant to kiss her.

Her mouth was warm, as their bodies shifted from rigid poses into a close embrace, softening together. This time he was not following her lead, but taking the initiative – and Alkestis responded with a receptivity very different from the way things had been before as his hands moved over her opulent curves. No longer the teacher, she trusted him enough to relinquish her former control. He disappeared their clothes, and lowered her to ground no longer gravelly sand and seashore scrub but gentle to their naked skin. Warmth flowed from him to her, and returned to him, spiralling gracefully upwards without fever or urgency until they flowered together into climax.

The ground on which they lay was a bed of brightly coloured, sweet-scented blossoms. Birds sang overhead in trees which had not been there when they began.

– Well, they say the Balance does the choosing. – Alkestis stood up. – You can sail a boat, I suppose? –

– Naturally. –

– Good. Simpler to turn the boat into something that can sail than try and reconstruct this pseudo-reality. –

They walked hand in hand to the seashore. A trim yacht bobbed a short distance out to sea: close enough that Alkestis could wade out. They climbed in, and he set the sail.

She was a beauty. He'd never sailed anything that responded so sweetly to the lightest touch on the helm, that managed so elegantly the delicate balance between speed and stability as she swooped across the dancing sea.

He helped Alkestis out into the gentle surf chuckling up the beach. She had repaired the ravages of her journey and the shipwreck, and looked very much the severe Lady Alkestis. Rieth looked at himself and realized that he still looked the stranded sailor, feet bare on the sand. She tucked her arm through his, and they began to walk across the beach.

Someone was coming towards them. Rieth did not recognize him until Alkestis sighed – Megarik. His illusions do not hold here. – He was shorter, less distinguished-looking, balding. Rieth understood suddenly why Megarik so resented him. Without those illusions of what everyone expected a wizard-aristocrat to look like, no one would have given Megarik a second glance. And if a man so much as suspected what lurked beneath Alkestis's prim exterior, he might well think her worth a struggle.

They halted. Megarik smiled at him smoothly. – You don't want her. Give her up. It'll be worth your while. –

Rieth waited for Alkestis to say something, and then realized that she was not going to. He was disconcerted. Doubtless Megarik could make it worth his while. But he'd thought that Alkestis would at least protest.

He shuffled his feet on the sand and thought about accepting the offer. Wrongness! He turned to look at Alkestis. – I regret I must decline. – Everything felt much better. In spite of Megarik's snarl.

– And I regret what we must do. – Alkestis took the other hand and they began walking once more across the beach, towards Megarik. His presence there was a wrongness in itself: Rieth looked at Alkestis. She gave him a small nod. Megarik vanished. – Is he all right? –

– Maybe a headache. Just back where he came from. –

Suddenly they were no longer on the beach but outside a small rustic cottage where an elderly man was sitting on a bench in the sun. He looked up at them. – I wondered when you'd get here. –

Alkestis sat down beside him and took his hand. – Kammeren dear. How stands the Balance? –

– You don't need me to tell you. –

– No. We had better go back, and prepare to harmonize the polarities. –

Alkestis stood up, letting go Kammeren's hand and taking Rieth's. He felt the world around him crack and slide and turn into swirling chaos, the only remaining reality the feel of her hand in his.

He opened his eyes. He was sprawled on top of her on a hard narrow couch. He could hear cats mewling outside the door. He was home.

Rieth leant back against her knees, purring almost like one of the cats as Alkestis rubbed the back of his neck. His so nearly disastrous involuntary sojourn on the Planes had taught him far more about the Balance, the burdens and powers of a wizard-major, and the bond between the two of them and the rest of the chain, than months or years of meek studying. As it had taught her the salutary lessons that needed to be relearnt again and again: and the one that perhaps one did not learn until the time came to pour out the filled cup. That one's choice of apprentice lay less within one's own will than she had believed, in spite of her arguments with Megarik. She had not known it in a way that mattered. Any more than she had known what Kammeren had told her years ago, that the teaching was not one way only.

Rieth took one of her hands and kissed the back, then laid it against his cheek. He needed a shave. 'Kestis, I'm sorry.'

'I suppose it's some advance that you've stopped calling me Lady Alkestis even in bed: but you still apologize far too much.' She tucked a straying auburn lock behind his ear. 'And I too little.' He turned and buried his head in her lap. She stroked the silky hair, remembering the moment when she had similarly turned at last to Kammeren. Recognizing that they were both under the Balance, both chosen.

•

CANDAS JANE DORSEY
Wishes

(1995)

One of Canada's leading science-fiction writers, whose best-known story '(Thinking About) Machine Sex' (1988) examines the impact on a woman of a technology that is created by men, Candas Jane Dorsey has also

published three volumes of poetry. 'Wishes' is a fantasy, but in it there are
no demons or dragons; this is the sort of fantasy that anyone might have.

If what I need is wish-fulfilment then what are the wishes I want to
fulfil? On this night I don't think that the solid shoulders of
muscular men or the long backs of slender tall women are necessarily on my agenda but I can think on them for a moment and decide.
Slot a few into the fantasy and see what happens. Only problem is I
keep thinking of people to slot in and they aren't fantasy material.
With whom would I want to be making love if I could have for the
moment everything I wanted, anyone I wanted?

Okay, it's a room with a double bed and soundproofing to start,
oh, hell, this is a fantasy, put us in a room with a great deal of
velour-covered padded surfaces. Lots of pillows, so on. Lovely big
windows to the outside (no one to look back in, thanks very much)
and perhaps a jacuzzi and sauna and shower and the like over thru
the door to the east, windows in that room too but tile not rugs,
light grey tile and silver fittings, with an upholstered bench over by
the window for massages, the idea is to have a place to play. Well,
okay, who's gonna be there with me? Oh, it has to be warm. So
that we can hang around naked without freezing. Okay, back to the
issue of with whom.

Well, first I'd want to be there alone a while. Read in bed. Pull a
duvet (synthetic fibre only, no allergens please) over me and sleep.
Quite a lot of sleeping and reading. (Bookshelves on one wall.)
Also walking in the fields, etc. Also eating meals prepared by . . .
we'll get to that. Anyhow so I get bored restless and horny.
Supposing. I never get bored and I'm more likely to want to work
but say I get horny. So, I want the door to open and in comes –

That's not so simple. Say I want a total stranger who looks thus
and so. Say I order up just the combination of looks and intelligence
that I can conceive of liking. See how intelligence creeps in there?
So I'm gonna hafta spend time with this person to see if they're
intelligent. After all, like Susan Sontag said, if I were to wake up in
the morning and realize the person next to me was an idiot, I'd feel
ashamed. So then if it's a total stranger and we're gonna sit around
for a while and talk and eat cookies I'd have to have clothes.

So a closet with some really good stuff in it. Lush Afghani
dresses. Gypsy stuff, but not too garish. Exciting tho, just in case

we get around to taking clothes off later. See, in case, now I'm assuming that this no-longer-naked-coming stranger has a choice, may not like me. What if?

Well, this is after all my fantasy. So say this stranger really likes me. And wants to make out. Which then gets even more specific. What kind of a fantasy is this? A straight heterosexual fantasy with a really fantastic guy who is muscular and attractive and believes in doing half the housework? Except in this fantasy for sure there are going to be servants because Mama ain't a'cookin tonight (except metaphorically) so there goes his *raison d'être*. So he's fantastically creative just like I am. But then there's the same problem I came up with earlier. Say I want to make out but something I said gave him a really good idea for some sculpture or something so instead he spends the night working in the adjoining studio? Then maybe I read a book or I get to work myself and in the morning we have a nice companionable breakfast (served by naked servants? but come on, what's a butler or a housekeeper without a tux or a belt to hang keys from at least, so there goes racy Utopia) and we discuss our work, and here we are back at the start again.

Now, I keep reminding myself that this is my fantasy. So back to the moment of confrontation again. Say this is going to be a far-out gay fantasy with this really great woman who is fantastic at everything she does including sex. But first I have to spend a certain amount of time with her seeing what turns her on, right?, and if we have anything in common. So somehow we get talking about kids, I guess cuz I see her stretch marks, and I tell her how I don't have any but a friend of mine dreamed I had twins. Then she starts talking about her little girl and how the father got custody, and she starts to cry, and because I really like her, right?, we established that before, I am feeling really bad too so I rock her and comfort her and pretty soon she goes to sleep and there I am working again, burning the midnight oil, because her story made me so mad and restless that I can't sleep. I just can't believe how a wonderful woman like that with a law degree and everything should be considered a bad parent just because of her sexual preference. I mean, do heterosexual parents do it in front of the kids? No way. So why assume gay people will? It's unfair. I write a letter to *Ms* about it and then go to sleep. Then it turns out that she is a morning person and has to be in court anyway so she's up doing her exercises the moment the sun peeks into those great big windows while I'm pulling the covers over my head. So she gets her lawyer suit back on and gives me a sweet little kiss and that's that for the possibility of sex with THAT stranger.

Wait a minute, what about movie stars? I mean, there's Donald Sutherland for a good start, love that long sensitive face and engaging mumble. I wonder if he ever really TALKS to people. Probably really the silent moody type. I hate it when someone won't talk with me, before after and during. And laugh! He's much too serious. Pretty, I must admit. But serious. What about a comedian? Who do I like? Who really makes me laugh? But you know about comedians, they hide behind a lot of yuk-yuk and then you go into the bathroom one day and they've o.d.ed on smack or free base or something, or worse still committed suicide. Then I'd be implicated. Look at what happened to that Cathy woman when John Belushi died. I've always wanted to have my picture in *Rolling Stone*, but not quite that way, thanks. What about a musician? Say, Michael Jackson, with those great legs. For dancing, I mean. He's never done a rock video with naked legs. They may not be much in real life. And he was a show-biz kid. What do I have to say to someone like that, whose life has been so different? And I was so disillusioned to hear he got his nose fixed. He probably has a real thing about physical beauty. And face it, I'm just your average-looking, out-of-shape Canadian woman. Canadian. That's a problem too, come to think of it. What do I know about Motown?

Okay, so maybe who I want in my fantasy is a friend of mine. Or at least somebody I know. Or someone I've met. Or even seen somewhere. Well, first I have to think of somebody I know who wouldn't mind being in my fantasy. I don't want to make anyone uncomfortable. I don't want one of my friends hanging back by the door and saying, gosh, I never thought of you THAT way, I mean, THIS way, I mean, I thought we were just friends. Or even, heaven help me, some near stranger like that nice Vietnamese restaurateur who has such a great smile. But that nice young etc. probably also has a great family at home, or maybe is into kinky sex, and I'm not, at all. Or maybe that university professor who always used to flirt a little? Well, I always liked his wife a lot and I'd have to figure out how to keep her out of this fantasy.

Oh, my wife wouldn't mind. Oh, my wife's in Tahiti. But I

know she's not because he's not taking the kids to day care, that's a cinch, he's here in my fantasy and that leaves the rest of the household to you know who. Oh, my wife and I have a trial separation. For the weekend. Sure. That's what they all say. You think the world is your oyster. You get the little woman all sewed up in household tasks and then it's out the door and trying to find adventure with a younger woman with no kids. Well, I may be counter-culture, mister, but I know there's no such thing as free when it comes to free love, so forget it. Go home and be nice to your lady; you don't know how lucky you are. You married men give me the pip, as my mother used to say.

Oh, God, my mother, she thinks I've settled down and here I am in this fantasy. Never mind, you don't have to tell your mother. But we're getting along so much better since I grew up. Well, she probably has fantasies of her own. Does she tell you her fantasies? Well, no, but if I look out those fantastic windows and across this little valley full of trees and solitude I can just see the roof of her little fantasy retreat sticking out of the trees. I wonder if she goes thru the same turmoil. I bet she has it all figured out.

Not fair. Stick to my own fantasies. My mother already gave me a lot, now I'm gonna steal her fantasies? Forget Mother, this is my big chance to live it up. So, *à nos moutons*. And where are the little lambs anyway who are supposed to be scampering thru this fantasy, this great love-nest, giggling and carrying on? Well, I'm not really happy with the idea of strangers or near strangers. Maybe one of my friends. Sometimes I feel mighty close to them, feel like putting my arms around them and . . . Well. Maybe. But the trouble is, I like my friendships pretty much as they are. I don't want to upset the apple cart. But I tell myself, look, this is a fantasy, you idiot. They'll never know. They will never know.

Okay, if I can believe that, then here we go. Hm. Aw, it's not feasible. Look, D spends the night in the hot tub reading Proust. I've never read Proust, but whatever turns you on. I got put off Proust by Monty Python skits. Well, obviously, for D, Proust and hot water are a better prospect for a racy night than I am. I knew that. D basically liked me for my mind anyway, and hates the way I do my hair. So it was doomed from the start. It was those great shoulders that made me think it would be worth a try. Okay, how about J? J has always had a sensual streak. So how about a back rub? Okay, I say. It's a great back rub. Almost greater than my physiotherapist gives. Nice hands. I love it when my friends take care of me. It's so warm and cosy and relaxed I fall asleep. When I wake up J and D are reading passages from Proust to each other. J loves D's shoulders. D loves J's mind, also buttocks. I wish them well and go downstairs for a late breakfast. They come down rumpled in a few hours and thank me for introducing them. No problem, I say.

So what about R? Too heterosexual. She'd freak out. Or M? Too monogamous. He'd freak out. And do I want to do that to a friend? Look, really, do I want to do that to ME? I mean, I have a certain image of myself, and it would take quite a beating if I have to accept that I'm the kind of person who'd lure some friend, someone, face it, who really trusts me, out into the country to some secluded love-nest and then try to misuse that trust, just to score? I mean, come on, this is ME I'm talking about. Nice me. Trustworthy me. Friendly, non-manipulative, egalitarian, non-threatening me. Child of the seventies, taking responsibility for my own actions and letting others make responsible choices without coercion or undue influence. How could I hold my head up if I flew in the face of everything I've ever believed? How could I ever call myself a feminist again? No, a friend would have to come into my fantasy willingly, of his or her own accord, and I would have to know that we were both getting into this with a clear idea of what lay ahead. I do your thing, and you do mine, and if we come together, it's beautiful.

By now I'm getting pretty tired of all this. Really I want to curl up with someone familiar and just relax. I already have a lover, after all. So who better to put into a no-holds-barred fantasy? Well, we're a little past the tearing-off-of-clothes stage. How many years has it been, after all? But I'm sure I could work something up. A seductive little dinner. A tremendously sexy outfit. On each of us. Great food. A little aperitif in front of the fire (soda for me, please). Gee, it's gonna be great. I'm really looking forward to it. If we can get away from town for a whole evening. After all, we're both busy people, and this love-nest I've worked up must not be too close to town or the glow of the city lights would be spoiling this wonderful view of the Milky Way.

Never mind, the important thing about this is it's a FANTASY. I'm completely free to do whatever I choose. There are no consequences. None at all. Everything can happen just as I want it to happen. There are no barriers. I can be outrageous if I want. I can be as free as my wildest dreams.

•

ANN OAKLEY
Where the Bee Sucks
(1995)

Ann Oakley is Professor of Sociology and Social Policy and Director of the Social Science Research Unit at the Institute of Education at the University of London, where for many years she has been working in the fields of gender, the family and health.

The author of many academic works, she is also a successful novelist and poet whose works include Taking It Like a Woman *(1984),* Telling the Truth about Jerusalem *(1986) and, most recently,* Scenes Originating in the Garden of Eden *(1993). Her views on the televising of her 1988 novel* The Men's Room *have been noted earlier.*

'Where the Bee Sucks' has been written especially for this collection.

Janice had lived in Brook Cottage for six months before she noticed the bees. She'd been very busy, with settling in to her new home and new job, and then there had been that business with her brother Damian apparently defrauding Mech-car, the firm he worked for, which serviced automatic car-cleaning machines. Thanks to Janice's intervention, Mosha Arid, who ran Mech-car, had agreed to let the Bickerstaffes pay the money back by direct debit. Damian was working in a hotel now, a health hydro in Cumbria, where he was responsible for maintaining water therapy for humans instead of cars. Janice herself had moved bravely away from her family in Birmingham and a failed love affair with a garage manager to take up a post as head of a library in a small town which served a large area of Lincolnshire. A little guilty, she stayed in regular touch with her parents. Mr and Mrs Bickerstaffe were actually not unrelieved to be shot of their worrying offspring. They'd just won a nice amount on the National Lottery and were planning to go up the Amazon with it.

Brook Cottage lay in farming country; the fields around it grew mainly sugar beet. According to a recent television programme which had featured several of Janice's afflicted neighbours, the fields had been oversprayed with a chemical called lindane, which got into the food chain by attaching itself to the fat globules in cow's milk and could be a cause of breast cancer in women. There'd been much talk about the programme in the library. Janice's young assistant, Graeme, had an aunt with breast cancer, and Aunt Frieda was undergoing a very nasty course of treatment at the moment at the local radiotherapy unit in Challingham. Because of staff cuts, the unit had moved from five times a week to twice a week radiotherapy, and no one knew whether this would work or not. Aunt Frieda's symptoms were a cause of constant distress to Graeme's mother, who thought she was going to get it too. They both drank a lot of milk. Graeme had stopped drinking milk after reading something which said that one per cent of breast cancers were in men.

That was the trouble about working in a library. You were surrounded by all this information. 'Put it away, Graeme,' said Janice, 'too much knowledge is a bad thing.' Was it? Graeme joined a local environmental group. He brought their leaflets in and asked Janice if he could display them on the notice-board which advertised second-hand fridges and spare kittens and mothers desperate to have their babies sat for. Janice let him put them on the notice-board. She liked to think she'd been innovative with the library. She wanted it to be a focus for the rural community. They now had special sessions for mums and toddlers and for children on their own after school, divided age group. They'd had most trouble attracting the teenagers, but Janice had expected that, coming from Birmingham. Young people today were a disaffected lot. Janice herself, being thirty, had been on the edge of the disaffected generation, not old enough to remember the days of family cosiness without TV when the radio blazoned out such mindless epics as 'Much Binding in the Marsh' and not quite young enough to appreciate the terrors of being reared for unemployment and the bleak amoral privatized deserts of neo-Conservatism.

She was a good citizen, Janice Bickerstaffe. Upright, except when her back played up due to an old dancing injury; a prompt payer of bills and contributor of odds and ends to the village's apparently seamless cycle of jumble sales, harvest and Christmas

and other gatherings, and not to mention the new dyslexia association that Mrs Farthing by Apple Farm had started up after young
Luke's disruptive behaviour with the horses had finally been given
a medical label. Once Janice had understood that car-boot sales
were not for selling car boots, she would have entered into the
spirit of those too, except that she didn't have any odds and ends
left and her own boot, of a prized but ultimately failing 1950s Mini
bequeathed by the garage owner, wasn't really big enough.

One night as she was sitting writing to her friend Lorraine in
Canada, she heard the bees. At first she thought she'd left the CD
player on when Simon and Garfunkel had finished, and then she
considered it could have been Mr Rigby, the shoe-shop owner next
door, trying to start his orange Skoda. She hadn't lit a fire, which was
unusual, but she planned on going to the Bull and Bush later with
Rowena, who made jewellery in an outbuilding on her father-in-law's
farm to escape the children. When Janice put her head against the
chimney-breast the noise got louder. The next day when she came
downstairs (with a slight ciderish hangover) there were about thirty of
them on the carpet, either dead or moribund, and when she came back
from the library in the afternoon they were on the bedroom floor too.
Ugh! Janice imagined how horrible it would be to tread on one of
those and squash them in the middle of the night on her way to the loo.

She rang the Council the next day. 'I don't know who I want to
speak to,' she began inanely, in the way of the town person, 'but I
think I've got a wasps' nest in my chimney.'

'Pest control,' issued the terse voice at the other end of the
phone. 'We contract that out these days, I'll see if the officer's
there.' He wasn't, but he rang her back and made an appointment
to come on Friday morning. Janice would take the day off, Graeme
could cope. She needed to get her hair done and see about the
hinges on the front gate as well.

He was an unattractive fellow with stumpy greasy hair and a curt
manner. He jumped out of his van (which he parked directly
opposite the cottage's front door, causing an obstruction), took one
look at the insect-littered floors, pronounced the word 'bees' and
then took her out and pointed upwards, where against the pale grey
Lincolnshire sky Janice could see a cloud of little black dots
circling the TV aerial stuck to the chimney.

'How do you know they're bees?' she asked.

'They're bees.' What was the difference between bees and wasps? Janice looked it up in the library later: bees are vegetarian wasps. They visit flowers to collect their food rather than doing it with insects. The unattractive chap lit three foul-smelling smoke pellets, one after the other, in Janice's sitting-room fireplace, charged her £15, and with a quick 'that should fix 'em', leapt back into his van and was gone just in time for Arthur Weldon's return from the fields with his new Triffit muck spreader. This was just as well, as Arthur would have had no patience with a pest-control van parked in his way, particularly after the humdingery he'd had flung at him by Patrice in the pub about his and other farmers' carcinogenic habits with lindane.

Janice swept up the bees. She picked one of them up and held it up to the light and examined it; but it was small and dark and dead and that was the end of it. She had a light perm put in her chestnut hair and proudly fixed the screws on the garden gate. She was oiling it just before *EastEnders* when her next-door neighbour, Peggy Elliot, walked past on her way to post a letter. 'Did he do his business, dear?' asked Peggy nosily, meaning, what business was he doing?

'Bees,' said Janice definitely, wrinkling her nose. After all, there were a lot of pests worse than bees.

At first she thought it was just the residue that continued to fall down the chimney, but after a few weeks she was obliged to confront the fact that the bees she came home to every day were no longer the ones that the unattractive fellow had impregnated with his smoke bombs, but a whole lot of new ones quite uncontaminated by the treatment of the Council's privatized pest-control services.

She rang the Council again. This time she knew who to ask for: 'Environmental services,' she pronounced firmly, 'pest control, please.' Even as she spoke these words, Mrs Weldon came in for a new Ruth Rendell, so Janice knew it'd be all over the village. 'Very difficult to get rid of,' Mrs Weldon informed her. 'We had them in 1964 when our Alice was born, I remember them buzzing when she caught German measles off that Brian in the post office. I hope this one's a bit cleaner than the last,' she said, picking up *Kissing the Gunner's Daughter*, 'I couldn't do with all the women's lib stuff in the last one, and that business about Rhoda Comfrey dressing up as a man wasn't at all nice.'

They sent the boss this time. He was an altogether different kettle of fish. 'Clifford Dunham,' he said, holding out a scrubbed soap-smelling hand with, as Janice noticed, a covering of bee-like dark hair on it. 'I'm the manager of Greenland Environmental and Farm Services. We do most of the pest control work for the Council round here.' He gave Janice his card, to prove who he was. It was larger than the average, with a neat green stripe round it and a new fax number in red at the bottom, to indicate urgency.

When Clifford Dunham had parked his van down the lane, he inspected Janice's bee problem thoroughly, beginning with the dead ones on her sitting-room carpet. '*Apis mellifera*,' he uttered knowingly, 'the common honey-bee to ladies like yourself. Circa thirty thousand known species, two hundred and fifty-three in the UK. A very social bee, I must say, as you can see from the remains on this charming carpet of yours.' The word 'social' had rather an ominous ring to it. 'The wrong chimney,' pronounced Clifford Dunham eventually.

'What do you mean, Mr Dunham?' interrogated Janice suspiciously, taking this as some sort of criticism of herself.

'The cast – we call the nest a cast,' said Clifford Dunham, leaning his furry bulk heavily against Janice's floral sofa from the Reject Shop in Lincoln, 'is in the chimney leading from the bedroom, so smoke pellets in the chimney in here would do no good at all.'

'Oh.' Janice didn't ask him how he knew where the cast was, since he did seem to know.

'We'll have to use chemicals. Is there any access?' They went upstairs to examine the bedroom fireplace, which was small and white-painted and very closed-off looking, locked into the chimney with a mass of silicone, courtesy of the garage manager (one of his leaving presents). 'Did you put this here?' asked Clifford Dunham, this time accusingly, pulling strands of it away with his clean-smelling fingers.

'Not me personally,' said Janice in self-defence. 'But yes, it was put there recently.' She watched the white gungy strips coming away with some embarrassment, and tweaked the counterpane on the bed behind her with a nervous tic.

Clifford Dunham drew himself up to his full height from his cramped position in the fireplace. Janice noticed how white and crisp his shirt was and how his tie and trousers, a smart navy blue, made him look like an aeroplane pilot. His face shone with good health and a pink-cheeked newly shaven look. Janice thought she could hear the bees buzzing in her ears again. 'I was just going to make a cup of tea,' she said, without planning to. 'I wonder, would you like one?'

She heard the leather of Clifford Dunham's shoes crunching the dead bees as they went downstairs. Was there a Mrs Dunham who scraped the dead bees off his shoes when he came home at night?

He drank his tea quickly, holding his tie to one side as he did so, to make sure no drips fell on it, though Janice had been careful not to allow any liquid on to the saucer. He looked out of the window at the trees at the bottom of Janice's garden. The wind moved their tops slowly against a misty bluish sky. 'The moan of doves in immemorial elms/And the murmuring of innumerable bees,' he said. 'Alfred Lord Tennyson, "The Princess". Except that they aren't elms, are they, Miss Bickerstaffe? Know about bees, do you?'

Janice had to admit she didn't; nor, actually, did she really want to. But she didn't say that. He put his cup down smartly on the shiny green melamine kitchen counter. 'Very interesting, bees are. We humans could learn a lot from them.' When he laughed the sound was that of a deep buzzing somewhere in the depths of his crisp white shirt, behind which Janice found herself imagining might lie a light covering of the very same smooth bee fuzz she could see, even now as she stood by the sink, on Clifford Dunham's hands.

What she didn't know, he intended to tell her. 'They live in colonies. Well, not all of them, some of them live alone, but *Apis mellifera* is a communal one. Every colony has only one queen, you see. The queen is bigger than the others. The others are the worker bees and the drones.' He laughed again, a queen-bee- or possibly drone-like sound. 'The workers are all ladies like yourself, the drones are all men. The ladies do the work, the men have all the fun. Out of the cast goes the queen, a virgin, and back she comes with all that . . . well, impregnated, you might say.' He fixed Janice with a meaningful look. 'Mind you, it's not funny what happens to the chaps when they have their fun.'

'It isn't?'

'It isn't. But we'll leave the details on one side, I think. Now back to your bees, your very own bees. We don't want you to be like the Old Man in the tree, do we?'

Janice looked out of the window at the non-elms. What a curious man he was.

'"There was an Old Man in a tree/ Who was horribly bored by a bee;/ When they said 'Does it Buzz?'/ He replied, 'Yes, it does!/ It's a regular brute of a bee!'"'

'I know that one!' she cried, like a child. 'Edward Lear, *Book of Nonsense*, isn't it!'

'It is, Miss Bickerstaffe, it is!' Clifford Dunham rubbed his hands happily. It transpired that whatever had to be done to Janice's bees couldn't be done there and then. Another appointment had to be made. Janice explained about her job in the library, and how she'd already had one day off for the fruitless wrong-chimney smoke-pellet exercise. 'Yes I can quite see that it's awkward for you. I'm sure we could do a Saturday to oblige. How about next Saturday? I might have to take Mrs Dunham to the new Asda, you know the one out by Swine Park, she wants to start her Christmas shopping. But I could come by with my gang in the afternoon. That is, if is suits, of course. It'll be a bit of a business, we'll need the triple ladder to spray the chimney. That's because of the queen's smell, her pheromone, you know. It lasts for seven years. Oh, and you'll need to strip the room.' He made it sound quite indecent. 'Take the curtains down, and the bedding away, and the soft furnishings, if you can.'

Janice did everything he said. She got up early to prepare the house, and then she went to Gateway and did her shopping and found herself in the alcohol lane, where she didn't usually wander, and she bought a six-pack of Carlsberg, and two bottles of Beaujolais Nouveau (she liked the pretty flower sign, it reminded her of the difference between wasps and bees), and a bottle of Hungarian Riesling which was on special offer. 'It'll come in handy for Christmas,' she explained to the girl at the checkout as she handed over her TSB visa card, thinking, as she did so, not about Christmas, but about Mr and Mrs Dunham in the Asda store not so far away, and about the triple ladders and the pheromone, and the drones and what happened to them on the queen's maiden flight.

When she'd put the shopping away, she had a bath and washed her hair. The perm was holding up well. She put on a white blouse with a lace collar and then took it off, and put a beige polyester one on instead. Underneath she wore a black body and black leggings and her M & S pixie boots. She turned this way and that and thought she cut a reasonable figure, and then she had a little laugh at the garage manager for abandoning her (though it was in fact she who'd abandoned him, needing a bit more adrenaline in her life than he could give her, though not quite as much as a person who was allergic to bees).

When the doorbell rang, instead of Clifford Dunham fresh from his exploits in Asda there was the unattractive fellow on the doorstep again. 'Mrs Bickerstaffe?' he asked contemptuously.

Janice couldn't be bothered to correct him. 'Isn't Mr Dunham coming?' She got a withering look for that. He brushed past her with a number of large rusty boxes. 'Keep an eye on the chimney, Ken!' Janice peered out past the dead spikes of the forsythia. A large man with a stance like a bull terrier was positioned in the middle of the road.

She followed the boxes upstairs. 'Still got the little blighters, have we?' She was sure he didn't believe her, didn't trust the mere word of a woman, didn't want to think his nasty smoke treatment hadn't worked. She stood there watching as he lit something else, and put it in the chimney and replaced the white lid and waited, narrowing his foxy eyes at her. The smell made her eyes water. Out of the window she could see Ken with his big feet on the road and his eyes on the chimney. For a while nothing happened and then with a big plop the bees fell to a man, as Clifford Dunham would later say, and the unattractive chap got his comeuppance as they all started to ooze with an angry buzzing round his smarmy hand. He called for Ken, and Janice had to fetch him, and more boxes were brought in, and the room filled up with buzzing, crawling and flying bees, going round in crazy circles and banging into each other like dented cars in a circus sideshow.

Janice went downstairs to get away from it all. Where was Clifford Dunham? He had no right to abandon her to these inefficient, disrespectful men who clearly knew less about bees than she, under Clifford Dunham's tutelage, had already learnt. In the kitchen she got angry and in the bedroom Ken and his mate hoovered up about five thousand bees. She went back upstairs towards the end. 'You'll get a few still,' said Ken, '*Mrs* Bickerstaffe. They're dead alright, but they can still sting for two weeks after death, so mind how you pick them up.'

'What about the scent of the queen in the chimney?' she asked.
'What about the chemicals?' They looked at each other hopelessly.
'I think you ought to ring Mr Dunham.' But just as she said it, they
could hear the van turning the corner of the lane. She went down
to let him in, and the two men came down after her, dragging their
boxes and chuntering in impenetrable Lincolnshire accents about
this not usually being the season for bees.

'It's all done, Cliff,' said the unattractive chap.

'Down like a man they came, did they?'

'But what about my chimney?' asked Janice with an echo.

Up in the bedroom there was no buzzing any more. A crowd of
dead bees lay in the grate. Then a little band of woodlice dropped
down as well, accompanied by a slab of roof insulating felt. Janice
shuddered. What else was up there? Where was – what had Clifford
Dunham called it – the cast? He stood behind her, manfully, and
then he inched forward and stabbed the dead insects with his
finger, searching, she imagined, for the queen. 'We'd better look at
the chimney, hadn't we? I had a quick look round the back before I
came in. I reckon the best access is from the flat roof if I can get up
there. Can I, Miss Bickerstaffe?'

Janice showed him the way out of the attic window, and climbed
out herself after him. She stood on the small square roof while he
manoeuvred himself up higher, and, grasping the apex of the roof
firmly between his navy-blue knees, moved himself like a cat burglar
along it. When he reached the chimney he stood up and peered
down it. Janice was afraid of his falling. She could hear Ken and the
other chap in the garden talking about who had phoned the other
one last night. The sun had just set and the sky was bright pink, and
the church bells rang suddenly, the new bell-ringers' group practising
for the display Mrs Farthing had arranged as a money-earner for her
dyslexia gathering. The air was full of pinkness and melody. Janice
smiled and looked at Clifford Dunham standing so majestically there
in his quest for bees, dead or alive, down her chimney. He took a
mobile phone out of his pocket, and flicked up the aerial, but she
couldn't hear what he was saying, because of the bells. Then Ken
and the other man came up with a big white plastic canister with a
sprayer attached and handed it to him, and he squirted a few gallons
of white liquid down the chimney, and came down from the roof
towards her with a look of queer satisfaction on his face.

They packed everything away in the two vans. Ken and the unattractive chap drove off first, both of them lighting cigarettes as they went. Janice wondered if he'd recovered from the shock. That'd teach him not to believe women! 'How much do I owe you?' she asked Clifford Dunham.

'Ah well, now, we'll have to work that out, won't we!' He asked her if he could wash his hands, on account of the stuff down her chimney, and the chemicals. Janice, who was working out what to say about not paying twice, found her train of thought interrupted by a question, which she proceeded to voice, about the nature of the said chemicals. 'Are all the women in Lincolnshire out of their minds?' queried Clifford Dunham. 'Mrs Dunham asked me the same question by the crackers in Asda.'

'Well, it could be serious.'

'So could your bees.' She handed him a towel, and thought he might be looking at the place on her body where any lindane might, even as they spoke, be resting. 'An allergy to bees isn't funny,' he went on, chattily. '"The bee is an insect; it lives in the same world with us." C. R. Ribbands, *The Behaviour and Social Life of Honeybees*. Bee Research Association, 1953. Though of course the best is the classic by Frisch, *The Dancing Bees*.'

'You're a mine of information, aren't you?'

'That's what the dancing is. A way of communicating. Yes, I must admit to being something of a mellitologist.' He laughed. 'Did you know, Miss Bickerstaffe, there are more than fifty books about bees in your library catalogue? Mind you,' he reflected, giving her back the towel, 'some of them aren't about bees at all. Take *Love of Worker Bees* by a Russian woman, Alexandra Kollantai, that's about socialists and communism and all that. Believer in free love, she was. An unhappy woman. No, nothing to do with bees at all.'

Janice thought about her alcohol supplies. It was nearly dark now, probably time for Clifford Dunham's tea. He leaned against the kitchen doorpost (his head, she noticed, was level with the top of the frame) and stroked his tie, settling it back against the white field of his stomach. 'Bees belong to the order Hymenoptera. Did you know that, Miss Bickerstaffe? *Hymen*, the Greek word for membrane. Only in this case it's the wings that are referred to.'

She swallowed quickly.

'I suppose you wouldn't have a beer, would you, to take away the scent of evil doings I've done this afternoon?'

He didn't want the Carlsberg: 'Not a man's beer,' he told her, 'more that of a drone.' He chose the Beaujolais, and drank the first glass quickly, just as he had his tea. They took the rest into the sitting-room, where he made an attempt at a conversation. 'Have you had the bees long?'

Janice told him, and a bit about herself, and her attitude to life and bees. But he didn't seem terribly interested, though he did look at her very hard, and she definitely felt he was enjoying himself. He lay back on her sofa for all the world as though it was his own. The doorbell rang, it was Peggy Elliot. 'I saw the vans, dear. Are you still having trouble?' Peggy craned her neck, craggy like a Christmas goose, round the doorway from the narrow hall into the sitting-room. 'Oh, I'm sorry, I didn't realize you had company.' Of course she did, thought Janice. Clifford Dunham's van was still parked down the lane.

'Mind if I give the wife a ring?' he asked, when she came back into the room.

'Go ahead.'

'Been a bit delayed, dear,' he explained into the navy-blue handset, colour-coordinated with his tie and trousers, 'difficult cast. You'll have to expect me when you see me. Good thing we bought the microwave, isn't it?'

He pushed the aerial down and put the handset in his pocket. 'You wondering why I wear navy blue, Miss Bickerstaffe? Don't deny it, I caught you looking at me just now. Don't blame me, blame P. Koch!' The laugh was very deep this time. 'Experiments, to test the insects' vision. Like man, and possibly woman,' (here he interspersed a light giggle) 'bees have trichromatic vision. They've three types of cells in their eyes, each sensitive to the three primary colours. P. Koch experimented with hives in six different colours. He found you get the most yield from navy blue. God knows why. Would there be any more of that wine left?'

When the church clock chimed seven, Clifford Dunham decided he ought to check on the state of Janice's bedroom before he went. The pile of woodlice was bigger, and now there was something that looked like a dead pigeon heaped on top. 'You'll get a bit of detritus for a while,' he told her, eyeing it with relish. 'Now, you're not to worry about it, just tell yourself all the little buggers are dead.'

'I won't worry,' she said, charmed by his protectiveness towards her.

'No, that's right,' he confirmed, taking a step towards her, and away from the dead pigeon.

'I'm grateful to you for coming,' she said, 'on a Saturday.'

'Anything to oblige.' The crispness of his shirt was just as she had imagined it, and when he kissed her she fancied there was honey on his lips. There were a few moribund bees clinging to the mattress, but he swept them off masterfully. His body was covered in hair. That had been one of the problems with the garage manager – not the main one, the main one had been the garage. Clifford Dunham's legs, particularly, were covered in it. 'Feature of bees,' he said, 'as opposed to wasps. Goes with the tongue.'

'The tongue?'

'Very well developed. In order to get deep into the flowers, you understand.' He stroked her body and admired her narrow waist, and that, apparently, had something to do with bees as well. 'Janice,' he said. 'Janice.'

She melted like a pot of warm honey. 'Tell me what happens to the drones,' she urged. 'You know, when they have their fun.'

Clifford Dunham took her hand and placed it on a part of him that wasn't hairy. 'This, in bees,' he said informatively, 'is very large.'

His wasn't small. She held it firmly. 'And?'

He parted her legs. 'They only mate once, once in a lifetime. So it's got to be good, you see.' He started moving inside her. 'Good, like this, like this, my little honeyed hymen.'

She folded her arms tightly around him and thought of the language and the sound of bees; the buzzing, the honey-making, the hierarchy of queen and workers and drones, and the love that did, or didn't go with it. She thought of Clifford Dunham on the roof of her house with his navy-blue phone and his big white can of chemicals plunging deep into the dark, rubbish-laden shaft of her chimney. The air seemed full of the scents of flowers and honey, and the moonshine that started to beam into the room from a lopsided white cheese of a moon turned itself into sunshine which speckled both their bodies with gold. Clifford Dunham took her breast into his mouth, and then came off it momentarily, like a surprised child, 'Where the bees sucks, there suck I,' he murmured. 'Or perhaps not, Janice, perhaps not.'

Janice reflected on the differences between a pest-control officer and a garage manager. To have a pest-control officer inside you, particularly one so knowledgeable about bees, was to be one with nature. Who wanted to be one with cars? She sighed happily and concentrated on being a queen. Peggy Elliot's horse neighed in the garden. Arthur Weldon drove his muck spreader home. In her bed in Daffodil Close, Challingham, Graeme's Aunt Frieda muttered about her pain and decided to set up a lindane action group. It seemed there was some relationship between the environment and how men treated it and how women felt, but in Janice Bickerstaffe's case the immanence of the moment when the pest-control officer spurted his non-chemicals into her would do for the time being.

'You still haven't told me what happens to them,' said Janice accusingly as Clifford Dunham climbed off. She noticed out of the corner of her eye a couple of bees attached to the edge of the mattress, but dismissed them along with the words of the bull terrier Ken about the apid capacity to sting after death.

'The only wasps that survive the summer are the young fertilized queens,' said Clifford, in a meandering kind of way.

'You're a very odd chap, you know,' she objected.

'Queens are fed on royal jelly, that's why they're queens. D'you know where royal jelly comes from, Janice? It's from the salivary glands of the worker bees. Regurgitated with sugar. What a lovely cocktail!'

Bile rose in her throat. She remembered what she'd been thinking about earlier. 'Do I have to pay VAT as well?'

'I'm a pest-control officer,' he said, 'and I'm here to control your pests.' He laughed and grasped her left buttock in a controlling action. In his jacket pocket on the floor the navy-blue mobile rang with an inquiry from Mrs Dunham about the whereabouts of the microwave operating instructions. When he sat up to retrieve the instrument, a dead bee bit into the hairy backside of Clifford Dunham's legs, which was a mistake for the bee, who had a mouthful, and for Clifford Dunham, who died of an unknown allergy to bee stings five minutes later without ever telling Janice Bickerstaffe what happens to drones who fertilize their queens. In any case, her bees came back the following spring, as the lingering pheromone, inefficiently uneradicated by Clifford Dunham's white liquid, and easily capable of cancelling out the scents of lindane and other man-made mischiefs, drew a whole new colony of the boring, buzzing brutes into her bedroom chimney from the copse beyond Apple Farm, which in its time had harboured many kinds of pests and rodents, and had seen them live and die and multiply, though not necessarily in that order.

ACKNOWLEDGEMENTS

A number of people helped us prepare this book by generously sharing some of the fruits of their own areas of research. They are Denys Johnson-Davies, Silke R. Falkner, Kristie A. Foell, Patrick J. Kearney, Andreas Lixl-Purcell, Ann Oakley, Simon Pettifar, Ann Marie Rasmussen, Alfred Thomas, James Thomas, Sarah Westphal and James Williams.

We should also like to acknowledge the individuals, publishers and agents who gave us permission to reproduce their works. These are as follows: 'Mitsou' by Colette, from *Mitsou*, 1919, copyright © by the Estate of Colette, translation copyright © 1995 by Marie Smith; reprinted by permission of Flammarion. 'Didn't Nelly and Lilly Love You' by Gertrude Stein, copyright © by the Estate of Gertrude Stein, renewed 16 July 1982; reprinted by permission of Calman A. Levin for the Estate of Gertrude Stein. 'The Villa Désirée' by May Sinclair, copyright © 1926 by May Sinclair; reprinted by permission of Curtis Brown Ltd, London. 'My Little Girl' by Edith Wharton, from *Beatrice Palmato*, reprinted by permission of the author and the Watkin/Loomis Agency. 'Marcelle' by Simone de Beauvoir, first published in *Quand prime le spirituel*, 1979, copyright © 1979 by Éditions Gallimard, English translation copyright © 1982 by Patrick O'Brian; reprinted by permission of André Deutsch and Weidenfeld. 'Sicily Enough' by Claire Rabe, from *Olympia 4* (April 1963), copyright © 1963 by Olympia Press; reprinted by permission of Mr J. P. Donleavy on behalf of the author. 'A Spaceship of Tenderness to the Moon' by Laila Baalabaki, translated by Denys Johnson-Davies, from *Modern Arabic Stories*, copyright © 1967 by Denys Johnson-Davies; reprinted by permission of the translator. 'I, a Woman' by Siv Holm, first published in Denmark by Stig Vendelkaers Forlag, 1965; English translation by J. W. Brown first published by Dell Publishing Co. Inc., 1967; copyright © 1965 by Siv Holm. 'Sex and/or Mr Morrison' by Carol Emshwiller first appeared in *Dangerous Visions*, copyright © by Carol Emshwiller; reprinted by permission of the author and the author's agent Virginia Kidd. 'My World of the Unknown' by Alifa Rifaat, from *Distant View of a Minaret*, translated by Denys Johnson-Davies, copyright © 1983 by Denys Johnson-Davies; reprinted by permission of the translator. 'Flesh and the Mirror' by Angela Carter, from *Fireworks*, 1974, copyright © 1974 by the Estate of Angela Carter; reprinted by permission of Rogers, Coleridge and White. 'An Old-fashioned Girl' by Joanna Russ, published in *Final Stage: the Ultimate Science Fiction Anthology*, eds. Ed Ferman and Barry Maltzberg, Penguin, 1975, copyright © 1974 by Joanna Russ; reprinted by permission of Joanna Russ. 'State of Emergency' by Verena Stefan, from *Shedding*, translated by Johanna Moore and Beth Weckmüller, London, The Women's Press, 1979, copyright © by Verlag Frauenoffensive. 'The Collector of Treasures' by Bessie Head, from *The Collector of Treasures*, published by Heinemann Educational Books Limited in the African Writers Series, copyright © by the Estate of Bessie Head, 1977; reprinted by permission of Heinemann Publishers (Oxford) Ltd. 'Black and White' by Nicole Ward Jouve, from *Shades of Grey*, London, Virago, 1981, first published as *Le Spectre du gris*, 1977; copyright © 1977, translation copyright © 1987; reprinted by permission of Éditions des Femmes, Paris. 'New York City in 1979' by Kathy Acker, from *Top Stories* 9, 1981, copyright © 1981 by Kathy Acker; reprinted by permission of the author and her agent, Georgina Capel of Simpson Fox Associates Ltd. 'A Lover's Ear' by Yuan Ch'iung Ch'iung, first published in *Zyzzyva*, English translation and copyright © 1985 by Howard Goldblatt, reprinted by permission of the translator. 'Kneel Down and Lick My Feet' by Amy Yamada, from *Monkey Brain Sushi*, ed. Alfred Birnbaum, published by Kodansha International Ltd, copyright © 1991 by Kodansha International Ltd; reprinted by permission of the author and Kodansha International Ltd. 'Our Secret' by Isabel Allende, from *The Stories of Eva Luna* by Isabel Allende, translated from the Spanish by Margaret Sayers Peden, copyright © 1989 by Isabel Allende, English translation copyright © by Macmillan Publishing Company; reprinted by permission of Scribner, an imprint of Simon & Schuster. 'Billets Doux' by Elizabeth Cook, from *Sex and the City*, ed. Marsha Rowe, London, Serpent's Tail, 1989, copyright © by Elizabeth Cook; reprinted by permission of the author and Serpent's Tail Ltd. 'Truck Stop' by Iva Pekárková from *Truck Stop Rainbows*, first published in Czech in *Pera a Perute*, copyright © by Iva Pekárková 1989, translated by David Powelstock, copyright © 1992 by David Powelstock; reprinted by permission of the author. 'Fetish Night' by Evelyn Lau, from *Fresh Girls and Other Stories*, Harper Collins Canada, 1993, copyright © 1993 by Evelyn Lau; reprinted by permission of the author and the author's agent Denise Bukowsky. 'Romances of the Era of Stagnation' by Svetlana Boym, first published in Russian in *Chego Khochet Zhenshchina*, 1993, copyright © by Svetlana Boym, 1993, translated by the author; printed by permission of the author. 'Harmonizing Polarities' by

L. A. Hall, copyright © 1995 by L. A. Hall; printed by permission of the author. 'Wishes' by Candas Jane Dorsey, copyright © 1995 by Candas Jane Dorsey; printed by permission of the author. 'Where the Bee Sucks' by Ann Oakley, copyright © 1995 by Ann Oakley; printed by permission of the author.

While every effort has been made to trace authors and copyright-holders, this has not always been possible. The editors would be glad to hear from any such parties so that any errors or omissions can be rectified in future editions of this book.

R.G.J. and A.S.W.